The last sinner

LISA JACKSON

KU-611-845

HODDER &
STOUGHTON

First published in Great Britain in 2023 by Hodder & Stoughton
An Hachette UK company

First published in the United States in 2023 by Kensington Books Publishing

1

Copyright © Lisa Jackson LLC 2023

The right of Lisa Jackson to be identified as the Author of the Work has been asserted by her in accordance with the Copyright, Designs and Patents Act 1988.

All rights reserved. No part of this publication may be reproduced, stored in a retrieval system, or transmitted, in any form or by any means without the prior written permission of the publisher, nor be otherwise circulated in any form of binding or cover other than that in which it is published and without a similar condition being imposed on the subsequent purchaser.

All characters in this publication are fictitious and any resemblance to real persons, living or dead, is purely coincidental.

A CIP catalogue record for this title is available from the British Library

Hardback ISBN 978 1 399 72778 5
Trade Paperback ISBN 978 1 529 30449 7
eBook ISBN 978 1 529 30450 3

Typeset in ITC Garamond

Printed and bound in Great Britain by Clays Ltd, Elcograf S.p.A.

Hodder & Stoughton policy is to use papers that are natural, renewable and recyclable products and made from wood grown in sustainable forests. The logging and manufacturing processes are expected to conform to the environmental regulations of the country of origin.

Hodder & Stoughton Ltd
Carmelite House
50 Victoria Embankment
London EC4Y 0DZ

www.hodder.co.uk

The
last
sinner

CHAPTER 1

October 2015
New Orleans, Louisiana

Faster!
I run, moving quickly.
Through the sheeting rain.
Crossing city streets.
Hidden by the shadows of the night.
Faster!
My heart's pounding, blood pumping through my veins as I splash through puddles and blink against the slashing rain.
I smell the earthy, ever-present odor of the Mississippi River.
Familiar and dank.
With my poncho flapping, my boots slapping through puddles, I run along the alleys and streets of the French Quarter.
Faster!
Streetlights are glowing, their illumination fuzzy in the rainfall, soft light reflecting off the hoods of a few scattered cars parked near Jackson Square, rainwater gurgling in the gutters, washing onto the street, and pooling in the potholes.
This city is, and always has been, my home.
And I loved it.
Until I didn't.
Because of *her.*
My stomach clenches at the thought of what I've gone through,

what I've had to endure. But now, after all this time, it's about to be over.

Faster!

With St. Louis Cathedral as my beacon, down the nearly deserted streets I fly. The cathedral rises high into the night, whitewashed walls bathed in light, its three familiar spires knifing upward to the dark, roiling heavens. From habit, I cross myself as I hazard a glance to the highest spire with its cross aloft, but all the while, I keep moving, the wrought iron pickets of the fence surrounding Jackson Square in my peripheral vision.

On the far side of the cathedral, I slip into narrow Pirate's Alley where a few lights in the windows of the shops are glowing, but the street itself is deserted, all pedestrians indoors, waiting out the storm.

It's fine, I tell myself. No, no, it's good, because in spite of the inclement weather, she will be coming.

I know her routine by heart. And I've double-checked to make certain that tonight she didn't vary from it, that her car is parked where it normally is three nights a week, so, tonight is the night. With the rain concealing so much, a wet shroud, I'll have more time and less chance of being observed, or worse yet, interrupted.

My heart is pounding, my chest tight in anticipation as I reach the end of the alley, near the Place de Henriette Delille. Here I wait, crouching low, catching my breath near the park. Swiping drops of rain from my forehead, I squint and stare across Royal Street, usually so busy with pedestrians, but tonight, thankfully, only spotted with a few brave souls dashing through the storm, all seeming too intent to get out of the downpour to notice me or even glance in my direction. It's too wet for most, a deluge, the wind-blown rain sheeting in the vaporous glow of the streetlamps, the pavement shimmering eerily, the night thick.

I check my watch, making certain I'm on time while water runs down my poncho to stream onto the cobblestones. My ski mask is tight over my nose and chin, but my hood is cinched tight around my face and no one should notice in the rain, though shaded glasses during the night might be considered odd. But this is New Orleans. Nothing here is really out of the ordinary. Anything goes.

Again I make the sign of the cross and let out my breath to count my slowing heartbeats.

And beneath my poncho, my right hand finds the hilt of my hunting knife, a sharp weapon with a thin blade that could whisk off the hide of an alligator and easily slice through muscle and sinew.

I've waited for this night for so damned long.

Now that the time has come, I'll savor it, that sweet, sweet taste of revenge. Licking my lips, my eyes trained on the building with the red door cut into a dimly lit alcove, a striped awning flapping with the stiff breeze, I wait. Then, I'm forced to move quickly, stepping deeper into the shadows as a man with a briefcase, head ducked against the wind, passes nearby. He's in a hurry to get out of the storm and doesn't so much as throw a glance in my direction.

I hear a siren in the distance and freeze, but the shrieks fade as the emergency vehicle speeds even further away, unimpeded by much traffic on this stormy night.

Anxiously I stare at the red door.

"Come on, come on," I whisper.

But she doesn't appear.

Nervous now, I check my watch again.

She's late.

Five minutes late.

Damn!

Come on. Come on.

Heartbeat pounding in my ears, I begin to sweat.

I'm breathing too fast.

Calm down!

Be patient.

But my nerves are strung tight, the muscles in my neck and shoulders bunched so tight they ache, my hand grasping the hilt of the knife strapped to my waist.

I know she's inside.

I passed her car, a little Subaru parked where she usually found a space when she visited the gym.

Noise!

Movement!

Out of the corner of my eye, I spy a couple dashing wildly through the storm. I turn quickly away to face the park just in case they glance in my direction and somehow see through my disguise. Sharing a shivering umbrella, they rush past, their coats billowing, the woman's laughter barely audible through the storm. Splashing by, they don't notice me.

Barely holding on to my sanity, I check my watch. Again.

Seven minutes.

Seven minutes late!

My pulse skyrockets. All my plans shrivel. Why would anything change tonight? She's always been prompt. I've timed her. On several different occasions. Like clockwork, she's always walked out the door within a minute or two of the hour.

I'm suddenly frantic. Unsure. Could she have left by another doorway? Because of the downpour? Did someone call her? *Warn* her? But no. No one knows what I'm planning. *No* one.

For a different view of the building, I cross the alley, but staring through the downpour, I see nothing out of the ordinary as I study the building with its recessed red door. Squinting, I look upward to the second floor where the yoga class is held. The lights are still on.

And then the red door opens.

She steps out and into the storm.

My pulse ticks up. My blood pounds in my ears and drowns out the sounds of the city, the rush of tires on nearby streets, the gurgle of water in downspouts, the incessant pounding of the rain. All I hear is my own thudding heart.

Eyeing the black heavens from beneath the flapping awning, she clicks up her umbrella and begins jogging, hurrying across Royal Street, her boots splashing through puddles, the umbrella's canopy shuddering with the wind.

She's running straight at me!

My heartbeat is in the stratosphere.

Saying a quick prayer, I withdraw the knife, my thighs tight, ready to pounce.

Suddenly her stride breaks and she veers sideways!

What!?! No!

Did she see me? Anticipate my plans?

No. A skinny, drenched cat, caught in the storm, gallops across her path before diving under the protection of a parked car.

Muttering a curse, she hurries forward again, her umbrella her shield.

Not a good enough weapon, I think. No. Not nearly good enough. She's barely ten feet away when I notice a shadow behind her, a figure running through the curtain of the rain.

What? No!

She's nearly to me.

I coil, ready to spring.

"Kristi!" a voice yells, and she half turns.

Startled, I lose my concentration.

Who is that? Someone who knows her? A witness?

No, no, no!

I flatten against the wall of the cathedral.

In a blink, she steps deeper into the alley, sweeps past me.

What?! NO!

I take off after her.

This can't be happening!

Tonight is the night!

I sprint. Faster. Faster.

Splashing through the puddles.

I've waited far too long for this to go wrong.

I won't be denied!

I'm only a step behind.

Suddenly, in a flash, she whirls.

Faces me.

My heart stops.

She peers from beneath the umbrella's flapping edge, her face hidden in the darkness, her words hard. "Who are you?" she demands. "Are you following me?"

Damn!

No time to answer.

The element of surprise is gone.

I leap forward, small knife clenched in tight fingers. As I do, I slash wildly, slicing the umbrella's canopy.

Just as she shoves the ferrule, the umbrella's sharp tip, straight at my eyes!

I duck.

The ferrule glances across my cheek and I stumble. Blood sprays, some onto the white walls of the cathedral as I land hard on wet cobblestones.

She jabs again! Throwing her weight into her makeshift weapon.

I feint, dodging the blow.

Spinning, I'm on my feet again.

I strike.

Hit her shoulder.

She yowls in pain and scrambles backward, flailing with the useless, maimed umbrella. But I hold on. Drive deep. As far as my blade allows. Twist the knife as she screams.

"Kristi!" A deep male voice yells. "Kris!"

What? Oh, shit! I waited too long!

The man who was following is approaching fast, his footsteps clattering, splashing.

"Kristi! Run!" the man orders at the top of his lungs. "Run!"

I have to finish this!

I yank the knife's blade from her shoulder, hear the sucking sound, cut myself in the process.

Still she flails wildly with that damned umbrella, its canopy flapping, its steel spokes exposed and glinting in the barest of light from a streetlamp, its deadly tip menacing, slicing through the air too near my face.

This is *not* how it was supposed to happen, how with one swift blow to her jugular or her heart she would die in my arms, how I would exact my revenge as she looked into my eyes and realized in her dying moments who had taken her life and why.

"Ruuuuun!" the man yells, and he is closer now. Too close.

I knock her umbrella away and, raising my blade, I pin her against the wall of the church with my weight. Blood streaks the white stucco. Her blood.

"You sick piece of—" She kicks upward, hard, the heel of her boot hitting me square in the solar plexus. The air rushes from my lungs. Still gripping my knife, I slice crazily, the blade whooshing through air as I land. Hard. Stunned. Pain radiating through me.

Hold on to the knife. Don't lose the damned knife!

But it slips from my fingers.

She is starting to come at me again, staggering upward.

I don't give her the chance to attack.

I ram her hard. Force her back against the church wall.

Craaack! Her head smashes into the wall behind her and she crumples, slithering to the street, leaving a red stain sliding down the stucco.

"No!" The man yells, springing forward, dropping the bundle he's been carrying, flowers and paper scattering in the wind.

Scrambling on the street, I find my blade just as Kristi's would-be savior grabs me, strong fingers circling my neck.

I thrust upward.

The blade cuts into his chest, through flesh, marrow, and bone.

"AAAAhhh."

Gasping for air, I rotate the blade. Hard. Force it upward.

His breath sprays me—air, spittle, and a few flecks of blood.

The hands at my throat fall away.

Blood from the cut on my attacker's chest rains on me, and I tear the knife from his torso to strike again.

He blinks. Horror giving way to rage. In a split second his fist slams into my face.

Pain cracks through my jaw, rattling down my spine. My legs buckle and I stagger to my knees.

He rounds on me again. Unsteadily. His legs wobbling.

I duck the wild swing. Thrust upward with my knife. Hit my assailant's thigh. Drive as deep as possible, all my weight into the jab.

He sways.

With all my strength, I force the blade to cut sideways, across the thick muscle.

Blood spurts.

More agonized screams.

And in the distance, sirens shriek.

Footsteps. Running. Hard. Fast. Splashing through puddles.

I fling the gasping man off and roll to my feet. From the corner of my eye I see that Kristi is rousing, blinking, her face ashen as she attempts to focus. "Oh, God!" she cries in agony as I stagger away. I see her stumbling forward, crawling to the dying man, cradling his head in her lap. "Jay!" she screams, her face in the dim light wrenched in pain as she holds him. "No. No. Oh, God. Oh, God. No, no, no!"

There isn't time to finish her. Already red and blue lights are flashing, washing the cathedral's walls in eerie strobing lights, lighting up the scene with its bloodstained cathedral walls, injured lovers, and scattered roses.

Without thinking, I pick up one of the long-stemmed buds. Then my mind clears. And I run. On unsteady legs, I sprint in the opposite direction of the police cars.

My face throbbing, I head to the route I've planned for months, fleeing down the alleys and streets, avoiding as many cameras as possible, head down, the raging storm my cover.

"Jay!" Kristi's anguished screams follow me.

But I keep running, slipping twice, righting myself and catching a glimpse of the luminous eyes of the same shadowy cat I saw before. This time it is peering from beneath a scrawny bush.

Bad luck, I think.

Kristi Bentz is still alive.

I've failed.

This time.

But only for a while.

Keep moving. Just keep moving.

Don't panic. Do not *panic.*

Next time, I think, *the next time you won't be so lucky, Kristi Bentz.* Stumbling, I hurry through the shadows and rain, dodging the few people I come across.

Still grasping my knife in one hand, I reach into a pocket with my other and rub the stones of a well-worn rosary. Praying, I cut down alleys and side streets, moving steadily forward. My heart is thudding, my jaw painful, but the glorious rush of adrenaline keeps me racing forward, putting much-needed distance between the cathedral and me.

Thankfully, because I took the time to find out, I know where the street cameras are located and keep my head low.

Under my breath I whisper, "I believe in God, the Father Almighty, Creator of heaven and earth; and in Jesus Christ, His only Son, our Lord; Who was conceived by the Holy Spirit, born of the Virgin Mary. . . ."

And then I disappear into the night.

CHAPTER 2

"Jay," Kristi cried. "No, no, no . . ." Someone was tearing her away from her husband. She had to talk to him. To explain. To tell him she'd made a horrid, horrid mistake. To let him know that she loved him. Had always loved him . . .

Forgive me. Oh, Jay, please, please forgive me.

But she couldn't get the words out.

Couldn't focus.

Was drowning in the rain.

"Get her into an ambulance!" she heard over the sluice of water gurgling in gutters and downspouts.

With an effort, Kristi struggled to sit up against the building. She was wet, her head aching, attempting to stay conscious, wanting to give way to the blissful blackness of not knowing, of being oblivious to this garish, harrowing night. She slumped again, her voice failing her, the dark night swirling around her, the palpitating sadness reverberating through her. "I have to be with him. Oh, please, God—" And then she let go, was vaguely aware of the cop giving orders. She felt her body being lifted and was barely able to hear voices and feel movement, heard the scream of a siren, though it was faint. "We're losing her," she heard, though the voice was distant, almost muffled.

She was in an ambulance? Was someone talking to her?

"Mrs. McKnight? Ms. Bentz. Can you hear me? Stay with me, now. Kristi? Kristi?" But the sound was far away, as if it were coming from another universe, and she was floating, gone again, giving in to the sweet unknowing, letting the grip of welcomed blackness surround her.

* * *

Over a week passed.

Kristi Bentz McKnight shivered. She was a widow.

And was barely aware of her father's arm as it tightened around her shoulder. She should have felt pain from her wound, but she didn't as she stood in the dismal cemetery. She couldn't feel, couldn't think, could only stare at the grave site where her husband was to be entombed. Numb to the October weather, heedless of the wind and prayers intoned solemnly by the parish priest, she waited, feeling nothing. Friends and family had gathered, all in black, all with sorrowful faces, all expressing grief and sympathy, but whose families were still intact. She saw it in the way a husband and wife would catch each other's gaze and link fingers, reassuring each other that they were still together. They were still alive. They still had a future together.

Kristi hated them for their normalcy. For their safety. For their feelings of relief that the tragedy that had befallen her hadn't befallen them. She blinked back tears of sorrow, yes, of anguish, but they were also tears of repressed fury.

Why Jay?

Why me?

Why us?

Dear God, why, why, why?

Closing her eyes for a second, grounding herself, she heard the priest's intoned prayers droning over the rush of the wind rattling through the branches of the live oaks lining the cemetery walls, felt the breeze against her skin and wished this had all never ever happened.

It was her fault Jay was dead.

She should be lying in the casket right now, not he.

It had been nearly two weeks since the attack, eleven days to be exact, where she'd gone through the motions of life, spending two days in the hospital after surgery to repair her shoulder. She'd gotten off easy, the doctor had told her; no artery, vein, or nerve had been severed and her muscles would heal, though scar tissue might develop. But if she worked at it, did her exercises, didn't let the muscles atrophy, she would be "good as new," the bright-eyed surgeon had pronounced.

She didn't think so.

And, Jay hadn't been so fortunate.

He'd given his life for her, leaping onto her attacker and bleeding out in her arms as the murderer had fled into the night. Jay's wound to his femoral artery had been fatal and no amount of guilt, nor prayers, nor feelings of ultimate despair had been able to bring him back.

Now, he was being laid to rest.

Another victim of a violent homicide.

Even the fact that the hospital had confirmed her pregnancy hadn't lifted her spirits.

The breeze lifted her hair from her shoulders and she looked up from the casket to the field of graying tombs and mausoleums that filled the cemetery, all mirrored by the gloomy sky and burgeoning clouds scudding slowly over the city.

She'd barely been able to function. She'd suffered a concussion and the muscles in her shoulder ached despite the fact that, in theory, there would be no permanent damage.

She'd been lucky.

That's what she'd heard.

Over and over again.

But it was a lie.

Food held no interest for her and her nights were sleepless, filled with nightmares of those horrid, panicked moments in the alley next to St. Louis Cathedral, a glorious edifice that had once been comforting to her, a landmark that helped her in her struggle with her faith, a symbol of God here on earth.

Now she avoided it, hated the huge white cathedral with its three spires knifing into the heavens as if reaching up to God.

Her heart shredded.

Each night as she fell into a restless sleep, she found herself once more in that fateful alley, again fighting for her life, the nameless attacker slashing brutally with his knife as the rain poured over them. Then she would see Jay, lunging forward, trying to save her as their assailant fled. Finally she would crawl over to her husband, cradle his head in her arms, and realize it was over as she witnessed his features fade to black and white. She heard herself screaming her denials. Not Jay. Not her husband. But she'd known his soul was leaving, had witnessed it so many times before, and each night, over and over again, while stroking back his hair with her bloodstained fingers, she watched him die.

A horror film forever on rewind.

It was so wrong. So very wrong. Her soul should have left the earth that night—not his. Not Jay's.

Except for the baby. Remember the baby.

God help me.

The truth was that as he'd lain bleeding in her arms, she'd vowed her love, begged him to hang on, that they had so much life yet to live. Together. But had he heard her? Over her cries for help and tears and his own labored breathing, had Jay known she loved him, had always loved him? Despite the ups and downs of their relationship, the passion and the pain? There had always been doubts, she knew, a past of breakups and reconciliations, but deep down, she'd always loved him. He'd known that.

Right?

While drawing his final breaths he'd had to have heard how much she loved him. Oh, God, she hoped so.

She surmised that he'd come to surprise her with flowers, that the strewn red roses he'd dropped had been his way of making amends for the fight they'd had.

Her throat swelled at the thought and she blinked against fresh tears.

As the first drops of rain began to fall, her father squeezed her shoulders and she sent a glance his way. He stood ramrod straight, his hair more salt than pepper these days, his jaw square, fine lines evident near his eyes and mouth, his gaze filled with concern. Beside him was his wife, Olivia, a gorgeous blond woman who stood stiffly in a long, black coat, her daughter balanced on one hip. The child, Ginny, Kristi's curly-haired half sister, so innocent, was turning one at the end of the month. Too young to be here, Kristi thought. Too little to recognize the enormity of it all. Perhaps best if Ginny didn't understand the life-altering sadness that would always exist, a dark cloak that would pale with time, but would forever be close, invisible but pervasive.

Kristi fought tears and failed. Unbidden, large drops filled her eyes to drizzle down her cheeks. Her relationship with Jay had not been perfect, they'd shared ups and downs, but she'd loved him fiercely and still did.

But now, he would never know.

Her throat was raw with the pain of that knowledge and the harsh words that had been said. At that thought her knees sagged and her father's strong arm held her upright.

She was aware of the final prayer, felt the priest's hand on her shoulder as he whispered condolences and reminded her that Jay was with God. She noticed the small group of mourners breaking apart, individuals and couples hurrying across the wet grass and concrete to their waiting vehicles, obviously relieved to have finished with this final good-bye, this obligation to the departed and his family. Now they could get on with their lives. It would be Halloween soon, and the holidays filled with good cheer and friends and family were on the horizon.

She resented them for it all and felt the bitter taste of envy rise in her throat.

She heard the quickly murmured condolences as mourners hurried past, and the growl of car engines starting, the buzz of tires against pavement as they all escaped, but she couldn't stop the horrid ache, or fill the dark void that was her heart. She caught a glimpse of Reuben Montoya and his wife, Abby, without their baby. Montoya was her father's partner, a man north of thirty with jet black hair, trimmed goatee, and intense, deep-set eyes. His wife was nearly his age, her red hair escaping from a black scarf. Montoya sketched the sign of the cross over his chest, then grabbed his wife's hand before striding away from the tomb.

"It's time to go," her father whispered into her ear a few minutes later when she and her small family were all that remained other than the men assigned to slip Jay's coffin into the tomb and seal it, men who huddled a few steps away, past another family's above-ground crypt. They were waiting, one smoking, avoiding her gaze.

She squeezed her eyes shut, stemming the hot tears.

"Come on, honey." Her father's voice was kind. Understanding.

Just leave me alone. Everyone, just leave me alone!

They couldn't understand her pain, the physical torment of heartache, the mental anguish of knowing that she should be in the coffin, not Jay. He was lying dead. She was alive.

Left to feel the void of the future.

Left to slog forward through platitudes, prayers, and grief.

Left so very alone.

He'd died saving her from a faceless, murderous madman.

"We need to go," Rick Bentz said, tugging at her arm, but she pulled it away and cast him a hard, meaningful glance as a new emotion crawled through her, a bright, hot rage that chased away the blackness, that battled with her self-torture.

"Leave me."

"Honey, we can't—"

"Dad. Just leave me," she bit out, and dashed her tears away with the back of her hand. "I want—I *need*—some time alone. With my husband."

"But—"

"Shh." Olivia gazed straight at her husband with eyes that, Kristi knew, had seen far too much, witnessed more anguish than any mortal person should ever have borne. "Let her be."

He opened his mouth to protest, but closed it again, finally seeming to understand. He let go of Kristi's arm. "We'll be in the car," he said against his daughter's ear, his voice husky as he planted a kiss on her cheek. "Waiting."

Kristi didn't respond.

Just stared down at the coffin.

Imagined that her once vital husband could hear her.

"I'll get him," she vowed. "I will get him. And he will pay." She bit her lip so hard it bled, then with bloodstained lips, bent down and kissed the smooth wood of Jay McKnight's coffin. "For you," she swore, straightening. "And for our unborn child."

She should have told him about the baby, Kristi thought, curled on the couch in her living room. Jay should have known that they were going to become parents by the following summer. But she'd kept the secret to herself. What had she been waiting for?

The "right" moment?

A big surprise?

How foolish she'd been. She touched her stomach, still flat as a board, the tiny bit of life within her undetectable at about eight weeks from conception. To be fair, she thought, she'd barely found out herself and then . . . oh, God. The fight. The horrible screaming match that had occurred before she'd left the house on the night of the attack.

She'd been leaving for her yoga class and what had started out as the same old argument about her working had escalated. She'd considered telling him about the baby that night, but had held her tongue because she'd known that her pregnancy would only amplify his reasons for not wanting her to work.

She wrote true-crime books.

He considered it dangerous and had warned her on various occasions that a convicted killer could be paroled or escape or have friends and Kristi was painting an ever-larger target on her back.

"These people aren't rational," he'd said, his eyes blazing, his lips tight with concern. "You can't trust them, no matter how 'good' they've been while serving time," he'd pointed out, while pouring himself a drink, a double scotch. Neat. His favorite.

"And they have friends," he'd continued, taking a sip from his short glass and pointing at her with a long finger. "Family members. People who would like nothing more than revenge against anyone they think exploits them. You make money from their mistakes, the pain of their loved ones. They're crazed. And they have weapons."

"Exploits them? Killers?"

"In their eyes, you're abusing them."

"Oh, Jay, stop it." That—his remark about abusing killers? Seriously? That had particularly stung and she'd longed for a drink of her own. Red wine. Her go-to when stressed, but that last night, because of her recently discovered secret, that they would be parents, she'd eyed the bottle but left it be.

"This is my job, Jay," she said. "It's not dangerous."

"You don't know that."

"And you don't know that it is. You're just paranoid."

"Am I?" He was getting angrier. Downed his drink. "What about Roy Calhoun, the author who wrote about that Chicago strangler? He ended up at the end of a rope, a noose hung from his own ceiling, dangling over a copy of his book, the pages all ripped out."

"One case?"

"How about Anne DeVille?"

"That was an accident," Kristi argued, really wanting that glass of wine.

"She went canoeing alone and was found drowned, her boat capsized. Her life vest missing."

"She was careless."

"Like you?" he'd said. "You've already published enough books. You don't need to write any more. Face it, Kristi, with every book you write, you're taunting someone in the shadows, profiting off their pain, throwing them and their families into the spotlight."

"I thought killers loved the limelight. I thought they got off on mentally reviewing their kills, that they loved to replay the suffering of their victims, that they got their rocks off by outplaying a game with the police."

"Some. But it's dangerous. These people are capable of unspeakable acts."

"I know."

"And you make them famous. Throw them into the spotlight again."

"I tell their stories, Jay. What are you saying?" she demanded, seeing deeper into his argument. "That I glorify them? Murderers? Rapists?"

"That they could object to you profiting from them."

"You don't get it, do you?" she'd flung back at him. "This isn't just a job for me, it's what I do. What I want to do!"

"Find something else. Something less dangerous."

"Oh. Yeah. Right. I can just imagine what you would do if I told you to find another career."

"I'd listen," he'd argued, and tossed back his drink.

"And then you'd do what you wanted. Well, consider yourself listened to." She'd grabbed her backpack and mat and stormed to the door. "And now I'm going to do exactly what I want."

"Kristi, don't!"

"Don't what?" she'd demanded. "Don't leave now? Don't write my story? Don't be the person I was meant to be?" She'd felt her temper rising, her anger exploding. "Maybe I should quit being Kristi Bentz and be satisfied with just being Mrs. Jay McKnight."

"Just?" he'd repeated.

"Yeah, like it's some big honor." And then she'd said it. The words that had haunted her since she'd spit them out. As she'd reached for the door handle, she'd glared at him and with all the venom in her heart said, "I don't know why I ever married you!"

And then she'd stepped through the door and into the night.

Less than two hours later Jay McKnight, the man she'd spat such hateful words at and the love of her life, lay dying in her arms. She wondered if he ever really trusted that she loved him with all her heart.

Of course as he'd lain bleeding in her arms, she'd vowed her love, begged him to hang on, that they had so much life yet to live. Together. Mentioned the baby. *Their* baby. But had he heard her? Over her cries for help and tears and his own labored breathing, had Jay known she loved him, had always loved him? That he would be a father?

Dear Jesus, she'd been a stubborn idiot. Their fight had been stupid. And it hadn't been the first. Her career and Jay's perceived danger of it had been the sticking point of most of their arguments, and more often than not she'd found herself finding solace in a bottle. They would fight, make up, make love, and she usually had ended up drinking too much.

Tears filled her eyes and spilled, as they had every day since the attack. She saw Jay's jacket, hung over the back of one of the dining room chairs where he'd always left it, and she blinked, carrying the jacket into the bedroom and reaching for a hanger in the closet.

Then she stopped, her fingers hovering over the bar holding all of her husband's clothes. This jacket had not been in the dining room earlier.

She was certain of it.

Right?

Her tired mind scrambled back to the day and the weeks earlier. The night of the murder Jay had been home, she'd left him, and yeah, the jacket could have been draped over the back of the chair as it always was. It was so common as to be part of the landscape. But in the intervening days between the night Jay was killed and today, she'd kind of cleaned up. Not entirely. She hadn't had the energy, but she was almost certain she'd hung this jacket in this closet.

Or had she?

A cold breath of unease brushed against the back of her neck, causing the hairs at her nape to lift.

No one had been in the house.

She kept it locked and—

Turning slowly, she surveyed the bedroom and studied the night table on Jay's side of the bed. Had things been disturbed? His watch was missing, but he'd been wearing it. His phone wasn't plugged into the charger as it, too, had been on him that night. And he'd been carrying his keys, which he sometimes left on the table beneath the lamp. She'd moved the remote to her side of the bed and everything looked the same except—

Her heart nearly jumped out of her chest.

Where was the picture that always stood on the nightstand, the small, framed photograph of Kristi and Jay on their wedding day, she still wearing her veil tossed back over her hair, he with his tuxedo tie undone and dangling? In the shot, they were laughing, sharing the joy of the day in the aftermath of the ceremony, and it was Jay's favorite picture.

Now it was gone.

Disbelieving, she strode across the room and peered at the floor around the nightstand, ignoring the dust bunnies that had collected. Her gaze scraped the entire area.

Nothing.

Oh. Dear. God.

With trembling fingers she opened the single drawer.

The photograph lay faceup on his e-reader, pens, notepads, and earphones. But the frame was cockeyed, the glass cracked, splintering in one corner. As if it had been dropped.

Or thrown.

She thought about their last argument.

The furious, ugly words spat out so harshly, intending to cut deep.

Had Jay been so angry with her for leaving to have thrown the picture against the wall, or so unthinking as to knock it over, and then what? Stuff it into the drawer when he'd cooled off?

Or had someone else been in the house, inside their bedroom? Fear crawled through her insides and she had to tamp it down. Once more she rotated slowly, like a toy ballerina on a jewelry box that was running out of power, slowly winding down. She eyed every inch of the room, her nerves stretched to the breaking point. She felt violated and scared and angry. Really angry.

Who would dare to come into her house? To mess with Jay's things? What kind of a—

"Calm down, Kris. Think. You can't prove that anyone was here. Find the evidence!"

"Damn it, I'm looking for it!" she said aloud.

She heard her voice, saw her image in the full-length mirror propped in one corner, and she gasped. She was wan, thinner than usual, all of her vitality gone. Her hair was a tangle and she couldn't remember when she'd last brushed it. She was still holding Jay's jacket in a death grip, her knuckles showing white, the collar of the jacket wadded in her clenched fingers.

She told herself to calm down. To not go off the deep end. To think like a rational person.

But her emotions were ragged and torn, her anger pulsing in her temples, her fear and outrage coagulating in her guts.

"Pull it together, Kris. You can do this."

Slowly her fingers unknotted and she tossed the jacket on the bed before walking through the house. Testing the doors and windows, scrutinizing every room and finding nothing more unsettling.

Yet.

But there were hours and days and weeks to come. She had to find some kind of inner strength. Finally she was convinced nothing else was out of place. She hung the damned jacket in the bedroom closet, then snapped blinds shut and pulled down shades before forcing herself to settle onto the oversized couch. Rubbing her shoulder, she recalled how the doctor had told her with a knowing smile that the wound was "healing nicely," and once more she'd heard again how lucky she'd been that her injuries hadn't been worse.

"Yeah, right," she muttered, but the headache that had come with the concussion was long gone and she could rotate her arm, lift it over her head, and even lift small items without much pain. "Lucky," she reminded herself.

Snagging the remote for the television and clicking it on, she watched the local news, but Jay's murder of two weeks earlier wasn't mentioned. Still a little edgy, she pushed herself from the couch and found her way into the kitchen where an unopened bottle of Merlot was waiting for her.

As it has been for half a month.

She felt the need of a drink, the anticipation of the buzz, the warm, cozy feeling of just a glass. Or two.

It wasn't just the life inside her that made her hesitate, it was the dance with alcoholism that had claimed her father, even though Rick Bentz was not her biological father.

"Close enough," she reminded herself as theirs wasn't what anyone would call a traditional family. She considered Rick her father; he'd claimed her as such and that was that. She wouldn't go down that dark path of her conception. At that thought she touched her abdomen. This child wouldn't know his or her father and that, in and of itself, was sad.

Scrounging in a drawer, she found her corkscrew, and opened the bottle of her favorite red. The scent wafted up to her and she remembered dozens of nights sharing a bottle with Jay.

Now she was a widow.

Make that a pregnant widow.

She lifted the bottle to her nose for a better smell, then walked over to the sink and poured, watching as the wine, so like the color of blood, streamed and swirled down the drain. She remembered all the blood that night. Hers. Jay's. Blending together from a random assault.

At least she thought the attack was random.

Jay's warning cut through her brain. *These people are capable of unspeakable acts.*

That thought stopped her short. She assumed that the attack against her was random, someone who'd intended to rob her, or do her harm, but only because she was walking alone on the street that night.

But maybe she was wrong.

Possibly she'd been targeted.

The police weren't sure.

And neither was she. But it didn't matter. Whoever had wielded the knife that night had ended Jay's life. That miscreant's days were numbered. One way or another, she was going to locate that sick son of a bitch and nail him to the cross.

Justice would be served.

Along with a satisfying slab of vengeance.

CHAPTER 3

"I'll just be a sec," Montoya said as he cut across traffic and slid the cruiser into a restricted space where paint was peeling from the curb. The mid-October sun was peeking through a haze of clouds, weak rays piercing the dirty windshield, the inside of the cruiser warm.

Bentz pointed to a signpost. "You're parked in a loading zone."

"Only spot available," Montoya said, his mouth a slash of white. "It's okay, Bentz. We're cops. Remember?"

Bentz didn't argue.

"If anyone gives you trouble, go all Dirty Harry on them and flash your damned badge. You're still working out, right? Hitting the big bag a few times a week?"

"Yeah." Bentz rubbed his shoulder. It ached a bit as he'd gone after the sparring bag a little too furiously this morning.

"Good. I'll be right back." And he was out of the car and jogging toward the door of a beignet shop where all kinds of pastries were on display in a tiered case behind the window.

As Bentz watched, Montoya pulled open the door, then hesitated, holding it open for a woman coming out of the shop. She was pushing a stroller with twin girls, both dressed in pink, both with curly black pigtails.

Then he disappeared inside.

For donuts? Beignets? Pastries?

What the hell was Montoya thinking? Bentz checked his watch. Eleven fifteen. A little late for a coffee break and early for lunch. Bentz drummed his fingers on the edge of the cruiser's window, all too aware of how time was passing, slipping away, minute by minute. And in those escaping seconds he felt the itch, that he wasn't doing anything productive while somewhere in the shadows his son-in-law's killer was out there.

Doing what?

Planning another attack on his daughter?

Or did he have someone else in his sights?

Was the assault random?

Or had Kristi or Jay been targeted?

And then, why? The question that burned through his mind in restless circles. Why? Why? Why?

His gut churned and his eyes were gritty.

He hadn't slept in days, not since Jay's brutal murder. According to Kristi, her husband had saved her life, breaking up the attack and being slain in the process. He might have survived the first wound to his chest, the short blade had barely nicked a lung. But the second gash, across his leg, severing his femoral artery, had cost him his life. The scene, rain drenched and blood soaked, bore out Kristi's telling of the horrific attack.

But if she was right, then the murderer had singled her out. Again, a random incident—wrong place at the wrong time?—or had she been stalked? Hunted? Had the killer been waiting for her?

So lost in thought was he that he didn't see Montoya return. The driver's door opened and his partner slid behind the wheel, handing over a paper cup of take-out coffee as he did. "Here." The aroma of freshly brewed coffee filled the interior.

"What is it?"

"Triple shot of espresso." Montoya glanced his way and dropped a white sack onto the console. "You need it. You look like shit."

"Thanks."

"I mean it." He slid the cruiser into gear and, with an eye to the rearview mirror, pressed on the gas and the cruiser slipped into traffic. "When's the last time you slept?"

"It's been a while."

"Define 'a while.'"

"I catch a few hours every night."

Montoya threw him a disbelieving look, but didn't call him out on the lie, just said, "Well, you're not doing anyone any good by draggin' your ass around as if it weighs two tons." Bentz started to argue, but Montoya shook his head. "Nuh-uh. Don't want to hear it. No excuses. I know your kid was nearly killed. I know your son-in-law didn't make it and I know that it's all personal. That you're obsessed with getting the guy so he doesn't strike again. You keep thinking about 'what ifs.' What if Jay hadn't shown up when he did. What if Kristi had left a little early. And you're makin' yourself crazy tryin' to figure out who did this and why. I get it. I've got a kid. I would feel the same way. But I'm tellin' you, man, you're not thinkin' straight."

"Is that all, Mother?" Bentz asked with more than a tinge of sarcasm.

"Ah, Jesus. Don't go there." Montoya sped through an amber light. "And no, it's not all. You haven't said it, but I know you think Father John is behind it all."

Bentz glanced out the side window. Felt his teeth gnash so hard his jaw hurt. Montoya had hit the nail on the head with that. "Father John" was an alias, of course, for a serial killer that had stalked the streets of New Orleans years before, a murderer who had been dubbed the Rosary Killer as the psycho had used the sharpened beads of a rosary to strangle his victims. Bentz had thought that he'd killed the bastard years before, deep in the swamp.

But he'd been wrong.

And now the terror the fake priest had inflicted upon the city so long ago had returned. Already there was one dead prostitute in his wake, his latest victim being Teri Marie Gaines aka Tiffany Elite, the unlucky working girl who had been caught in Father John's web and ended up strangled. The same marks, unique marks, had bruised her throat, a pattern of little cuts that mimicked the bead pattern of a rosary that had appeared on the victims years before. Also, a hundred-dollar bill, with Ben Franklin's eyes blackened out, had been left at the victim's apartment.

Father John's signature.

A mocking display meant to taunt Bentz and had ended up haunting him.

Now, the "Rosary Killer" was back, a ghost of a murderer who had eluded Bentz in the past, who had disappeared and now resurfaced, Rick Bentz's own personal white whale.

Or, unlikely as it seemed, was the killer who had staged Tiffany's body so perfectly a copycat, a killer who had studied his mentor's methods and style to a T?

Bentz couldn't help but wonder if that killer had decided Bentz's daughter would be his next victim.

Even though she hadn't died, Kristi had been permanently wounded. Not only physically but emotionally as well.

"Dear Jesus." He shoved his hand through his hair in frustration.

Every time he'd seen Kristi, his heart twisted. Oh, she'd always put on a brave face, but he'd been able to look through her facade. He'd recognized the bone-tired weariness no amount of makeup had been able to conceal. He'd noticed the wan pallor of her skin, the dark smudges beneath her eyes, the lack of animation in her expression.

She'd always been lively—a "firecracker" or "pistol" while growing up—and reckless and headstrong as a younger woman. Now she seemed a shell of the woman she'd once been.

He suspected that despite her arguments to the contrary, she was experiencing survivor's guilt, an emotion that had been his own burden for years whenever he thought of his first wife, Jennifer, Kristi's mother. His eyes narrowed as he remembered Jennifer. So beautiful. So vain. So filled with deceit. Her lies . . . He stopped himself, wouldn't allow his mind to wander down that dark and twisted path. He forcibly turned his thoughts to the present and to the simple fact that someone had nearly taken Kristi's life and had, instead, made her a widow.

His fists clenched.

That sick son of a bitch would pay.

Bentz would make sure of it.

His stomach twisted again and he felt a rising swell of fury. Along with a jab of impotence at the thought of Father John or even a copycat stalking the streets of his city again.

Montoya cut into his thoughts. "There're beignets in the bag. Plain, a couple of apple, and some chocolate. Help yourself. A sugar rush wouldn't hurt you."

Bentz took a sip of the hot coffee. Wished it was bourbon. Passed on the beignets. Already the coffee was mixing with the acid forming in his stomach and he figured a sugar-coated, fat-fried almost donut wouldn't help. "Thanks."

"No worries." Montoya hit the brakes as a bicycle rider cut in front of him. "Idiot!" he muttered under his breath as the bike angled into a side street. "I should cite him." Then he took a deep breath and, for once, didn't chase the offender down. Montoya was still a hothead and he ran on adrenaline and testosterone, but since he'd become a father, some of his sharp edges had smoothed a bit. Fingers tight over the wheel, he shot his partner another glance and got right back up on his soapbox. "I'm just sayin' take care of yourself, okay? Then you can take care of the case."

Montoya had a point, Bentz grudgingly thought. It was all true that he hadn't slept in days aside from a few catnaps here and there. At night his worries compounded, driving any chance at sleep away. Though he rationally knew the murderous attack wasn't his fault, he couldn't help but feel a needle of doubt prick deep into his soul, a sharp little reminder insisting that he was somehow responsible, that it was up to him to keep his family safe.

Another sip of coffee. "Message received."

"Really? You're going to take my advice?" Beneath his goatee, Montoya's lips twisted and his dark eyes flashed as he switched lanes.

"Maybe."

"And maybe not." Montoya's earring winked in the weak sunlight that managed to pierce through the windshield. "What is it you don't understand about 'random attack'?"

"Don't believe it," Bentz said. "Not when one victim is the daughter of a cop and the other victim works with the force." He shook his head. "Not random."

"Prove it then. And while you're at it?" He shot another hard look Bentz's way. "Get some fuc—effin' sleep." He scowled. "Shit." Then let out a disgusted huff. "Abby's trying to get me to clean up my language. Y'know, for the kid. Ben's too young to understand but"—he shrugged—"who knows what he's picking up?"

"I hear ya."

"Do you? About takin' care of yourself? I hope so."

"Working on it," Bentz assured him as Montoya parked.

"Well, for Christ's sake, work a little harder, would ya?"

Montoya threw the tennis ball the length of the yard, a long, narrow piece of property that extended from the back of the shotgun house he shared with his wife and kid. Abby was talking about moving, getting a bigger place, maybe thinking about having another child. "I'd love a daughter," she'd told him in bed this morning. "Or another son. Benjamin will need a sibling."

Montoya wasn't convinced. At least not yet. The kid was way too young to deal with a brother or sister, even given another year, at least in Montoya's opinion.

And the world they lived in was tough.

Climate change. Social unrest. A recent flu outbreak. Overpopulation. Wars around the world.

Was it wise to bring another kid onto the planet? He was of the opinion that Ben was enough. At least for now.

Their dog, Hershey, a chocolate lab that was beginning to show his age, bounded after the ball, loping through the patchy grass to retrieve the prize in the gloom of coming evening, then bring it back. Hershey's muzzle was graying and he spent a lot of time lying in the sun on the back porch.

"Get it!" he said as the dog snuffled through the grass. "You can find it." The ball had lodged between a crepe myrtle tree and Benjamin's plastic trike near the back fence. "That's it. You got it! Now, come on. Bring it back." Tennis ball in mouth, Hershey loped back. "Good boy." Montoya ruffled the lab behind his ears, then walked inside where the scents of bacon, onions, and tomato sauce still lingered from dinner.

Outside the bathroom he nearly ran into Abby, who was hauling a towel-wrapped Ben on one hip. "Hey, big guy!" He ruffled his son's wet hair and the kid gave him a wide smile that showed two tiny lower teeth just breaking through his gums. The grin melted Montoya's heart.

Benjamin gurgled something indistinct.

"Did you hear that?" Montoya asked, and joked, "I think he said 'DaDa.' Clear as a bell."

"Dreamer." Abby laughed, a sound Montoya still loved. "Okay, 'DaDa,' if you say so. Now, why don't you get him in his pj's and ask him to enunciate a little more distinctly, huh?" she said, handing Montoya the boy. "I'll deal with cleaning up our bathroom where Hurricane Benjamin hit."

"You got it." He winked at his wife, then carried Ben into the nurs-

ery, a small room next to theirs that was definitely too small for a second crib no matter what Abby said. Placing his son on the changing
table, he then struggled to get the wriggling baby into a diaper and
pajamas.

"You're a wiggling worm," he accused, finally wrestling Ben's head
through the pajama top.

The baby giggled, as if he truly understood.

Montoya picked up his son and scooped up the damp towel before hanging it on a hook near the door. As he did, the cell phone in
Montoya's back pocket vibrated.

He almost didn't answer, then thought better of it and placed the
baby into the playpen in the living area.

No caller ID on the screen.

"Hello?" he answered, rolling a ball toward his son in the playpen.

"Bro?"

Montoya's stomach dropped. "Cruz?" he said, recognizing the
voice he hadn't heard in over a year.

"Yeah," his brother whispered, breathing hard, as if he'd been
running.

"Cruz, where the hell are you?" Montoya couldn't remember the
last time Cruz had called him. Maybe on his last birthday? Maybe the
one before. Cruz had always been a loner, a rogue, sometimes referred to as "the black sheep" of the family.

"Look, it doesn't matter where I am. Not now," Cruz said, keeping
his voice low, as if he were afraid someone other than his brother
might hear. "I'm in trouble. Deep shit, man."

Montoya's back muscles tightened. "What?"

"I can't explain now. But I want you to know I'm heading
your way."

"Why?" This sounded bad.

"Because I need your help. And you can't tell anybody, okay? Not
anyone in the family and not Abby. Not your partner. You got that?"

Oh, shit. "Are you ser—?"

"Serious? Is that what you were going to ask?" Cruz demanded,
his voice tight, and Montoya imagined his brother's face, a muscle
jumping near his temple. "Hell yeah, I'm serious. This is no joke.
Okay?" A long shaky breath. "Holy Mother of God, I think—no, I
know—I'm about to be arrested for murder."

"What?" Reuben said, disbelieving. Sure, Cruz had gotten into more than his share of scrapes with the law in the past. But homicide? Never. "Murder?" he repeated. "What're you talking about? Who died?"

His question went unanswered.

The phone was already dead.

CHAPTER 4

Bentz caught sight of the moon, not quite full, rising high over the city. Then he snapped the blinds shut and checked his watch. After midnight. He cracked his neck, glanced down at the papers piled on his desk and the glowing screen of his laptop, then walked down the short hallway to the master bedroom. Olivia had turned out her reading light and was lying on her side of the bed. He thought she might be sleeping, then heard her say softly, "Give it up, Rick. You don't have to be a superhero tonight. Come to bed."

If only it were that easy. "I will in a few."

She sighed as he pulled on the door, leaving it open just a crack. Then he crossed the hall and peered into Ginny's room.

Moonlight filtered through the blinds, striping the room, and he was reminded of bars in a jail cell and he pushed that image aside.

His daughter was curled at the bottom of the crib, her springy blond curls on the exposed sheet. On silent footsteps, he avoided stepping on several dolls and blocks and coloring books, crossed to the bed, lifted Ginny up, and kissed her smooth forehead. Her tiny little lips moved and her eyes blinked open for just a second, eyelashes fluttering before she sighed once more.

"Love you," he whispered, returning her to the crib and watching as she settled into sleep again. "Good night, sweetheart," he said under his breath, his heart nearly aching at the innocence of her.

How it all changed when life interfered.

His jaw tightened as he thought of his older daughter, a grown woman who knew martial arts as well as her own mind. He'd made sure Kristi was skilled in the use of firearms, but he'd never been able to tame the fearlessness in her. She was beyond courageous to the point of being reckless.

And this one . . . His heart squeezed and he closed the blinds, leaving the room in darkness other than for the fairy princess night-light that glowed near the closet. He left the door slightly ajar as he headed back to his den, making a pit stop in the kitchen where, of course, he found no beer in the refrigerator.

A good thing, he reminded himself as he settled back into his desk chair and heard it creak against his weight.

He went over the case notes on Jay McKnight's murder and found nothing new. His son-in-law had been stabbed in the chest with a sharp, short blade, then sliced in the thigh, the upshot being that he'd bled out from the wound to his femoral artery. The street cameras that night caught images of the assailant, a man—well, possibly a woman, it was impossible to tell. The killer had been dressed in a black poncho and had been wearing a ski mask and dark glasses to cover his face. Sunglasses with reflective lenses. In the middle of the night in the pouring rain.

Bentz's eyes narrowed.

He saw no evidence of a clerical collar in any of the footage, and the few witnesses the police had tracked down had only noticed a dark figure running, nothing more.

Bentz stared at a still from a camera located at a pawnshop not far from the attack; it gave the clearest image of the man in the poncho, but it was still grainy, in black and white, the rain a curtain distorting any features that might have been visible.

Leaning back in his chair, he rotated the kinks from his neck to hear his spine crack.

Kristi insisted that the attack was random, just some nut-job, but Bentz wondered. Could she have actually been the target? She admitted that going to the class at night was part of her weekly routine. As for Jay? He'd come looking for her. She didn't know why except that they'd had a fight and he was probably coming to patch things up. The scattered roses, a dozen red blooms, seemed to suggest just that.

So what if Kristi were the target? Not a random victim?

Bentz's blood ran cold at the thought.

Who would want to harm her?

Possibly some dirtbag whose story she told in one of the books she wrote. She'd always been fascinated with true crime and spent hours, days, weeks, and years researching a subject, exposing the inner torment of the killers and their victims. Could she have crossed paths with a psychopath who didn't like how he'd been portrayed, or a maniac who became fixated with a pretty woman asking questions about him?

He made a note to put together a list of her enemies, starting with the felons portrayed in her books. A side note reminded him to check with their families as well. Siblings, parents, and children often took offense at their lives being studied or, as they saw it, dissected and abused for Kristi's personal gain, their lives exploited. He glanced up at a bookshelf mounted near the window where signed copies of her books were so proudly displayed. Although he worried about her chosen line of work and about how closely she became associated with convicted killers, he took pride in her accomplishments. His gaze scanned the spines, and as he did, he recalled those freaks whom she'd exposed to the world, some of whom he'd helped put behind bars. The Chosen One, a killer who had dubbed himself that not-so-humble name, or Hamilton Cooke, a doctor who had killed his wife. Bentz had nailed Cooke and the bastard had been convicted. Kristi had written about both cases. Recently Cooke's conviction had been overturned, which really bothered Bentz. The surgeon was a stone-cold killer; Bentz knew it and had proved it.

There were others as well, for example Ned Zavala, the Bayou Butcher, or Mandel Jarvis, an ex-pro football player who "accidentally" killed his wife and blamed Bentz for his conviction.

That just scratched the surface.

To be truthful, it could be a dozen other killers whom Bentz had sent up the river and were now free.

Unless it was more personal.

He chewed on the inside of his lip. Thought hard.

Maybe he was barking up the wrong tree.

And maybe, just maybe, Father John was back. He stared at the spine of Kristi's book *The Rosary Killer,* and a knot tightened in his stomach.

He needed a list of the subjects of her books along with other enemies she may have made in her life.

The same went for her husband. As Bentz recalled, Jay had left some broken hearts along the way, including jilting a woman to whom he'd been engaged. That had been years before, of course, but what was the old saying? "Revenge is best served cold," or some such crap.

But he couldn't discount it.

He couldn't discount any suspect.

He flipped over the page of his legal pad and wrote quick reminders on a clean yellow sheet. Again he thought about the murderers who might be connected to him, convicts he'd put away and were out of prison. They ate at him. Could the killer be one of the psychos who had sworn they would make Bentz pay for arresting and convicting him?

Once again, he studied the spines of Kristi's books. More than a couple of the cases had been made into television movies and had been intertwined with his investigations. That had been only natural. Also her own life had been in jeopardy on more than one occasion.

Bentz's jaw slid to the side and he felt the burning in his gut again when he considered how many times he'd already thought he'd lost her, how often a woman of her age, young, athletic, and healthy, had faced and cheated death.

But the Grim Reaper was nothing if not determined. Patiently so. Because he always wins in the end.

I study my wound in the mirror.

A bright red scar runs from my eye to chin, compliments of Kristi Bentz. The slice is raw and red, but will heal. Luckily my eye was saved. Wouldn't droop. And I know how to take care of wounds; I understand how to help the injury heal and reduce its scarring. Though vanity is a sin, I can't help but take pride in my looks—yes, I know, another sin. Add it to the list. The truth is I usually spend more hours working out than I do praying.

I will have to change that, I think as I take out my favorite weapon, that perfect little knife, and sharpen it on the stone. *Scritch!* The blade rubs across the hard surface. *Scritch! Scritch!* Faster and faster, scraping the edge until it's razor sharp. *Scritch!*

Perfect.

I think about that fine, deadly edge and consider the night I last used it.

On Jay McKnight.

I managed to escape on the night I attacked Kristi Bentz, although I worried that the police with their cameras, computer enhancements, legions of troops with guns, cars, helicopters, and dogs would hunt me down. Arrest me. Cage me.

So far I've escaped.

I didn't chance going to a hospital to get stitched up. No urgent care, or clinic, or even visiting a veterinary supply store. I know what to do. The US government helped me out on that score. I was a medic in the army. I learned. I practiced. And I was able to apply that knowledge and those skills to the thin cut running down the side of my face. With a little surgical tape and glue, I pulled the skin together. Ever since I've tended to the area meticulously, gently massaging my skin and applying vitamin E as if I was in post-op care for plastic surgery. I've laid low, which I planned in advance—another convenient trip out of town for those who asked—but I've also avoided sunlight and recuperated, staying inside, even forgoing my usual workout routine for now.

And I prayed.

Oh, how I prayed. Over and over as I healed.

Asking for guidance.

Begging for a sign.

Hoping to atone.

Now, not for the first time today, I make the sign of the cross and whisper, "In the name of the Father and of the Son and of the Holy Spirit. Amen."

It's been over a week since I'd taken Jay McKnight's life and I've replayed the scene in my mind hundreds of times, maybe even a thousand. McKnight's death hadn't been part of the plan. Never before had her husband, or anyone else, interrupted that bitch's walk from her three-night-a-week yoga class to her car. I know. I followed her for weeks, making certain her routine was always the same.

So why on this night had McKnight tracked her down?

Had he known?

It was all just bad luck, I decide as I gently apply more of my healing ointment onto the scar, then wipe my fingers and make my way from the tiny bathroom to the main living area of my apartment, a converted old carriage house that backed the property, the access only visible by one neighbor, an infirm elderly woman on the other side of a thick hedge, but there are a few holes in the greenery and I've seen her peering through them as she gardens. Luckily, lately she can't pry. Not since her last stroke, which was all the more convenient as she'd been hauled off to a nursing home where she was recuperating and rehabilitating. Hopefully she wouldn't ever return "home."

Which would be perfect because, before that fortunate little bleeding in her brain, Bessie Cawthorne was getting a little nosy. Sometimes if the old bat was out in the garden trimming or deadheading her flowers, she'd call to me, ask me how I was, to which I always answered, "Fine" or "Busy" or whatever. At times I'd caught her peering through her blinds, especially if I was leaving late at night. That's when her curiosity got the better of her and she'd always ask the next time she ran into me, what was I doing, where was I going, that sort of thing. I'd been able to fend off her questions fairly easily for the most part.

And now, at least for the foreseeable future, she won't be a problem.

Aside from the old lady, there aren't too many others to worry about. A lawn service with a variety of gardeners mows her yard and blows debris off our shared driveway. But the workmen wearing ear protection were always trying to finish as quickly as possible, never even glancing at the short alley and brick fence that surround this private spot.

My biggest concern had been Bessie's scrappy little dog—a terrier of some sort—and an infernal beast with bristly gray fur, curious dark eyes, and a penchant for watching my every move. As soon as I open the gate, there he is, peering out the kitchen window from his seat on the banquette, paws on the glass. Sometimes the damned dog barks—a high-pitched, irritating noise—and I'd rather he didn't alert the old lady to my comings and goings. Especially at night. Not that I'm in the alley all that often, but still, the less notice, the better.

However that problem is solved. At least temporarily. Someone in Bessie's dutiful family took the irritating mutt away.

And now that the dog and Bessie are gone, my life is simpler.

Aside from the sorry fact that Kristi Bentz is still alive.

That's a problem.

I try to convince myself that it's all for the best, that I should savor this moment. I'll get to her in time, but for now, isn't it better that she is grieving, feeling the pain of the loss of her husband?

Sure, it is, I tell myself as I walk into the kitchen and reach into the small refrigerator and pull out a bottle of cranberry juice—not that sugary stuff, not the "cranberry cocktail" that is touted on TV, but pure, tart cranberry juice. I dilute it with filtered water, then carry it to the tall café table where newspapers are spread, opened to pages dedicated to the murder that occurred in Pirate's Alley. I peruse them again—there's nothing new, thank God—then fold them and pull out my laptop to check the latest reports. I scroll through the news reports, not only for New Orleans, but nationally. Just in case.

Here, in this apartment, I have secure Wi-Fi under an alias—everything in this tiny apartment is listed under an alias, of course. I can't help but smile at that. Who would think? I've gone to such lengths to hide, so that no one will ever suspect. Sipping the juice, I find that Jay McKnight's homicide has receded from the national interest. No column inches dedicated to his death. And checking social media, I find his bizarre murder is no longer trending.

Good.

The fickle public has moved on to other more topical and salacious scandals, mainly those involving celebrities. Jay McKnight's brutal demise is, for now, forgotten.

Except by his wife.

And the police.

They would still be searching, examining every tiny clue, every microscopic shred of evidence. How ironic, as Jay McKnight had worked in the crime lab, a forensic specialist. I smile. All McKnight's knowledge and expertise about crime scenes and blood spatter and DNA analysis and whatever wouldn't help him now, would it?

I lift my glass and silently congratulate myself on a job well done. Well, sure, it wasn't exactly what I'd planned, but it would work. It might even work better.

Because Kristi Bentz is suffering.

Good.

Her pain—that is what matters.

So maybe I didn't fail after all. Maybe, instead, I've increased the agony.

Which is perfect.

"To me," I say aloud, and wish I had just a tiny shot of vodka to add to my drink, "and to all that is to come."

I can't wait.

And then I make the mistake of turning on the television and am faced with another clip of one of the movies made for television, a cheesy replication of the crimes that Kristi Bentz wrote about in her books.

"No!" I say, and smash the glass against the floor. "No! No! No!" As I stare at the television, my good mood, like the glass, is shattered, and I feel the walls closing in. From the outside, pushing in on my brain. I close my eyes and grab my head to stop the pain. Anger surges through my blood, pounding in my ears.

I fall to my knees, feel the liquid seep through my pant leg, and whisper, "Our Father, Who art in heaven, hallowed be Thy name. Thy kingdom come, Thy will be done, on earth as it is in heaven. . . ."

Bentz glanced at the clock. Almost two a.m. He yawned and stretched at his desk, rubbed his chin, and felt the stubble that he'd have to shave in what? Five hours? He needed to go to bed.

He would.

In ten minutes.

First, he pulled up the pictures of mourners at Jay's funeral for the third time tonight. They were photos that had been discreetly snapped from a cell phone by one of the cops watching the crowd from a distance. He studied each of the mourners, as he had the day of the funeral, and told himself the killer wouldn't be so bold as to risk exposure there.

Or would he?

Would his fascination, whatever the hell sick compulsion that caused him to assault Kristi and kill her husband, drive him to be a witness to the rite? No one looked out of place. He'd IDed everyone in attendance at the grave site and taken note of the mourners at the church. He had no pictures of the inside of the nave, but the same cop taking shots of the entombment had also clicked off dozens of photos of people leaving the church. Some he didn't recognize, but most were identified, people who knew Jay, friends, co-workers, and family, or others who were there to support Kristi.

Tired to the bone, he reached under his desk to his briefcase, quietly zipped it open, and found the small flask he kept in an inner pocket. Telling himself it was just this one time, he took a long swallow.

For years he'd been on the wagon, never touching a drop, but then he'd slipped, drinking a beer or two while investigating the 21 Killer's crime spree. He'd told himself he would stop, put down the bottle and never pick it up again once that case was solved.

But it hadn't happened.

So far he'd been able to pace himself, but he would quit again.

Soon.

But not tonight.

Not when he thought Father John might have come back to haunt New Orleans.

Oh, good God, Bentz, he's not a frickin' ghost. You don't believe in that shit.

If not the fake homicidal priest, then who?

He scrolled to pictures of the crime scene for Teri Marie Gaines, and his stomach twisted as he viewed her half-nude body, the bruising and little cuts on her neck, her eyes fixed.

This was how Father John liked to see his victims.

So why the vicious attack on the street? Maybe there was no connection at all; it could be that his thinking was muddled because of the Teri Marie Gaines murder. He glanced up sharply to the books on the shelf and zeroed in on the spine of Kristi's book about the Rosary Killer.

Was there a connection there, or was he grasping at straws?

Could Kristi's book, with her detailed, thorough analysis of Father John, be not just an account of the killer's crimes but a blueprint for a copycat?

Or was there no connection whatsoever?

He thought about his promise to his wife, to himself, about turning in his badge and retiring. They'd discussed it; he'd mentioned it to Montoya. But it never seemed to be the right time and now . . . no, not now. Not until he found out who'd nearly killed his daughter, not until he'd brought the scumbag who had made Kristi a widow to justice. No way.

Shoving his hands through his hair in frustration, he let out a heavy sigh, then took another nip from his flask. He was getting nowhere.

He heard a faint cry from Ginny's room, the results of the bad dreams she sometimes experienced. He kicked back the chair and made his way to her room to find her as he had earlier. Once again curled at the foot of her crib in the fetal position. "Silly girl," he whispered. He stared at her for a long while, watching her sleep, her lips moving, her breath steady. He wanted to ruffle her tiny curls, but resisted and returned to the den. At his desk he took a final sip and then, as the booze warmed his bloodstream, capped the flask, returned it to his briefcase, then headed for the bathroom to brush his teeth before he slipped into bed, hoping that sleep would come easily.

But he wasn't betting on it.

CHAPTER 5

In the rain, Jay touched her.

Caressed her.

Kissed her, but she backed away, daring him to catch her.

Then they were running, laughing, dashing through the thick drops pouring down on the city. She turned, smiling, catching sight of his dark figure through the shower.

"Catch me if you can," she yelled over her shoulder as she turned the corner at the cathedral and raced into a dark alley that seemed to grow narrower and narrower.

Jay's voice echoed from behind her. "Kristi, ruuuuun!"

But her legs were suddenly wooden and she noticed that the raindrops had turned to rose petals, falling and dancing against the white walls of the church to stain it red and run, like rivulets of blood, to the cobblestones, swirling around her feet, a garish eddy encircling her. She tried to call out to Jay, but her voice was muted.

She spun, turning in slow motion to search for him through the storm, but the figure that appeared was cloaked in black, his arms spread wide, his poncho stretching into wings just as he swooped, his fingers becoming talons, razor sharp and glinting—

Kristi awoke just before the killer struck.

Her heart was racing, sweat collecting at the roots of her hair.

She flung an arm across the wide bed, but it was empty.

Cold.

Tears sprang to her eyes and she sniffed loudly, swiped a hand under her nose in the darkness, and fought the urge to break down. It was a nightmare. The same hideous dream that chased her through her troubled nights. It shifted with slight variations, but essentially, she awoke each night, her heart thudding wildly, the vivid scenes holding tight to her brain as she roused.

A glance at the clock.

4:47.

"Too early," she told herself as she walked to the bathroom and listened to the house creak and moan in the predawn hours, as if the cottage they'd shared, too, was in mourning.

"Oh, stop it," she said aloud. "You're acting like an idiot."

Still, despite her sudden burst of bravado, she wondered if she'd ever sleep again, if this cozy little house would ever seem like home again. She'd so loved their little cottage and now . . . oh, God, now what?

She saw his aftershave on the shelf to the left of the mirror, reached for the bottle, opened it, and smelled.

Bad idea.

All sorts of images came to mind. All of him. She capped the bottle quickly, considered throwing it away, but replaced it, leaving it on the shelf where it belonged. The thought of getting rid of anything of his was mind numbing. She wasn't ready. She just couldn't do it. Not yet. Her throat grew thick and she wished, just one more time, she could feel the touch of his hand against her cheek.

Instead, she thought of the baby—the child he would never see—and she nearly crumpled. Grasping the edge of the sink, she forced herself to stand upright. The hole in her heart was just so, so huge.

Taking in a shaky breath, she stiffened her spine, then splashed cold water on her face. She saw her reflection in the mirror over the sink. Pale and hollow eyed, hair wild, breathing still uneven. "Pull it together," she told her reflection, then went to the kitchen where she drank a full glass of water and eyed the coffeemaker.

Not yet.

She should try to go back to bed.

Catch up on her sleep, but she knew it to be impossible.

For the time being, this—waking up in ultimate despair and fear before five in the morning—was her new, if unwanted routine.

"You can do this, Kris. Move on."

She heard Jay's voice as clearly as if he had been standing in the kitchen next to her and was, as he always did, patting his pockets to make certain he had his phone and keys before leaving for work. She imagined his sheepish smile when he found his phone not in his jacket but on the coffee table where he'd left it the night before. "Someday I'll figure this out," he'd say, scooping up the phone, planting a kiss on her cheek, and winking at her. "See ya later, gorgeous!" and off he'd go.

Feeling hollow inside, she walked through the living room where vases of dying flowers and piles of cards had been left on the coffee table, making the place seem like a mausoleum. But she couldn't deal with them. Not yet. Not this early. In the kitchen she tossed back two Tylenol tablets to fight the headache that had been her constant companion since the attack. Along with keeping up with yoga and tae kwon do, she'd taken up running again, but it was too early to hit the streets and she didn't have the energy. Then again she couldn't stay in the house another minute, couldn't remain where the memories of her husband surrounded her, where she could see him, hear his voice and know it was all in her head, that he was never coming back.

She grabbed her keys and cell, threw a coat over her pajamas, and headed to her car where, once behind the wheel, she drove the city streets. She bought a cup of decaf coffee at a drive-through, then wound her way through the familiar, but now-quiet French Quarter, inching along Decatur Street where she looked through the park to the cathedral, bathed in lights that washed up the tall black spires. And the alley, that dark, narrow street.

There.

There is where he died.

Where my life ended.

"*No, Kristi,*" he said as if he were sitting in the passenger seat. "*Where it begins. Where your new life, and that of our unborn child, starts.*"

"Is it?" she asked the ghost beside her. "And how do you know about the baby? I didn't—I hadn't told you."

She glanced at the seat. It was empty. If she'd expected to see any watery image of her husband, she was disappointed. She kept driving, wandering through the city in the predawn hours, circling back past the French Market District and seeing a few people on the street, some lights in restaurants where workers were preparing for the day. "Any advice?" she said, hoping to conjure up her husband's spirit, but he didn't appear, not even in her mind. "Oh, God, you're going out of your mind," she told herself, and drove home, never once touching her coffee.

Instead she told herself she could go down a worrisome path to crazy land where she talked to dead people she created in her imagination, or she could find a way to move forward with her life.

For herself.

For the baby.

Once home, she threw on her running clothes, eyed the disaster in the living room, but couldn't face reading through the condolence cards and best wishes and messages of hope for the future. It was all just such bullshit.

As the sky started to lighten, she took off down her regular running path, along a course she'd carved out for herself in this quiet neighborhood of New Orleans. Her cottage was located in the Garden District and she ran along streets lined with live oaks and followed the route of the St. Charles Streetcar for several blocks, then cut over to the river. By the time she reached the still-dark waters of the Mississippi, she was breathing hard, her body sheened in sweat, the sun rising higher and chasing away the fog. The demons that haunted her nightmares withered away and she felt that with the dawn came a new beginning, for her. For her child.

"That's my girl."

She nearly missed a step when Jay's voice whispered through her head, almost stumbled, and she slowed, half expecting to see him approaching, running to catch up to her, but, of course, he didn't. "Pull yourself together," she reprimanded, then picked up her pace again, listening to the sound of her feet slapping against the sidewalk and cursing the fact that she'd left her earbuds at home. She usually listened to music or a podcast while jogging, but she was just so out of sync these days she'd forgotten them, even left her phone at home.

She finished her loop, returning to her street and the little cottage she and Jay had purchased in the last two years.

With three small bedrooms, one bath, a wide front porch, and an attic that had been converted to an office where she spent hours researching and writing, the house had been perfect for them.

The backyard was large but manageable and private, with a tall fence and even taller shrubbery that created an oasis and would be perfect for the children they'd planned to have. At that thought she touched her abdomen and told herself it was all right that her child would grow up not knowing his or her father.

Kristi herself had been raised in a family that was far from traditional and she'd made it. This child would, too. She'd make certain of it.

Jay's ghost was right: it was time to get on with her life.

First things first. She collected the mail that had piled up in the box and left it on the coffee table with the unopened envelopes. Then she disposed of all the flowers that had been delivered and were now dying, tossing the dried-out blooms into the garbage and pouring the dirty water down the sink. Next she tackled the live plants, spreading them around the rooms, adding water, and checked her phone, noting that she needed to text or call a few friends. Finally she hit the shower, scrubbed off the sweat and tears, shampooed away the rest of her lingering sadness, and rinsed the pain away—at least she hoped she did. That was her intent.

When she was finished, she towel-dried, gave herself a pep talk, got dressed, and eyed Jay's clothes. She'd keep a few things—his flannel shirt she sometimes wore, his favorite tie and . . . Sadness threatened to overtake her, so she slammed the closet shut and headed to the kitchen.

"You can do this," she muttered, snagging up the remote and snapping on the TV as she passed through the living room. She poured the dregs of her now-cold coffee from McDonald's down the drain and found the makings for a smoothie by scrounging in her refrigerator, where piled-up casseroles and desserts vied for space, but weren't what she needed. Still, she managed to find solace in the loud whir of the blender as the last kiwi, a few blueberries, a couple of leaves of spinach that hadn't wilted were whipping to a froth along with an overripe banana and some yogurt that had been decidedly past its pull date.

Then she sat down at the table and, sipping her concoction, sorted through the mail. Bills, advertisements, and more cards. Condolences from faraway friends. She opened them all with a kitchen knife and read the kind words, heartfelt and touching, friends with whom she'd lost contact over the years and only kept in touch occasionally, sometimes with Christmas cards, others through social media, Facebook and Instagram and such. College and high school friends she'd barely seen in the past few years, people she'd worked with or who knew her father and had drifted away.

She set them aside and halfway through the pile found an envelope without a return address. Stranger still, there was no postmark, as if the card had been personally dropped into the box.

Odd, she thought, slitting the white envelope open to expose a card on deckle-edged paper, as if it were a wedding invitation. No words were on the outside, just an inked drawing of a single black rose.

What was this?

She flipped it open.

Inside, the card was inscribed with a single Bible verse written in careful calligraphy:

> *~For the wages of sin is death*
> *Romans 6:23~*

"What the—?"

Her blood turned to ice.

Who would send such a dark, damning message?

With trepidation, her skin crawling, she studied the card and envelope but caught no clue about who'd sent it. No—not sent it. Left it in her mailbox. Boldly stepped onto her front porch and left the card in her overflowing box.

Maybe it was a dark joke. A prank. After all, it wouldn't be the first, but it was sick and, she thought, evil. The message cruel.

She turned the card over, but there was no information on the back and she felt as if it had been handcrafted, not purchased in any shop or store. The message had been created for her, about her husband.

No, she thought, this was not a sympathy card, not intended for condolence. This particular piece of paper was a warning.

Intended for her.

She sucked in a sharp breath. Though she tried to argue with herself, she'd worked on too many weird real-life crimes not to see some validity in her thoughts. She wasn't letting her imagination get the better of her as she stared at the card with the black rose inked onto the thick white paper. She was facing the mind-chilling truth.

The attack on her hadn't been random.

Someone was seeking his sick kind of revenge.

And her valiant husband had lost his life defending her.

Sadness stole over her, but it quickly gave way to anger. Who the hell was behind this? Why? And God, why did Jay have to die? Seething, she climbed the stairs to her office under the eaves, fired up her iPad, and found the app for the security cameras Jay had installed around the house. Studying the recent footage, she found what she was looking for. Amid the deliveries by the postman and florists was a figure clad in black, wearing a ski mask and poncho, dark glasses covering his eyes as he avoided looking at the camera as if he knew where it was, then slid the white envelope through the mailbox slot.

She froze the frame, but saw nothing identifying about him. Nor was there any vehicle parked in the view of the camera. But she had a time stamp and would send a copy of the footage along with the card to her father, who would go through hell and back to nail the murdering prick.

"We'll get you," she vowed to the gray image. "And when we do? Hell will be waiting."

CHAPTER 6

Montoya came in hot.

He barely spoke a word as he stripped out of his leather jacket and dropped into his desk chair. These days, due to recent and on-going renovations in the department, he and Bentz shared an office, their desks pushed together, their privacy nil.

Bentz leaned back in his chair. "Somethin' up?"

"Yeah." Montoya's dark eyes flashed. "It's personal."

"If you say so." Bentz wasn't one to pry, and with his partner, he rarely did.

"You got a smoke?"

"I quit," Bentz reminded him.

"I know, but—"

"So did you."

"Maybe it was a bad idea. I could use, I mean really use a Marlboro about now." Scowling and agitated, Montoya rolled his chair up to the desk, and turned his attention to the monitor of his computer. "What've we got?"

"On Jay McKnight's homicide? Nothing new."

"Shit." Montoya frowned, lips tight in his goatee.

Bentz waited, started scrolling through e-mail. Montoya would say what was on his mind. He always did. After he smoldered a while.

It didn't take long.

"Okay, fine!" Montoya said, almost exploding. He kicked his chair back and stood, a vein showing in his forehead. "It's Cruz, okay?"

"Your brother?"

"Who else? How many other Cruzes do you know?" He ran a hand through his short-cropped hair. "Jesus, could the guy ever settle down, y' know? Be like a normal man? God Almighty, I swear—" And he did, rattling off invectives in Spanish in a loud, long rant with Bentz only understanding a few of the words. He didn't need to. He got the message.

Footsteps in the hallway heralded the arrival of Brinkman, a heavyset, ponderous detective who was a pain in the butt. "Problems?" he asked with obvious pleasure. He was dressed in jeans that had seen better days, a polo shirt, and rumpled jacket that was a size or two too small.

Montoya glared at him. "I thought you retired!"

"Soon."

"Not soon enough!" Montoya said, then smelling the scent of a recently smoked cigarette, asked, "You got a smoke?"

"For you?" Brinkman laughed, his lungs rattling. "I thought you quit."

"I did."

"Good. Then fuck off."

"You're in my office," Montoya reminded him. "*You* fuck off."

Brinkman pursed his fat lips and raised pudgy fingers close to his head where he wiggled them. "Oooh. Sorry," he said in a mock apology. "Touchy today, aren't we?"

"Always." Montoya glared at him.

Brinkman gave off another series of laughs that ended in a coughing fit, but he walked off, leaving Montoya visibly steaming.

"Let's get out of here." Bentz was already pushing back his chair.

"And go where?"

"Anywhere. You need to cool off."

"Oh, fu—Okay, fine." He slipped his arms through the sleeves of his jacket.

Once in Bentz's Jeep, Montoya slipped on his sunglasses and leaned back in his seat. "So, really, where are we going?"

"Out to visit Dr. Sam. I texted. She's expecting us."

"Didn't we already talk to her?" he asked, but it was a moot question.

They both knew it. Soon after Teri Marie Gaines's body had been discovered, Bentz had contacted Dr. Samantha Wheeler, a radio psychologist who went by the moniker of Dr. Sam. A radio personality,

Dr. Sam dispensed her brand of counseling to those who called in during her show, *Midnight Confessions.*

In their recent interview with her, Dr. Sam had insisted she hadn't received any calls from the murderous fake priest. "Security's really tight at the station and all of the callers are screened," she'd assured them, "and anyway I would have recognized his voice." She'd given a little shudder. "I'll never forget it," she'd said, her expression turning dark, her gaze settling on a middle distance only she'd been able to see. Years before, Dr. Sam had been the Rosary Killer's ultimate target and Bentz figured she still would be.

If Father John were still alive.

"So what do you think has changed since we talked to her a couple of months ago?" Montoya asked, then answered his own question. "Oh, right. McKnight's murder. I'm telling you it doesn't feel right to me. It's off, y'know?" When he saw Bentz about to argue, he held up his hands. "I know, I know. You're linking them but I'm sayin' that's bogus."

Bentz shot him a skeptical look. "And you think we've got two killers."

"Maybe . . . but you gotta admit, the MO is *not* the same. We've got the guy who dresses up like a damned priest and makes an appointment with a hooker, then before they can get down to business, he strangles her with a rosary—a rosary, Bentz, something sacred, at least in my book. Then he leaves a C-spot with Ben Franklin's eyes blacked out. Weird shit." He shook his head as he thought about it.

"So?"

"So, on the other hand you've got a random attack on the street. Yeah, the guy was wearing black, and yeah, the murder took place next to the cathedral, but it just doesn't match up."

"He could've changed over the years. Maybe he's still stalking pros, y'know, in the priest's getup, but then he has this other part of him that isn't interested in rituals so much as just getting back at me."

"By?"

"By killing my daughter."

"That's a stretch, man," Montoya said, stroking his short beard, "a real stretch. . . . Oh, pull over here." He pointed to a convenience store on the corner and before Bentz had parked, Montoya unhooked his seat belt. He threw open the door and jogged inside. Within minutes he was out again, cigarette clenched between his lips. He paused to light up, took a deep drag, then he jogged back to the car. Before he climbed inside, he inhaled again, then crushed the butt out and slid into the SUV.

"All better?" Bentz asked as they drove off.

"Yeah. Almost." He reached into the bag and pulled out a chocolate bar, which he unwrapped, and then broke off a piece and promptly tossed it into his mouth. "Now."

Bentz took a corner, then slowed for a group of musicians, hauling instruments in cases, who were jaywalking across the street. As he drove to the Lakeview area of the city, he prompted Montoya, "You were telling me about Cruz."

"Right." Montoya nodded, as if to himself. "Always been in trouble. It just seems to hunt him down and find him. Well, you know. You met him."

"A few years back." Bentz remembered Montoya's brother. Taller than Reuben and more muscular, with eyes as dark as the night and a nose that looked as if it had been broken more than once, Cruz had roared into New Orleans and Montoya's life on a motorcycle only to disappear again. As far as Bentz knew, Montoya hadn't heard from him since.

"He called. Last night." A muscle worked in Montoya's jaw.

"And?"

"And he's in some kind of trouble. 'Deep shit.' That's what he called it. Says he's gonna be arrested for murder and he's heading my way. Then he hung up. Just like that. I called him back. No answer. I tracked down a couple of my other brothers." He scowled and gave his head a sharp shake. "No one in the family has heard from him in years." He broke off another chunk of the chocolate and ate it in one quick swallow. "This is just like him, y'know. Just like him."

"Did he want you to help him?"

"All he said was that I wasn't supposed to tell anyone, including the family and you."

"But you just did."

"I'm telling you, but I didn't explain it to my brothers. Hell, what could I say anyway? Think about it? All they would have would be questions and I don't have any answers."

"Where is he now?"

"Wouldn't say."

"When is he going to get here?"

"I don't know! I told you everything he told me, okay? So, let's drop it."

Samantha Wheeler was breathing hard as she jogged to keep up with Rambo, her eighty-pound mutt they'd adopted just last year. Black, shaggy, and energetic, he was a genetic mixed bag, the most obvious breed some kind of shepherd. They'd "walked" near the shores of Lake Pontchartrain but, as usual, the brisk pace had quickly morphed into a jog as the eager dog strained on his leash.

Her heart was pumping, legs feeling the strain as she gazed across the wide expanse of water. God, she loved living near the lake; she took in deep breaths, smelling the brackish scent and watching an undulating V of geese flying high overhead.

Her cell phone hummed in her pocket and, still jogging, she yanked it out and, expecting a text from one of her sons complaining that he'd left his homework or lunch at home, she nearly stumbled. The message was from Detective Rick Bentz of the New Orleans Police Department. He and his partner were on their way to her house.

Her stomach dropped.

This could only mean one thing: another victim of the Rosary Killer had been discovered. *Not again! No, no, no!*

Years before when she'd been his target, when he'd called in to her radio program, she'd been terrified, a single woman stalked by a sadistic killer, but in the intervening years she'd gotten married, had children, lived a relatively quiet life that she adored.

Now? Her blood turned to ice. Yes, recently Bentz had called her, warned her, asked if she'd heard from the killer. The answer, of course, had been a resounding "No!" and she didn't want to think that the madman was back.

"Come on," she said to the dog, cutting their regular route short and heading through the neighborhood of tree-lined streets with large, private homes. Her throat was suddenly dry and the sweat that broke out along the back of her neck was more from a sudden case of nerves than from exercise.

She urged Rambo faster along a side alley to the street where her home, a historic mansion, stood three full stories, and was graced with a wraparound porch on the street level. Above the porch was an upper veranda, and above that, on the third floor, arched windows peered out from a mansard roof.

Ty loved the place because of the security. The grounds were fully fenced with wrought iron and a hedge, and the house and gates equipped with cameras and alarms. Sam called it "the fortress," which Ty didn't think was all that funny. Too bad, though, the name had stuck. Both their sons referred to it as such, and she'd even had a small engraved sign custom made and given it to Ty one Christmas.

Nonetheless she had to admit that the over-the-top security might be what they needed. She didn't believe that the monster who called himself Father John was back after all these years, but why else would Bentz be stopping by? He and his partner Montoya had already talked to her, warned her when Teri Marie Gaines was murdered a few months ago, the crime, according to the police, was a perfect duplicate of the previous homicides when the Rosary Killer had been on his rampage. But then there had been talk of a nun being killed by the man posing as a priest and that seemed out of character for him.

Then again, what did she really know about the psyche of a serial killer?

Was all the terror happening again?

She shivered inwardly at the thought and closed her mind to it. There was no reason to borrow trouble because, as her mother had warned her, trouble was bound to come your way.

But she had to admit, once in a while, she'd thought someone might be following her, had felt unseen eyes watching her every move. She'd told herself that she was just being paranoid, that after what she'd been through and considering the world they all lived in today, she was letting her fears, her subconscious, rattle her. She took several deep breaths and told herself to get real, to live in the moment, to not let the horrors of the past ruin today or tomorrow. Her life was too good to let thoughts of some maniac from the past destroy it.

At the house she pressed in the code to unlock the gates to enter the compound. When she was in the house, she locked the door and waited, unleashing Rambo and hearing him pad to the kitchen where he lapped water noisily from his dish.

Poised at the door, she spotted a black Jeep pull into the drive. Detective Bentz was at the wheel, his partner, Montoya, in the passenger seat. As the cops climbed out of the SUV, she opened the door and Rambo came scrambling back, his claws clicking on the tile floor.

"Stop," she ordered the dog. "Sit."

Rambo slid to a halt and waited as the men arrived on the porch. No introductions were necessary. She asked them inside and they all went through the foyer where the staircase wound upward to the back of the house, which, over the years, had been remodeled to an open-concept kitchen and family room with French doors leading to the enclosed garden. A squirrel was scolding from the low-hanging branch of a magnolia tree, so Rambo lost interest in the visitors and was laser-focused on getting outside. She opened the door and the dog shot through, barking, the hairs on his nape stiff, his eyes on the squirrel.

She offered coffee or water or even sweet tea, but the cops declined as they took seats on stools at the island and she cradled her own steaming cup on the other side, her back to the stove.

Bentz got down to it. "Have you heard from Father John? Called into the show? Sent you anything?"

She was already shaking her head. "We've been over this before," she said, remembering the night the cops had come by with the devastating news that another woman had been killed in the same manner as had Father John's victims so long ago.

"I thought he was dead. That he died in the swamp. That you shot him."

Montoya said, "His body was never recovered. And we talked to you about the recent homicides that we think he *might* have committed."

Bentz flinched.

She knew that many had been fascinated by all news of her attacker, had pored over reports of the search of the bayou where the killer had been shot. The cops had done their due diligence, the theory being that the murderer had been eaten by alligators or other swamp creatures or washed out to sea. "He hasn't contacted me."

Bentz raised an eyebrow, his stare intent. "You're sure?"

"Yes—well, no, not a hundred percent, but I don't think so." As a radio psychologist, she accepted on-air questions during her program, *Midnight Confessions,* and that's where Father John first connected with her. Since that time security had been beefed up, every phone call, e-mail, text, or other communication double-checked, and then there was the chilling fact that she was certain she would recognize his voice, that it was forever etched in her memory, that she would never forget it.

"So what happened?" she asked, but knew with dead certainty that someone had been killed, probably another prostitute strangled by a rosary. Sam's blood curdled at the thought, her heartbeat accelerated. He had to be dead. The monster had to have been killed in the bayou that night; he couldn't be alive. Her lungs constricted and she clenched her coffee cup so hard her fingers began to ache. "Another murder?" She set her cup onto the counter.

Montoya was nodding. "Yeah, but we're not sure it's connected to the Rosary Killer," he said.

Bentz's jaw tightened almost imperceptibly while Montoya explained about the homicide in Pirate's Alley.

"I read about that," she said, and to Bentz, "I'm sorry for your loss. That's rough. Is your daughter okay?" What a dumb question. She saw the answer in Bentz's eyes. Could almost hear his thoughts: *No. Of course not. Who knows if she'll ever be "okay" again. She lost her husband and nearly her own life in a brutal attack. So, no, she's definitely* not *okay.*

But he said, "She's still working through it."

"She's been through a lot of trauma," Samantha said, silently adding, *and so have you, Rick Bentz. So have you.* "She'll probably need grief counseling. I can recommend someone."

"I'll let her know," Bentz said as the dog scratched at the door and she let him in. Rambo, the traitor, sidled up to the spot between the two bar stools where the cops were sitting and, nose in the air, hoped for attention, or more likely some morsel of food to drop.

"You here alone?" Bentz asked.

"Kids are in school. Ty's out of town." She explained that her husband, a freelance journalist, was often away, sometimes on the other side of the country, sometimes the other side of the world. Currently he was in Canada, but was due back the following week. "So it's just the boys and me. Well, and Rambo." She glanced at the dog. "He's great company but, as you can see, not much of a guard dog."

At the sound of his name, the animal's ears pricked forward.

"Well, nothing's changed. He hasn't called into the program. And it'll be a moot point soon."

Montoya asked, "How so?"

"The station just sold. A deal's been in the works for months, but just two weeks ago it was signed and everything's changing. All pre-recorded playlists and the like. It's a whole new world, you know. No more *Midnight Confessions,* at least not the way it has been."

"Meaning?" Bentz asked.

"That I'll be doing podcasts. Some of the most interesting cases I've worked on."

"Including Father John?" Bentz asked, his eyes narrowing thought-fully.

"Of course," she said. "He's my first."

"That might not be a good idea."

"It's already a done deal. All recorded."

"Really?" Montoya said.

"Uh-huh. It starts airing in the first week of November."

CHAPTER 7

"It's only been a little while," Bella said from across the café table at the small bistro where Kristi had agreed to meet her for coffee or, in Kristi's case, sweet tea. "You'll be fine." But the expression on her pixie-like features didn't convey the same rosy outlook as her words. "You've been through worse. . . . Well, not worse maybe, but a lot." She flashed a smile as she reached to the top of her head and adjusted the band securing the ponytail that held her black, springing curls away from her face.

"This is different." Kristi dunked her straw in her tea and looked through the window to the street where people were bustling past an area of outdoor tables with umbrellas. She thought about being a widow, she thought about being pregnant, and she thought about the disturbing card she'd received.

"I know it's different. Of course it is." Bella was nodding, trying to cheer her up, but Kristi wasn't in the mood. Maybe it was just too soon. All she knew was that Bella's usually infectious rosy attitude was failing to scale the wall of Kristi's unhappiness. "But come on." She reached a hand over Kristi's wrist. "What do you say we go for a mani-pedi," she suggested, and seeing that Kristi wasn't responding, added, "Or a long bike ride or hike, maybe? Whatever you want."

"Don't think so."

"Not today, but hey, what about next week? Jay, he wouldn't have wanted you to grieve like this."

Kristi's head snapped up. She caught Bella's gaze in her own. "How do you know that?" she demanded. "You don't. No one does."

"Ouch." Bella recoiled. "Hey, I'm your friend. Just trying to help, and yeah, no one knows what Jay would have wanted for sure, but I'll bet he would have wanted you to move on. To find happiness." She managed a smile that didn't quite meet her eyes. "Hey, Kristi. Remember, Jay was your McKnight in shining armor."

The joke fell flat.

As many times as Kristi had said the very same thing, now, after he'd given his life saving her, it stung. "Listen, Bella, I know you think you're helping, but I'm struggling, okay?"

"Of course you're—"

"No, no. Just hear me out. You don't understand. Jay and I? We were having . . . problems. I didn't think they were that serious at the time, but . . . we'd had a huge fight that night and I said some things, some awful things that I can't take back." Her heart ached deep in her chest. "And now I never can."

"Oh, Kristi, all marriages are difficult, have their ups and downs and—"

"Did you hear me?" Kristi cut in sharply. "I said I can never take back those hateful, spiteful words." And in that instant they came back to haunt her: *I don't know why I ever married you.*" She pushed aside her glass. "I've got to go."

"No. No, you don't." All the pseudo joy Bella had exuded left her face and her eyes turned serious. "Everyone has fights. Every marriage is a constant workout. If you care about someone, if you're passionate for them, if you truly love them, you're honest with them and . . . and you disagree. Sometimes it gets pretty awful, but it's honest and it's raw. It hurts. But that's life."

"And in this case, it's death," Kristi said. "There's no making up, Bella. What I said, what we fought about, it's out there and it . . . it can never be called back."

"Okay, fine, but you don't have to punish yourself."

"Don't I?" she threw back, aching inside. God, she hated this!

"Maybe you should join a grief support group."

"Not yet," she said. She knew all about them from doing research on the 21 Killer, a heinous murderer who had recently stalked the streets of New Orleans.

However, Bella was on a roll. "Listen, I have the name of a counselor. Dawn Aguillard, and she's great. I went to her when Sean and I were having trouble. You remember?"

Bella and Sean had nearly broken up because of financial issues that resulted in his affair with a co-worker, but somehow they pieced their marriage back together. Bella swore that her counselor helped her get over her anger, find a way to forgive her husband, and take him back.

Kristi said, "That's different."

"Is it? Grief is grief. And I was grieving for my marriage, but she, Dr. Aguillard—Dawn, she had me call her Dawn—she helped me through it. God, she's just the best. The best! I'll text you her contact information."

"You don't have to."

"I know, Kristi. But I want to. You know I do." She pulled her phone from her back pocket, pressed several keys, and looked up. A fresh smile was pinned to her face. "Okay. You call her. There's no reason you have to go through this alone, and if you don't feel comfortable talking with me or other friends or even your dad, you can talk to her."

Kristi's cell phone dinged, indicating a message had been received.

"I don't know that I'll call her."

"Okay, okay, I get it. I really do. You might need more time. Sure. But the way I see it, you're avoiding fun, avoiding life."

"Oh, give me a break. I am not."

Her friend's knowing eyes narrowed. "Fine. Truth time. I'm worried about you. Okay? And so are Sarah and Jess."

"I'll be fine."

"Will you?"

"Yes! Jesus." She stood suddenly. "Let's just pay the bill and go."

"Why?" Bella demanded. "Do you have a million things to do?"

"Yeah, yeah, I do," she lied. "I'm late on a deadline."

"It'll wait."

"I need to let the dog out."

Bella's eyebrows drew together. "Really? I thought . . . didn't your dog . . . Geez, Kristi, you don't have to lie."

"I didn't mean . . ." She let the sentence fall away and didn't argue, because of course right now she had no dog. All of the pets that she and Jay had adopted had passed on. "Sorry."

"If you don't want to go, just say so. What's with you? You never were one to make excuses or lie, for God's sake."

"Okay, okay. You caught me. It's not that I don't want to go, it's just that right now . . . I just can't."

Bella flipped a hand up as if to say, "Whatever." And then she said, "It's whatever you want, Kristi. Who am I to try to talk you out of living the rest of your life as a monk, er, a nun?" Her eyebrows arched. "Just your best frickin' friend. But, hey! Go! Go on. Get out. Go home." She made shooing motions with her hands. "Hole up in your house by yourself if that's what you want."

"I do. It *is* exactly what I want."

"Fine!" Then Bella calmed a bit. "Look, you just survived a horrific attack and lost your husband, watched him die in your arms, for God's sake. That's . . . that's unthinkable. Horrific. The worst! But even so, there's so much to life, so much to live for."

Kristi's eyes grew hot. She thought of the baby. Her baby. Jay's. Growing inside her. "I'll be fine," she insisted, and her voice sounded rough. "I know I've got some things to work through, but . . . but I'll be fine." She was on the edge of telling her friend about her pregnancy, but didn't. It seemed traitorous somehow, that Bella Lyons would know the truth and Jay wouldn't. Not ever.

Of course she would have to tell Bella—or someone—soon enough, she thought as she pulled her debit card from her wallet. But not today.

Definitely *not* today.

"Look, Jess and Sarah and I, we're thinking of starting jogging. Like at least once a week, maybe more. You already run, right? So why don't you join us?"

"I'll think about it," she lied. Right now, she couldn't think of anything worse than getting together with her friends and doing anything where there would be hours to talk about their lives, their husbands, their children, their joy. Not yet.

"And you know, if you ever want to do a show, promote your next book or whatever? The producer at the station is interested." Bella looked hopeful, as she always did. Though she sold ads for the station, she seemed to think it her mission to find guests for the local talk shows. This wasn't the first time Bella had suggested Kristi make herself available for a television interview.

Today, Kristi wasn't in the mood. "Another time."

"Promise?"

Kristi shot her a look. "No. But if I ever consider it, you'll be the first to know."

"Cool," she said, though the way Bella muttered it, Kristi was pretty sure her response to the offer was anything but chill with her friend.

They split the bill and hugged good-bye, but there was definitely a stiffness to the embrace that had never been there before. "You take care of yourself, okay?" Bella asked as she released her. "And you call me, or text, if you need anything. I mean it. *Anything.*"

"Sure. You got it," Kristi lied, and holding her jacket tight against the wind, hurried back to the spot where she'd parked her car, just off the French Quarter. She passed open-air shops and galleries and eyed the neon sign for a psychic. Glowing yellow letters over a blue crescent moon.

She paused for a second, considered making an appointment for a session, then dismissed the thought.

"Afraid of what you'll find out?" Jay's voice asked.

"Never," she said loudly, and an older man in a hat and overcoat walking in the other direction sliced a look her way. She lowered her voice. "The whole psychic crap thing isn't real, you know that, you're a scientist for God's sake." And then she heard herself. "And you're not real, either." She considered telling him to leave her alone but wasn't certain that's what she wanted. Besides, the conversation, at least his side of it, was all in her mind.

Right?

She kept walking, her coat billowing in the breeze, and told herself that she didn't believe in psychics or the paranormal, or any of the otherworldly things she'd found so fascinating in college. But that wasn't true, was it? Didn't she have the uncanny ability to see a person's color change to gray just before he or she was about to die?

"You're a fruitcake," she said as she reached her car and unlocked it remotely. This time, thankfully, no one heard her.

Except Jay, who said, *"You might not want to piss off all your friends, Kris. There's a good chance that you're going to need them."*

"Oh, yeah? And how would you know?"

"Because I know you, Kristi, better than anyone does."

"Is that right? Then you'll get it when I say I don't think you're real. Okay. You're just a manifestation of my guilt or my grief or whatever. But you are not real."

"Whatever you say."

She started the car and began to pull away from the curb only to hear a loud, impatient honk as a pickup whizzed by.

Kristi's heart bounced around in her chest.

The Silverado's tires hit a deep puddle, throwing up a curtain of water that rained all over her car.

She told herself to get a grip and then checked her mirror before managing to meld into traffic.

All the while she told herself that Jay wasn't with her, that she imagined his voice, that she was *not* going mad.

But she didn't believe it for an instant.

"I'm tellin' ya, cuz, I haven't heard from him," Luis said as Montoya, on the other end of the wireless connection, paced on his walk from the front of the house to the street, cell phone pressed hard against his ear, as if the more tightly he gripped his phone, the more likely he'd get the answer he was looking for. "Not for years. We were tight in school, yeah, but, you know, life goes on. Look at you. A damned detective. *¿Quién lo hubiera pensado?*"

"Who would have thought?" Montoya repeated in English, but grinned nonetheless.

"Yeah, man, you were bad-ass. *Un gran alborotador!*"

Montoya couldn't deny it. He was a troublemaker. Probably the worst in the family. Except for Cruz.

"And now you're a cop. *¡Increíble! Es un maldito milagro.*"

Montoya laughed. "Not incredible. Not a miracle," he said, and sobered. "Just let me know if he shows up or calls or texts. If you hear anything."

"You got it." Luis hung up and Montoya closed his eyes in frustration. He should take Bentz's advice and let it go. Cruz would show up when he damned well chose, but still, why would the jerk-wad call in a panic, tell him he was going to be arrested for a homicide, insist he was heading to New Orleans, and then just disappear, become a goddamned ghost in the wind?

Cruz always had been an egocentric prick.

Growing up.

In the military.

In college.

Every damned where.

Why would he change now?

The answer was simple: he wouldn't.

Cruz Montoya played by his own rules, and his brother knew from personal experience that bending or breaking every rule just never worked out.

Never.

"Seriously, Dad. I'm okay. Thanks for the offer."

"Maybe tomorrow?" her father suggested when she didn't agree to drive over to his place for dinner. "Ginny would love to see you." The concern in his voice pulled at her heartstrings.

"Maybe," she said, thinking of her half sister, the imp. She loved that kid. Kristi forced a smile into her voice even though she didn't feel it. A headache was beginning to form behind her eyes and she leaned against her desk in her office, her gaze sliding to the stack of legal pads where she'd taken notes on her next book about the 21 Killer. "Give Ginny a hug from me. But don't count on tomorrow. Maybe next week. I've got a ton of stuff to do around here."

"But you have to eat and Olivia makes a mean jambalaya."

"No arguments there." But even the mention of one of her favorite dishes didn't interest her. She had no appetite. "I'll text you. Promise." Staring through the window into the night creeping through the city, she ended the call feeling empty and lonely and wondered if she should have accepted her father's invitation to dinner. Just for something to do. To get out of the house. She would have except she didn't want to fall into the trap of running back to "Daddy" every time her life turned upside down. She was a grown woman. A pregnant grown woman, she reminded herself.

She snapped off the lights in the office and walked downstairs to the bedroom.

Pausing at the door, she felt another cold gust of loneliness and disbelief rush through her as she stared in the semidarkness to the bed, mussed as she hadn't bothered making it, the duvet half sliding to the floor.

Oh. God. She braced herself against the door frame, then refusing to break down again, stiffened her spine and walked into the room.

Jay was gone.

She had to face it.

Get on with her life.

She snapped on a bedside lamp and set her jaw against a fresh spate of tears.

"No more," she said aloud, even though her voice trembled.

Reluctantly she opened his closet and stared at the neat row of sports coats and shirts hanging just as he'd left them, the jeans folded on the top shelf, his shoes placed tidily beneath his dress shirts. Her own closet was a mess in comparison. Dresses and blouses hung haphazardly, hats and purses strung out over the shelves, her shoes and boots lying wherever she happened to kick them off.

She slipped one of Jay's shirts from its hanger, a light blue chambray he'd worn just two days before he died, and held the soft fabric to her face, lost for a second in the smell of him, his aftershave still clinging to the collar.

"Come on, Kris, pull yourself together." His voice was so clear, so close, she half expected to feel his fingers on her shoulder, the warmth of his breath against her nape.

Instead she felt nothing. She stepped out of her own sweater and donned his shirt, rolling up the sleeves, returning to the living room to watch TV. Her thoughts strayed, as they always did these days, and by eleven she couldn't stand staring listlessly at the boob tube a second longer.

She slid out of her jeans, but still wearing Jay's shirt, she tumbled onto the bed where she tried to read a book. No reason to turn out the light because she was convinced that tonight was no different than all the other nights since Jay's death, that sleep was unlikely to come and even when it finally did, it would be riddled with horrific nightmares of that bloody and harrowing night. But the book couldn't hold her attention, her eyelids heavy. No surprise there. She hadn't slept in what seemed like forever. She tossed the novel aside and, convinced she would never drift off, that she was destined to be forever sleep deprived, she turned out the light to stare at the ceiling. But when the quiet of the night surrounded her, she fell into a deep, dreamless sleep.

Creaaak!

The floorboards were groaning against someone's weight.

"Jay?" Kristi mumbled into the pillow as she opened a bleary eye. What was he doing creeping around at . . . she glanced at the bedside clock. God, it was after three in the morning and—

Her head cleared.

Her heart stopped.

Jay wasn't in the house. He would never be in the house again, but someone or something was.

She was suddenly wide-awake and straining to hear as she lay in bed.

Was that a footstep?

Or her imagination?

Was someone breathing hard?

Or was it the sough of the wind through the magnolia tree outside her window?

Only one way to find out.

Slowly and quietly, she rolled out of bed, bare feet landing on the carpet.

The room was cold. She shivered and sensed a stirring in the room, something out of sync.

The back of her mouth turned to dust as her eyes adjusted to the darkness and she saw a movement, a shifting of shadows at the window. The blinds moving with the breeze, filmy light from the streetlamp filtering through the window to ripple in undulating stripes across her mussed comforter.

What? The bedroom window was open just the faintest of cracks, the curtains moving only slightly.

Really? Hadn't it been closed? The latch didn't work all the time, but she had shoved the sash completely closed just before the horrible rainstorm on the night of Jay's death, what—like about two weeks ago, going on three? In the time since, she hadn't touched it. Hadn't felt any breath of air seeping in.

So . . .

Her heart stilled.

She glanced around the room.

Nothing seemed out of place.

Right?

But the hairs on the back of her neck raised.

She thought about finding Jay's jacket misplaced and the shattered glass in their wedding picture. Her stomach twisted and she paused, again listening, but hearing nothing out of the ordinary. On silent footsteps she walked to the dresser where Jay kept a dish for his keys and pocket change. The dimes, quarters, and nickels seemed the same, the spare set of keys untouched, a thin layer of dust visible.

And yet . . .

She felt something, a shift in the atmosphere, as if someone was or had been inside, as if unseen eyes were watching.

Again, she strained to listen, but only heard the pounding of her pulse in her ears.

"Now you're being ridiculous," she whispered, but slowly opened the drawers. First Jay's—underwear, socks, T-shirts, shorts, nothing out of place, everything neatly folded and stacked. Three drawers undisturbed. Nothing changed since she'd found his jacket in the dining room a while back.

Still . . .

She opened her side of the shared dresser. Sweaters and scarves, jeans and T-shirts, all tossed in, half folded and stuffed into lower drawers that were forever too small. Looked fine.

She let out her breath.

Opened the top drawer filled with her bras, underwear, and socks, all in a tangled pile as always. No way to tell if it had been disturbed. That thought brought a bad taste to the back of her mouth.

Don't be ridiculous. It's nothing. For God's sake, don't freak yourself out.

She shoved the drawer closed and it stuck.

Nothing unusual there, overstuffed as it always was.

Cardboard?

"What the—?"

Pinching the edge of the obstruction, she pulled out a white envelope.

Blank.

Like before.

She slid out the card with, again, a black rose, hand drawn across the thick paper.

Her insides went ice-cold as she flipped it open and read the message:

> *~For the day of vengeance is in my heart, and the year*
> *of my redeemed is come.*
> *Isaiah 63:4~*

Dropping the card as if it had burned her, she watched in horror as it fluttered to the floor.

He'd been in her house.

Riffled through her underwear drawer.

Left his sick missive and . . .

Oh, God, he could still be inside.

CHAPTER 8

Kristi froze.

Didn't move a muscle.

Every sense heightened, her nerves stretched to the breaking point, she concentrated, listening, peering through the doorway to the rest of the house.

Nothing.

No sound of breathing.

No movement she could detect.

Nothing she could see.

Was whoever left the card hiding in her house?

But no . . . surely she would have noticed.

Her mind whirled backward to the previous day, the meeting this morning with Bella, the errands she'd run—a few groceries, gas for the car, stopping at the gym to cancel Jay's membership, then coming back and heading up to the office where she'd spent most of the afternoon.

There had been rooms she hadn't gone into—the spare bedroom that she'd thought they would convert to a nursery and the small closet-like space where Jay had made his office.

Was someone in here, even now? Watching her through a crack in a door or from behind a curtain? Silently she crept through the house, searching the extra rooms and closet.

Nothing.

She pulled the door to Jay's office closed.

Click.

Then, again, more faintly. *Click.*

What?!?

She held her breath, ears straining over the jackhammer that was her heart.

Gathering her courage, she poked her head around the corner to the living room. Empty. Same with the attached dining area, so she stepped into the kitchen.

Something was off here.

Something didn't feel right.

Throat tight, she slid a butcher knife from the magnetic strip over the stove and peered out the window to the backyard.

Layers of darkness, only broken by the patches of light from the windows, a branch moving with the wind, leaves dancing. But no dark shadow creeping at the fence line, no whites of eyes visible.

You're imagining things.

But then she noticed the door to the garage. Unlatched. Moving slowly inward. Damn! She raised her knife, but as the door swung open, yawning into the blackness that was the inside of the garage, no one appeared.

She moved closer.

Heard a rustling.

Felt the cold as she reached through the door and, with the butcher knife raised in her right hand, snapped on the light with the left.

A dark shadow flitted near the rear of her Subaru.

She bit back a scream.

Not a person, though.

Way too tiny.

Unblinking eyes stared out from beneath the rear axle.

A cat?

No—a kitten?

Fuzzy and black, scrawny and, it seemed, as scared of her as she was of it. "Oh, Geez," she whispered, letting out her breath. "What're you doing in here?" She bent down and tried to grab it, but it scooted away, hiding in between the tires near a puddle of oil that had stained the cement floor. "Come on," she said, but the scared cat wouldn't move. "So how did you get in?" she asked, and rocked back on her heels, eyeing the unfinished walls where some of the plywood had started to gray, and she noticed the door next to the garbage cans, the one she used to haul them outside.

Always closed.

And now ajar.

Obviously how the kitten gained access.

But why was it open?

She straightened, walked around her Outback, and pulled the side door shut, the way she always did after taking out the trash bins on the day her garbage was hauled away, the only time she used the door.

So why wasn't it locked?

The dead bolt turned as it always was?

Had she been careless?

That was possible, she supposed, as she'd been distracted ever since the night Jay was killed.

Her fingers tightened over the hilt of her knife again.

So who had been through here?

Obviously the person who left the card in her underwear drawer.

Once more her skin pimpled in revulsion and she wondered if the intruder had taken any of her panties or a bra. Shuddering inside, she double-checked to make certain the garage door was locked again, then walked around her car and into the kitchen, leaving the adjoining door open for the cat. Bending down and peering to the dark space under her car, she said, "You can come in if you want."

Two small unblinking eyes stared back at her. "Tell you what. I've got something you might like." Then she straightened, found a couple of small bowls and filled one with water, the other with milk, and left them just inside the doorway next to her boots, beneath the pegs where she hung her jacket.

Just to be on the safe side, she did another thorough search of the house, found no one hiding, then went upstairs to her office and searched through the footage from the camera again. She'd looked once, when she'd received the first card, but hadn't been able to ID who had left it.

Now, she scrolled through the last two days of footage, but there was nothing; obviously whoever had left the card had accessed the house through the unlatched window. Well, that was going to end right now.

No way could she get a repairman out within the hour, so she found a YouTube video on how to fix the latch—too difficult; she didn't have all the parts, but she could take the existing one off and install another, once she bought one. In the meantime, she took four heavy nails and a hammer from the garage, then went to work, hammering the nails to the sides of the window, so that they stuck out over the sash and prevented it from opening. Then she tried pushing the window open.

It didn't budge.

Once more, really putting her muscles into trying to force the sash upward.

Again it held.

A temporary solution, but effective. She thought about Jay's gun, a small caliber that he kept in a case up in the closet, locked away. She could use it, of course. Her father had taught her about firearms when she was growing up, but she didn't much like them. She'd find another way to handle the situation.

"That's my girl." Jay's voice was clear as a bell and for once she didn't tell him to leave her alone, he was a figment of her imagination. "Okay, then, what's next?" she said to the empty room. "Huh? Tell me: what would you do from here?"

Find that son of a bitch and bring him to justice!

Not Jay's voice. Her own plan.

She thought about returning the hammer to its spot on the garage wall, but decided against it. Instead she ran her fingers over the flat head to the sharp claw, then opened the drawer to her nightstand and slipped the hammer inside.

Just in case.

Red silk, or a leopard print?

She held up the tiny dresses, each on a hanger, and pressed them to her body as she stared into the full-length mirror standing next to her makeup table in the alcove that had once been a closet.

Did it really matter? Her client wouldn't care and the clothes would go into a heap onto the floor, unless he wanted a slow strip tease, then she would make certain they would fall into a neat puddle. And if he was rough and wanted to tear at her clothes? She'd make him pay. Oh, she'd make him pay. In more ways than one.

Her dresses weren't cheap. Not that she cared. Not really.

She shopped at the best consignment stores in the city as well as online, under an alias, of course. "Gently used" or "barely worn," some with designer labels, though usually, she saved those for her steady customers.

Cocking her head to one side and imagining how she'd look in tonight's persona, she decided on the red, shaking the hanger under the soft lights, watching the fabric shimmer seductively. She showered, toweled off, slipped on a wig cap, then, seated at her expansive makeup station, added her face prosthetics—thin, sculpted silicone pieces that added shape to her cheeks, chin, and nose. It was a long process as she took care in blending the silicone, trimming it, and melding the edges so that they became seamless, invisible to the naked eye. Next her teeth caps and dark contact lenses, then her makeup, a red lipstick to match the dress, a fine layer of gloss, deep gray shadow, and eyelashes that were black and thick. Satisfied that her face was the way she wanted it, that no one would be able to recognize her, she dressed with care, checking her garters, the push-up bra, and slipped on the dress, making certain it fell over one shoulder and draped deep to display her cleavage. Next she put on the black wig—thick and full, piled high with soft tendrils falling loose around her face, and stepped into four-inch clear stilettos.

Finally, she eyed her array of jewelry—most of it cheap costume stuff, but a few pieces much more expensive. She decided on a silver ankle bracelet and a slave-girl bracelet for her upper arm. Of course she'd wear her Apple Watch with its blingy band for the opposite wrist, add oversized hoop earrings, and just to spice things up a bit, a silver necklace with a bejeweled cross that settled seductively between her breasts.

After the finishing touches, she checked the mirror again and smiled. Perfect!

"Hello, Helen of Joy," she said in a low whisper, and smiled, reveling in becoming her alter ego. This was her act, not just as if she were on stage, but a form of her own personal rebellion, and it felt good. *So* good. She was careful, of course she was. She had to be. She had too much to lose if her true identity was ever revealed. She eyed her reflection and liked what she saw.

After all, she wasn't in it for the money.

As for the sex?

It was okay—even exciting at times.

But usually not. And secondary.

Because all of this was for the thrill of getting away with this, her alter ego. She loved the little edge of danger that fueled an adrenaline rush, the heart-pumping excitement that was lost in her "real" life.

Tap! Tap!

She heard the knock on the door and pasted a sultry smile on her face, double-checking the mirror once more to see that every detail was just right, then pulled the curtain across her staging area and whispered under her breath, "showtime."

At the door she paused, took in a deep breath, and slid the dead bolt to peer into the darkened hallway.

A tall man in a poncho stood waiting. "I'm here for Helen," he said in a low voice that caused a little spark that started in her tailbone and sizzled up her spine.

"You found her." She let the door fall open and stepped back as he came inside.

In that second she sensed something was wrong. He wasn't what she'd expected from a john. This tall man in dark glasses was wearing a clerical collar beneath a poncho, a slash of white as if he were with the clergy. It was a little more than theatrical and she thought he was wearing thick face makeup—concealer of a sort—as if he were hiding acne, or some other facial imperfection, maybe even a tattoo? But why? For vanity's sake? Or because he could be recognized? Warning bells clanged in her head. She'd read about some freak who'd dressed as a man of the cloth and had strangled women with a rosary.

Surely this wasn't the guy. No way. She couldn't be that unlucky.

"I'm sorry, Father," she said, covering her case of nerves, which only increased as she watched him slowly slide the dead bolt into place. "I was expecting someone. Is there—" Was his hand in a pocket? Did he have a gun? A knife? A damned sharpened rosary? "Is there something I can do for you?"

"Yes." His voice was low. Almost sexy.

Still, the mood was off.

She wasn't buying it.

"I think there's been a mistake," she said. "I don't do business with a . . ." She motioned with her hand to his clerical collar, so stark and white. "Not a priest." Even for her, that was a bridge too far.

"Why not?" He was advancing and withdrawing whatever it was from beneath the poncho.

A crisp hundred-dollar bill. As if that were enough. What was with this guy? Then she noticed the bill was marred. Ben Franklin's eyes had been blacked out with a marker or something.

Oh. Jesus.

He laid the bill on a small table, then retrieved something else from his pocket, a rattling of glass and then deep red rosary beads winked in the light.

Her heart stopped for a second. "Not in my wheelhouse," she said, backing away. "This isn't happening. Take your money. No harm, no foul, Father."

"We had a date," he reminded her.

"Right. But I changed my mind and—"

"You can't. We had an agreement."

No money had changed hands, but she knew he wouldn't accept that. "Listen. You need to leave," she said firmly, her voice no longer a whisper. "Just go."

"Why?"

"I told you—I don't do priests." Not even freaks dressed up in clerical garb. "Get out." She pointed to the door and saw a smile crawl across his face. An evil, determined leer that turned her blood to ice.

Time to end this.

Time to end it *now*!

She pushed a button on her watch, which connected her directly to 9-1-1.

Too late!

He leaped, the rosary over her head, encircling her throat. She kicked upward. This was not happening!

She felt the strand tightening and his weight against her body as his muscles flexed, drawing the beads—so sharp—into her flesh. No. No. No! Struggling, she flailed, reached behind to the makeup counter, her fingers knocking over tubes of lipstick and bottles of nail polish to the floor.

Desperately she tried to breathe, to suck in any air as he pressed forward, determinedly walking her backward.

She was light-headed, her lungs on fire.

The noose tightened.

Why? Why was he hurting her?

Blackness converged as she reached the alcove, the curtain parting, her buttocks pushed hard against the edge of the counter. Makeup jars clattered, rolling, falling to the floor, crashing, powder exploding, the room swirling.

Fight! You have to fight!

Her lungs felt as if they would burst.

The overhead light, dimmed, came into view, then seemed to swim away.

She scraped at her neck with her hands, tried to curl her fingers around the chain cutting off her air, but she couldn't pull on the chain cutting into her throat.

He's going to kill you. You have to fight, Helene, you have to get away!

She scrabbled and kicked, but her movements were sluggish and he was so strong . . . so damned strong. And agile.

He squeezed tighter.

Help me. Please . . . someone . . . help . . .

His face was near hers as he bent her over the makeup counter, her spine curved back impossibly.

The world swam behind her eyes.

Her hands fell to her sides, limp on the counter.

She saw her own reflection in his sunglasses.

The tip of one finger touched the edge of a bit of rough metal, long and sharp. Her damned nail file.

Gathering all her strength, she forced her fingers around the file, and as his breath was hot against her face, she swung her arm upward and struck, jabbing the file deep into the flesh of his shoulder.

She heard him yowl in agony, felt a jerk on the chain at her neck. And just after that nano second of satisfaction in wounding him, the world went black and the pain was gone.

CHAPTER 9

Bentz stared at the two cards lying on his dining room table. Each was in a plastic ziplock bag, a black rose inked onto thick white paper. He'd read the inside messages, each a veiled threat wrapped in some Bible verse. Each received by his daughter.

His insides turned to jelly.

"One came in the mail?" he said, clarifying what his daughter was saying as he pointed to the first missive she'd received. "And the other one was in your dresser drawer? He'd been in your house and left it there, in your bureau?"

Jesus Christ. The nutcase had been in her house! He tried like hell to quell his rising sense of panic. The whole morning had gotten off to a rocky start. The baby had fussed all night with a runny nose and Olivia had brought Ginny into bed with them. Then after a sleepless night, Bentz had gotten up, run through the shower and just started making coffee when he'd gotten a text that Kristi was outside, that she wanted to talk to him. So here they were in the dining room, two cups of coffee untouched on the table near the damning letters.

Kristi nodded, buried her hands in the pockets of the jacket she hadn't bothered to take off. "Right. He was in my house."

Bentz tried to remain calm. Found it impossible. "Why didn't you tell me about this earlier?"

"I noticed the first one in a bunch of other mail I'd ignored," she said, meeting his gaze across the table. "Don't know how long it had been there. Maybe a week." She shrugged and he knew that she'd lost track of time, had been in a fog since the attack and murder of her husband. "Yeah, it creeped me out, but I didn't think I needed to come running to Daddy, you know." She offered him the hint of a sad smile. "I'm a big girl, right?"

"Who was nearly killed less than three weeks ago."

Leaning back in her chair, she leveled her gaze at him. "Well, yeah, there's that."

"And the other card." He pointed to it. "That was actually in your drawer in your bedroom, tucked in with your . . ."

"On top of my underwear, wedged in there." She made a face, offended. "Sick-o."

"Kristi—"

"Dad, don't," she said, cutting him off before he could even ask her to move in. She'd heard it before. "I know you're going to tell me to be careful and I will be, but I'm not coming back here, okay?" She explained about nailing the window shut and planning to get it fixed. She also told him she was having the locks changed, getting a new security system with updated cameras, digital footage, and alarms, and that she'd contacted a local shelter about getting a dog, one that would get along with cats as she'd recently taken in a stray kitten.

He was undeterred. Worried sick. "You should have told me about it when you received the first one."

"I know. I thought it was just a prank, or a mistake or something," she said a little defensively. "I mean, I've gotten weird letters before."

"Never left on your doorstep, or in your drawer," he pointed out. "This . . . this . . . *maniac* . . . person knows where you live." And that scared the hell out of him.

"I know." She checked her watch. "Look, I've gotta run. Literally. Bella wants me to start jogging with her three days a week. Stupidly I said yes. Well, actually I didn't say anything and she took it as a yes." She scraped her chair back. "And I've got a call in to a new security company. They're supposed to call back and set up an appointment and I do work, you know."

"You're a writer. I think your schedule's pretty flexible."

"It is," she admitted sharply, "but I'm trying to get back into it. It's been . . . it's not been easy."

He nodded. "I, uh, suppose not."

"But I thought I should bring you these"—she motioned to the cards—"ASAP."

"Right." He didn't want her to leave, felt impotent. But she was nothing if not headstrong. She'd made up her mind. "Okay, but if you ever want to crash here—"

She held up her hand and stood. "Yeah, Dad, I know. Your door is always open."

"Right."

"And I appreciate it. Really. But . . ." She sighed, looked for a second like she might break down, but cleared her throat. "I've got this handled. Really."

He didn't believe her for a minute, but just then Olivia appeared, disheveled, her wild curls framing her face. She was yawning as she cinched the belt of her robe over her nightshirt.

"Coffee," she said. "God, what a night." Then she spied Kristi. "I thought I heard you." A smile stretched over her face and even in all her disarray, or maybe because of it, she was, without a doubt, at least in Bentz's opinion, the most beautiful woman he'd ever met. And that included Jennifer, Kristi's mother, herself a knockout. "Are you making breakfast?" she asked, shooting her husband a look.

"Not for me. I was just telling Dad I've got to go," Kristi said, keys in hand. She and Olivia had bonded over the years, though when her father had first started seeing his now wife, Kristi hadn't accepted the woman who would become her stepmother. For a while it had been difficult for them all, Bentz thought, though eventually Olivia had won over his hardheaded daughter and the rough edges of their relationship had smoothed. "Look, I'll take a rain check." She forced a smile, then looked back to her father. "Dad, you're on, maybe next weekend."

And she was out the door.

Olivia turned to him, her gaze skating across the cards still lying on the table. "What was that all about?" she asked.

He explained about the short meeting with Kristi, everything she'd told him, and as Olivia picked up first one card, then the other, examining it through the plastic, he added, "But she's lying."

"Lying?" Her eyebrows drew together. "About what?"

"I don't know. Maybe things are worse than she admitted, but she's holding out."

"Are you sure?"

"Yeah." He was. "I know my daughter and when she lies, she forces herself to stare straight at you, hold your gaze, you know? As if to convince you that she's telling the truth by not looking away. She's done it since she was about fourteen when she was sneaking out, or meeting a boy or generally getting into trouble. She thought she could look innocent and sincere enough to fool me."

"But you were too smart for her, is that it?" Olivia arched a knowing eyebrow.

"Yeah." He nodded, catching the sarcasm. "That is it."

"I don't know. Kristi's pretty damned sharp." But her playful attitude changed as she studied the Bible verses and looked up. "This is serious, Rick."

"You're telling me." At that moment Ginny let out a cry from their bedroom.

"Oops. Duty calls. I'll get her and you pour me a cup of coffee."

"You go get the coffee," he told her, and pushed his chair back. "I'll see to our daughter."

For a reason he didn't want to examine too closely, Bentz needed to hold the baby, press his nose into her cheek, and smell the baby-scents of her, to keep her close. That was the problem with children. They eventually left. He remembered the first time he'd held Kristi as a newborn infant.

Never had he felt such joy.

And never had he felt so vulnerable.

Neither feeling had ever left him. And now Kristi, whether she admitted it or not, was drowning in her grief. He knew it would take time for her to heal, of course. Hadn't he been there himself? But he hated to see her hurting and he was worried sick about her safety.

Ginny was crawling to the side of the bed, dragging her ratty pink blanket with her, when he reached the bedroom. "Hey, sunshine," he said, and scooped her up to hold her close, the blanket dangling. "Who's my big girl?"

"Me!" she cried in delight.

"That's right, honey, you sure are."

This one, he thought, carrying her into the living area, he could protect. For the moment. But his other daughter?

God, he hoped he could.

He'd have to find a way. His arms tightened around his youngest. Have to.

She'd lied to her father.

Again.

God, when would she ever learn, Kristi wondered as she drove home. Yes, a security tech was scheduled, but she wasn't going jogging with Bella or anyone else for that matter. Not yet.

Her stomach was queasy and she attributed the slight case of nausea to her lying and, of course, the pregnancy.

Soon she'd go to the ob-gyn to confirm what she'd learned in the hospital, and talk to a specialist who would give her more information about her pregnancy. Then she would give her father the happy news, but she wasn't ready yet. Telling anyone about her baby, Jay's baby, seemed a bit of a betrayal somehow, since she'd never been able to confide in her own husband.

"Don't go there," she said, and drove home.

To an empty house. She and Jay had each had pets when they'd gotten together, but over the years the animals had aged and eventually passed on. As a couple, they'd talked about adopting another dog or cat but hadn't gotten around to it. Jay's half-blind dog Bruno had been his constant companion when he and Kristi had reconnected, and she'd had wonderful Houdini, her black cat who'd always had a hint of mystery, plus little Hairy S, a scruff of a terrier mix.

All now gone, she thought sadly.

As was Jay.

But there was the new little kitten and soon, hopefully, another dog.

With renewed determination, she shook off her melancholy and walked into the house, hesitating inside, but sensing no one had entered. The technician wasn't due for another couple of hours, so she decided to take Bella's advice and go for a run. She even considered calling her friend, but thought better of it. She wasn't ready for company yet, but she would be and soon. She'd need her friends and she'd just have to gut through all their happy little stories about their lives, the tales of their husbands' foibles, their kids' accomplishments, the constant struggle with their co-workers and bosses, even their pets' hilarious antics. It was time to get out of her own whirlpool of self-pity and get on with her life. True, her life was somewhat isolated and lonely, the nature of being a writer, and the subject matter of violent crime could be a real downer, but she'd just have to make an effort.

She discovered the kitten curled on her bed, a little fluff of black fur with round eyes that was already burrowing into her heart, a female that she'd dubbed Lenore in honor of one of her favorite poems by Poe.

She spent some time petting the little purring beast, then located her favorite Nikes, kicked off by the back door, slipped them on, and took off, running through the neighborhood and following her usual route. She noticed the houses as she passed, many with pumpkins, even jack-o'-lanterns on the porches.

There was a new strength in her pace, a fierceness in her stride, a determination to find herself. And not only that, she thought as she crossed the streetcar's tracks, then jogged under the canopy of huge live oak trees and past the grand old homes of the Garden District, but she was going to quit moping around and find the son of a bitch who had killed her husband, the prick who had robbed her unborn child of ever knowing his or her father.

At the corner of Washington and Fourth Street, she had the sensation she was being followed, but a quick look over her shoulder told her that she was imagining anyone tailing her. That was the problem. Ever since the attack, she'd felt unseen eyes upon her and she'd been jumpy. Paranoid.

Then, discovering that someone had actually been in her house to leave her the disturbing card only increased her case of nerves.

She cut past Lafayette Cemetery with its graying marble tombs and wrought iron fence, then headed back to her house where she showered and dressed. Next up? The local animal shelter where she intended to find a big, fierce-looking dog, one that would run with her, cuddle with her, and most of all, deter anyone from daring to think they could ever break into her house again.

Once more she thought about the attack, the notes she'd received. Personal messages, aimed at her. Not Jay. He was just, to the assailant, collateral damage. She'd been the target that night. She thought back. She'd been late coming out of the dance studio, had to settle up a problem with her bill with the instructor, and when she'd stepped onto the street she encountered a downpour. Using her umbrella, she'd dashed across the street, run down the alley and, she was certain, the attacker had been waiting. And not for a random victim, no. Otherwise she wouldn't be receiving the cards.

So whoever killed Jay had targeted her.

But why then, when he'd entered her house, long enough to leave the message in her underwear drawer, hadn't he stuck around? Why hadn't he waited for her and attacked? Why would he be playing this cat and mouse game when before he'd tried to kill her? Why the change in attitude?

The answer came in Jay's voice, echoing inside her head. *"Because it's his sick mind game. He wants to terrorize you. Now that he missed his mark and killed me, he wants to torment you. He's playing with you, Kris."*

Did that make sense?

"What about this makes sense? He's toying with you. Getting off on it."

"Sick-o," she said aloud, and made her way up the stairs to her office and heard a soft mew from the floor below. "Oh, Lenore." She'd been so lost in thought she'd forgotten about the kitten. Hurrying down, she found her attempting to climb the steps. "You'll get it. Soon," Kristi assured her, then scooped up the little black cat and headed up again. Once in her office she stood in front of the built-in bookcase where copies of her true-crime novels were shelved. Still holding and petting the kitten, she eyed the spines and thought back to the cases. Several of the murderers she'd written about were dead, so she discounted them. Not that a loved one, a member of the killers' families, or close friends couldn't have taken up the sword and sought revenge, but they were in the second layer of suspects.

"Who, who, who?" she whispered, kissing the kitten on its head while studying the volumes. Her gaze fell on *The Bayou Butcher*, her book on Ned Zavala, who had been tried and convicted of slaughtering a member of his family, cutting his sister up and freezing her parts before using them to hunt alligators. Zavala, like so many convicted killers, had sworn his innocence and, years later, his mother had recanted her testimony, swearing it was her dead husband who had committed the crimes, Zavala's stepfather. She swore he was behind several other women who had gone missing on the bayou but had maintained her silence until Corrin Hebert's massive heart attack had taken his life.

Nonetheless, Ned Zavala had served most of his sentence and was only paroled because of good behavior while behind bars.

She slid into her desk chair and turned on her laptop and initiated a quick Internet search of the ex-con. Sure enough, he was living in the area, at the same address as his mother in a small town southwest of New Orleans. Zavala had always blamed Rick Bentz for locking him away and had been outraged that Kristi had written a book and used the name the press had given him for its title. He'd sent letters to her publisher, had always insisted that he wasn't guilty, and was incensed that anyone was profiting from his tragedy. The letters had stopped three years ago. Just about the time he'd been released from prison.

She reached for a new legal pad from the stash she kept in a drawer and started a list of potential suspects. Ned Zavala's name was at the top. She also included his address and where he worked, all info she found easily as she paid for an Internet private eye service. Ned's employment history had been spotty, working through a temp agency at jobs at hardware and sporting goods stores, working in an oyster-processing plant, once driving a forklift for a construction company.

She wondered. No one, including her father, had been able to prove that Zavala's stepfather, Corrin Hebert, had been the killer, but it was possible as Hebert had been a big bear of a man with a mercurial temper. He'd hunted alligators and anything that moved in the bayou. He'd been a suspect, but the evidence had pointed to Zavala, who had no alibi and some of his dead sister's blood on his jeans, evidence he'd sworn had been planted. His mother, finally, had said

Hebert had done the deed, filled a vial with blood he'd taken off the dead woman, dripped it onto the jeans, and told his wife he'd kill her and the rest of the brood if she so much as said a peep. She'd believed him.

Now Ned was taking care of his housebound mother, the very woman whose silence had kept him locked up. Good old Mom.

A weird twist of fate, Kristi thought, turning the idea over in her mind.

Kristi bit her lip and absently stroked the cat.

Maybe the state of Louisiana had gotten it right after all. Maybe Zavala actually had been the Bayou Butcher. Or maybe he was just pissed that he'd spent years in prison for a crime he hadn't committed. Rick Bentz had sent him up the river. Kristi Bentz had profited from and sensationalized the bizarre crimes.

But there were others as well.

She leaned back in her chair and perused the other books she'd written where the convicted murderer in the story was now out, a free man. *The God Complex and Murder* was the story of Hamilton Cooke, a brilliant surgeon with a genius IQ, who had been convicted of homicide in the brutal murder of his wife, but the evidence had been thin and circumstantial and with an appeal and new attorney, his conviction had been overturned. Dr. Cooke was working on getting his license to practice medicine reinstated.

He was handsome, arrogant, and cold, and Kristi, to this day, believed he'd murdered his wife for a hefty life insurance payout. Over a million dollars. But he'd proclaimed his innocence, of course, and threatened to sue Rick Bentz and the New Orleans Police Department for false arrest, and Kristi Bentz for profiting from his tragedy and the "incredible miscarriage of justice!"

Kristi didn't buy it.

Hamilton Cooke was shrewd and never let his public outrage die. When his story faded from the news, it was he who always pumped it up again, giving interviews on television or for the newspapers, keeping up several social media platforms, polishing his infamy into a burnished stardom of sorts.

Her gaze moved to the next book about another local murderer, but before she could think about Mandel Jarvis, a pro football player who'd been charged and convicted of killing his model wife, her cell phone jangled and she saw Zera Stern, her agent's name, flash onto the screen. Zera was young and ambitious and had only been with Kristi a short while. And she always talked a mile a minute.

Before Kristi could even say hello, she heard, "Is it true? Is the Rosary Killer really alive? Oh, my God, Kristi, is that the person who attacked you? Who killed Jay?" Zera was incredulous. "I thought—I thought he was dead. Father John, I mean. Killed in the swamp or something. Wasn't that right? Didn't your father shoot him? Or alligators eat him or something?"

"Yes, but—"

"No 'buts.' Now we have a sequel. I mean, I hate to be that person, the agent that sees dollar signs in every tragedy, but this . . . Oh, my God, no one can tell this story like you. I know you must be feeling raw. Good Lord, you haven't even recovered fully from the attack yourself, but a tragedy like this is a horrible, horrible turn of events. I know your life is turned inside out and I can*not* imagine the grief you're going through. Unthinkable. Just unthinkable. But, you do see my point, right? That you can make lemonade out of lemons, so to speak, spin this thing on its ear, and find a hint of a blessing in this terrible turn of events."

"Oh—I don't know. And no one's certain that whoever killed Jay is the Rosary Killer. It's still all under investigation."

"But he's back, right? There have been other homicides that fit his MO and the police are looking into the idea that he's returned, almost from the dead! This story will practically write itself because you—you, Kristi Bentz—are smack-dab in the middle of it."

This was all too fast. "Nothing is certain."

"Yet. But it will be. Have faith," Zera said, her voice having a kinder edge. Then, of course, she was back to business: "Just tell me you'll think about it," she insisted. "You don't have to give me an answer right now, of course, but I want to shop the idea around, you know, before someone else gets the idea and it'll happen, you know it will. Drake Dennison would love to get his teeth into this one."

"I know." Drake Dennison was another true-crime author, one who had reached more than a modicum of success, a recluse who was an expert on serial killers. However, Drake had lost some of his

luster once Kristi began her own career. As the daughter of a homicide detective and herself a victim of more than one psychopath, she
was more in demand, and though she'd never met Dennison, she'd
learned that he resented her.

"This could be big. I've already talked to your editor and believe it
or not the publisher had already discussed rereleasing *The Rosary
Killer*, you know, because those made-for-TV movies on some of your
books? They're coming out again—this month! Wait—in a week or
two? Remember?"

"Of course." How could she forget? The previews had been shown
twenty-four/seven, it seemed. And four of her books that had been
turned into made-for-TV movies were going to be shown in rotation
during the last week of the month, just before Halloween, all part of
Murder Month, a promotion for the network. She'd seen the promos
for *The God Complex and Murder, American Icon/American Killer*,
The Bayou Butcher, and of course, *The Rosary Killer.*

Zera was still talking at a breathtaking pace. "This is a no-brainer.
I've already got a call in to your editor." Zera was pressing her case
about Kristi writing a sequel to *The Rosary Killer*. "And truthfully,
Kristi, as I said before, you're the only one who can tell the story the
way it should be told. You wrote the first one, you're intimately involved, and it could be . . . could be like a catharsis for you and what
you're going through. You could work your way through it."

"It's way too early."

"I know, I know. Seriously, I do, and I feel for you, I do. You know
I do, but I'm just saying that an opportunity has presented itself.
Unique to you, so just tell me you'll consider it, okay? Can you do
that much?"

Kristi bit her lip. "It feels wrong."

"Too soon. It's just too soon. I know. I shouldn't have brought it
up. But, there it is. Give yourself some time, but think about the future. You're a widow, now, sadly—"

A widow. She recoiled from the word.

"—and you have to think about what's best for you."

And the baby.

Involuntarily her hand cradled her abdomen, her thoughts straying to the child growing within her. She blinked, surprised that tears
she'd thought had all dried sprang to her eyes.

"I'll give it some thought," she said.

"Good. Good. Keep me informed, okay? Let me know how you're doing, how the investigation is going?"

"I will," Kristi promised as she disconnected and stared blankly at the phone. Her agent was right, of course, but it all seemed surreal. Nonetheless she heard Jay's voice again; this time he was telling her that this was, indeed, her story to pen.

She just hoped she could discover where the killer was hiding and expose him before he harmed anyone else.

Only then would she think about writing the *Rosary Killer* sequel.

CHAPTER 10

Bentz's stomach roiled.

Just as it always did when he walked into the scene of a homicide.

No matter how many years had passed, no matter how many gory scenes he'd witnessed over his career, his reaction was always the same and oftentimes he'd end up hurling on the street outside. His reaction was a concern for Montoya and a point of amusement ending with ridicule from Brinkman, who could see a victim carved to ribbons, eye the scene and smoke a cigarette afterward as if it was all nothing.

This scene was no different.

"Who called it in?" he asked his partner as they stepped inside the small apartment in the French Quarter. The victim, a white woman somewhere between twenty-five and her mid-thirties with exaggerated makeup and a short dress, lay face-up on the floor.

"Roommate," Montoya said, careful to step around the body.

"And first on the scene?"

"That would be me," a young patrolman in a crisp uniform said. "Ray Connors." He was standing in the doorway to the apartment and couldn't have been more than twenty-five, a fresh-faced black man with a shaved head and athletic build. "Got the call. Came over. Talked to the roommate. Saw the victim. Called it in." All business.

"Who found her?"

"Roommate." Connors checked a notepad. "Sherilynn Gordon."

He answered Bentz's question before he could ask. "She's in the patrol car outside. Thought you might want to talk to her."

"Good. We do," Bentz said. He and Montoya had gotten the call, shown up here, and after signing in to the crime scene, donned protective footwear and walked carefully so as not to disturb physical evidence as the Crime Scene Unit was on its way. As was someone from the coroner's office. Now, they surveyed the small studio apartment with its eclectic bits of furniture that included a wide bed, one chair and a desk with a lighted mirror and jars of makeup, nail polish, brushes and the like, scattered across the surface, some on the floor next to the victim, the obvious results of a struggle.

"She was wearing a wig," Montoya said, staring at the victim's face. "Jesus, I think I know her." Then he shook his head, crouching down to get a closer look.

"What?" Bentz, too, leaned down for a better view as he eyed the dead woman's neck. The telltale marks were there, deep impressions, contusions in a specific pattern, that he knew were of the beads in a rosary. "It's him," he said, looking up. "Father John." The same sick-o who used a sacred, holy artifact to kill.

Bentz glanced to a side table. Sure enough, the C-note was there, complete with Ben Franklin's eyes blackened. "Son of a bitch." He straightened and fought the urge to vomit. He'd known the bastard was back, had seen the evidence at the previous scene where Teri Marie Gaines aka Tiffany Elite had been killed. "You know her?"

Montoya was shaking his head. "No, I don't 'know' her, not personally, but I think I've seen her." His eyebrows were knitted, his lips pursed. "Like she's famous or something. Wait a second. She's wearing contacts, one's slipped. Her eyes aren't brown, they're blue. And . . . look." He pointed to a spot by the dead woman's nose. "Her skin's peeling off here or . . ." He glanced up at Bentz. "She's wearing a prosthetic?"

"You sure?"

"Don't know."

"You think she might be famous and tricking?" The woman was obviously a prostitute.

"I don't know, man." He was still studying the woman's face and from the looks of it, thinking hard. "But I've seen her. I'm sure I have."

"Any ID?" Bentz looked over at Connors, who was still standing in the doorway.

"Yeah—her purse is in that closet." He pointed to a door near the bed. "There's a wallet inside. I looked at it. The name on the driver's license and credit cards, health cards all say Helene Laroche. The picture on her ID doesn't match the vic and I thought maybe she'd stolen the purse, but I talked to the roommate. She confirmed that she's Ms. Laroche."

Bentz felt as if he'd been sucker-punched.

Montoya let out a long, low whistle. "I knew I recognized her."

Bentz hadn't. Her disguise was too complete. But he knew the name. Helene Laroche was a bit of a legend around these parts. Helene Sands grew up dirt poor, as a preteen and teenager, always in trouble with the law, dropped out of high school despite an off-the-charts IQ, married and divorced twice, and then met Hugo Laroche, who was old enough to be her grandfather and rich enough to be one of the city's biggest patrons of the arts and donor to all kinds of charity causes and universities. Laroche's grown children had been scandalized by the affair and marriage and the city had been abuzz with gossip as just two years ago Hugo had dumped his wife of nearly fifty years for the young porn star.

As the coroner arrived, followed in short order by the crime investigators, Bentz and Montoya walked outside to the sultry October afternoon. The sky was gray, the heat oppressive for this time of year, humidity higher than usual.

Bentz felt sweat trickle down his neck and tugged at his suddenly too-tight collar.

Connors walked them to the cruiser where a tall, leggy woman with short, spiked red hair, sunglasses, and glossy, nearly colorless lips was taking a long draw on an e-cigarette. A female officer, short and stocky, stood next to her.

"Wouldn't stay in the car," the female cop said as they were introduced to Sherilynn Gordon, Helene Laroche's roommate.

"It was like a sauna in there," Sherilynn complained as she motioned toward the cop car.

"Sorry, ma'am, I thought we were on our way downtown."

"We are," Bentz said. Already a crowd had gathered, all with cell phones, all taking videos and pictures of the police activity. "Go ahead and we'll meet you there."

"What? No! The station?" Sherilynn was shaking her head, tiny lines of worry around her mouth. "I freak out at police stations. Freak the fuck out! Besides there's not much more to tell you. I came back here and found her and called nine-one-one." She took another hit from her device, and saw the crowd. "Oh, shit! A fuckin' TV crew."

Sure enough a van from a local station was rolling into a parking spot and Bentz thought he saw a reporter he knew, next to a female photographer, camera lifted. All of that was nothing, though, as cell phones from all the lookie-loos were hoisted high and before the five o'clock news aired, videos of the activity would be streaming on the Internet.

"Downtown is better," Bentz said.

As if Sherilynn, too, finally got it, she said, "Okay. Fine. But I don't know what else I can tell you. I've done nothing wrong."

"It's just for a statement," Montoya said. "Won't take long."

She sized him up: goatee, leather jacket despite the heat, diamond earring, and that Montoya swagger.

"You're a cop?" she said almost incredulously, though he'd shown her his badge. "You work vice?"

"Homicide."

"Hmm." Somewhat satisfied, she said, "Can't you just take my statement here? Now?" she demanded as the coroner's SUV rolled up, a news van on its tail. "Oh, shit. More TV is here. This is turning out to be a fuckin' three-ring circus!"

"That's what I mean," Montoya said. "Probably best to talk in private."

Sherilynn adjusted her sunglasses and took another hit on her e-cigarette, a thin cloud of vapor roiling around her as she exhaled. "Fine. Let's go. But make it short."

They didn't.

The interview at the station took over two hours with Bentz and Montoya both in the room asking the questions.

Sherilynn Gordon's story was straightforward: She and Helene had known each other in high school. They'd both gotten into boys, drugs, and trouble, not necessarily in that order. Helene, gorgeous, had "married up" as Sherilynn explained it, trading husband one, a successful electrician, for a second husband, who owned his own insurance company, and finally landing "the big fish," meaning Hugo Laroche, who had sold his software company years before for upwards of fifty million. "That is if you believe him," Sherilynn had said with a sneer, indicating she didn't.

"He lies?"

"Let's just say stretches the truth, to make himself look better, if you know what I mean. Brags about it."

"You don't like him."

"I've never met him." She eyed Montoya across the table. "What does that have to do with anything?"

Bentz ignored her question. "Did he and Helene get along?"

"I don't know." She cocked her head. "But obviously things weren't exactly perfect, right? I mean it must not have been all sunshine and roses. Otherwise . . ." She shrugged, let the sentence trail off.

"Otherwise what?"

"She wouldn't be back in the business, right? Obviously there was trouble in paradise."

"Do you know what that trouble was?" Bentz asked.

"You do know the story about a bird being trapped in a gilded cage, right?" She stared at Bentz as if he were the most dense man on the planet. "She was twenty-five. He was seventy something." Her gaze sharpened. "What was the trouble in paradise? You tell me."

They asked a few more questions and learned that, of course, Helene didn't get along with her husband's grown children, hated his grandchildren, despised his ex-wife, and wasn't that fond of her husband. According to Sherilynn, she'd taken up turning tricks for the thrill of it.

". . . she certainly didn't need the money. She rented the apartment, paid for everything. All I had to do was keep it in my name, so the old man wouldn't find out. And she was picky. Didn't just take a date with anyone. They had to 'intrigue' her, that's what she said. She definitely wasn't in it for the money." Sherilynn scoffed at the idea. "And I don't think it was for the sex—she could've gotten that anywhere. It was just that she was getting away with it. Being Helen of Joy, y'know? She told me once that she felt freer, less like she was selling her body, when she was with johns of her choice rather than with her own husband. Limp Dick. That's what she called him." A tiny smile touched the corners of her lips. "What does that tell you?"

What, indeed, Bentz thought. "So how did she usually hook up with her dates?" He couldn't see her walking the streets.

"She has, I mean, had, a Web site." When they didn't respond, she said, "Helen of Joy NOLA. Google it."

Montoya was already on his phone. As the Web site came up on the screen, his eyebrows inched upward.

"So you found it," she said.

"Do you know who she met up with last night?"

"I already told you. I had no idea. We kept our business separate and that was her idea. She had to keep things on the down low, cuz she didn't want the old man finding out. He woulda blown a gasket, y'know. If he didn't have a heart attack himself, he would have killed her."

"Literally?" Montoya asked.

"Financially," she said. "And as much as she hated the old man, she sure did love his money."

"So she gave you no clues as to whom she was seeing."

"How many times do I have to tell you? No. We each have our own place, right? We just use the studio for, you know, entertaining clients. We keep to a schedule and don't interfere with each other."

"But you saw her some of the time."

"Once in a while. We'd catch up for coffee or a drink, but it didn't happen often. We each have, had, our own lives."

"Did she ever mention a priest?" Bentz asked.

"What? A priest? What the hell are you talking about? Oh." She stopped short. Snapped her glossy-tipped fingers. "I know about this. Saw it on the Internet. A fake priest, right? That's what you're talking about. Not a real one. A guy who committed a lot of murders way back when. Oh, Lord." Her head swiveled, her gaze moving from Montoya to Bentz. "That's it. You think he killed Helene."

"We don't know," Bentz said.

"Holy Mother of God." She blanched.

Montoya said, "So it's important, if you know anything—"

"But I don't. What's with you two that you don't understand common English. I don't know anything about her clients. And that was intentional. We had a deal, Helene and I. No pimps. And we never talked business." Her eyes were round and she actually looked scared. "I have no idea who she was seeing."

Unfortunately, Bentz believed her. He glanced at Montoya, who had gotten more intense during the interview. It seemed like his partner was finally starting to understand that Father John, the Rosary Killer, was back in New Orleans.

And he was back with a vengeance.

Try as she might, Kristi couldn't concentrate on the sequel to her book about Father John, nor could she get her head into her new book, and it wasn't because Lenore was batting at her bare toes with a tiny paw while hiding under the desk. No. Her agent's suggestion that she drop everything and concentrate on delving deep into the sequel was still too new of an idea to even think about writing. For God's sake, the investigation was just starting.

However the real problem was that she was too caught up in her own life, the fact that she was now a widow.

She'd told herself that she just needed to bury herself in the work to get through the too-long days and harrowing nights that she spent, sleepless, the claw hammer now under her pillow, the kitten usually under the covers with her. She'd checked with the neighbors, several vets and rescue groups, along with posting online. No one yet had laid claim to the cat and, with each day that passed, Kristi hoped more and more that no one did.

She eyed her desk where notes, books, newspaper clippings, and magazine articles were scattered. She was still in the research phase on her book about New Orleans's most recent string of murders. She'd spent several weeks on research while organizing her notes, adjusting the synopsis she'd written about the 21 Killer, a grotesque serial killer who murdered twins on their twenty-first birthday. 21's reign of terror was over, thank God, and Kristi's publisher was interested in the story, but as Kristi sat in her office, going through the evidence against 21 and digging into his psyche as to why he would kill the twins, she found her mind straying and finally, hauling the kitten, gave up and headed downstairs where she poured herself a glass of water and checked the time.

The tech from the security company she'd called to upgrade the system had canceled the first appointment as there had been a foul-up in the shipment of some essential part of her new security system, but the part had come in and the technician was supposedly on his way.

He was over half an hour late, though, the digital display on her desk clock registering 2:47. Just as she thought about calling the company, she received a text from an anonymous number, indicating "Lance" was on his way and would arrive by 3:00.

Good.

Maybe the new system would ease her mind and she would sleep better.

"Fat chance," she said aloud as reports of the return of the Rosary Killer had overtaken the local news and were permeating via the Internet to the national level. Many people, including her father, had speculated that Father John had survived in that bayou where it was thought he had died only to return to New Orleans and wreak havoc on the city.

"As if we don't have enough," she said.

Worse yet, the rumors were flying that the killer had taken his vengeance out on Rick Bentz, the detective who had unmasked and nearly killed him, by murdering Jay McKnight, Bentz's son-in-law. And, of course, those maniacs who fed on bizarre murders were all over social media, chatting it up, making it worse.

"Careful, Kristi, those maniacs are the people who buy your books." Jay's voice echoed through her brain, clear as a bell. After being silent for two days.

"I know," she said under her breath, then checked her e-mail where Zera had left her a quick note:

Good news! *Rosary Killer* is definitely going to be reprinted. Early as next summer. Publisher already promoting. Let's talk!

Not now.

A headache started at the base of her skull.

It was all too much.

She decided to hang it up for the day.

The story would wait, she told herself. Every day she was feeling a little stronger, a little more like her old self. She'd even agreed to meet with her friends for coffee in a couple of days after declining drinks and karaoke, which sounded just awful. She hadn't liked it when she was single in her twenties and was certain it wasn't for her. Besides, she was avoiding alcohol for the baby's sake, though there was nothing she wanted more than a tall drink to numb her mind and her body from the grief. And the guilt.

"Baby steps," she told herself.

The doorbell rang and she hurried down the stairs, and rather than just fling the door open as she usually would, she peered through the sidelight and saw the repairman, in a gray uniform stretched tight over his middle. Around five-nine, wearing thick glasses, shaggy black hair showing signs of silver, he stared back at her. Three or four days' worth of a beard darkened his jaw and a badge on his uniform proclaimed that he was Lance with Eastside Security and Alarms.

She opened the door a crack, noticing that the day was hazy.

"I'm Lance with Eastside," he said, the name on his uniform confirming that he was, indeed, Lance, the laminated badge he offered her that included his picture in agreement. "I texted."

"Right." She nodded, but was still unsure. Didn't move from blocking the doorway, though the van he drove had the logo, phone number, and name of the security company painted along its side.

"Sorry about the mix-up a couple of days ago." Lance shrugged, his expression slightly perplexed about the whole situation. "Parts, right?"

"Until I can put in a whole new system."

"Well, it's tough, you know, to get parts for old equipment. Stuff comes from all over the world these days, so what're ya gonna do?" Then he glanced to the side. "Oh. Hello. What's this?"

"What?" She watched as he took a step to the side of the door, leaned down, and picked up a vase of flowers—roses and baby's breath—that had been tucked close to the house, just out of her viewpoint from the cracked doorway. Straightening, he said, "I think these are for you?"

Kristi wasn't surprised. She'd received bouquets and live plants for the better part of two weeks, but she'd thought maybe they'd stopped coming. This was the first delivery in four days.

"I'll be right back," he said, and headed back to his van.

She followed him with her eyes as he retrieved equipment and tools, then left the door open for him and carried the flowers inside just as her cell phone jangled. She left the vase on a side table near the front door.

Answering, she kept her gaze on the technician. He seemed okay, but she was still unnerved, trying to be uber-careful these days.

The call was from Bella. "Hey, just letting you know that we're actually doing it. Tomorrow, at six in the morning, if you can believe that, because Sarah has to be at work at seven forty-five."

"What?"

"Running! We're going to start at Crescent Park six a.m., sharp. That's when it's supposed to open, and from what I've heard it has great jogging and walking paths." It did. Kristi had run the span of trails and bridges with great city views. Bella continued, "Thought you might want to join in. You're the expert."

"Six?" Kristi repeated, watching as the boxes of security components grew and the repairman suddenly looked up at her, obviously waiting to speak with her. "Look, I doubt it. Not tomorrow. Maybe another time? But I have to run now. I've got someone here."

"Wait!" Bella said. "I need to ask you something. From the producer of the morning show at the station."

"What?" Kristi asked, holding up a finger at Lance to indicate she'd be off the call shortly.

"Renee-Claire, the host, would love it if you would do a show. And soon. It's almost Halloween and we're doing all kinds of spooky stuff at the station and on *Bonjour, New Orleans!* And since you're the resident author who writes about serial killers and I know you, they thought I could convince you to be on the show."

"Oh—God, I can't think about that now," Kristi said.

"Yeah, I know it's a bad time, but they're really interested! I mean *really*! I think they've even talked to your publisher or agent or something."

"What? Uh . . ."

Lance was still waiting.

Kristi said, "I can't . . . I mean . . . I'll call you back," and she ended the call.

"Sorry," Lance apologized by rote, then said, "I see you've got an older system. As in ancient. Are you sure you just want to upgrade it a little? You could really use a new state-of-the-art system."

"Yes, yes, I do." Kristi tried to turn her attention back to the problem at hand. "But I was told that couldn't happen immediately."

"We're backed up."

"Right. So I need something temporary," she reminded him. "I just want a system that works now, even if it's not state of the art. Just a tweak to what I've got until I can have a new digitalized system."

"Okay," he said, nodding. "That's what the scheduler said. I'll need access to your Wi-Fi, and is your electrical panel in the garage?"

She walked him through the house and told herself this was all normal for the type of system she could afford right now with what was available, something more than the do-it-yourself setups, but not a system capable of securing Fort Knox. At least not yet. However, he had her second-guessing herself and just being around him made her nervous. It wasn't anything he said directly, though he was a little intense, but she didn't feel comfortable with him checking out her house, moving from one room to the next, testing cameras, the alarm with its sharp screech, and motion detectors.

It's all part of his job. It's what you're paying him to do, she thought.

She told herself that she was overreacting, that she was being supersensitive because of the recent trauma she'd been through, but by the time he had commented on the nails in her bedroom window with, "Wow. I see you've got some old-fashioned security here, but it's the kind that can kill you if you're trapped by a fire," he was beginning to bug her, even though he was joking. He finally finished by remarking that she should change out the backup battery every year and have someone double-check the system regularly, then took the time to explain how it worked, showing her how to turn off the various areas in the house. He reminded her once more that though he'd upgraded her existing system, she really should spring for something more high-tech. "This system has its flaws and is really old."

"I know. It came with the house when we bought it."

After he double-checked his work he handed her a thin instruction manual for the new parts that was printed in six or seven different languages and left.

Relieved to see him go, she watched him through the sidelight of the front door as he spent another fifteen minutes with paperwork and on his phone before he backed his van out of the driveway and turned down the now-dark street. Once his taillights disappeared, she changed her security code and tested the app on her phone that linked her to the system.

Everything seemed to work.

"Thank God," she said aloud, and thought that maybe now her father would be happy. If that was even possible.

Her phone buzzed again and she recognized the number of the animal shelter. "Hello?" a bright voice said. "Is this Kristi Bentz?"

"It is."

"Hi, it's Heather at the animal shelter. And I think we may have found the perfect dog for you. A two-year-old neutered male, around eighty pounds and a love. He's part Staffordshire terrier, pit, you know. And . . . from the looks of him, he's got a little lab, or boxer, or both, we're really not sure. Haven't done any DNA on him, you know."

A dyed-in-the-wool mutt, it seemed.

The woman was going on about the dog. "His name is Dave and he came in from another shelter. He's been quarantined and already seen by the vet. He's healthy, neutered, and you could meet him tomorrow if you're still interested."

She didn't hesitate, said she'd fill out the application online and be at the shelter in the morning, and disconnected. The picture of Dave came through in less than a minute and in that instant she fell in love with a floppy-eared, caramel-colored dog with a black snout and a pink tongue lolling from one side of his mouth. He looked like a mutt. Pure and simple. Maybe part lab. Maybe part pit bull, but definitely a mutt. And—because of his silly pose in the picture—not that intimidating. But that was okay, she thought. This dog would guard her, yes, but have to get along with her newly adopted kitten and be gentle with children as well.

Absently she touched her still-flat abdomen.

A baby was coming.

CHAPTER 11

A tall, rawboned man with wide shoulders and a shock of snow-white hair, Hugo Laroche was stoic as he stood in the doorway of his home, his body blocking entrance to the mansion, a three-storied brick house painted a pastel pink and trimmed in black wrought iron filigree.

"Homicide?" he repeated as Bentz and Montoya stated their reason for arriving on his doorstep. His jaw was tight, his eyes dry, his shoulders square as he learned about the death of his wife. "You're saying Helene was murdered?" he asked, a muscle working in his jaw.

"Yes," Bentz said, and kept more information to himself, including his theories about Father John.

"That's . . . impossible. I mean . . . who—?" He let out a sigh and wiped a hand across his forehead.

"That's what we're trying to find out. We'd just like to ask you a few questions."

"Yes . . . yes, of course." Stunned, he led them inside, down a massive hallway to a door tucked beneath the sweep of a grand staircase. "We can talk in here," he said. "No interruptions."

They stepped into a large den equipped with a massive flat screen that took up most of one wall. On the opposite side of the room, French doors framed by floor-to-ceiling windows opened to a private pool area that was surrounded by a rock wall. Palm trees shaded the scattered tables and lounge chairs and a massive waterfall emptied into the pristine waters of the pool.

Laroche motioned Bentz and Montoya into the chairs facing the television, which was tuned into a financial news channel. He picked up a remote, muted the volume, and said, "Can I get you anything? Sweet tea, a soda, or something stronger?" He made his way to a built-in bar located between massive bookcases. A fireplace now empty stood on one side of the room, and a desk was pushed into a corner with a view of the private gardens and glistening water.

Bentz and Montoya declined the drinks while Laroche poured himself a tumbler of scotch and added two ice cubes. While waving them into the two leather recliners, he sat in an executive desk chair that he rolled from behind his wide desk. After taking a deep swallow, he said, "Tell me. Where and when did this happen?" Then he held up a hand. "And for God's sake, how did it happen? She told me she was spending the night with her sister in Baton Rouge, they were going to do shopping and spa-ing, manicures, pedicures, facials, and massages, that sort of thing, then have drinks, and she didn't think she'd want to drive. Told me she'd be home sometime this afternoon. In time for dinner." He glanced at his watch. Saw that it was nearly four. His eyebrows quirked. "I wasn't even worried. Dear God . . . is this for real? Can I . . . can I see her?"

He seemed more curious than grief-stricken, Bentz thought. Not that he was acting, it just seemed that Hugo Laroche wasn't all that concerned.

As if he'd read Bentz's thoughts, he said, "This is terrible. Horrible, but—" He took another swallow from his drink and moved the swivel chair back and forth, just slightly. "—I'm not surprised."

"You're not?" Montoya asked.

"She's a risk taker. Helene always pushed the envelope, if you know what I mean."

"I don't." Montoya leaned forward in his seat.

"I met her at a strip club. No big deal. My wife and I were having problems, and I started, well . . ." He paused, searching for the right word. "You know, looking for action."

Bentz kept his face neutral.

"So I saw Helene dancing and I met her." He looked away, to a middle distance only he could see. "She called herself Helen then, of course."

"Of course."

"That was before she added, 'of Joy.'" He shook his head at the thought. "So, anyway, we went out a few times and she wanted to do everything extreme. To the max. I'm not just talking about sex but, you can imagine, that was fantastic. She wanted to do parasailing and rock climbing, parachuting and helicopter skiing. Whatever it was, she was in." He got lost in thought for a second, swirled his drink. "She was exciting, you know. And in bed? Like I said, we role-played, and well . . . did things I'd only dreamed about, you know? She's always, always up for a good time and likes to spice things up. Even, you know, with more partners. Three-ways or whatever. Took me to a couple of orgies." His eyebrows shot up. "Wild." Another long drink. More thoughtful swirling of the ice cubes and movement of the chair. "She was like an addiction. I couldn't get her out of my head. She wanted to get married and I guess I thought that would be a good idea. I could tame the tigress, so to speak, or at least have her for my own."

He shrugged. "You probably know the rest. I divorced Beverly and that cost me a pretty penny, let me tell you. My kids, Vince and Marianne, disowned me, at least at first, but wow, I had Helene." He was nodding to himself. "Until I didn't." He took another swallow, draining his glass. "That's the trouble with taming the tigress. She's always looking for a way to escape and make her way back to the wild."

The tigress? Really? Bentz asked, "So you knew she was seeing other men?"

He snorted. "I suspected, but didn't want to believe it. Then my son, he showed me a link to her Web site. Helen of Joy. Oh, she was wearing a disguise, y'know, a wig and makeup, but I recognized her."

He stared off to the middle distance again, a sadness stealing over his features. "I confronted her and she didn't deny it, told me to 'deal with it.' That's what she said, 'deal with it' or she'd divorce me or I could divorce her, she didn't care. She liked the lifestyle here—well, hell, who wouldn't—but she would give it all up because she figured I'd pay through the nose to keep the divorce clean. She had stories she could tell—remember those orgies?—and she wasn't afraid to talk to a reporter or two." He cleared his throat. Frowned into his empty glass. Then walked to the bar for a refill.

"There's something more," Montoya pressed because they both felt it.

Laroche's shoulders slumped as he fixed his drink and he swore under his breath. "Oh, fuck, yeah, there's more." A muscle was working in his jaw as he started to sit, then thought better of it and stood next to the cold hearth. "She has—er, had—pictures. Videos. They would ruin me. I sit on the boards of several charities and still have a seat at Laroche Software, the company I sold. Hell, it even still has my name on it. This is New Orleans, I know. People think anything goes here, but . . . well, no . . . some of those videos." He shook his head.

"Where are they?"

"She hid them."

"Does anyone know where they are?"

"Not that I know of." He took a drink.

Montoya was taking notes. "Did you know about the apartment?"

"The one she shared with the other whore?" Leaning a shoulder on the mantel, he nodded. " 'Course I did. I had her followed. Private investigator."

"We'd like to see his reports."

They heard the front door bang open and then quick footsteps down the hall. A woman of about forty sped into the den. In shorts and a loose T-shirt, her black hair scraped into a messy bun, she slid to a stop in the middle of the room. She had to be Marianne, Hugo's daughter. The resemblance to her father was unmistakable—intense blue eyes, strong jaw, wide shoulders and slim hips, a swimmer's body. "Dad?" she said, catching a glimpse of her father before casting her gaze at Montoya and Bentz. "What's going on here?"

"These are detectives from the police department," he said. "They're here—"

And then he caught himself. "This is my daughter, Marianne."

She went barreling on. "This is about Helene, right? Because she was murdered?"

"Well . . .well, yes. But how did you know—?"

"And you're talking to them? Without a lawyer?" Her eyes snapped blue fire. "Jesus Christ, Dad, for a smart man you can be so dumb sometimes."

"I've got nothing to hide."

"Oh, hell, are you fucking serious?"

"How do you even know about it?"

"Geez. It's all over the news!" She faced the cops. "This interview is over. Right now. Got it? If you want to talk to Dad again, or anyone in the family, we'll have representation with us." To her father, she said, "Call Alan. Tell him what's going on, but he probably already knows. I'm surprised he hasn't phoned you. Warned you to keep quiet."

"I said I have nothing to hide, Marianne. Nothing."

"Well, it's gonna get ugly. Or uglier. Helene's finally been exposed for the whore she is. Helen of Joy? Oh, save me!" Rolling her eyes, she let out a disgusted breath. To the detectives, she said succinctly: "Now, please, leave."

Bentz pulled out a card, handed it to her. "We want to talk to all of Helene's family and—"

"We are *not* her family. Not related to her. I wouldn't even call her stepmom, okay. She's over a decade younger than I am." She threw her father a weary look. "Oh, Dad. How could you have—?" And then Marianne caught herself. She focused on Bentz. "We'll come down to the station," she finally said. "We'll set it up through Alan Thayer, our attorney."

"Okay. Good. We have more questions for your father and your brother and you, Ms. Laroche."

"It's Mrs. Petrocci now. And I'll gladly give a statement, but only with my attorney present." Her eyes narrowed. "Do we get to see the body? You know, like ID it?"

Her father's head swiveled. "What do you mean?"

"How do we know it's even Helene?" she demanded. "It isn't like she hasn't run off before and we think something horrible happened to her only to discover that oops, it was all a mistake. She was just off doing some weird thing, 'taking me time' or going to the mountains in fucking Kentucky to 'clear my head,'" Marianne pointed out, making air quotes. "And she was always coming up with some weird disguise, altering her looks so she couldn't be seen or recognized, like she was some big movie star or something. Give me a break." She let out a breath and when her father was about to say something, added, "Or . . . or what about that time she chartered a private yacht off Miami because she wanted to experience the Bermuda Triangle? Huh? When there was worry about a damned hurricane! What about that? Every time she left without a word. To do something weird or bizarre, something to get herself noticed! Holy shit, none of us ever knew if she was alive or dead when she took off on one of her head-game trips. That's what it was, you know. She was always playing head games!"

Hugo had the decency to look sad if not grief-stricken. "Helene is a . . . well, she was . . . an independent spirit."

Marianne let out a loud, disgusted breath. "A whacko, that's what she was!" To the police, she demanded, "I want to see the body! I want to know that she is really and truly dead. It wouldn't surprise me if the poor dead girl is some kind of body double or something, and in two or three days once the press has sensationalized the story, she waltzes back in here and swears she was just gone on some kind of life-changing journey, a walk-about in Australia or met with some great shaman in India and learned about the true meaning of life or some such bullshit." She crossed her arms over her chest. "And I'll want to see the body!"

"We'll arrange it," Bentz said.

"Good. And if it is Helene," Marianne said, glaring at her father, "may she never rest in peace."

"Man oh man, she was just a kid," Montoya said in the morgue where the stripped-down body of Helene Laroche lay on a metal table.

Hugo Laroche and Marianne had already visited, the corpse wheeled into the viewing room, a sheet pulled down from her face. Bentz and Montoya had been there, witnessed the reaction of both father and daughter.

"Yes, yes, that's Helene," Hugo had said, a catch in his voice, and though he'd remained dry eyed, he'd blinked rapidly.

Marianne had wended her arm through her father's in what Bentz thought was an out-of-character display of comfort. Lips pinched, face a little more wan than earlier, she'd nodded, her messy bun jiggling. "Yeah," she agreed, at least for the moment convinced that her father was, indeed, a widower. "It sure looks like Helene." And then she'd frowned, her eyebrows slamming together. "I want a DNA test on the body."

"Marianne!" Hugo had been aghast. "You can see . . ."

"Can I?" Her eyes had narrowed in suspicion. "I know it's over the top, but we're talking about Helene here, Dad. Anything's possible." Turning her gaze to Montoya, she'd said, "You're going to do an autopsy anyway. Right? Isn't this all kind of standard in a homicide case, you know, to separate out the victim's DNA from that of the attacker if any was left at the scene?"

"You've been watching too much *CSI* and *Law and Order* or whatever on TV," her father had charged.

Montoya had held up a hand. "We'll handle it," he'd assured her before they'd left.

Father and daughter had shuttled quickly away, out the door of the viewing room, their footsteps echoing in the hallway before fading, and the body had been returned to the morgue where the detectives were now standing, staring down at what remained of Helene Sands Laroche. And Montoya was right. Without makeup or her wigs, the prosthetics on her nose and cheeks removed, she looked younger than her years.

"Yeah." Bentz was staring at the corpse and shaking his head, knowing that the psycho who had killed so many was at it again. All because Bentz's aim had been off just a fraction, but enough to allow the pathetic piece of human garbage that was the Rosary Killer to survive. If only the bullet would have found its mark on that murky night in the bayou, or if only the alligators had feasted on the wounded man. But no. Father John was back. "This is not a copycat."

"Probably not."

"Let's get out of here." The morgue was cold and sterile with tile walls and shiny, brutal-looking instruments—stainless steel saws and scales, forceps and scalpels, scissors and hammers. Tools of the trade for autopsies, but Bentz imagined them as weapons. They'd seen enough.

Though the autopsy wasn't complete, the toxicology screen not processed, it seemed obvious that Helene Laroche had died from asphyxiation, the result of being strangled by what appeared to be, at least in Bentz's mind, a rosary, most likely a homemade one with sharpened beads and piano wire for string.

He'd seen it before.

A long time ago.

Outside the day was gray and overcast, still warmer than usual for October, the wind steady and quick. The talk by the weather forecasters was that there was still a chance for a hurricane this year. That thought was grim; hurricanes here, despite all the recent upgrades to the city's defenses against huge storms, were a cause of major concern and stretched city services, including the police department, to the limits of their capabilities.

They reached Montoya's Mustang and Bentz slid into the passenger seat. "All right," Montoya said as he started the car and the big engine roared to life. "I'm convinced. Rosary is back." He wheeled out of the lot, gunning it to slide into a spot in heavy traffic.

This wasn't good news, but at least Montoya and Bentz were on the same page.

"But I'm not sure he was behind the McKnight homicide."

"No?" The truth was Bentz was on the fence about that as well.

"MO is too different."

"What are the chances that we've got two whackos dressed as priests?"

"Slim. Okay, I'll give you that." Montoya's head swiveled and then he cut across traffic to make a quick left turn.

"Hey!" Bentz shouted as an angry horn blared. In all the years they'd been partnered together Bentz had never gotten used to Montoya's aggressive driving.

"Plenty of room."

"Tell that to the guy in the BMW who's flipping you off." Bentz nodded at the silver car speeding past, the driver, a seventy-ish man sticking up his middle finger.

"Moron," Montoya said, irritation in his voice.

"I think that's what he's saying about you."

"The difference is I'm a cop."

"He doesn't know that."

"And I don't have time to make him aware of that fact," Montoya snapped, glancing at Bentz.

"Whoa. You gotta problem?"

"Not just one." Montoya glared out the bug-spattered windshield and, instead of heading back to the station, pulled into a vacant spot across the street from their favorite take-out place, known for its barbeque shrimp, po'boys, and red beans and rice. "Let's eat."

"Don't you have to be home?" Bentz's watch said it was just after five. They were officially off duty.

"Already called Abby." He shut down the engine. "You?"

"The wife's expecting me, but I can tell her I need to work late."

"Do that. Po'boy good?"

"Yeah. Shrimp."

"What else?"

"Fries and a . . . Coke." He wanted a beer, thought better of it.

"See you inside." Montoya climbed out of the car and jogged across the street.

Bentz, yanking his phone from his pocket, did the same and once he was in front of the red and white awning, phoned Olivia, telling her not to wait dinner on him and asking if he could pick anything up for her.

She declined, mentioning leftovers. "I've got plenty here in the fridge. So don't worry about it."

"I'll probably be an hour, maybe longer. Don't know. Something's up with Montoya. Don't even ask what, because I'm in the dark." That was stretching the truth; Bentz guessed Montoya's attitude had something to do with his brother, but he wasn't sure. "Listen, Livvie, if I'm gonna be longer, I'll text."

"Okay. See you after a bit," Olivia said, her tone not frosty, but a little frazzled, and he heard his daughter babbling in the background. That gave him pause and he felt a pang. He should be home with his wife and little girl. But he still had to keep his older daughter safe. Torn, he slipped his phone into his pocket. Once this was over, once he'd nailed Father John for good and was assured Kristi was out of danger, then he'd retire.

He owed it to Olivia and Ginny.

It was time.

Long past, he decided, following his partner into the restaurant.

Inside he found Montoya already seated and facing the front door from a corner booth at the back of the long, narrow restaurant.

As Bentz wound his way through a warren of tables, he glanced past the line of booths and through an open back door where the gray day was visible and the scent of cigarette smoke drifted inside. The evening crowd was gathering, half the tables and booths filled, the buzz of different conversations interrupted by bursts of laughter and the clink of glasses or rattling of flatware.

And over it all, he smelled the sharp, inviting scent of alcohol.

He shut it down.

Told himself not to give in.

It was just stress.

He'd had his last drink the other night.

"Okay, what's up?" he asked as he slid onto the bench opposite his partner. "You hear from your brother again?"

"Cruz?" Montoya gave an irritated shake of his head. "Nah. No one's heard from him. It was almost as if the call was a prank." He frowned, dark eyes worried. "But it was him. I know it and he wouldn't have made a joke of it."

"What then?"

"You."

"Me . . . ?"

"Yeah, you. You're taking the case too seriously."

"Hold on." Bentz lifted his hands, palms out. "You're saying I'm taking the murder of my son-in-law and the attack on my daughter too seriously? Are you kidding? We're talking about my kid."

"I know. And you're losing your perspective."

"What?"

"You're all over this Father John angle, but there's more to this case than the obvious," Montoya said. "You're so laser focused on him that you're not seeing the big picture."

"Oh, Jesus, are you going to try and convince me that there's two killers again? We've already been over this." His temper was rising, but before he could say anything further, a waiter, a scrawny kid of about eighteen or so with a bad case of acne, picked up the plastic placard indicating their table was #43 and left two large glasses filled with ice and soda and a couple of red plastic baskets lined with paper and filled with po'boys and piles of steaming French fries.

Montoya dug into his sandwich while Bentz, simmering, snagged a bottle pressed to the wall at the end of the table, shook it, then squirted a thick stream of ketchup over his fries, nearly smothering them. Who was Montoya to tell him how to run an investigation—a case involving his own kid? He ate half the order of fries in silence, then tore into his po'boy.

Montoya had been wet behind the ears when they'd first teamed up. A hotshot, show-off, with little experience, lots of bravado, way too much testosterone and, Bentz admitted grudgingly, good cop instincts that Montoya had honed over the years.

Of the two of them, Montoya had been the one to go off half-cocked, to run on emotion rather than rationality, and Bentz had always had a cooler head and been able to rein him in.

Not so anymore it seemed.

When had that happened?

When a maniac killed your son-in-law and tried to slice your daughter's throat, that's when.

He took a long swallow of Coke. "So what are you suggesting?"

"I just think it might be smart," Montoya said after swallowing another large bite, "if we broke the case up. Think of it as two cases, okay? You work on the Father John angle because we know he, or a dead-ringer copycat, killed Teri Marie Gaines and Helene Laroche."

"And what? You'll concentrate on Jay's homicide, is that it?"

"That's exactly it." Montoya's gaze was hard, piercing. "You're too close to it and you know it."

He did. But he didn't want to think about it. He ate another handful of fries and seriously considered a beer.

"Come on, man, you won't be out of the loop, but you need to step back, okay?" Montoya wasn't giving up. "We'll discuss all the cases. Yeah, of course, but we treat them separately. For now. Until there's a stronger connection." He finished his sandwich and wiped his fingers with a napkin.

Bentz didn't like it—not one bit. The whole idea made him twitchy inside.

"If this wasn't personal, you'd suggest the same thing. Hell, if it was my family we were talking about, you'd lobby to get me thrown off the case for 'my own good' or to 'keep the case clean, not compromise it with personal bias.'" He leaned back and met Bentz's gaze. "Right?"

Bentz hesitated.

"Right?"

"Maybe." He hated to admit it, but if he did force his emotions to a dark corner of his brain and examined the case with clear mind and unjaundiced eye, he had to concede that Montoya was right. He was too close to the case; he knew it. But that didn't stop him from wanting to chase down Jay McKnight's killer.

Despite all that logic and conforming to police procedure, he couldn't help but feel deep in his bones that Father John was the murderer who had taken Jay's life.

And despite all protocols, he had to step over the line.

Screw Montoya.

Proper procedure be damned.

Bentz knew in his gut that his daughter was in a killer's crosshairs, her life in serious danger.

He'd do anything he could to save her.

And Montoya would do it for his.

So, again, screw Montoya.

CHAPTER 12

Kristi met Dave.

And fell in love.

The big, floppy-eared mutt acted as if he'd been waiting for her all of his short life. Besides running in circles as if he'd lost his mind when she was allowed to see him in the shelter's exercise area, he leaped up and down on the sparse grass.

"So how is he with cats and kids?" she asked Heather, the handler, as he took another turn around the yard. He was running full speed, kicking up dust with his big paws. All sleek muscle and shiny gold coat, he looped past them, doing five full laps before settling down and sitting, tail sweeping the yard as he gazed up expectantly, practically begging her to scratch him behind those bat-wing ears.

"Oh, I don't think you have to worry," Heather said. She was a woman of about sixty. Compact and taut, with tattooed vines of ivy crawling up her sinewy arms and her silvery hair shaved on one side, she beamed at the dog. "He was introduced to Albert, our resident cat, weren't you, honey." Patting his thick neck, she added, "Barely noticed that Albert was nearby. And he's good with kids. A couple came in with a toddler yesterday to meet him, and he was a perfect gentleman, but the two-year-old freaked and they decided on a smaller dog—a beagle, but it wasn't Dave's fault. He was gentle as could be." She gave the dog's broad head a scratch, then grabbed a leash hanging from a hook on the fence.

"Great." That was good news. "So not much of a guard dog?"

"Oh, God, no." Heather laughed, showing off a slight gap in her front teeth. "He's big, so his size could be intimidating, of course, but just meet this big fella once and you know he's a sweetheart. He'll roll on his back and want a belly rub from just about anyone." Her forehead wrinkled slightly. "Is that a problem?" She was snapping the leash onto his collar.

"No, no, it won't be," Kristi said. Better a dog who appeared intimidating rather than one who was actually ferocious. "When can I pick him up?"

"Tomorrow morning? He's been all cleared by the vet, his shots updated, and since he was already neutered, he's almost good to go. After we got your application, I did a drive-by of your place and saw that it was fenced, so"—she shrugged—"all that's left is the paperwork and the adoption fee and he's yours. We can be ready as early as ten."

"I'll be here."

"Fantastic." Heather smiled. "He's a great dog."

And soon he'll be mine, Kristi thought, leaving the exercise area and walking through the squat building to the small parking area. Dave might not scare off any intruders, but he would be company and maybe help fill that huge hole in her heart that had been with her for weeks.

She unlocked her Subaru remotely and slid into the warm interior.

The dog wouldn't replace Jay, she knew that—no pet could, no man could—but maybe Dave would help, at least a little. Retrieving a pair of sunglasses from the console, she said, "So what do you think?" and slid the Ray-Bans onto the bridge of her nose.

For the first time in almost three weeks, Jay didn't answer.

"You coming to bed?" Olivia asked from the doorway.

Bentz glanced up from his computer in the den. The room was dark, only the computer's monitor offering any illumination. Once more he'd been studying pictures of all of the guests at Jay McKnight's funeral, some new ones taken by a couple of Kristi's friends, hoping to spot something he'd missed before. Had there been someone he'd missed, someone lingering in the cemetery during the burial ceremony or inside the cathedral before and after the service? He'd wondered if the killer would be so bold as to show up, possibly keeping himself at a distance. Or had he been one of the mourners? Even someone dressed as a member of the press and huddling nearby? The cemetery with its raised tombs and sculptures had made hiding all too easy. Bentz forced a smile at his wife. "I'll be there in a few."

She arched a disbelieving eyebrow. "Seriously?"

"Yeah. Seriously." He nodded and saw her cross her arms under her breasts.

"Why do I have the feeling you're placating me?" she asked. "I'm smarter than that and I know you, Rick Bentz."

She wasn't mad, just mildly irritated, her eyes sparkling despite the forced set of her jaw. They'd put Ginny to bed hours ago, he realized as he glanced at the clock on his computer screen and saw that it was after midnight, nearly twelve thirty. But he'd been compelled to work through a knot in the case, or as Montoya thought, two cases. Try as he might, Bentz couldn't get it out of his mind that the two were entwined.

"I thought you were going to retire," she admonished softly.

Uh-oh. He leaned back in his chair. *Here we go again.* The same argument they had been having for a long, long time.

"I am. I mean, I will."

She sauntered into the room, backlit by the hall light, arms still crossed, and rested a hip against his desk. "When?" The sounds of the house at night, hum of the refrigerator in the kitchen, ticking of the old clock in the front hallway, occasional rush of a car as it passed on the street outside, closed in on him. Through her thin robe he saw the outline of her body, felt a stirring deep down, the same male response she always elicited no matter how many years they'd been together. He studied the slope of her hip, the mound of her breasts.

"Soon. I swear." They'd had this argument for the past several years. He could leave the department at any time. Full retirement. Spend more time at home. Teach if he wanted to. Consult. But . . . he flat-out loved his job.

"You've been saying 'soon' for what? Five years? Six?" Now the smile faded from her eyes. "You're not going to leave the department until they force you to or"—she drew a deep breath—"until you're killed in the line of duty. We both know it."

"You know I can't leave now, Livvie. Jesus, not after Jay's murder. Kristi was nearly killed herself." He pushed back his chair, stood, and heard his back pop.

"I wouldn't ask that," she said as he rounded the desk.

"Good." He drew her close.

"But when this case is over, when you know Kristi's safe and Jay's murderer is either dead or behind bars, you'll retire."

"Yeah," he said automatically, and ignored that niggle of doubt that wormed through his mind. "I will." He placed his forehead against hers and tried to kiss her, but she put a finger to his lips, stopping him short.

"Promise?"

"Yeah. Sure." She smelled so good of soap and some faint perfume that he equated with her and always turned him on.

"I'm going to hold you to it."

Her eyes held his. Wide and intelligent, so deep they seemed to scrape into his soul and possibly ferret out any lies he might concoct.

"I know."

"You have Ginny now. She's going to be one soon, almost walking, and you're missing so much of it." She sighed. "And you have me. Kristi, too, of course, but in your zeal to protect her, please, Rick, don't forget us."

"I—I couldn't if I wanted to," he said with raw truth. "And I don't want to."

She seemed to believe him, to understand, and she drew her finger away and kissed him, her lips warm and pliant before parting.

He was lost then.

Picking her up, he carried her into their bedroom and kicked the door shut. Together they rolled onto the bed and for the next few hours he forgot about Father John and Jay McKnight and Helene Laroche and Teri Marie Gaines. He was so lost in the touch and feel of his wife that he even, for the moment, let his worries for his firstborn slide into the farthest corners of his mind.

For the first time in the better part of a month, Rick Bentz slept long and hard, his worries melting away with slumber, his wife's warm body snuggled next to his.

His cell phone hummed across the night table.

Opening a bleary eye, Montoya saw that it was one in the morning. He snagged the phone off its charger hoping not to wake his wife, but he heard her mumble something unintelligible into her pillow.

He didn't recognize the number.

Almost hung up.

Then, with an instinct reserved for siblings, he rolled off the bed and eased into the hallway. The dog gave a soft "woof," but Montoya quieted him with a quick, "Shh," and padded outside to the back porch where the night was clear, only a few stars visible over the ambient light glowing up from the city. "Hello?"

"Bro."

"I knew it was you!" Montoya said, sighing. "Where the hell are you, Cruz?"

"On my way."

"It's after one in the morning."

"Not here."

"As I said, where the hell is that?"

"Mojave."

"Mojave," Montoya repeated, his mind still blurry from sleep. "Vegas? You're in Las Vegas?"

"No. At least not anymore."

"What the hell's going on? The last time you called me you said you were wanted for murder, that you were involved in some homicide."

"I'm not. I didn't have anything to do with her death."

"Whose death?" Montoya asked, his heart suddenly in overdrive, his mind spinning horrible scenarios involving women covered in blood. "What are you talking about?"

"It was an accident."

He froze. Cruz was sounding more like a suspect, a guilty party all along. "What was an accident?"

"I'll tell you all about it when I get to New Orleans. I should be there in two, maybe three days. Possibly sooner."

"It's not that long of a drive."

"Being careful. Back roads."

"I don't know what you want me to do," Montoya said. "You know that if you're wanted I'm going to have to advise you to turn yourself in." For the love of God, Cruz didn't expect his brother to compromise a case, did he?

"I'm not wanted. At least not yet."

That was a relief.

Or a lie.

Montoya couldn't stop that deep-seated worry that gnawed at him, right in the middle of his gut. He longed for a cigarette, anything to calm his nerves. "Who's dead? Where did this happen? Why the hell are you involved?"

"I'm not. Not in her death."

"Who's 'her'?"

"Look, the less you know, the better. For now."

"Then why the hell did you call me in the first place?" Montoya demanded, his voice rising and his temper flaring. Cruz was and always had been trouble, more trouble than he himself had ever thought of being.

"I didn't want to just show up and freak you out."

"You're doing that now."

"I'm just giving you a heads-up. I figured after my last call you might be worried—"

"The whole damned family's worried sick, Cruz. What the hell's wrong with you?"

"You tell me!" he snapped, obviously on the edge. "I'll see you soon. I'll explain then."

"You sure as hell better—"

But the connection was severed and Montoya was left not knowing any more than he had ten minutes earlier before he'd answered the phone. Who was dead? Some woman with, as yet, no name. Some woman Cruz had been somehow involved with. And that woman had been murdered. Out west somewhere.

Knowing he couldn't sleep, he slipped back into the house and grabbed his laptop, brought it out to the porch, and sat in the porch swing where he heard a truck rumbling by on the street and farther off the sound of a train gathering speed. There was an occasional voice and he saw, through the slats in the fence, his neighbor's yard cast in flickering shades of gray from the old man's television, which was always on, day or night, muted, thankfully, as he kept his curtains and windows open.

He Googled recent homicides of women in the western states, concentrating on the day Cruz first called him and the week before that. Then he started filtering down the news reports, Googling Cruz's name, and got nowhere. Sadly, too many people were the victims of homicide in this country.

Rocking gently back and forth on the swing, he thought about it. Where would Cruz be in the West? Why had he gone there? The last time Montoya had seen him, years ago, he'd been burned by a woman who'd stolen his motorcycle and had left him stranded here, in New Orleans.

But he'd taken off after Lucia Costa, a woman who had been a nun at St. Marguerite's, a girl he'd known in school years before.

When Montoya cross-referenced her name with the recent murders, he found the headline:

WOMAN FOUND SLAIN NEAR TRASK RIVER
BOYFRIEND WANTED FOR QUESTIONING

Boyfriend?

Montoya skimmed the story. Yes, the body of Lucia Costa had been found on the banks of the Trask River in a remote part of Oregon. She was the apparent victim of homicide and Cruz Montoya was being sought as a person of interest.

The story ran at the end of last week, an earlier one several days before, but Cruz had called him over a week before that. So he'd known about Lucia's death.

And was involved.

Enough to be on the lam.

Shit!

Montoya stopped rocking and felt the knot in his stomach tighten. The police department involved would certainly be looking into Cruz's family, everyone remotely connected with Cruz, including his brother, a cop in the New Orleans Police Department.

Great . . . just fuckin' great.

He knew that as bad as things seemed now?

They were sure to get a helluva lot worse.

It's not enough, I think as I slip into the vestibule of the old church, the door creaking on rusted hinges before closing behind me with a soft, almost final thud. Kristi Bentz's pain wasn't enough.

In the narthex, I pause to stare through the sanctuary to the altar, now dark of course, and I think of the funeral I attended, that of Jay McKnight. I watched the mourners from my vantage point, my eyes drawn to Kristi Bentz. I witnessed her tears, the tremble of her chin, the way she fought to stand tall but eventually crumpled against the strong, straight form of her father.

At the thought of Rick Bentz, my stomach curdles, and it's all I can do to tamp down my burning need for revenge.

At the cemetery I was a ghost, hiding behind the tombs and sculptures, observing from a distance, trying to wring out the last drop of satisfaction from seeing the pain on Kristi's white face, the hard expression of her father, whose lips had been tight, his jaw set, his hands balling in frustration.

Yes, that had been satisfying.

For the moment.

And seeing that she's nervous, worried about me, that is exciting! I feel a sizzle of adrenaline in my blood at that thought. I watched as that moron from the security company worked on her house, fiddling with sensors and cameras and alarms.

Rudimentary.

I will have to be a little more careful, but that's not a problem.

Slipping through the tombs as the mourners gathered in the cemetery was more than a little exciting, I'll admit it. I enjoyed watching Kristi Bentz grieve. And since then, viewing her from a distance and witnessing her falling apart had great appeal, but little satisfaction.

It's not enough.

As I walk to the altar through the ancient pews of the empty church, I think of the torment I've put her through, but it's still not enough for all that she's taken from me. The scales are far from even. Yes, it's good to see her pain, I think while absently tightening the cincture more securely around my cassock. But I need more. As I always have.

Once at the altar, I kneel and pray.

I'm grounded here in this sacred place, so close to God. Centered again.

I light a candle and watch the tiny flame flicker and dance in the darkness.

This candle and my prayer are not for Jay McKnight's soul.

Nor is it for any other person living or dead.

No, this tiny light is for clarity and divine blessing.

And it's also for strength. My strength. To carry out my purpose.

Watching the tiny, flickering flame, I whisper, "In the name of the Father, and of the Son, and of the Holy Spirit. Amen."

CHAPTER 13

Dave was waiting for her, his tail sweeping the floor in wild anticipation after she'd signed all the adoption papers, paid the fees, and taken information about his microchip and vaccination status.

"Look who's here," Heather said to the dog, who, as she snapped the leash on him, turned crazy circles.

It was all Kristi could do to corral him into her car and drive him home. He commanded the passenger seat of her Subaru, and she cracked the window for him with a warning that in the future he'd have to be restrained.

Once at the house, she snapped on a new collar and ID tag she'd bought at the pet store, then walked him through the rooms, putting out a dish of water near the back door, then letting him run crazy circles around the backyard. A squirrel scolded from a live oak before scampering across the fence, startling two sparrows who flew in a whirlwind of feathers from the bird bath to the branches of a pine tree where they settled noisily.

After he'd run some of his excess energy off, she brought him into the house and went into the bedroom to retrieve Lenore. The kitten was already aware of the dog, her muscles tight, her eyes round and intense on Dave. He showed interest and sniffed as the cat, still held by Kristi, hissed and showed her small, needle-sharp teeth.

"It's gonna take some time," Kristi said to the dog, who wagged his tail and pressed his nose closer. After another round of hissing, he got the message and backed off, settling on the floor and whining. "Good boy," she said, but decided to keep the animals separated for a while. "Just give her some time. She'll fall in love with you, too."

Which might be a lie for all Kristi knew, but patience and time was the key, and though patience was far from her strong suit, right now she had all the time in the world.

Well, not quite.

In six or seven months there would be a new little human in the house. She had yet to be seen by her ob-gyn, but she'd made an appointment. Then, once she heard that the pregnancy was viable and going as it should, she would tell her dad that he would soon be a grandfather. She imagined that he would welcome the news, but his anxiety about her safety and raising a child on her own would only ratchet into the stratosphere.

"So deal with it," she told herself, and Dave thumped his tail, his eyes on hers. "You," she said to the kitten, "get to hang out in the bedroom while I take this guy"—she hooked her thumb at Dave— "on a walk."

Which quickly became a run.

Dave, as excited as he was, couldn't mosey, and so they jogged through the streets near her house and she decided she now had a running partner. Who needed Bella and Sarah and Jess? She now had, floppy ears flying, pink tongue lolling, indefatigable Dave to gallop happily along beside her as she jogged.

For the first time since Jay's murder, she felt her spirit soar a bit, and when she considered the future, it didn't seem so bleak. No, she didn't have her husband and that pain, she suspected, would always exist at some level, but she did have her new dog, and the kitten, and in a little over half a year, a brand-new baby.

"Things could be worse," she confided in the dog, her shoes slapping against the sidewalk, her thighs beginning to burn as she ran. "It could be raining." It was getting harder to talk and run, so she cut through the park and turned back toward the house and slowed the pace. By the time she let herself in the back door, she was breathing regularly. Dave buried his nose in his water dish and slopped it everywhere. "Some people might say you have a drinking problem," she teased, ruffling the mutt behind his ears before sopping up the mess with a kitchen towel and tossing it into the laundry room basket.

She carried a glass of water into the bathroom, where she showered and then, with a towel wrapped around her, swiped at the bathroom mirror where moisture had collected due to the fact that the fan wasn't working, a project Jay had said he would take care of on an ever-growing list of household tasks that he'd never gotten around to. She cracked the window and immediately an alarm went off.

And the dog started barking like crazy.

"Right." The new security system. "Crap." She turned off the alarm, slammed the window down, and latched it, and as she did, she noticed movement in her peripheral vision, a shadow flitting against the fence.

Every muscle in her body tensed.

In a nanosecond the shadow was gone.

What the devil?

She dropped the towel. Grabbing her robe from a hook on the bathroom door, she threw it on and raced through her bedroom and down the short hall to the living area where Dave was going nuts at the slider. Jumping and barking, the hairs on his nape and back raised, his tail stiff. She looked outside but the yard appeared to be empty and the image—what was it? The billowing tail of a black coat? The hem of a trailing skirt? Or the flap of a poncho caught in the breeze?

Oh. Jesus.

She opened the door and Dave shot out, bounding down the single step, flying across the flagstones of the patio, rounding the corner to the side of the house where the gate stood open. He raced through hot on the trail of whoever had dared enter. She ran after, barefoot, holding her robe together with her hands. "Dave!" she shouted. "Dave! Come!" But he was halfway down the street. "Dave!" she screamed, still running after him as he reached the intersection. Her heart was beating in a wild tattoo as he barreled into traffic.

No! No! No!

In her mind's eye, she saw him being hit. Maimed or killed.

Brakes squealed.

Horns honked.

People shouted.

A woman screamed from a bicycle and skidded, barely missing Dave as he flew across the lanes.

"Oh, God!" Kristi increased her pace, didn't care that the robe was flying open exposing her bare body, was only concerned for her dog.

"Dave! Come!" she cried, frantic as she saw the dog reach the far side of the intersection.

Ignoring the traffic signs, she held out her hands to stop traffic and dashed through the spaces between the vehicles.

"Are you crazy?" she heard as she reached the park, gasping, her heart pounding, her mind screaming. Where the hell was he? "Dave!" she screamed. "Dave, come!"

But he was gone.

She asked a jogger and a mother pushing a double stroller with twins if they'd seen the dog, but both had shaken their heads and hurried by, the jogger moving swiftly, the mom on her phone and eyeing Kristi as if she had just escaped from a mental hospital. Kristi didn't blame her. She was naked under the robe and too many people had caught glimpses of her body as she'd run, her feet were bare and muddy, her hair wet and wild. She wandered aimlessly on the paths that cut through the thickets and past a fountain, still calling out for him. But the dog could be anywhere, a mile away in any direction, and he'd barely been at the house; he wouldn't know his way back.

She hadn't grabbed her phone, wasn't wearing her watch, couldn't call anyone to help. If she couldn't find him, she would have to go back to the house and get her car, start driving around and calling shelters and vets.

Heartsick, she did one quick lap around the park.

Nothing.

She tried to bolster her flagging spirits by reminding herself that Dave was wearing a collar with her name and number and he was micro-chipped. And if someone called her right now, a Good Samaritan who was looking to return him, he or she wouldn't be able to get through. They would have to leave a message, wouldn't they?

With one more sweeping glance around the park and noticing a thirty-something woman who was quickly shuttling her toddler away from the crazy woman in the dirty bathrobe, she gave up. There was nothing to do but go back home, retrieve her phone, get in her car, and start searching. Maybe someone had found Dave and had already left a message, or taken the dog to a shelter or a vet's office.

She had to put her faith in the fact that someone would find him.

Someone would bring him back. Or . . . what if the dog caught up with the intruder? Her heart turned to ice. What if the intruder was the same person who attacked her, who killed Jay, who had been in her home and left her the cards with the dark rose? "Don't go there," she said aloud.

"Hey!" a sharp male voice called from behind her. "Is this your dog?"

She spun quickly and found a tall man holding a belt as a makeshift leash hooked around Dave's collar. Her knees nearly buckled in relief. "Dave!" she said as the dog strained at the belt, leaping toward her.

"Guess so," the tall man said, walking closer, Dave's momentum propelling him forward.

"Yes, yes!" she gasped. "Oh, God, thank you!"

"No worries."

"But where?"

"He came right at me. Worried me for a sec." He handed her the belt as she threw her arms around Dave's neck.

"At you?" she asked, and a niggle of apprehension skittered up her spine. Who was this guy? "Why?"

"Don't know, but he bolted out of a copse of live oaks and ran like a bat outta hell, straight at me."

"And stopped?"

"Yeah. I thought he might be some kind of attack dog, but"—he shrugged, broad shoulders moving beneath a short jacket—"obviously not."

"Obviously." She straightened and took a good look at the man, in his thirties, she guessed, with jet-black hair that brushed over the collar of his jacket and deep-set eyes that were hidden by reflective sunglasses. His beard shadow was long past the three-day mark. He had an edge to him, a tension beneath disreputable jeans, a faded black T-shirt, and scruffy jacket. No smile in that hard jaw, no spark of humor in his expression. There was a toughness to him, evident in a nose that had been broken at least once and a tiny scar near his left eye.

I know you. The thought ran through her head, but she couldn't place him.

"You're Kristi Bentz." Not a question. For a moment she thought he might have recognized her—she'd been in the paper often enough and her picture was on the jacket of some of her books—then realized he guessed her identity because her name was etched on Dave's collar.

"Right. And you're—?"

"Doesn't matter." The barest hint of a smile, just a fleeting slash of white in his dark jaw. "Just a guy who found your dog." She couldn't tell because of the glasses, but she got the impression he actually winked at her. "So—you got this now and I gotta run."

"Wait," she said, but he'd already turned and was jogging away. "Your belt—"

"Got another one!" he called over his shoulder, then disappeared behind a thicket. She was left holding on to the belt buckle while staring after him. "Weird," she said under her breath, then noticed a woman in running gear backing away from her and she realized she looked like an escapee from a mental ward in her bare feet, flimsy robe, and holding on to a muddy dog by a belt.

"Let's go," she said to the dog, and began tugging on the makeshift leash. Dave happily trotted beside her as she picked up her pace and retraced her steps back to the house, all the while ignoring the stares she received from passersby, people in cars who gawked, or pedestrians giving her wide berth. Two teenaged boys, roaring by in a pickup raised high overhead, actually honked at her, waved and laughed.

Oh, get over it. This is New Orleans. There is no weird. Anything goes.

Or so she told herself as she reached her house and saw that her side gate was still hanging open. Probably the slider, too. Again, she thought of her new little kitten. "Lenore," she whispered, worried sick as she jogged across the lawn, grass bending under her feet, to stop and latch the gate behind her. If she lost the cat, too . . . *No! No! No!* She couldn't bear it.

The slider door off the kitchen was closed.

Kristi stopped dead in her tracks.

She'd left it open, hadn't she?

She'd hit the alarm, shutting it off, then flown out of the house after the dog and hadn't even thought about closing the door.

Yet it was.

The back of her arms goose-pimpled.

Who had closed the door?

And was that person still inside?

She wished she had her phone and thought for a second of going to a neighbor's, then considered the state of her undress and walked to the door and slid it open. Unlocked. "You stay," she said to the dog, who was wiggling to get inside. "In a sec." Then she stepped into the kitchen and, spying the kitchen knives on a metal strip over the stove, she tiptoed to the range and pulled out the butcher knife. Then she paused. Barely daring to breathe, she didn't bother with any lights, but swept her gaze through the adjoining rooms.

Nothing.

Everything appeared just as she'd left it.

The house was quiet.

Still.

Dave was wriggling near the door, ready to bolt inside. And wouldn't that be best? The dog able to sniff out anyone—

She paused, realizing what seemed off. Everything was too quiet. While she heard a bit of exterior noise, traffic, a lawnmower several houses down, further away sounds of construction workers and equipment, inside there was not a sound.

Not even the hum of the refrigerator.

Her stomach tightened again, and motioning to the dog, they slowly made their way through the dining area and living room, entry hall and Jay's study. One hand on the stranger's belt that was now Dave's leash, the other holding the knife in a death grip.

Her bedroom door was slightly ajar and she thought she'd left it that way. She stepped through, Dave gave off a sharp bark, and something brushed against her ankle. She jumped, her pulse skyrocketing as she spied the kitten, backing up and hissing.

"Oh, Jesus, you scared me," Kristi said, and picked up the fluff of fur as her gaze swept the room. She grabbed her phone off its charger and slipped it into her pocket. "Come on," she whispered to Lenore, and unhooked the belt from Dave's collar. The house was empty. No one had intruded. The cat and dog and she were all safe.

"Then why was the slider shut?" Jay's voice, which had been a few days silent, was suddenly back.

"I don't know," she said. "Not now, Jay." Then she caught herself, talking out loud to her dead husband. She really was going nuts. "Pull yourself together!" she whispered, then cringed. Now she was talking to herself!

With the cat in one hand and her knife in the other, Kristi walked through the two bathrooms, throwing back the shower curtain in the main bath, and then climbed the stairs to her office, where nothing looked out of place.

So why was the door shut?

Who had bothered? A neighbor? Someone passing by?

The slider was in the back of the house, unseen from the street, and if her father or one of her friends had stopped by, wouldn't they have waited? Or called? Or texted?

She scrolled through the menu on her phone.

Nothing but a couple more requests from reporters.

"Forget it," she said, and took heart in the new security system. If someone had really been inside, she'd have evidence. He or she would be caught on the camera mounted over the back door.

After ensuring that all the doors and windows were latched and locked, she checked her phone app, which was linked to the security system, but it didn't seem to be working.

Every nerve in her body tightened. She double-checked the app, but no images appeared. "What the—?" And then she realized how quiet it was in the house, how dark. Why wasn't the refrigerator humming? She glanced around as she walked into the bedroom. Hadn't she left on a single lamp? Why wasn't the digital display on the clock on Jay's night table glowing with the time of day?

She hit the light switch.

Nothing happened.

"What?" A burned-out bulb? But the clock. She checked. Not unplugged. Just dead.

She left the kitten on the bed, walked to the bathroom, and tried the separate switch for the shower light.

But the shower stall remained dark.

Her feeling of disquiet increased.

She hit the bedroom switch. The overhead light didn't snap on. Nor did the TV come to life as she tried with the remote to switch it on.

Nothing electrical was working.

"Well, crap."

What the hell happened while she was gone? And who was behind it?

Back in the bathroom, she pressed the GFI switch located over the counter and again, nothing happened.

Not good.

Locating a second GFI switch in the kitchen, she attempted to reset it, but once more pressing the red button did nothing. The whole damned house seemed to be without electricity, so she went into the garage, dog on her heels, found the electrical panel on the far wall, and discovered the main circuit breaker switch for the entire house had been turned to the off position.

Her stomach knotted.

Obviously someone had thrown the switch intentionally.

Why?

To freak her out?

Well, if that was the case, mission accomplished.

But who was behind it?

She flipped the switch and heard a series of clicks in the house as appliances turned on, humming to life, and as she walked into the kitchen she noticed a tiny light on the coffeemaker glowing, the digital clocks in the stove and microwave blinking, a lamp in the living room burning again.

Once more she did a quick search and, at first glance, nothing seemed out of place, nothing stolen. Her purse was on the couch, where she'd flung it the night before. Credit cards and cash accounted for. Her computers were as she'd left them, TVs on their stands, jewelry, such as it was, untouched, her keys all hanging where they should be. She checked and saw that nothing seemed to be missing, nothing stolen, everything appeared to be in its place.

But as she walked past the front door, she caught a glimpse of the flower arrangement that had been left on her doorstep a few days earlier, the vase of red roses and baby's breath that the tech from the security company had discovered and handed to her. She'd set the vase on the entry table, never paying much attention to it. Now she noticed the baby's breath was missing and in its place, tucked between the red blooms, was a single black rose.

What!?!

The contents of her stomach curdled.

She noticed a card was sticking up between the rose's thorny stems and her pulse quickened as she approached and pulled it from the bouquet.

It was decorated with a single black rose.

Her pulse began to thunder in her ears as she opened the deckle-edged paper and read the missive:

~Shout against her round about; she hath given her hand. Her foundations are fallen, her walls are thrown down; for it is the vengeance of the Lord. Take vengeance upon her; as she hath done, do unto her. Jeremiah 50:15~

Fear clenched her insides for a second, then her roiling stomach rumbled and she raced to the bathroom to heave over the edge of the sink. Tears burned her eyes as she lost the meager contents of her stomach and leaned heavily against the counter. She stared at her reflection in the mirror: ashen skin, her auburn hair a tangled mess, her eyes round with fear, her robe not only thin but muddy, her feet still bare and covered in dirt.

Not only had someone been in her house, but he had been here for the single, sick purpose of terrifying the living crap out of her.

And, unfortunately, he'd succeeded.

CHAPTER 14

Montoya had just pulled out of the station's lot and was on his way to the crime lab, the place Jay McKnight had worked, when his cell buzzed. A quick look at the screen flashed Bentz's name and number. He clicked on, but before he could answer, Bentz said, "I just got a call from Kristi. There's been some kind of break-in at her house. I'm in the bayou checking with the locals to see if they've noticed any newcomers." Montoya knew what that meant. Father John had once had his own place in the swamp, a lair where he hid out. Bentz continued, his voice stern. "I'm leaving now. On my way back, but I'm a good thirty—maybe forty minutes out. Either head to her place yourself or send someone."

"Got it. I'll be there in ten."

"Good." Bentz clicked off.

Montoya, behind the wheel of his Mustang, flipped on his lights, sped through two yellow lights, and was at Kristi Bentz's home in under five minutes.

He banged on the door and she opened it just a crack.

"Oh. I was expecting my dad," Kristi said as she finally opened the door. "I called him."

"Yeah. He'll be here ASAP." Montoya checked his watch. "He knew I was closer, so he called me." He offered her a smile, but she didn't return it. In all truth, she looked like hell. Her hair was wet and she seemed too small for her T-shirt and jeans, almost shrunken in them. "Tell me about the break-in."

"It really wasn't a break-in. I left the door open," she admitted, wincing as if the truth actually hurt her. "A mistake." She swung the door open wider, stepped aside, and he nearly tripped over a short-haired dog with oversized ears and bright, inquisitive eyes. "It's okay, Dave," she said, patting his head. "He's a teddy bear," she admitted to Montoya. "And the reason I left the door open. Wide open, I'm afraid."

"Maybe you should have gotten a guard dog."

She glanced at him and looked away. "Can't have a dog that's ferocious. There are lots of little kids in the neighborhood."

Since when had she paid any attention to her neighbors? As far as Montoya knew, Kristi was a bit of a loner, and because of her history, had been all about her privacy. "We can talk in the kitchen," she said, and he heard the door shut and click into place behind him. "You want something?" she asked. "Coffee or—?"

"I'm good. Just tell me what happened and, yeah, you'll have to repeat it when your dad gets here."

"Yeah, I know."

He took a seat at the island while she poured herself a glass of water.

She explained about adopting the dog, losing him, chasing after him into the park, the stranger having found him and then discovering that someone had been inside, leaving everything untouched other than the note and flower in an already delivered bouquet. "I opened the card, realized what happened, so I locked everything, cleaned up, and called."

She handed him a card inside a clear plastic sandwich bag and he recognized the black rose, inked onto the same paper. Inside was a cryptic Bible verse, a different bit of scripture from the previous missives, but still about vengeance.

"Do you have any idea who would send this to you?" he asked, covering old territory.

"No."

"No enemies?"

"Enemies? As in someone who would attack me, kill my husband, and then go about terrorizing me?" she said, shaking her head. "No."

"What about family members?"

"What?" she threw back at him, then rolled her eyes. "No. My family adored Jay. Every last one of them."

"What about his?"

"Oh—God, they thought he was the best." But she paused, her eyes clouding over a bit.

"There's someone?"

"No, not really." She thought for a moment. "Okay, there's one cousin who hated him for some reason. I never knew why. His name is Greg."

"Greg McKnight?"

"Yeah. I think he lives in Alabama. Mobile, maybe, somewhere around there. But Jay hadn't heard from him in years and whatever happened between them was all a long time ago. Maybe high school. I think Jay ratted him out and he got thrown out of school, maybe ended up in juvenile detention. Jay was always a pretty straight shooter. Greg? Not so much."

"You ever meet him?"

"Only a couple of times. The last was at a family wedding about three years ago."

"What about Jay? He keep up with him?"

"No. Not even Christmas cards or anything like that. I think the wedding was the last time Jay had seen him, too."

"And—?"

"And what happened at the wedding?" she asked, and shook her head. "Nothing. They didn't speak, at least not that I know of."

Montoya decided to check out Greg McKnight. The department already had a list of all of the family members and people close to Jay, as well as to Kristi, the information collected right after the homicide, but Montoya would double-check. A long shot, but you never knew how deep hatred ran, how old emotional scars might reopen and ooze.

"What about people who might have a grudge against you?"

She took a sip of water and thought. "Well, there are those people I've written about or interviewed. Murderers who could take offense, but most of them are either dead or locked up. Dad and I have talked about this and Jay and I fought about it, but it's what I do." She met his gaze. "Basically I work alone. Here. In my pajamas or sweats a lot of the time. I don't have any work enemies."

She seemed perplexed and he made a note to double-check on the subjects of her books, some of which had become best sellers.

"No rival? No person who feels a grudge against you, maybe for your marriage, or your fame?"

"No." She shook her head.

"Nothing personal?"

"No—I told you that." She frowned, her eyebrows slamming together thoughtfully. "Look, I've stepped on a few toes in my life. I knew there were girls in high school who hated me and some in college, I suppose, and for a while everyone in Jay's family had a thing against me, but that was years ago, because I broke up with him for a while before we got back together, but no one who would kill him or try to murder me. None of them went psycho that I know of. They've all moved on. So this—it—it just doesn't make sense."

"The same with your professional life?"

"I told you. I work alone. And as for rivals I guess there's always that. Jealousy or something." She sighed and scratched the back of her neck. "The only person I can think of who might be remotely jealous of me professionally could be Drake Dennison, I suppose." But she was shaking her head.

"He's a writer?"

"Yeah, another true-crime author. I've never met him, but about the time that I was getting some fame, after the Rosary Killer book, and I'd come up with another idea or two, the publisher dropped Dennison." Montoya's interest sharpened and she must've recognized it, because she added quickly, "He wasn't alone. Publishing was going through a hard time generally speaking, the market shrinking, and a lot of authors suddenly couldn't get a contract."

"But you could," he said.

"Right. I'd been a victim, my dad's a homicide detective, so it could be perceived that I have an advantage, an edge, I guess. But I heard through a writer's chat group I'm on that he might be publishing again, that he has a contract with a new publisher."

"Is Dennison religious?"

"I wouldn't know. But—I think one or two of his books had some kind of religious overtones." She bit her lip. "Not sure about that, though. But—wait. He did want to write a book about the Chosen One," she said. "He was pissed that he didn't get the contract, that the publisher wanted me to write it as I was involved, you know."

Montoya remembered the case well. The killer had been a real nut-job and went around killing people as martyred saints had been slain. It was sick and ugly and the public had eaten it up.

"Does he live around here?"

"No. I mean, I don't think so. In the South somewhere. Wait a sec. I'll be right back." She hurried out of the room, dog on her heels, and he heard her footsteps as she continued up the stairs. She was back in less than two minutes holding a hardback book that she handed to Montoya. The title was *Too Little, Too Late,* by Drake Dennison. The pages had yellowed, the paper jacket ripped slightly.

Kristi explained, "This is Dennison's last book that I know of. It was written about four, maybe five years ago, I think."

Montoya flipped the book over to view a black and white picture of the author in his early thirties. He had thick dark hair, tinted glasses, and a heavy beard and mustache. His smile was slight and mysterious and the entire head shot seemed staged. His bio was short, that he'd studied criminology at LSU, had worked as a private investigator and settled in Atlanta, where he was currently working on his next book.

He glanced up at her. "It says he's working on his next book."

"Maybe he was."

"And maybe he wasn't?"

"I don't know." She shrugged. "Probably he had something going. Writers write, whether they have contracts with publishers or not. And at the time that this book was published," she said, pointing to the hardback in Montoya's hands, "some authors had begun to move on to self-publishing, or podcasts or whatever. I don't know that he did, but he must have a new book in the works if he's got another contract. But I probably shouldn't have said anything. I don't know him. He's a recluse. That was part of his deal—you know, an air of mystery that surrounded him."

"Is he still that way?"

"Again, I don't know."

He thought about it. Made a mental note to check out the author. "Anyone else you could think of?"

"Who might resent my career? Sure, I suppose, but no one that I know about, no one who would try to terrorize me. And . . . and certainly no one who would kill my husband!" She let out a frustrated puff of air.

"How about online?" he asked. "You've got Twitter and Facebook, Instagram accounts and the like."

"Of course."

"Anyone there hassling you?"

"Hassling? You mean like a troll?" she asked, then shrugged. "You know how it is these days. There's always someone online ready to be a hater, but if you're asking if there's anyone in particular who posts inappropriate stuff?" She thought about it a second, then shook her head. "Not really. Nothing that's so out of line it stands out."

"I'll take a look," he said, and studied the card in his hands. Bible verses. What was that all about? Could Bentz be right, was Father John or whoever was copying him also doing a side number on Kristi? Had he morphed over the years into something more than the killer obsessed with Dr. Sam, who killed prostitutes bizarrely with a rosary?

That part had really bothered Montoya. He'd been raised Catholic and the religious symbols and artifacts were sacred to him. The fact that the killer had impersonated a priest made his blood boil. Yeah, he no longer attended mass, but his kid was baptized in the church and Montoya still had his own kind of faith all wrapped up in Catholicism. And he liked it that way.

Was it possible that the same whack job turned his attention from Dr. Sam to focus on Kristi Bentz, who had not only written about him but was the daughter of Rick Bentz, the detective who had nearly killed him in the swamp all those years ago?

Montoya told himself to keep an open mind as Kristi's cell phone vibrated and scooted across the kitchen counter about the same time a black kitten hopped onto a bar stool, then the counter. "Nope," Kristi said, glancing at the phone number appearing on the cell's screen and scooping up her kitten. As if she needed to explain, she said, "It's my agent again. I'll call her back." She must've seen the question in his eyes and she added, "Zera—that's my agent—she wants me to do another book, a sequel to the one on the Rosary Killer. You know, because she thinks he might be back and I have this unique perspective, but"—she shook her head, her wet hair sliding over her shoulders—"I think I'm too close to it, not ready."

"Have you got copies of the books you wrote?" he asked. "Maybe I should read them."

"Sure. Tons of author copies. I've got them upstairs," she said, and was off again before he could tell her it could wait. Again Dave padded after her up the stairs, then back down as she returned to the kitchen, this time with an armload of her own books. "Take them," she said, stacking them on the counter next to him.

"Thanks." He eyed the titles, then asked, "Which ones should I read first? What I mean is," he explained, tapping the top of the stack, "which book is about someone involved—the suspect or family members or friends or whatever—who threatened you or made you feel uncomfortable?"

"Oh, geez, too many to mention," she said. "I wasn't exactly popular with the killers."

"Okay—but if you were to read them?"

"What order? Okay." She eyed the spines and pulled out the first. "Okay, well, this is *The Rosary Killer*; if the murderer is alive, he'd probably be really pissed. But"—she shook her head—"we think he's dead." She put that book aside and pulled out another. "This is *The Bayou Butcher,* about Ned Zavala. Everyone in his family was upset about the book, and yeah, he threatened to sue me and 'fuck' me up." She used air quotes. "Swell guy." She set that book aside, too, as she looked over the other titles. "Oooh. Now here's one. *The God Complex and Murder.* It's about Hamilton Cooke, kind of a big deal surgeon before he was convicted of killing his first wife." She thought about that. "Ended up collecting insurance money and marrying the second wife, Reggie Lucerno, who was his lawyer."

"Lucerno? Oh, right. She was married to someone else at the time," Montoya said, nodding.

"Aldo Lucerno, big businessman in town. Inherited an oyster-packing business. 'The Oyster King.' That's what they call him. He fought the divorce and lost. After all, Reggie is an attorney." She added *The God Complex and Murder* to the suggested reading pile while perusing the other titles. "Oh. Here you go. Here's another." She pulled *American Icon/American Killer* from the rest of the stack. "Mandel Jarvis—his story."

"The football player turned preacher."

"The football player turned killer turned preacher." She placed it with the other books she'd suggested, then studied the remaining four titles. "Yeah, I'd start with these because they all happened here, in New Orleans. The others are from other places in the country."

Montoya was nodding. "Okay. So now, tell me about the guy who found your dog."

"What about him?"

"He was here at the house before you, right?"

"No, he was at the park."

"But he could have followed you?"

"I guess," she said. "But I don't think so."

"Why wouldn't he give you his name?"

"I don't know."

Montoya frowned. "The only reason I can think of for him to keep his name from you is that he had something to hide."

"Or he just didn't want to get involved."

"He already was. He put the dog on a makeshift leash and waited for you." He felt his eyes narrow. "It's a little off." More than a little, he thought as he heard the screech of tires on the street, an engine shut off, and the sharp rap of knuckles on the front door. He glanced over his shoulder. "I think your dad has arrived."

He was right. Through the sidelight he saw Bentz pacing back and forth on the front porch, one hand raking fingers through his hair.

"Here we go," she said under her breath as she headed into the foyer.

Kristi let Bentz into the house and he grabbed her, holding her tight. "That's it," he said. "You're coming home with me. You can live with Olivia, Ginny, and me until we get this whole thing sorted out."

Though she had collapsed into his arms, she extracted herself and shook her head. "No, Dad, that's not gonna work. This is my home."

"And it's not safe." Bentz didn't bother hiding his worry. "Obviously." Then he spied the dog, seated at the edge of the sectional, his tail wagging wildly, his eyes fixed on Bentz. "Don't tell me this is your guard dog."

"Sit down, Dad," she suggested, heading back to the kitchen, her father following.

After Bentz took a seat next to Montoya at the island and she'd deposited two glasses of water that they hadn't requested in front of them, Kristi went through the whole story about the lost dog, the stranger with the belt as a leash, the fact that the electricity had been turned off, and discovering the card in the flowers, one more time. As Kristi explained what happened Bentz's eyes grew darker, his lips compressed, and the faint lines in his forehead became more pronounced. He let her speak, then peppered his daughter with questions:

Why had she left the door open behind her?

Who had left the flowers?

Was she sure nothing was missing?

Why the hell didn't she demand the name of the stranger who had "found" her dog?

Did she trust the tech who had set up the new security system? Could he have planted the flowers? Did the vase say where the delivery had come from?

Had she gotten any weird calls?

What had she seen on her app for the security system?

And on and on.

To Kristi's credit, she handled her father's near-inquisition without freaking out. In fact, the more questions Bentz threw at her, the stronger and more quick to answer she appeared to become, and when he tried to throw a little blame her way, she responded sharply.

"What were you thinking, leaving the door wide open?"

"I wasn't, okay? I was worried about the dog. It was his first day. My mistake. It won't happen again."

"You can't let—"

"Dad, I know!"

"It's just that someone's targeting you. I mean, Jay's already—"

"Dead? Is that what you were going to say? Murdered? I know. I get it. More than anyone. I'm faced with him being gone every day, Dad. Every damned day. I'm usually careful, but I screwed up. Okay?" She paused and took a deep breath. "No one feels worse about it than me!"

Bentz's face softened slightly. "Okay, okay, this isn't a blame game, honey. I'm just—"

"Isn't it? Because it sure seems that way to me." She leaned over the counter, getting closer to him, nose to nose. "Look, I know you're worried sick. I know you think that I was attacked and Jay was killed by the Rosary Killer, yeah—" She was nodding, agreeing with herself. "—I get it, okay. And you have every right to feel that way. I know you feel some sort of guilt that you didn't protect me, that you hoped and thought that Father John was long dead. But don't. You've done a great job of taking care of me and I—if I never said so before, I appreciate it." She held her father's gaze and Bentz drew in a deep breath. "But I'm going to be fine. Here. With—Dave. Oh, and Lenore."

"Lenore? Who's—?" Bentz asked.

"She's here, hiding under the ottoman."

He swiveled on his bar stool and looked.

So did Montoya. From his perch he spied two gold eyes peering from beneath the tufted leather footstool.

"You adopted a cat, too?" Bentz said.

"Kind of the other way around." Kristi walked to the living room, got to her knees, and eased the little black kitten from her hiding place. "Actually, she adopted me." As she straightened, holding the little clump of fur, she explained about finding the cat cowering in her garage and concluded with, "I'll be fine here."

"We'll keep this," Montoya said, pointing to the plastic-encased card, "and we're going to need a copy of the footage on your camera, and a description of the man who found the dog. Maybe talk to a police artist."

"I don't think he had anything to do with it," Kristi protested.

"Nonetheless," Bentz interjected, thinking. "And we'll dust for prints, even though I doubt he left any. But everyone makes mistakes. Even the best." He glanced at his daughter and Kristi blushed, understanding it was her father's olive branch for her leaving the house unlocked.

Kristi got another phone call and she scowled at the screen.

"Problems?" Bentz asked, immediately going into cop mode again.

"No." She shook her head. "I recognize the number. A reporter."

Bentz rubbed a hand over his jaw, his beard shadow scraping. Obviously he wanted to plead his case again, to have his daughter move in with him, but Kristi's set jaw and folded arms gave him pause. "I'm only ten minutes away. Make sure you get the security system reset—it shouldn't be connected to the main switch."

"Got it."

"And I want to talk to the people who set this up. Did they connect

the system to the main electrical switch? Seriously? What kind of id-
iots are they? What was the name of the company? The technician?"

"Dad, stop! I'll deal with them!"

But Bentz was on a roll. His eyes slid to the dog, who had sidled
over to sit at his feet. "Any chance you could take him back? Get a
Rottweiler or a Doberman or maybe a pit bull."

"The people at the shelter think Dave's part pit. They're a very
loving breed."

His jaw worked. "He just doesn't seem . . . oh, Jesus." Dave had
rolled over, exposing his belly, hoping for a rub. His tongue lolled,
and his tail was still sweeping the floor even as he lay upside down.
"See what I mean?"

Kristi actually laughed for the first time since Montoya had arrived. "Yeah, but . . . come on. Give it a rest, okay?" Then her expression turned serious again. "I'll be careful. I swear."

Bentz scowled at the dog, but finally relented and petted his wide
head. "Fine, but I'm going to order more patrols in the area and if
you notice anything out of the ordinary, you call. Got it?"

"Got it."

Montoya picked up the card. "So what about the belt? The one
used as a leash. I think we should check it for prints, see if the 'Good
Samaritan' is in the system."

"My fingerprints are all over it," she said, but found the belt and
handed it to him.

Montoya took the worn strap of leather.

It seemed familiar somehow. But an old belt? He turned it over in
his hands, saw the discoloration of the leather, the small cracks indicating it was old, and then, near the buckle, he spied an area where it
looked as if someone had carved initials: AM.

His muscles froze.

Alejandro Montoya.

His great-grandfather. "This is the belt?" he clarified, his throat
tight, but he knew the answer.

"Yeah." She nodded, her eyebrows knitting at the question. "Of
course."

"What?" Bentz asked, picking up that something was wrong.

Montoya could barely believe it. "I think this was my great-grand-
daddy's belt." He remembered seeing pictures of the old man wear-

ing it while riding his horse in the hay fields seventy or so years earlier. "So that means the person who found the dog and brought him back is my brother, who inherited the belt." His jaw was so tight it ached. His brother had lied to him. Cruz had been nowhere near the Mojave when he'd called. His back teeth gnashed in anger as his brother had played him for a fool. "It looks like Cruz is already back in New Orleans."

"So the question is: What was he doing here at Kristi's house?" Bentz said, deadly serious.

"That's one, but I think the first question and the most important one is: Why didn't he tell me he was already in New Orleans?" Montoya said, but that was a lie and he knew it. The most important question for Cruz was a lot darker: *Did you kill Lucia Costa?* Cruz, of course, had already sworn that he hadn't killed anyone and would certainly insist that he was innocent. So, Montoya thought darkly, the second question was obvious and just as gut-wrenching: *Then why the hell did you run?*

CHAPTER 15

Kristi stared at the aftermath of the police searching her house. Several techs had come over while her father and his partner were still questioning her. They'd taken fingerprints, clicked off pictures, examined the electrical system, checked the yard for footprints, and gone through the footage from the new security device. When the electricity had been shut off, the alarms had been silenced due to a flaw in the system—but the cameras, before they, too, were disabled, had caught images of the intruder. He was in black, a poncho covering his frame, a ski mask and sunglasses guarding his identity, the hint of a beard visible, but he seemed to know where every camera was located and had attempted to turn his face away before his visage was recorded.

"There's got to be something here," her father had insisted, but the prowler had managed to hide his identity.

"You really think he's Father John?" Kristi had asked, obviously skeptical as she eyed one of the blurry images from the camera on the app she'd downloaded to her cell phone.

Bentz had scowled. "The MO's the same."

"Copycat, possibly," Montoya interjected.

"It's been a long time," Kristi had pointed out. "Why now?"

Throwing up a hand as if the answer were evident, Bentz had said, "Because he's a psycho. He doesn't need a reason."

Kristi hadn't bought it, but had held her tongue. Because Dad had been too raw, too worried about her.

Eventually everyone, including her father, had left, and Kristi, after being cautioned a dozen times by her father, had locked the doors behind them.

Cruz Montoya had rescued the dog? Montoya's brother? She did remember talk of him now, but it had been a while. Once she was reminded though, she saw the resemblance to Reuben. Cruz was taller, leaner, but, it seemed, more battered. They both were intense men, that much was obvious, but Cruz had less of a swagger and more coiled energy, or at least, that's what she'd sensed.

She wondered how he had ended up with her dog.

And ended up at her house.

He hadn't explained, but her last name and telephone number had been etched into Dave's ID tags. Somehow Cruz had taken that information and figured out her address.

"He's a private detective, remember? He can get that kind of information." Jay's voice again. As clear as if he were standing in the kitchen next to her.

She'd ignored her phone most of the day while dealing with Dave and then the police, but now she scrolled through her texts and found one from Bella asking her out to dinner.

Let's meet at Rico's! Dinner and drinks and much needed girl talk. Here she'd added a wineglass emoji.

We could all use a little time to unwind, right? Sarah's in, but Jess can't make it. Work, again. Her boss is the worst! Bella inserted a frowning emoji face, but Kristi wondered if Jess was just making an excuse as she'd been in an on-again, off-again affair with the man she worked for whether he was "the worst" or not.

And speaking of bosses, mine would love it if you would come for an interview b/c of cable movies of your books, reprint of RK book, and possibility of him returning to NOLA. Here she'd inserted a frightened emoji face and praying hands, pleading with Kristi to consider the offer.

Kristi considered, but declined. She didn't want to even speculate about "RK," the Rosary Killer, returning and wasn't ready to explain about the intruder today. If Bella ever learned about the cryptic religious notes she'd received, the veiled threats all wrapped up in Bible verses, and let it on to her boss at the station, Kristi would be plagued to do an interview, which, maybe someday, she'd consent to. No doubt her publisher would love it when the book was republished. But not yet. Not until she'd figured it out a little more herself. Nor did she want to expose the fact that she wasn't drinking. No one knew about the baby yet, and she wasn't ready to share the news with her girlfriends. First she needed to see the obstetrician, an appointment she'd scheduled for later today, and then, once she'd learned for certain that the pregnancy was on track, she'd tell her father. After that, she'd let her friends know.

Right now, she still wasn't in any kind of mood to celebrate, so she came up with an excuse that only stretched the truth a little and texted back:

Thanks. Sorry. Can't tonight. New dog—Dave—already escaped once today. Have to get him used to the place. Maybe next time?

She took a quick picture of Dave looking up at her and sent it along, almost as if she had to prove to Bella that she wasn't just putting her off.

Which—to be truthful—she was.

But just for now.

She'd get back to her friends. She knew she would. Right now, though, she had more important things to do rather than socialize. For the first time since Jay's brutal death and the attack, she felt energized, once again ready to tackle the world, and most importantly to uncover the truth and unearth the lowlife who had ruined her life by taking away her husband.

Her interview with Montoya had turned her thoughts around. She'd been so busy grieving and feeling sorry for herself, so dulled by her own pain, she'd lost her need for the truth, her desire to find Jay's killer, to expose him and bring him to justice.

But that had changed today.

First things first, though, she thought, checking her watch and realizing that if she didn't step on it she'd be late for her first appointment with her ob-gyn. A pang of guilt and remorse cut through her as she'd always imagined Jay would be with her for her visits to the obstetrician.

She told herself to shake the feeling, changed, and drove under threatening skies to the clinic, a three-story brick building that had been constructed in the seventies and shared a parking lot with

St. Ada's Hospital, a looming structure built before the turn of the last century. The hospital was attached by a covered walkway to a church with matching yellow stucco siding that had gone gray in spots. The church's bell tower knifed upward, its spire seeming to pierce the ominous low-hanging clouds.

Kristi parked and hurried inside where she filled out paperwork and waited and eventually was seen by a nurse, who took her vitals and drew blood, then by Dr. Vale, a heavyset woman with intelligent, nearly black eyes, dark skin, and graying hair clipped away from her face. In a lab coat over neon-pink scrubs, rimless glasses perched on her nose, the doctor was as cheery as the day outside was drab.

"Everything's right on schedule. It looks like the baby will arrive the very end of April or early May," the doctor said, wobbling her hand back and forth after the exam. She offered a bright smile along with a prescription for prenatal vitamins. "I'll see you in four weeks," she suggested.

As Kristi left, she felt a bit of buoyancy in her step for the first time in days despite the fat drops of rain beginning to fall. The thought that the baby growing within her was healthy, that she and Jay had created this special little miracle, lifted her spirits despite the gray day.

She made her way to the car and found a flyer jammed under the wipers, then noticed every other car in the lot had been plastered with the same yellow sheets. "Great," she muttered, plucking the sodden paper from her windshield. She was about to wad it up when she saw that it was for a rally at a local church. And who was the preacher? None other than Mandel Jarvis, the ex-football star who'd been convicted of murdering his wife and whom Kristi had written about in *American Icon/American Killer*. The thought turned her stomach sour, because, she thought, her telling of his tale had brought even more attention to him, brought him into more prominence. She read the information. The Newcomers' Worship Event was to be held on Friday night at seven p.m. at the New Faith and Glory Church of Praise, which was located on the highway to the airport, almost to the Kenner city limits.

She slid into the car, engaged the engine, and flipped on the wipers.

Mandel Jarvis's congregation was large. He had a huge social media presence and a cable television show, so it seemed odd to her that he would spend any effort on slapping flyers on cars. Why bother with individuals like her who would just throw the papers away? Why not spend more money advertising online?

She glanced around the lot and saw other people hurrying through the rain to their cars. An eighty-ish man using a cane hitched his way to an older pickup. He saw the flyer and tossed it to the ground in disgust. A woman in her sixties was holding her sweater over her head as she dashed around puddles to her white sedan, got inside, then opened her door and swatted at the flyer before dragging it into the car with her. But she paused before starting the vehicle and, like Kristi, read the message before driving out of the lot.

Odd, Kristi thought, then turned her gaze to the hospital where people came and went in a steady stream. She glanced at the sodden flyer on the passenger seat. Jarvis's picture was included and a Web site address, then symbols for Internet social platforms. Maybe Jarvis was covering all of his bases, searching for followers through modern means via the Internet, as well as older methods such as these flyers left on windshields and, no doubt, stapled to telephone poles and left in grocery stores.

Again she looked through her rain-spattered windshield at the people heading in and out of the hospital, most walking on their own accord, but some with walkers, others being pushed in wheel-chairs, one man turning gray before her eyes, and she knew that whatever was ailing him would win. And soon. She turned her atten-tion to a twenty-something couple laughing and carrying cups of cof-fee as they strolled past, the woman in a sweater, jeans, and boots, the guy she was with in shorts, a thin rain jacket with a hood, and flip-flops, an umbrella barely keeping them dry.

Her heart twisted as she thought of Jay and how many times they'd walked the streets of the city, talking and laughing and care-free. And it had all ended with angry words hurled at each other, her storming out, and him dying in a pool of blood and scattered roses at St. Louis Cathedral.

She let out a sigh and blinked back tears.

More people passed and she studied them, strangers walking by in groups or alone. A redheaded woman getting out of a sleek black Audi, her husband holding the door. Maybe this wasn't such a bad place to look for new members of the church; people with ailments who were facing their own mortality and entertaining thoughts of life after death might be a rich source for finding new followers.

Again she stared at the church attached to the hospital. Catholic. Steeped in tradition. Not some newer born-again faith, that, as far as she knew, was concocted while Jarvis was behind bars. Maybe the mouthful that was the New Faith and Glory Church of Praise drew those who were more of the born-again crowd. From her research, she knew that Jarvis had started the group while he was incarcerated, a small number of convicts that had grown over the years he'd been locked up. Drawn by his fame and charisma, more and more people came on board. By the time he was freed, he had nearly a thousand followers, some still in prison, others freed and spreading his word. And now many more. Once he'd become a free man, could access television cameras and the Internet as well as create news and proclaim that he would be exonerated completely through the acceptance and blood of Christ, his fellowship exploded, growing exponentially. Like sinners looking for redemption. Followers who were nearly rabid in their faith and trust of this one man.

Again she saw the couple from the Audi and the wind caught the woman's hair, snatching it away from her face.

With a start, Kristi recognized Reggie Cooke, the statuesque lawyer, in high-heeled boots and a camel-hair coat. The man beside her? Hamilton Cooke, taking the crook of her elbow in one hand while holding an umbrella aloft. Reggie shook off his hand and strode through the double doors of the hospital a step ahead of him. Frowning, Cooke followed, closing the umbrella and shaking off the rain in the vestibule before he, like his wife, disappeared inside.

Kristi stared after them before starting the car. She'd just slid the gearshift into reverse to back out of the space when she spied another person she recognized: Aldo Lucerno—at least it looked like him, in sport coat and dark slacks, as he slipped through the hospital doors.

Was he following his ex-wife and her new husband?

Were they going to meet?

Or was the situation random?

Or had the tall man with jet-black hair and swarthy complexion been someone else? Had her willing mind just leapt to the idea that Lucerno was lurking nearby? She'd never liked him, and when researching her story on Hamilton Cooke, she'd been put off by not only Cooke but Lucerno as well.

"Odd," she thought aloud, then glanced in her rearview and hit the brakes as an elderly woman in a lavender pantsuit and pushing a walker appeared in the mirror's reflection as she inched through the parking lot.

Kristi's heart nearly stopped.

She'd been distracted and hadn't noticed the woman.

"Pull yourself together," she warned, and once again backed up, put the car into drive, and pulled out of the lot. She drove home barely noticing the traffic, nor the rain that was coming down faster and harder. Sliding a glance at the wet flyer, she thought maybe she'd attend the newcomers' event.

She'd been idle too long and ennui didn't suit her. If she wasn't busy, she was antsy. Kristi hated to admit it, but her agent was right. She needed to work again. Now that she was healing physically and, she supposed, emotionally, it was time to get moving.

She wondered about Mandel Jarvis.

Had he really found God?

Did he truly believe in the teachings of Jesus Christ?

Was he a reformed sinner?

Or a clever scam artist?

If she were a betting woman—and she was—she'd put all her money on the latter.

". . . so I'll be home late," Montoya said, his cell phone propped between his shoulder and jaw as he sat at his desk.

"How late?" Abby asked.

"Don't know. Got to run down a few leads, but I'll try to be there before the baby goes down."

"Good."

He heard the exasperation in her voice and the baby wailing in the background.

"He needs a father, Reuben."

"He's got one." He hid his own irritation. "I'll be there."

"I'm holding you to it," and then she cut the connection without her usual, "Love you."

"Love you, too," he said, as was his custom, then turned his attention back to his computer screen and notes. Since being called over to Kristi Bentz's place, he'd spent most of the day double-checking alibis of the Bentz and McKnight family members, and all the alibis were solid. Even Jay's cousin in Alabama, Greg McKnight, had his story backed up by "friends" at a bar on the outskirts of Mobile. Greg hadn't attended Jay's funeral and had nothing good to say about his "dick-wad" of a cousin and, Montoya noted, had a rap sheet, priors that included a few misdemeanors and one felony for assault out of a dispute with his neighbor. In the argument over tree debris, Greg had cut down the branch of a magnolia that had grown over the fence line, then when the neighbor objected, had taken off after him with a chain saw. In the ensuing wrestling match, he'd cut himself with the saw and ended up with fifteen stitches in his thigh, the neighbor only suffering a black eye, cut lip, and loss of a tree limb.

Greg had done six months in county and eventually moved. Montoya tapped his pencil on his desk and studied the mug shots and driver's license photos of Greg McKnight, with his long face, scraggly blond hair, and slight sneer—none of which made him guilty. Though Montoya didn't dismiss him as a suspect completely, he had to admit the chance of Greg McKnight driving down from Alabama, laying in wait for Kristi, then attacking her and killing his cousin on the streets of New Orleans was pretty slim. Jay wasn't supposed to be on the street that night.

Montoya tore through Kristi and Jay's life, turning it inside out, going through everything from their bank records, phone calls, and texts as well as Twitter and Facebook accounts, all the while searching for anyone who had made negative comments or reposts or tweets, someone whose anger made him or her stand out as a potential suspect.

While Bentz was half convinced the attack and murder had to be attributed to Father John, believing that psycho had somehow resurrected himself from the swamp and reappeared after years of being in hiding, Montoya wasn't so sure. The MO of the attack on Kristi and Jay was all wrong. Father John wasn't a knife-wielding psycho. His "work" had always been well thought out and ritualistic and had conveyed a weird, outré religious theme. The Rosary Killer had been intelligent and organized, not the type to send out dark greeting cards no matter how warped and deviant he was.

Where was the rosary? The hundred-dollar bills with Ben Franklin's eyes darkened to black? And what was with the funereal greeting cards with their signature black roses? Was the ink blocking out Ben's eyes on the C-note the same as used in the drawing of the roses on the dark greeting cards left at Kristi's house? He wondered, made a note to check.

He reread the cards again—yes, they had religious overtones as the missives were warnings, Bible verses twisted into ominous threats.

No, Montoya didn't think the attack on Kristi Bentz or her husband's homicide was the work of Father John.

Then who?

Who, who, who?

That was the problem. He'd come up with a few anonymous trolls online who continually barraged Kristi's Twitter account with nasty comments, people the department was still attempting to ferret out. And there were several other suspects connected to Bentz who could have killed Jay, killers Bentz had arrested and helped convict, many of whom had voiced their loathing and hatred of the cop who relentlessly hunted them down. Most, though, were still behind bars.

But there were a handful who had, for one reason or another, been released.

The first Montoya considered was Ned Zavala, a man who'd escalated from assault to homicide and was out after serving his time and was on parole for good behavior.

He glanced at the stack of books Kristi had given him. He picked up a copy of the tome dedicated to Zavala: *The Bayou Butcher,* a psycho if there ever was one. Montoya had been a part of the case, but Bentz had been lead detective who had brought the killer down.

Montoya had seen a lot of bad shit in his career, people capable of unbelievable cruelty, and Zavala was right up there. He'd been a butcher at one point in his life and the body they'd found in his freezer had been sliced with a meat-cutter's precision and wrapped in butcher paper, some of the parts even filleted.

Even now the story got to him. And he'd never really bought the story that Zavala's mother had sworn to, that her dead husband, a brute named Corrin Hebert, had done the deed—some unbelievable story about Hebert taking his victim's blood and drizzling it over his stepson, Ned's, jeans.

Upon his release Ned had sworn to get back at Rick Bentz, the detective who had zeroed in on him. He might have regained his freedom, but his wife had left him, hauling his kids to Alaska where they remained estranged, and Kristi's book had ensured that people forever saw him as the Bayou Butcher.

Now, Zavala was taking care of his dying mother right here in New Orleans.

Could something have set him off?

Would he have actually come after Kristi and then been surprised by Jay and killed him instead?

Maybe . . . but maybe not.

Leaning back in his desk chair, he rubbed the back of his neck and tried to dispel the feeling that he was barking up the wrong tree, that maybe Bentz, with his damned Rosary Killer theory, might be closer to the truth.

And what the hell was Cruz doing at Kristi Bentz's house? That worrisome thought had chased him around all day, nagging at him, picking at his brain. Cruz had said he was coming to New Orleans and had told Montoya when he arrived he'd call him, but no— he ends up with Kristi's damned dog on their great-grandfather's belt.

What was that all about?

The belt was lying on a corner of his desk, the hand-carved initials visible from his vantage point.

He'd thought about calling the authorities in Oregon. Shit, he didn't have much choice but to inform them that he'd heard from his brother, but he was waiting until Cruz contacted him again. He'd be in deep shit for that—called on the carpet at the very least—and he was running out of time and excuses for not notifying the officers in charge.

"Fuck," he said under his breath, and told himself to give Cruz until the morning, then deal with his latest mess. This time a homicide. Of a woman he'd known for over half his life, maybe longer.

Montoya glanced at the clock and told himself to put thoughts of his brother aside. For now. He had work to do.

The door to the office he shared with Bentz was hanging open, and through the opening to the hallway he heard noises indicating the shift was changing. Cops going off duty, more coming on, so the outer hallway was loud with footsteps, conversation, and bursts of laughter. Cell phones jangled and every once in a while, from a distance, a sharp voice would cut through the din, someone shouting angrily, usually a person protesting his arrest, or the loud voice of a friend or family member of the dirtbag being hauled to jail. All of this over the scream of saws and the rapid-fire bursts of a nail gun as construction continued.

Enough to give him the start of one helluva headache.

Chaos, that's what it was.

Pure chaos.

CHAPTER 16

Montoya's back ached and he felt as if he'd been spinning his wheels all the damned day.

"I'm telling you, it's Rosary," Bentz said when he returned and noted his partner's frustration.

"You got any proof of that? That Father John is back?" Montoya asked.

"Not yet. But . . . it's just gotta be."

"Maybe." Montoya wasn't going to discount any theory at this point.

Bentz spent less than fifteen minutes at his desk, checking his computer and in-box, then was on his feet again. "I'm meeting a guy. Rents old cabins on the bayou and he might have met with Father John."

"And you know this how?"

"Anonymous tip came in. Ride along?"

"Sure." He gathered his jacket, keys, and sidearm. They walked through the halls, past other cops, and around the construction site that had been cordoned off with thick plastic sheets. Workers behind the semi-opaque curtain were closing up shop, turning off equipment and packing up toolboxes.

Outside it was still daylight. Late afternoon, a lazy breeze blowing in from the gulf followed Montoya to Bentz's Jeep. "How far is this?" Montoya asked as he slid into the warm interior and Bentz got behind the wheel.

"Over an hour." Bentz slid a pair of sunglasses over the bridge of his nose. "That okay?"

"Yeah." It wasn't. He'd have to let Abby know that he wouldn't make it home for Benjamin's bedtime. But that was the job. Traffic was heavy in New Orleans, but Bentz picked up speed after they passed through the city limits, the sun setting low in the western sky, the strip malls and subdivisions giving way to larger tracts of land, small farms, and more isolated houses. Bentz explained that they were meeting with Cyrus Unger, the owner of a dozen or so cabins in the bayou.

"So the tip came in. Anonymous, but the number was tracked. To Unger. In his original message he said he might have seen a priest asking about a cabin, but he wasn't too interested in coming in to talk at the station and I thought it might be a good idea to have a look around myself. Unger, he's not happy that we're coming, but he finally agreed." He slid a look in Montoya's direction. "I think Unger might be working a side hustle or two. Poaching or drugs or something that makes him uneasy around the cops."

"But he called it in."

"Homicide is a long way from some petty grift or killing an alligator without a tag or taking a bear out of season or dealing meth." The road curved in a wide arc that cut through fields of rice growing in ponds where the tops of crawdad traps were visible. As the farms disappeared, they drove into the bayou, where the last rays of a dying sun pierced through the swamp. Pale cypress trees, their branches draped with Spanish moss, loomed, growing out of the dark water where duckweed and spider lilies seemed to float.

Using his GPS system, Bentz cut off the main road to a narrow gravel lane that wound through the trees and over an ancient wooden bridge barely wide enough for the SUV, and drove another mile into the swamp.

"You really think Father John would live this far from the city?"

"Don't know, but he's comfortable in the swamp." That much was true; the killer's original lair, a rustic cabin, had been located deep in the bayou and, Montoya had thought, he'd died in the swamp.

"Here we go." The beams of the Jeep's headlights washed onto a long, low cabin, once white, but now grayed with age. A porch that listed a bit covered the entrance and a faded red sign hanging over the door announced that this building was the office. Other signs had been nailed to the siding, and as Montoya climbed out of the

SUV he read the hours of operation along with notices that this establishment sold live bait and cold beer.

He also noted that the neon vacancy sign was lit and humming slightly. Mosquitoes were definitely on the attack despite a bug-zapping device that crackled with the death of a new unseen victim as he passed.

Before he and Bentz could climb the one rickety step to the porch, the door swung open and a balding man with a flushed complexion, bulbous nose, and a burst of freckles over all of his face waved them inside. "I'm Cyrus," he said as they introduced themselves and showed their ID, which he examined with a jaundiced eye. "But ever'buddy 'round here calls me CU, y'know—my initials. Like 'see you.'" He snorted. "Started in grade school. The other kids thought it was real funny and it stuck. So, I just roll with it. I mean, what're ya gonna do? Know what I mean?" He wore an orange T-shirt and battered jeans held up by suspenders that stretched over a protruding belly. His beard was gray and thin, his feet slipped into moccasins that had stretched and looked a size too big. As they stepped into the office, he closed the door quickly behind them, pulled down the shade, and with the click of a switch killed the vacancy sign. "We need a little privacy," he explained, "and some of my guests, well, they get a little squirrely around cops, if ya know what I mean."

Montoya did.

The office itself was small with low ceilings and smelled of tobacco, fish, and dust. A counter ran along one side of the room, a refrigerated case on the opposite wall stacked with cold drinks—soda, beer, water, refrigerated snacks that included processed cheese and sausage, and bait. Next to the cold drink case was a chest freezer stuffed with frozen waffles, pizza, corn dogs, ice cream sandwiches, and more bait.

Nuts, pretzels, M&M's, cigarettes, and chewing tobacco were also available and displayed beneath the glass top of the counter, while behind the register was a wall-to-ceiling display of hard liquor bottles and packages of ammunition, all tightly locked behind Plexiglas doors. A bulletin board held curled and yellowed business cards, photos of hunters with dead alligators or deer, or fishermen with their catches, along with a piece of paper offering CU's cabins for rent with his phone number on tabs at the bottom. The paper was missing four or five slips where potential customers had torn off the information. Not exactly high-tech, the kind of advertising one did in local grocery stores.

"Come on back to the livin' room," Cyrus suggested.

They followed him down a short hallway where supplies nearly blocked the path to an area that was a rustic studio apartment, a bed pushed into one corner, couch and recliner stretched across the opposite wall, television on a swiveling stand so that it could face the recliner or bed.

The kitchen was an alcove with a microwave, mini fridge, and hot plate, and over the scents of mildew and dust, the smell of recently fried fish still lingered.

Sliding doors opened to a large deck built over the water of the swamp and decorated with hanging lights and another couple of bug zappers.

"So tell us about the priest," Bentz suggested after letting CU know the interview was being recorded.

"I'm not sure he was a priest." CU settled into his recliner and stared out the window to the darkness beyond.

"What made you think he was?" Montoya asked.

"He was dressed all in black, no collar—just black pants and shirt, which isn't all that odd these days, but there was something about him that made me think . . ." He let his voice fade off for a minute. "It was all odd. He called, asking about a cabin, which isn't weird, of course, said he'd heard that I had one from a friend of a friend, though he never gave any names. Again, that's not out of the ordinary. But it felt fishy to me. I've got a pretty good inner bullshit detector and this guy—he set off all kinds of alarms. I figured he was hiding something, but hey—not my business.

"Anyway, I don't advertise on the Internet or anything high-tech, try to keep my business on the down low, if you know what I mean. Local stores and shops know about me and I even put up some flyers with my phone number across the bottom, where you tear it off and give me a call. But he didn't do that either.

"Came in on foot. No damned vehicle. Now *that's* unusual." CU stared out the back door to the swamp, recalling. "He said he caught a ride with a buddy and that's still fine, but the buddy didn't stick around, didn't show his face, so I'm a little suspicious. Then he asks about a cabin and he was real clear that it had to be remote, maybe only got to by boat, and I do have one but it's rented. Yearly tenant. Pays on time. I'm not kicking him out, if you know what I mean." Scratching his beard, CU said, "So I showed him what was available—got cabins all along this bayou, y'know, but he wasn't interested. They were all too near civilization." He pulled on his lower lip. "Some of these places are a quarter mile in, no one around, if you know what I mean, but he seemed to think they were too accessible, and he said he needed a place where he could be completely alone, a place to meditate, just him and God."

"Is that why you thought he was a priest?"

"Hell, no. You don't have to be part of the clergy to want to communicate with the big guy upstairs. Uh-uh."

"So why?"

"Like I say, it was his mannerisms. The way he talked to me, kind of like he was my mentor. Like some kind of role model—trying to be friendly, but a little standoffish, if you know what I mean."

Bentz shook his head. "I don't."

"It was as if he wanted me to think that he was on the up-and-up, even spiritual, but it seemed off to me."

"I don't get why that would make you think he was a priest."

"Oh, no, no. That's just it, I think he wasn't a man of the cloth at all, not a priest, not a pastor, not a damned rabbi."

"So?"

"I think he wanted me to think he was, and then I caught him sketching the sign of the cross." CU motioned the cross over his own ample chest. "But it was real obvious, y'know, didn't look natural, and I got the feeling he wanted me to see it. Like to convince me or something."

"Why?"

"You tell me. He just had this little smile on his face. Serene. But fake as all shit. And 'course I couldn't really read his expression, what he was really thinkin', cuz I couldn't see his eyes on accounta those shades he wore. Big. Reflective. And then he left, the same way he came, on foot. Said he was gonna call his buddy for a ride and headed off down the lane. He was gone about five minutes when I heard a car start up."

"His friend was waiting," Montoya said.

"Uh-uh. It was his car."

"And you know this how?"

For the first time since they walked into his establishment, CU smiled. "Because I got it on tape."

"Tape?"

He leaned forward, hands on his jean-clad knees. "Out here we can get some unsavory types, if you know what I mean. People think they can take advantage cuz there ain't many people around. Think they can rip people off and no one's the wiser. It happened to me a couple of times. Before I installed the cameras."

Montoya couldn't believe it.

"You have pictures of the guy?" Bentz said.

"Better than that," CU said with a cunning smile that showed a gap between tobacco-stained teeth. "I just happened to get his vehicle in the shot, too."

CHAPTER 17

"I'm just telling you to send me something, okay?" Zera insisted as Kristi held the phone to her ear and stared out the window of her office.

"I said I'd try."

"I know, I know. And I wouldn't push you, but it's important, you know, timing is everything."

Kristi spun her desk chair around to stare at the opposite wall. A flat screen TV was front and center, taking up wall space over a bookcase/credenza where her Wi-Fi connections, DVR, and old DVD player were positioned. Arranged on the top of the credenza was an array of her favorite pictures, framed and facing forward.

She focused on a shot of Jay she'd taken while they'd been on a trip to the Grand Canyon. Jay's hair was caught in the breeze, his jaw covered in beard shadow as he squinted toward the lowering sun over the canyon's rim. Her heart twisted and she suddenly realized Zera was still talking.

"—won't take you long. I'm just asking for a few pages. That's all I want. If the idea needs fleshing out, then we'll do it at that point, but it's important that we jump on this. Now. Strike while the iron's hot, so to speak."

A headache started to pound behind Kristi's eyes.

Zera was still pushing Kristi for a sequel to her book on the Rosary Killer.

Kristi swiveled her chair back so she again was facing her messy desk.

"Look," Zera said, "I've got a couple of editors who are asking and

I've heard through the grapevine that there are other authors who are interested in writing the story, who are already submitting proposals."

"Let me guess," Kristi said without much enthusiasm. "Drake Dennison."

"That's one of the names that's been mentioned. Dennison is in New Orleans now, you know."

"I didn't." Kristi was surprised. "I thought he lived around Atlanta somewhere."

"I thought so, too. But it's always been a guessing game with him. Ever mysterious our boy Dennison, but I think he moved in the last year or so. A colleague mentioned it; he's friends with Dennison's agent, who doesn't let much out about his client. It's all part of the 'Dennison mystique,'" Zera added sarcastically, and Kristi imagined the agent making air quotes around her phone.

"Save me." Kristi rolled her eyes. "That might have flown years ago, but in the age of the Internet, with Facebook—oh, excuse me, Meta—and Instagram and Twitter and book lovers' groups and mystery blogs and podcasts and whatever, it seems impossible."

"I'm just saying," Zera said. "And he's not the only one who is talking about a new book on Rosary. I even heard a whisper about a movie. Made for TV."

Kristi should have been enticed. She wasn't. "That's already happened. They can dust off that old made-for-TV thing."

Zera snorted. "An episode of a cheesy true-crime cable show. This would be different."

"If you say so."

Zera continued, "I'm telling you, Kristi, the vultures are circling. If you don't do this, half a dozen other authors will."

"I hear you."

"Good. So just send me something!"

"I will." It was a lie. Kristi knew it as she disconnected. Zera would be pissed at her, okay, but if Kristi figured out who was behind the attack on Jay—yes, possibly Father John—there would be a whole new story to appease her agent. A sequel to *The Rosary Killer*? She wasn't certain of that, but both she and Zera knew that from her unique perspective of victim and new widow due to the attack, she would be able to get a publisher interested in the story, no matter what or who the competition.

If she could put the pieces together.

And if she didn't get hurt or killed while doing it.

Absently, while the kitten hopped onto the windowsill, Kristi rubbed her shoulder where her assailant had thrust his blade, just before killing Jay. "I'll get you, you son of a bitch," she said under her breath. "If it's the last thing I do."

"No, Kris. Not the last thing." Jay's voice again, ringing in her ears. Reprimanding.

"What?" she bit out angrily, mad that he wasn't here, that he was haunting her instead.

"The baby. You have to think first about the baby."

Oh, God. She let out an exasperated breath as Lenore stepped onto the top of Kristi's messy desk. Jay was right, of course. She couldn't put herself into any kind of danger, not now. Though reckless when it came to her own safety, she couldn't, wouldn't, place her unborn child in peril.

Frustrated, she threw her pencil and startled the kitten, who leaped straight up and landed back on Kristi's work space, her back arched, her needle teeth exposed as she hissed. "Oooh. Sorry." Kristi reached for her, but Lenore scuttled behind the stack of books Kristi had pulled from the shelf and left on a corner of her desk. Copies of the same books she'd given to Montoya.

Kristi paused. Studied the spines of the hardbacks.

Was Montoya right? Could Jay's killer be tucked into the pages of the books she had written over the years? What were the chances of that?

Not great, but better than the odds of some family member hiding in the shadows of St. Louis Cathedral, pouncing and committing assault and murder as Montoya had suggested. Ridiculous, though she supposed he couldn't know that. Still, the idea rubbed her the wrong way, that anyone in her family or Jay's was homicidal.

So who was behind the attack, then?

Who hated her so much as to try and murder her?

"Not just you, Kris. It could be your Dad who is the ultimate target." Jay's voice again. *"He's made more than his share of enemies in*

the course of his career, and what better way to get back at him than to hurt you? Do your research. Think with a clear head. If you're going to do this—and you know you will—then do it right."

"Oh, shut up," she said, her lips curving in the hint of a smile as she remembered saying the same thing jokingly to her husband when they'd argued and she'd ended up realizing he was right.

Twirling the wedding ring on her finger, she sighed. "I do miss you," she admitted, and felt her throat close. Again. Before allowing herself to devolve into tears, she blinked rapidly, then picked up the first book in the haphazard stack on her desk: *The God Complex and Murder.* "Hamilton Cooke's story," she said to the room, and saw Dave perk his head up from the dog bed she had placed under a window. She smiled and rolled her chair over to the bed and scratched the dog behind his ears. "I'll tell you about it sometime," she said, and Dave's tail wagged.

Kristi remembered interviewing Cooke, a supposedly brilliant surgeon and a total egomaniac. Cooke used his status to his advantage, creating an alternate personality, always keeping people guessing, forever in the news and the subject of Internet, television, and radio interviews and speculation, while behind bars and especially since he'd been out. He'd become a quasi-celebrity of sorts and seemed to revel in all the attention.

"Dr. Ego," she whispered under her breath.

Kristi had met him several times during the course of writing the book, had interviewed him and he'd come across as smooth, a man who under the pretense of humility was always making certain everyone in the room knew how smart he was, that in fact, he was a genius. And, of course, a brutal murderer. He'd been so arrogant as to think that he was convincing Kristi of his innocence, when exactly the opposite had been true. He was just one of those people who thought because his IQ was in the stratosphere that he could fool everyone because they were, if only in his own estimation, of lesser intelligence.

Kristi had seen right through him. She had let him think he was manipulating her into his way of thinking, when exactly the opposite had been true. The more he told his well-practiced story, the more false it rang, but she never let him know it. She saw through his well-practiced charm and knew the twinkle in his eye wasn't be-

THE LAST SINNER 165

cause he was clever, but because he thought he was pulling a fast one on her.

In one interview at the prison before his release, she'd listened raptly and allowed a small smile to play on her lips, gazed into his eyes as if he were a god, and he'd not been able to help himself, thinking he was so damned smart and charismatic. Because he'd assumed that he'd captivated her into believing his bullshit, he'd even allowed her to tape the entire conversation despite his attorney's vociferous objections.

Cooke was just that self-involved.

She searched through her computer files, found the interview in which Cooke had agreed to speak to her during the time he was appealing his original conviction. Kristi hit play and there he was, Dr. Hamilton Cooke, dressed in a prison uniform, his demeanor comfortable and even relaxed in a plastic chair, cinder block walls as a backdrop as he spoke into the camera she'd been allowed to set up. She'd sat on one side of a small table, he on the other, her voice and all other sound picked up by the microphone, only the doctor visible.

Cooke's features were even, his nose pointed, nearly aristocratic, his black hair having silvered, his smile pinned on to a clean-shaven face with a strong jaw. Tiny crow's-feet fanned from blue eyes that had kept Kristi in sharp, almost inquisitive focus.

He'd never faltered during the interview, his story unchanging.

Cooke had sworn that his wife, Beth, had slipped and fallen in the shower, hit her head on the tile surround, and died before help could arrive. His daughter had been the person who found her. Hamilton, who had been outside in the back, by the pool house, had come running upon hearing his daughter's screams. He claimed he had tended to Beth, trying his best to save her as the frantic daughter dialed 9-1-1.

It was all for naught.

She watched the recording for what had to be the twentieth time as he explained. "Sadly," he said, his lips pulling into the slightest of frowns, "she was already gone when the EMTs arrived." He stared straight into the camera. "A freak accident. That's all." He shrugged. "The police made more of it than there was."

The police being Kristi's father.

The trouble with Hamilton Cooke's story was that the medical examiner had begged to differ about the extent of Beth Cooke's injuries, that they were inconsistent with a fall and more likely the result of blunt force trauma from a weapon that was never located—a hammer of some kind.

And Cooke had been convicted. Largely because he'd insisted on testifying and thinking he could convince the jury that he was innocent. They, too, had disagreed, and when Kristi had interviewed him he was in the process of appealing his conviction. He'd seemed to think that her book would help and he kept referring to his story.

"So glad we could do this," he said on the recording, allowing himself to smile sadly, just enough to show off the hint of a dimple. "So we can set the record straight, you know. My first attorney botched the case, horribly." He'd said the phrase as if it tasted bad. "Poor choice." His eyes darkened a bit, a little shadow skating through the blue orbs only to disappear in an instant. "But that's behind me. I've got new representation and she's dedicated." His chin lifted a fraction of an inch. "She'll make certain justice prevails."

That attorney, Reggie Lucerno, had arrived not ten minutes into the interview. A tall, striking woman with scraped back red hair, mile-high cheekbones, and wide green eyes that snapped with intelligence, she strode into the small interview room. Her high-heeled boots clicked against the floor as she walked, a long camel-hair coat billowed, and a cloud of outrage surrounded her, all of which was caught in the camera's eye. "I can't believe this! I told you no interviews." Rolling her eyes to the ceiling, she said, "Sometimes I wonder why I even try."

"Reggie—" he'd begun, but she cut him off.

"This"—she'd made a quick back and forth motion with her hand over the table, to include Kristi—"this is over! Now! You can't go talking to the press or . . . or some what? Novelist?"

"True-crime writer," Kristi corrected, and she remembered standing and extending her hand as she introduced herself. "Kristi Bentz."

"Bentz?" Reggie had repeated as the light had dawned. At that point she'd ignored Kristi's outstretched palm and turned her furious gaze onto her client. "As in Rick Bentz? The detective who fucking arrested you? For the love of God, Hamilton—" Outraged, she glared at Kristi. "As I said, we're done here. This is over." Snapping her head toward the doorway, she shouted, "Guard!" Then to Kristi in a more modulated voice, "This is outrageous." Jabbing a finger as she walked closer, the heels of her boots clicking ominously across the floor, her image no longer visible on the screen, only Cooke's face, flushed with anger, caught on camera.

"Outrageous," Reggie repeated, her voice a hiss but still being recorded.

Kristi remembered how infuriated the attorney had been, her lips knotted, a little tic appearing over one eye, none of which was recorded, of course. Reggie had leaned in close. "We'll sue."

"Do it," Kristi had said, irritated herself and not intimidated in the least. Who the hell did this woman think she was? To Hamilton she said, "I'd like to take this up later."

"Uh-uh. Not gonna happen," Reggie insisted, and sent a hard look at her client, silently warning him to keep his mouth shut just as a burly, uniformed guard hurried through the doorway. His hand was on the Taser strapped to his belt. "Trouble?" he asked, eyes scanning the room.

"No trouble," Kristi assured him. Gathering her recorder and briefcase, she ignored the lawyer and said, "If you change your mind, I'd love to continue this."

Reggie gave a soft, bitter laugh. "In your dreams. When I said this was over, I meant permanently." She turned her attention to the guard. "We're done here. My client is finished with the interview. Please escort Ms. Bentz out."

And that had been the end of the interviews.

Kristi had tried and been declined.

Reggie Lucerno had been as good as her word.

A powerhouse of an attorney, she had managed to have Cooke's case retried on appeal and get his conviction overturned.

During that second trial, covered widely by the media, rumors had surfaced linking Hamilton and Reggie romantically, despite the fact that Reggie was already married to Aldo Lucerno, a self-made millionaire who had become New Orleans's "Oyster King." Those rumors had been denied, of course, by both client and attorney, but like a bad smell, lingered, and the hounds of the press were always on the watch, prowling after the attorney, who just happened to divorce her husband during the weeks and months leading up to the trial. This created more of a buzz, keeping Hamilton Cooke in the national spotlight, though never again had he been interviewed.

Cooke's conviction had been overturned, and handsome, arrogant Dr. Hamilton Cooke became a free man even if the question of "did he or did he not brutally murder his wife?" hung like a cloud over him. Only after his release did he and Reggie confirm their relationship, and within three months of Cooke walking out of the prison, the couple tied the knot in a private ceremony on a Florida beach, both tanned and barefoot, she in a gauzy white dress, he in a tuxedo, his shirt open-throated, his tie dangling. They married surrounded by tall palm trees, glittering white sand, and clear, aquamarine ocean.

The media had not been invited, but the paparazzi had hovered, and a bold photographer had managed to take some intimate shots before being gruffly forced to leave. Too late. Pictures of the "private" wedding had been splashed across the tabloids and shown in quick spots on entertainment news segments.

Cooke, with his attorney/wife at his side, threw his attention into regaining his medical license and starting a charity for those who had been wrongly imprisoned. With Reggie's help, he'd finally collected the benefits from the hefty life insurance policy he'd carried on his first wife, reportedly two million dollars—enough money to give an unhappy husband pause, plus, of course a motive, especially when that husband was facing divorce, possible financial ruin. Add to that the fact that in the months leading up to Beth's death, Hamilton Cooke had increased the coverage on his wife. It all smelled very, very rotten.

Reggie, fiercely protective of her client/husband, and senior partner in a small law firm, was quick to threaten lawsuits against anyone who smeared her new husband's name or stood in Hamilton's—or her—way.

And that included her ex-husband, who was livid that she'd paraded her affair in front of the press, damaging his reputation. Aldo Lucerno had been vocal at the time of the divorce and fought dissolution of the marriage citing personal, religious, and business reasons, claiming he would be financially ruined as well as publicly embarrassed. In truth, Aldo had come out of it well, his brand of canned oysters catching national attention and distribution. Now, according to Kristi's research, he was worth over ten times what he had been at the time of the messy divorce.

Nonetheless he, like his ex-wife and her new husband, had been livid at the thought of a book being written putting his family in a bad light, and the scandal of his wife's infidelity had been brutal enough without Kristi writing a book about it. A lifelong resident whose ancestors had immigrated to New Orleans centuries earlier, Aldo was adamant that no one, including Kristi Bentz, besmirch the Lucerno name. "Don't even think about it," he'd warned when she'd tried to interview him at his home, a huge, sprawling, plantation-style house on manicured grounds hidden behind a wall of a fence and a gate that only opened by electronic command. She'd been forced to stay in her car at the gate, but Aldo, at five foot ten or eleven with clipped dark hair, had emerged from the home, walked stiff-backed down the brick drive, and stared at her through the elaborate wrought iron gate. "If you print anything about my family," he'd said, "I'll have my attorneys ensure that not one word of your book ever gets published."

Kristi had refused to be intimidated. "We'll see about that." After a short exchange, she'd driven off and written what she'd seen as the truth driven by the facts of the case. All the threatened lawsuits never materialized. The book had been published and became a best seller.

Of course Reggie had remarried quickly. Now she and Hamilton made their residence in a historic three-story home built by a famous architect in the 1880s. Completely renovated, but keeping all of its original charm, it claimed a private courtyard, pool, five bedrooms and five baths, and had been featured in several architectural and cultural magazines, the spreads including shots of the loving couple who owned the prestigious home.

And it was only a few blocks from Kristi's cottage, in a more prestigious part of the Garden District. She hadn't realized he lived so close to her and the thought was disconcerting, but she shoved it aside. For now.

So, what about his daughter? Lindsay? She'd been a child, preteen when she'd discovered her mother's body.

Kristi searched the Internet. After the second trial, Lindsay Cooke was barely mentioned in the press and seemed to be in college at a small school in the Midwest and avoiding the limelight that her father so adored.

Kristi spent the next couple of hours reading articles about both Hamilton and Reggie Cooke, scrolling through one after another on her computer screen. She also checked out Hamilton Cooke's social media accounts and Reggie Lucerno Cooke's law firm's Web site. Clicking through all the information on the couple, she saw photographs and watched short videos, all of which seemed slick and polished, as if professionally created and edited to show Reggie or Hamilton in perfect light. Older shots were included and displayed an earnest Dr. Hamilton Cooke in medical scrubs, often with a young patient. In the more recent images he was always dressed casually, his hair longer and peppered with gray, an easy smile and a noticeable twinkle in his blue eyes.

Kristi leaned back in her chair. She twiddled a pen as she thought about Cooke. She believed to this day that beneath Cooke's suave and debonaire veneer lay a cold-blooded killer, a man who thought he was smarter than everyone else in the room and had the credentials to prove it. Cooke was a sociopath with a dark and murderous side.

During the time when she'd researched *The God Complex and Murder* Kristi had discovered that Cooke's first wife had planned to divorce him. Beth Cooke had confided as much to her sister, only two weeks before her tragic, fatal accident. She had even set up an appointment with a prominent New Orleans divorce lawyer, but had died three days before the meeting.

Not, in Kristi's estimation, a coincidence. She looked again to her computer screen where the most recent image of Cooke was still displayed. It was another professionally crafted shot of him seated at his desk, leaning back in his chair, a tiny almost condescending smile playing upon his lips, his dress shirt unbuttoned at the collar, his sleeves rolled up. Behind him, warm pine walls were decorated in framed diplomas and awards.

As she stared at the picture, Kristi felt that same cold sweep of wariness she'd experienced when interviewing him behind the prison walls, that she was staring at a facade, that beneath the warm, friendly exterior was the soul of a cold-blooded killer.

Hamilton Cooke hated her. He'd made no attempt to hide his fury that he thought she'd betrayed him in her portrayal of him in her manuscript.

Reggie, of course, had threatened to sue after the book had been published and became a best seller.

He apparently had thought that only his interviews with Kristi would be included in the final draft and he'd objected vociferously to Kristi talking to his daughter and once-upon-a-time friends, along with his first wife's most trusted confidants and especially Beth's sister.

Upon receiving and reading an advance reading copy of Kristi's book, Cooke had gone ballistic, insisting that Kristi had twisted the truth, and made him appear in a bad light, by warping the facts and creating an aura of malice around him that was far from the truth. He charged her with irreparably staining his reputation and distorting who he was as a physician and a member of the community. In his estimation, her portrayal of him was light-years away from the image he tried so valiantly to portray.

But would he go so far as to attempt to murder her?

She wondered, still fiddling with the pen.

Hamilton Cooke was capable of homicide. No doubt about it. Despite the second trial jury's findings, Kristi believed Cooke to be an egomaniac, a psychopath, and a murderer who was cold enough to kill his own wife.

But was Jay's murder his style?

An attack on a street on a rainy New Orleans night?

It was one thing to off your wife in the privacy of your own swanky gated residence, another to hide in the rain-drenched shadows and slice with a knife in a very public spot.

That point bothered her. Though she believed the attempt on her life had been conceived and executed with thought—only the weather and Jay's arrival at the alley not part of the plan—the entire attack still seemed a little random, not as precisely executed as she would have expected from the uptight perfectionist that was Dr. Hamilton Cooke.

"Keep an open mind. You don't know what he's capable of," Jay's voice reminded her.

"Oh, what do you know?" she demanded. "You're dead. Right? A damned figment of my imagination."

She could almost hear Jay laughing at her consternation.

Almost.

But not quite.

She stood and stretched.

The kitten, who had been curled on a pillow near the window, opened one eye.

Kristi picked up the tiny bit of black fluff and heard Lenore start to purr. Kristi pressed her lips into the soft fur of the kitten's tiny head just as she felt a wet nose against her leg.

"Uh-oh," she said, glancing down and finding Dave looking up at her, his tail slowly swinging side to side. "Do you think you need some attention?" She set Lenore onto her pillow again, then scratched Dave's ears. "Yeah, I suppose it's your turn, eh? Maybe you and I should go for a walk."

The dog was on his feet in an instant, twirling in circles near the door.

Only then did she glance outside and realize that night had fallen.

"Great," she said under her breath, but she wasn't going to live her life in fear.

No way.

CHAPTER 18

Montoya knew that Abby was pissed.

He didn't blame her.

And yet, as he and Bentz drove back to the city, he couldn't help thinking that they were finally making progress, that what they'd learned from Cyrus Unger, CU, would finally put them on track.

Bentz, too, was pumped. He was driving faster than usual, thank God, instead of like an old man, and the lights of New Orleans were visible through the windshield. They'd already called in the license plate of the car CU had taken pictures of and had copies of everything on his camera's footage. Including the 2005 black Chevrolet Impala with out-of-state plates.

By the time they reached the station, Bentz half jogged to their office, Montoya just a few steps behind. "Now we're cooking with gas," Bentz said, as much to himself as Montoya as he kicked out his desk chair and switched on his computer. He was still eyeing the screen while calling to find out if they'd gotten an owner for the car that had shown up on the footage from CU's camera near the edge of his property.

The preliminary check had shown that Florida had no record of a 2005 Impala with the plate numbers listed, and on closer look, the tags had expired by a month. So the plates were stolen and placed on a stolen car as well—possibly switched. It was after hours, but Bentz called their guy who dealt with the DMV and cross-checked that kind of information. The call was short. "Still no answer," Bentz muttered, frustrated, and leaning back in his desk chair. "So our guy steals a car in Florida, switches the plates, and drives to New Orleans." He scratched his jaw where a silvery beard shadow was showing itself. "He must've left his own car there."

"If he had one."

"Or maybe the car was here and he brought the stolen plates back here to Louisiana, found a car, and stole it as well."

Montoya pulled up the image of the license plates again. "Maybe we've got it wrong," he said, enlarging the screen. "Take another look." When Bentz had come around and stared at the computer image, Montoya pointed to the screen. "Could one of those eights actually be a three that has been doctored? Painted to appear, at least from a distance, to be an eight?"

Bentz's eyes narrowed. His lips compressed into a razor-thin line. "Let's find out."

Montoya was already on the phone to double-check.

Sure enough, within the hour they had a hit.

"Bingo," Montoya said, pleased. "Looks like we have a winner, one Opal Guidry, original owner was her husband Harold. But the car isn't a Chevy Impala."

"So what're we looking for?"

"2004 Oldsmobile Alero."

Opal Guidry turned out to be a seventy-five-year-old woman originally from Tallahassee who owned that year and make.

Bentz was on the phone in an instant. He got hold of Mrs. Guidry, who knew the plate was missing and thought the plate might have been stolen here as she'd moved permanently to New Orleans a few months back. Possibly they had been swiped while she was at the grocery store or at the church she not only attended, but where she volunteered her time.

Bentz seized on that point and stared across the widths of their desks at Montoya once he'd disconnected. "The church," he pointed out, "is Our Lady of the Grove." His eyes narrowed. "Just a few blocks from Lake Pontchartrain and Dr. Sam's house."

"So you think Father John is using this place as what—his cover?" Montoya asked. "The guy's not a real priest."

"I know. But if anyone saw a guy dressed as a priest in the parking lot, no one would make note of it."

"Maybe not." But Montoya wasn't certain. Wouldn't a guy dressed like a priest, someone unfamiliar to the parishioners, cause attention? What about the real priests or the church secretary or someone?

As if reading his mind, Bentz said, "Remember Father John would only be around at night, most likely, trying to stay out of sight, especially from the other members of the clergy, right?" He was nodding to himself, a hard smile curving his lips. "We're closing in. I can feel it."

"Let's hope," Montoya said, though he still had doubts about Bentz's old nemesis being resurrected only to wreak terror on the citizens of New Orleans again. To Montoya, it didn't make enough sense to become a working theory.

Not yet.

He gathered his things, getting ready to head out. He'd missed Benjamin's bedtime again, but he'd be there if his son woke up in the middle of the night and would stay until Ben roused in the morning.

"Dr. Sam's last show is on Halloween. Two weeks from Friday," Bentz was saying as Montoya patted his pockets making sure he had his keys, wallet, badge, and phone. "Over that next weekend—in November—she's putting out her first podcast."

"You think Father John will call in before she signs off for good?" Montoya was already walking to the door.

Bentz didn't hesitate. Gave a swift nod, his expression grim. "Oh, yeah," he said, "I'd bet my badge on it."

It probably wasn't a great idea to be running alone on the city streets in the dark, Kristi thought, but the dog was already hyped and she needed to stretch her legs and clear her mind. Besides, it wasn't all that late, she thought, checking her watch. Barely seven, but the sun had started setting earlier.

"This'll have to be a short one," she said to Dave, heading downstairs and hearing his toenails click on the wooden steps as he followed. "And then we'll all have dinner."

Oh, God, she *had* to quit talking to her pets.

Just like she had to stop acting as if Jay were actually speaking to her.

She hated to admit it, but maybe Bella was right. Maybe she should start getting out, seeing people who were alive and start having real conversations!

"Good luck with that," Jay's voice came to her, but, for once, she ignored it.

Leaving the cat behind, she armed the alarm, patted her pockets to make sure she still had her keys, phone, and a small flashlight that doubled as a weapon with its sharp-edged rim around a light that nearly blinded it was so bright.

Then she and Dave set off.

Outside the air was clear, smelling faintly of moist earth, wet leaves scattered on the sidewalks, as she ran past other homes, windows glowing in the night, landscape lighting competing with the streetlamps. Cars came and went along the neighborhood streets, headlights flashing bright, taillights glowing a softer red. Nostalgia crept into her heart and mind.

She and Jay had jogged these streets together at night, sometimes stopping at their favorite bar for a nightcap, sometimes racing to the river, and try as she might, fit and fleet as she was, Kristi had always lost. "Next time," she always swore, breathing heavily near the bend in the river, sometimes bent over with hands on knees as she gulped in air. "Next time, Jay McKnight, I'm going to beat you." He'd always laughed and more often than not, drawn her into his arms to kiss her passionately before taking off and racing home again, letting her win and pissing her off even more. Then, once inside, another long kiss and with passion rising, they'd stripped, leaving a trail of clothes to the bedroom where they'd made love until they were spent. Her heart pounded at the memories and she jogged lost in a cloud of melancholy.

Never again, she thought, her throat swelling.

"It's okay, Kris. You'll be fine," he said, his voice ringing in her head. *"Remember me. But let me go."*

"I can't," she whispered. "Jay, we're going to have a baby."

"I know. And you'll be a great mom."

Would she? She wanted to argue with him, but came back to earth. He wasn't there. He would never be there. That voice in her head? It was her own, projecting what he would say, and she could listen to it, yet. Pretend for a second or two. But the voice in her head finally made sense. She had to let him go.

Casting aside her sadness, she ran past the wrought iron gates guarding Lafayette Cemetery, where trees rose above graying tombs, and she felt an unworldly chill, a breath of wind against the back of her neck. Ridiculous, she knew, as she glimpsed the tall trees rising high, branches webbing over the graying tombs that lined walking paths. Shuddering, she crossed Prytania Street and with Dave galloping gamely beside her, cut a new path, one she hadn't used before, a route that led her to the address she'd memorized and the tall house belonging to Hamilton Cooke. It, too, was secluded, hidden behind a tall brick wall, but she caught a glimpse of the mansion within, interior lights filtering through sheer curtains on the windows and piercing the filigreed posts of the porch to cast weird, woven shadows on the lawn. She paused, running in place, breathing hard, staring through the bars of the gate and upward to a second balcony and the French doors of an upper room.

The curtains shifted slightly and she realized someone was on the balcony, the tip of a cigarette visible, red and glowing, the smell of smoke seeping through the thick night air. A tall woman or a man? She couldn't tell, but had the feeling that she had been noticed and was being watched.

Dave whined and tugged on the leash and Kristi began running again, realizing that though Hamilton Cooke lived eight or ten blocks from her, the distance, as the crow flew, was much shorter.

So what?

No big deal.

Ten blocks or twenty, what did it matter?

She ran home at a quicker pace, only slowing when she reached the corner of her street. At the corner, beneath the streetlamp, she leaned over, hands on knees, and breathed deep, slowing her heartbeat as Dave strained on the leash, sniffing at the shrubbery that lined one yard. "Okay, okay," she said, and walked toward her house.

As the cottage came into view, her heart twisted. She remembered walking through the place when she and Jay had been looking to move from their apartment. "It's perfect," she'd told him as they'd walked through the rooms.

"You think? Isn't it a little small?"

"What? No! Look, you have an office and we can get a hide-a-bed or a Murphy bed for guests and we can convert that empty attic into kind of a loft/work space for me. It will be perfect."

"What about kids?" he'd asked.

"We'll figure it out. Oh, come on, Jay. We've been looking forever. This is the place!"

He'd laughed, run his fingers through his hair, then said, "If you're sure."

"I am! I love it!"

"Then we'll put in an offer!" And he'd wrapped his arms around her and spun her in the living room.

She hadn't lied. She had loved the house. For the few years they'd been here, she'd absolutely adored this little spot. A lump formed in her throat. But she'd loved the house because it had been theirs. Together.

"It's time to move on, Kris. You know what you have to do."

She walked the half block to her house and slowed at the edge of the yard, the grass sprinkled with leaves and a few sticks from the last storm. Hard as it was, she needed to pull herself together for the baby's sake. While keeping Jay's memory alive for her child, she had to get on with the rest of her life. Part of that might be moving out of the cottage. She and the baby needed a new start, a fresh beginning, their own place to make new memories so that she wasn't surrounded by the past and reminded of a future that would never be. She would have to find a house or condo or apartment that hadn't been invaded by the person who had taken her husband's life, the nutcase who seemed determined to terrorize her.

But, there was more.

Running away from the past and building a new future wasn't enough.

Somehow she had to unmask the unhinged prick who had killed Jay, bring him to justice, and purge him from her life, and then find a way to carve out a new life for herself and her child.

"I'll do it," she said to the night air. "I swear. I'll do it."

"That's my girl," she heard Jay say, but his voice was far away and faint. A whisper. As if he, too, were letting go.

She turned her head to reply to him, as if he were right beside her, and caught herself. He was gone. Of course.

"Get real," she whispered, and started up the walk, tugging on the leash.

It tightened.

Dave didn't budge.

Growled instead.

His hackles rose, hair standing straight up on the back of his neck and his lips curled as he stared, long and hard, across the street to the alley separating the neighbors' lots.

A little shiver raced down Kristi's back.

She squinted, saw nothing, not so much as a shadow.

But the dog gave out a low growl, his gaze still fixed on the dark alley.

"It's nothing," she said, as much to herself as the dog. "Come on."

He didn't move.

"Dave!" she said more sharply. "Come!"

Wait!

Did she hear something? A whirring sound?

Her heartbeat kicked into overdrive before she saw the bicyclist round the corner, reflective spokes whirling in the incandescence from the streetlamp, headlamp glowing like a demon's eye. She relaxed a little. The bicycle whipped past, illuminating the street in an eerie light and offering a quick glimpse to the alley across the street, where a dark figure appeared, only to blend into the night in a nanosecond.

What?

Had she really seen someone in that split second, a person dressed in a long black robe?

A priest's cassock?

Her heart stopped.

She took a step backward.

Blinked.

The person, if indeed it had been someone, was gone. Vanished. Darkness enclosed the alley again.

She swallowed. Searched the gloom. Saw nothing. Not the hint of movement. Nor did she hear the hasty retreat of footsteps, just the cool sough of the wind rattling brittle branches of surrounding trees and the faraway hum of traffic. But her throat was dry, goose pimples crawling up the backs of her arms. "Come on," she whispered to the dog, her voice tight. When he didn't budge, she gave a quick tug on the leash and he followed reluctantly.

Once inside, she threw the dead bolt, then disarmed the security system so that it was no longer in the "away" mode, but still would alert her if anyone tried to enter through a door or window.

"It's your imagination. That's all. You just freaked yourself out," she told herself, but double-checked the windows, doors, and closets, even under the bed.

She might have convinced herself except for the dog. Dave was still on edge, running into the living room window to press his nose between the blinds. She snapped them shut more tightly, unhooked his leash, then walked to the kitchen and poured herself a glass of water.

It was nothing!

But her heart was still pounding as she hung the leash on its hook near the back door and felt suddenly alone. She even thought for half a second about calling Jay before reality set in.

"This is all such bullshit," she said, her voice cracking.

Tentatively, the kitten peered out from behind the couch. "There you are." Picking up Lenore and carrying her into the bedroom, Kristi flopped on the bed and reached for the remote to turn on the TV. As the screen came to life, she opened the drawer of her night table, pulled out the claw hammer, and tucked it under her pillow.

Just in case.

The dog is a problem.

As I run through the darkened streets, I realize I should have taken that mutt out when I'd had the chance, but he'd been too fast, gotten away from me, and I had work to do and it had to be done quickly. I thought he might be lost forever as he took off like a shot and I couldn't risk chasing him down, or being seen. Besides I had work to do in the house.

But I'd been wrong.

And tonight, that damned cur had caught scent of me hiding in the shadows, had alerted her that I was there.

A stupid, stupid mistake.

I could have been caught and all the years of planning, the anxious nights, the second-guessing myself, and finally the attack at St. Louis Cathedral would be for naught.

I take the time to remove my cassock and stuff it into the case. Slowly I let out my breath.

Still I'm sweating, my breath coming in short bursts, but as I cross St. Charles Avenue, I slow, gather my wits, and make the sign of the cross over my frantically beating heart.

I can't afford to mess this up.

Too much is at stake.

I've gone too far.

So I'd had to flee, racing through the shadows, certain that the couple entwined in each other's arms in the parked sedan with its windows fogged had caught a glimpse of me.

But maybe not.

They'd been so involved, and the eye I'd seen, the woman's eye peeking around the head of her lover, might not have focused on me. Even if she'd seen me, it would be a blur and she couldn't identify me.

No way.

Or so I tell myself as I round a corner and slow as there is more traffic, more cars, more beams from headlights cutting through the darkness, more people on the street. It's not as if I haven't been a public figure. Here in New Orleans because of my history, my face is all too recognizable.

I must remember that in the future.

A man walking another damned dog, a huge beast with yellow eyes, teenagers laughing, arms linked, a mother pushing a stroller over the uneven sidewalk pass me by, and one of them could ID me. I have to be cool. Walk as to not attract attention.

Blend in.

Breathe.

I tell myself I don't look that out of place. This is New Orleans, after all, practically anything goes. People carry satchels and bags and briefcases all the time. No one knows what has been in mine.

Yet.

But they will. Oh, they will.

And very soon.

CHAPTER 19

Cruz Montoya glanced up and down the street, saw nothing out of the ordinary, no cop cars in the nearby convenience store lot, no obvious stakeout with plainclothes officers of the law watching the motel. He thought, for the moment, he was safe, so he quickly jay-walked across the two lanes of sparse traffic, then jogged across the pockmarked parking lot of the cheap motel he'd chosen on the edge of the city.

Three battered pickups, an old Volvo station wagon straight out of the seventies, and two dirty sedans, one with several dents and missing a taillight, were parked in the lot of the dive of a motel, the place he had called home for the last twenty-four hours. The nondescript L-shaped building had been built sometime in the previous century when cinder blocks, cement porches, and flat roofs had been all the rage. Once painted aqua, the facade was faded and dirty, home to drifters, himself included. He'd already checked the exterior and discovered where the two security cameras had been mounted, though he doubted either was in working order.

Cruz had already witnessed a drug deal going down behind the building and, he was certain, a couple of prostitutes with clients in the end unit. A young blonde and an older, weary-looking redhead, both of whom had approached him, the blonde more shyly, the redhead all business.

He'd declined in each case.

The fewer people who saw him, the better and, he figured, as he surveyed the place, all the other residents felt the same. Though each unit had a large plate-glass window, not one curtain was open.

No, those who took temporary refuge at the All-Day-All-Night Inn were of the same opinion, curtains drawn, doors locked, the only illumination coming from the corner office where a neon vacancy sign shone red and the interior was awash in an unworldly fluorescent glow.

Cruz unlocked the door to his room, stepped inside around his Harley to flop onto the bed. He'd pulled his bike into the room just to make certain no one caught a glimpse of it from the street. Though the idea of anyone looking for him here was remote, it wasn't impossible, and until he could figure out his next move, Cruz figured it was better to be safe than sorry.

That thought soured in his gut.

There was enough sorrow, enough regret already.

His thoughts strayed to Lucia.

He'd found her irresistible, not to mention, beautiful, happy-go-lucky, fervently religious but a bit naughty. As he thought about her, his jaw clenched, the scar over his heart tearing a bit. But he wouldn't go there. Not now. Not ever. What was done was very much done. Whatever part he had played in her death would haunt him for the rest of his life.

His cross to bear.

But first, he had to find out who had murdered her, what sick son of a bitch had set him up.

He unwrapped the pulled pork sandwich he'd purchased from a take-out barbecue joint down the street, then tore into it. It was good, the savory sauce had just the right kick, but he didn't really care. He just had to fill himself after the long journey on his bike and stretch out on the bed, saggy as it was. His body ached, his back sore from the endless hours of riding, some of the miles on smooth, straight interstate, others on twisting back roads when he'd felt it necessary. The important thing had been to keep a low profile, not cause anyone, especially a cop, to notice him.

So far, so good.

But his luck wouldn't last. He cracked open a bottle of Coke and took a long gulp.

He'd sold his original bike for parts in northern California, then bought this smaller, older Harley and started out cross country.

He'd made it to New Orleans.

And then his good luck had run dry.

What were the chances of finding Rick Bentz's daughter's dog in this huge city? He'd parked in a lot, stopped for a chili dog and a beer, and on the way back to his bike, run into the mutt who had been in and out of traffic.

And then he'd run into Kristi Damn Bentz, or whatever her name was now. She was married, he'd thought, having noticed the ring on her finger. Though he hadn't given his name to her, she had studied him, might even have recognized him as there was a strong family resemblance between all the Montoya brothers. And there was his belt. He shouldn't have left it with her as it was unique, hand tooled, his great-granddad's initials carved inside.

Stupid mistake!

He tried not to dwell on it, or the fact that Kristi Bentz with her tousled wet hair, flushed face, and bathrobe was sexy as hell. He'd heard once from his brother that she'd inherited her mother's good looks. Cruz didn't know the woman, but he could vouch for the beauty.

Not that it mattered.

But his brother might get the message that he was in town, and Cruz's being in New Orleans would matter to Reuben, he thought, taking another bite of the sandwich. He would have to come clean to his brother sooner rather than later because Reuben would soon realize Cruz had lied to him if he put two and two together, which was all very likely.

Reuben had always been a smart son of a bitch.

"Hell." What was he going to do about his cop brother?

There had been a time when Reuben had been more inclined to break the law than enforce it, but those days were long gone, and so somehow, Cruz had to get him on his side.

He finished the sandwich, wadded the greasy paper wrapper, and tossed it into the trash.

Could he trust his brother to help him rather than arrest him?

Time would tell.

Dinner consisted of frozen chicken nuggets she'd blasted in the air fryer, half an apple, and a bottle of vitamin water. "Not exactly gourmet cuisine," Kristi confided in Dave as he'd scarfed down a ration of kibble and two of her nuggets while the kitten picked at some kind of canned "tuna delight."

After leaving her single dish in the sink, she headed for the shower and, by the time she was out, towel-dried and in pajamas, most of her earlier worries had receded a bit. In the living room, she eyed the dying flowers, then tossed them all into the garbage, rinsed the vase, then flopped onto the couch with her phone.

Finally, she checked her texts, scrolling through, then saw one voice message from a number she didn't recognize. She listened to the taped message from a producer of a local news program inviting her to be a guest on their morning talk show as the author of the definitive book on the Rosary Killer. "Brenda thinks this would be a great opportunity for you to promote your book. She'd love to discuss it with you." Brenda Convoy was a reporter for WKAM who had worked her way up from a reporter at large to hostess of the morning show.

"Don't think so," Kristi said. She didn't feel up to pinning a smile on her face and talking about the killer she'd thought was dead and gone. And invariably the questions might turn personal, to the attack at the cathedral and the loss of her husband. Nope—not yet. Not when her grief was turning to a dark, simmering rage.

She thought of being assaulted.

Of the cryptic, evil cards.

Of someone invading her house.

Of Jay's murder.

Her blood boiled and she found she was gripping her phone so hard that her knuckles were white, her hand aching.

"You sick piece of . . ." She blinked back tears of anger and decided she had to do something.

Anything.

Don't get mad, get even.

The old quote ran through her mind as she headed up the stairs. *Think, Kristi. Think. Try and keep your emotions out of it!*

Of course that was impossible, but she gritted her teeth and told herself she would no longer be a victim. She would take the bull by the horns and be proactive. She'd never in her life run from a fight and had the scars to prove it, so yeah, she'd been handed a helluva blow with Jay's murder, but it was time to quit licking her wounds and find out who the hell was behind this—who left the damned cards? Who the hell wanted her traumatized?

Who wants you dead?

It's not just the cards.

Whoever is behind this attacked you and wants you dead.

"Not without a fight," she muttered, up in her office again.

She fired up her laptop.

Her father thought the Rosary Killer was behind Jay's death, had sent the cards with their twisted meanings.

She couldn't get her head around that theory.

Why would Father John return? Why would he target her? Not Dr. Sam, who had been his original and ultimate target? Had the bullet in the bayou changed his thinking? After all these years, having somehow survived a grisly near-death in the swamp, would he really show up in New Orleans again? Where had he been? Recovering and lying low—but for years? Or had he been incarcerated for another crime—no, if that had been the case, her father would have known about it, the police in whatever jurisdiction where he'd been captured would have gotten in touch with the New Orleans PD and the FBI if a known serial killer had been located.

The questions pounded through her brain.

And remained without answers.

None of it made any sense.

She thought about Montoya's theory that the killer could be one of the killers she'd written about, someone who was now free.

Who would hate her so much?

Who lived within the area?

She thought of the hate mail she'd received over the years, of the interviews that had turned sour, of the angry threats. One in particular, at the end of an interview, seared through her brain.

Ned Zavala, the Bayou Butcher, had glared at her as the interview had ended. A big brute of a man with stringy, dishwater-blond hair, deep-set small eyes, and crooked yellowed teeth that seemed too small for his wide face with its off-center nose, the result of a recent fight. He'd abruptly stood, towering over her, the table between them suddenly seeming minuscule. His hands had been cuffed, chained to the leg of the table, so he was hunched a bit, like a lion poised to pounce. He'd pinned her with his watery gaze.

"You better tell the truth, missy," he'd said, spittle gathering at the corner of his mouth. "You better stick to the facts. Don't you lie about me. My family's already fucked up, so don't you add to it."

She'd gathered her things quickly. "I just write the truth."

"Don't you twist it. Don't even think about it. Corrin. You look at my stepdaddy. He's the one who done this. Corrin Hebert. You talk to my ma. She'll tell ya!" His meaty fingers had opened and closed rapidly, as if he'd wanted to choke the life out of her. "You tell it straight or I'll come lookin'. Ya hear? And I'll catch ya. And, believe me, you won't like it when I do."

She believed him and had left the tiny, claustrophobic room as he'd yelled, "Jest cuz I'm locked up, don't mean I can't find ya. I got friends, y'know. Lots of friends. You cain't hide." His voice had taken on an oily, threatening quality and chased her down the hallway as she'd walked quickly down the locked corridor and finally out of the prison.

She already knew he lived in the area, in a small house on the bayou, the place owned by his mother, the woman who had changed her testimony and pointed her finger at her dead husband, just as Ned Zavala had predicted. And now, he was taking care of her as she was dying from some sort of cancer. At least that's what Zavala claimed.

However, as Kristi thought about the night she was attacked, the murderer cloaked in a wet poncho, she didn't think Zavala was the killer. When she'd seen him he'd been immense, a thick layer of fat over hard muscle. Her assailant hadn't been that big; she'd had no memory of bulk.

Zavala could have trimmed down over the years.

And remember his final threat. About his friends.

Still, it didn't seem right. Her book had been printed as Zavala had been arrested and convicted for the homicide. In the book Kristi had suggested law enforcement should take a hard look at him for the other women who had disappeared from the area over the years that he'd been a free man. Why else would the disappearances have stopped once he'd been locked away? So, she had to consider that

Ned Zavala was still carrying a grudge and was somehow triggered into attacking.

But why?

Because of the resurgence of interest in the case? Because during Murder Month on cable TV, the case of the Bayou Butcher would be available on cable and streaming?

The swamp usually calmed him.

The still waters and smell of the earth, vegetation decomposing, the sounds of insects humming, and fish jumping were balms to his nerves.

But not tonight, he thought as he polished the stones of his special rosary, handcrafted with love, dedication, and skill. The stones glittered a bloodred in the candlelight, the edges honed razor sharp.

Perfect.

Of course.

His radio was tuned to a classical station, but he'd change it soon. So he could hear her voice, the clear, dulcet tones of a jezebel, they called to him like a siren's song.

It had been years since he'd had serious contact with her—the murderess who had killed his sister. He'd sought to put an end to her before, and his attempt had ended badly, with him nearly dying. If not for the good graces of a man who poached alligators for a living and the healing powers of his wife, he might not have survived. The couple, always at odds with the law, had refrained from taking him to a hospital, nor had they questioned the bullet wounds in his body, for they themselves had a few hidden scars they'd received compliments of the local authorities. And the woman, Maizie, had believed him to be a true priest, a man of the cloth.

Their cabin, hidden deep in the swamp, downstream from where he'd been shot, had proved the perfect cover, a hiding space no one had found. The man had connections and secured himself a new identity in exchange for the work of smuggling poached alligators to butchers and skinners and tanners of the beasts' thick hides. He'd learned skills of healing from Maizie and from Willard, how to do trade in an underground community, to work the system from the shadows, to learn new skills that would only help him to reach his ultimate goal.

From the illegal alligator trade, he'd moved on, adopted several aliases, and roamed around the south. From Tampa and Jacksonville, to Richmond and other points north, he'd spent his years, but eventually, lured by that siren's song, he'd returned to New Orleans, and Willard and Maizie of course, paying them one last visit. And he'd found his way back to reside here, in a cabin built much like a child's tree house, upon thick gnarled limbs reaching over the water. The floor was uneven, planks nailed deep into the limbs, mosquito netting hung over the two windows. This was not his only place of residence, of course, but the one spot in the world where he felt completely free and unfettered, the place where he could let down his carefully crafted guard. The place where he could be himself. Glancing at the wooden walls where his disguises were hung carefully on pegs, he eyed the gray wig, the brown beard, the old man's suit pants and jacket draped over a folding walker. He had many disguises to go with his multiple personas for those times when he had to be out in public and couldn't risk anyone recognizing him.

He checked the time, still several hours before she was on the airwaves throwing out bogus, evil advice to strangers, people who called in to the station with serious problems, life-altering problems on which she spent two to five minutes, in between commercial breaks, handing out her own kind of witchcraft, the untested psychobabble of a would-be celebrity shrink.

It was hokey.

It was false.

It was all for show, for money.

And it was evil.

She needed to be silenced.

Forever.

And not just retired from radio land to the newer, more fashionable mode of a podcast where she could reach even more innocents. Oh, no.

He would do it, he thought, breathing on one sharp bead and polishing it until it shined bright in the candlelight. And at the same time, he'd get back at Rick Bentz, that dirty cop. Father John knew all about Bentz's sordid past, about his sins in LA, how he killed a kid, mistaking a toy gun for the real thing, before the New Orleans Police Department hired him. What kind of a detective does that?

Bentz had run Father John to the ground once before, but wouldn't get a second chance.

His jaw was so tight it ached. He could almost taste the sweet flavor of satisfaction when both Dr. Sam and the dick-wad cop were dead. He looked around his small lair, lit by candles, the sound of water lapping and mosquitoes buzzing, the night calming as he prayed for patience. He would bring her here to sacrifice her.

Her own home was far too dangerous.

Finally, after all the long years, she would pay for her sins.

In her own blood.

He rocked back on his heels.

First, though, he needed to play a little mind game with her.

Perhaps tonight?

He hadn't waited all this time to have it end without her understanding the extent of her sins, her knowing what she'd done, even if his patience was growing paper thin.

Just be patient, he told himself. He would lie low, wait for the final show, and then make his move.

Surprise them all.

Not just Samantha, but that dirty cop who'd dogged him forever, too.

And the woman who had profited off his story—the filthy cop's daughter.

Kristi Bentz had nearly died the other night.

But luck had been with her and she'd managed to escape.

That would never do.

Of course, her husband hadn't been so lucky.

Retribution, he thought, feeling the hint of a smile crawl across his lips. He stood and peered into the dark bayou and the wound that was healing in his shoulder.

Retribution would be his.

And it was long, long overdue.

CHAPTER 20

Late into the night Kristi researched the subjects of her books who now lived in New Orleans. There were few. Less than a handful. She looked again at the spines of her true-crime books and the one that caught her eye was *American Icon/American Killer*, the Mandel Jarvis story.

Once a pro football player, next a convicted murderer, and now a local televangelist. And he had found God in prison, even become a minister of some church that, because of his fame, had a solid following.

She pulled out the book and flipped through the pages, but she remembered most of the details of his case. Mandel had been a smart, charismatic, and athletic kid who grew up poor but had worked hard, the oldest of five brothers whose incredible skills as a defensive end in football had earned him a four-year ride to LSU and a third-round draft pick in the NFL. His pro career had just started to take off when it ended with a life-altering knee injury that no amount of surgery, rehabilitation, or painkillers could overcome.

He'd become a celebrity of sorts, showing up on a lot of talk shows, a fit, good-looking man who was featured in a few TV commercials and even modeled for a while. A recurring part in a television series introduced handsome, sexy, bad-boy Mandel Jarvis to a new legion of fans that he fed through the Internet and social media platforms. For a while, at least in New Orleans, Mandel Jarvis was everywhere and far more famous than if he'd continued his football career.

His incendiary romance with Filipa Petrovic, a gorgeous Serbian runway model, threw him into the international spotlight. The fact that Filipa hadn't quite gotten out of her previous marriage and was rumored to be pregnant with either her husband's or Mandel's baby caused the gossip seekers and their publicists to salivate while tabloid sales soared, and the ratings of entertainment news on television or the Internet whenever the couple was featured hit the stratosphere. Filipa and Mandel were everywhere, at least that's how it had seemed to Kristi at the time.

Filipa had managed a quick divorce and married Mandel in a very public ceremony on a Greek island. No baby was ever born, no mention of a miscarriage. Nothing about it, and Kristi suspected the whole "Is she or isn't she preggers?" had been part of a publicity stunt.

The marriage of Mandel and Filipa had been stormy from the get-go, rumors flying that the bride had experienced ice-cold feet and had wanted to bolt on the morning of the nuptials. Whether it was all just talk, or a carefully leaked story by Mandel's publicist, no one ever knew. Mandel and Filipa said their vows on the island with a thousand candles lighting the centuries-old church, Filipa gorgeous in a designer gown that showed, through a webbing of intricate lace, the entire slope of her back, her pale hair partially braided to fall in her signature loose, messy curls. Mandel, arrow straight, his shoulders wide, his waist narrow, was dressed in a black tuxedo, his smile mysterious, his dimple showing through beard shadow, his mocha skin gleaming.

And from that point on, the marriage had been rumored to be stormy, a union of two beautiful people with enlarged egos and more than a dusting of fame, a couple who regularly walked the red carpet and whose relationship was always on again/off again. It was grist for a rumor mill that kept grinding to keep the public interested. In the four years of their marriage there was constant talk of affairs and drugs, gambling debts and orgies. All the while two red-hot tempers were forever igniting.

It had all come to a head early one Sunday morning just before Christmas, when they had argued. The fight had escalated to the point that neighbors heard yelling and screaming, and a gunshot through the heart that had ended Filipa's life.

Mandel had admitted to accidentally killing her in an act of self-defense. He swore they struggled over her handgun and it went off in the fight. The gun, a Glock, was registered to Filipa. There was a record of her purchasing it the year prior to her death, but there had been questions about the actual firing of it. The prosecution's expert insisted the trajectory of the bullet, blood splatter, and gunshot residue did not support Mandel's claim, while the defense had their own celebrity expert who came up with a differing scenario.

In reading over the court transcripts and studying the evidence, Kristi believed Mandel Jarvis probably hadn't intended to kill his wife, but murder her he did during the heated argument that had turned so violent and eventually fatal.

Kristi had sifted through the evidence after the trial, then walked through the crime scene at the historical home in the French Quarter where the homicide had been committed.

Rick Bentz had been the detective who had arrested Jarvis and provided the evidence for the prosecution. Upon his conviction he'd sworn to get back at Bentz and anyone else involved in the "false arrest."

Kristi had written the true-crime book. Jarvis had threatened lawsuits against Kristi, her agent, the publisher, anyone he could name to block the publication of *American Icon/American Killer.* But the lawsuits had never materialized.

Jarvis had been found guilty of manslaughter, served four years of a ten-year sentence, and gotten out for good behavior. While in prison he found God, became a minister of his own church, and managed, through the help of his publicist, to spread the word outside the prison walls. By the time he walked out of the gates to a newfound freedom, he had a huge following of over twenty thousand believers. Today the membership of his church boasted more than a hundred thousand due to broad television coverage of a reformed sinner preaching the gospel, living the good life, and promising salvation.

Now Kristi flipped open the book to the midsection where photos of Mandel Jarvis filled the pages. Pictures of him from infancy, through childhood with his brothers, in college in full uniform, again as an NFL pro athlete, his disarming smile ever-present. Then shots of Filipa and the wedding on the Greek isle, celebrity head shots, some candid photos of the couple, and finally the police images of the bloody crime scene, a New Orleans mansion forever stained by murder.

She snapped the book closed.

In the nearly five years since his freedom was regained, Mandel had lost none of his swagger. He had married his current wife, a B-level actress with whom he'd been rumored to have been involved while married to Filipa. Despite his tarnished reputation or possibly because of it, Mandel Jarvis was still considered handsome and "cool," and today he maintained his innocence, that the cops set him up somehow. Today he was a major player in the community, preaching about God and police brutality and the corruption of the system. Despite finding the "path to heaven through Jesus," he still seemed filled with hatred for the police, prison system, and specifically Rick Bentz.

Worse yet, *American Icon/American Killer,* timed for publication just as he was released from prison, was a best seller and brought more attention to him, which he had turned to his advantage, using his fame or infamy to preach against sin, corruption, and the American legal system, all the while growing his congregation exponentially.

So would he, after all this time, still be harboring a grudge so deep that he would risk everything he'd gained—millions of dollars, a wife and son—for revenge? Was he deranged enough to think he could turn a second murder around to his advantage? Had he been lying in wait for Kristi and when things went sour, killed Jay either intentionally or accidentally? Besides, Mandel Jarvis was a muscular black man, who was just over six feet and about 220 pounds. She hadn't been able to see the attacker's face, nor skin tone, but she didn't think he was that size, not that heavy and certainly not that tall.

But she could be mistaken. The night had been dark, the rain a downpour, visibility practically nil. And she'd been freaked out of her mind, fighting for her damned life, concerned only about saving herself and her unborn child, not in her right mind.

She froze.

Thought about how she'd reacted that night, how intense her need to save herself and her child had been. She would have killed her attacker if given half a chance. Anyone would have.

Right?

And another thought struck her—what about one of his rabid fans? A loose cannon or a deadly minion? Some religious nut who thought he or she was doing God's bidding by attacking her? People were crazy these days, oftentimes starstruck and worse yet, fiercely loyal. They thought nothing of brandishing weapons—anything from knives to assault weapons—all in the name of a cause. She eyed the TV where Mandel had riled up the parishioners, all standing and saying praises to the Lord. Was it such a leap to think anyone of the thousands who were in the audience, either live in the church, or watching remotely on television or computer screens, would take up arms against the enemy of their presumed savior?

It was sick.

But a definite possibility.

She turned to her laptop and found a YouTube video of one of Reverend Mandel's shows. He stood at the pulpit, a handsome man in a light aqua suit, dark shirt and tie, and after a short sermon and prayer he came down to a main stage where he was backdropped by a group of musicians and a choir in crimson robes with silver stoles that glittered under the lights.

Music swelled, Mandel preached, and the choir sang, members swaying slightly with the beat. The camera panned the studio audience where the flock was on their feet, nearly dancing as they praised the Lord. It was an inspiring performance, but Kristi wondered if at least one member of the church's congregation could be a fanatical zealot with a homicidal streak.

Mandel had publicly decried Rick Bentz and the cops in general, and he'd never failed to mention that Kristi Bentz's book was all a fabrication, lies perpetuated by her father and glossed over by a publisher interested only in book sales, the bottom line, and best-seller lists. He'd called it a "continual travesty of justice" and each time he spoke, every time he was interviewed, any time he mentioned the "tome of Satan," book sales would spike and he'd be feeding the "greedy maws of hypocrisy, exploitation, and mendacity."

As she stared at the screen, she couldn't help but wonder if any one of the people watching the Reverend Mandel speak was a fervent believer and a killer.

Or could it be the minister himself?

She walked into the living room and peered out the window to the alley where she'd thought she'd seen the dark figure. No one was loitering. No one could get into the house, but she glanced around the room to the spot where the bouquet with the black rose that included the card had been. Now the space was empty. The police had taken the vase and blooms.

Who the hell had left them for her?

There had been no florist's card tucked between the roses, no printing on the tissue paper and cellophane, nothing etched into the vase, no identifying marks whatsoever. As far as she knew, no fingerprints had been found on the glass, but her father had insisted that there could be a trace of DNA or something on the card, on the vase, on the damned flowers.

Kristi doubted it.

Whoever had left the bouquet was a risk taker, someone bold enough to leave the vase on the porch, but that didn't mean he was careless.

Just determined, she reminded herself, and very, very deadly.

CHAPTER 21

The double doors to Our Lady of the Grove Church were open when Bentz pulled into the nearly empty parking lot. A thicket of live oaks surrounded the little church, while its spire needled high into the heavens where the sky was morning blue, broken only by the remains of a jet trail beginning to disintegrate. The gravel lot was nearly empty, but he spied an older Olds Alero parked near the raised porch.

Opal Guidry's car.

It wasn't alone. A dirty Dodge Ram pickup, once painted black but now sporting one white fender, sat at the far end of the lot near a gate to a small cemetery wedged between the back of the church and a park. The truck was old, the tailgate dented, the body muddy despite the ancient mud flaps behind the back tires.

Bentz killed the engine of his Jeep, grabbed his iPad, and crossed the space to the porch, his footsteps quick against the concrete steps. Inside, he paused, crossed himself from habit, and strode into the nave.

A small birdlike woman in a housedress was standing a few rows back from the altar, above which a huge cross was suspended. Her back was to him as she polished the back of the pew in front of her, and as she did the smell of pine wafted to him.

"Mrs. Guidry," he said, and she started, whipping around to peer at him with wide, owlish eyes covered by thick glasses, one hand flattened to her chest. "Didn't mean to startle you."

"Well, you did."

"Sorry. I'm Detective Bentz," he introduced himself, showing his ID. "We spoke earlier on the phone."

"Oh! Yes, yes." The hand over her heart fell away as she let out breath. "I didn't hear you. Of course. But, please, call me Opal." A tiny cross dangled from a fine gold chain and glittered in the hollow of her throat, and her teased white hair didn't quite hide the hearing aid tucked into her ear.

She dropped the oily rag she'd been using into a nearby bucket. "You're here about the car. I mean my license plates," she guessed. "My stolen plates." Her lips pursed into a knot of disapproval. "Who would steal them? I mean why? And here? Right out of the church's parking lot! At the Lord's house." She made tsking sounds with her tongue.

Bentz asked, "You know they were taken while you were here?"

"No. Well, not for certain, I suppose, but it's the only place where I leave my car unattended for any length of time and sometimes I'm here at night." Her eyebrows raised over the rims of her glasses. "Still, why would anyone do such a thing?" More tsking. "The world today." With a sigh, she ran her gloved fingers over the top of a hymnal in the book rack fastened to the back of the pew. "Let's talk outside," she said, glancing at the altar. "Not here. Not in the Father's house." Before he could respond she was yanking off her rubber gloves, stuffing them into her bucket, then moving swiftly, pushing up a padded kneeler and walking to the side of the nave.

He followed her past the stained tracery windows and out a side door to a grassy area between the trees. Two graying concrete benches were arranged near a fountain, now dry. "Here we go." She dusted off a few dry leaves and sat on the shaded side of the seat. "This is my husband's bench," she explained.

From the corner of his eye Bentz caught sight of a middle-aged man in jeans, a flannel shirt, and red baseball cap who was raking leaves between the trees of the park.

"Harold, he was my husband, may he rest in peace," she continued, bringing Bentz's attention back to her. Opal's smile was faint, as she dusted off the plaque that stated the bench had been dedicated to the memory of Harold Guidry. "I come here to talk to him sometimes. I know that sounds silly, but . . . We were married fifty-six years before he was called home." Again she sighed, her expression suddenly melancholy.

"Called home?"

"To heaven, of course." She adjusted the hearing aid and straightened her shoulders. "Now, Detective, tell me, what is it you want?"

"I was wondering if you'd ever seen this man," Bentz said, taking a seat next to her as he retrieved the photos of Father John from his pocket. "Anywhere. Maybe here. Or at your house? Even when you were out shopping?" He handed her the pictures, though they were all over ten years old. Included was the fake priest's driver's license picture, which was older still.

She eyed the photos, frowning, then slowly shook her head. "No—I—I really don't think so."

"Take a look at this," he suggested, and handed her his iPad. On the screen was a picture of Father John that had been enhanced with age-progression software. There were several pictures of his face, his hair grayer and thinner, deeper creases around his eyes and mouth. Bentz had also asked for head shots with more facial hair, a beard and a mustache, one with a goatee.

Opal swiped through the screen, studied each picture carefully, her eyebrows knitting over her glasses, her expression thoughtful. "I don't know," she said finally. "I don't think I've ever met this man, but"—she bit her lip and swiped back to the enhanced picture of Father John with a beard—"it's possible." She handed Bentz back his iPad. "Sorry. I wish I could be of more help to you. I really do. But"—she lifted her small shoulders—"I really can't say."

He'd expected as much. "Would you mind if I had someone look your car over? Check for prints?"

"Oh, no. Have at it. Anything to help."

"We would have to take your fingerprints as well," Bentz said, "for comparison and to rule yours out."

"Oh, I know. And no need to worry. Mine are already on file," she said, nodding. "I taught second grade for thirty-two years. And sure, that would be no problem."

"And you never saw anyone hanging around the car who shouldn't have been?"

"I already told the policewoman who called that I didn't. That hasn't changed." She fiddled with her hearing aid, answered a few more questions, and Bentz thanked her, then eyed the bench on the opposite side of the fountain. It, too, held a plaque, slightly burnished and dedicated to the memory of Marjorie Laroche, with the inscription, BELOVED MOTHER.

"Do you know anything about this bench?" he asked, motioning to the empty concrete seating area.

"Oh. Yes. That's for the Laroche family." Her eyebrows were knitting. "Well, it was. Beverly Laroche, while she was still married to Hugo, mind you, bought it. Actually, as I understand it, this whole area"—she motioned to the area where paths wound through the trees—"was gifted to the church, the archdiocese, I think, but she specifically wanted it to be attached to Our Lady, which makes sense."

"Who gifted it? Beverly?"

"No, no, Marjorie, she was a widow, Beverly's mother-in-law." Her lips pursed in disapproval. "Of course that was before he divorced her to marry that little tart Helene . . . Oh!" As if she realized she'd devolved into gossiping, she stopped suddenly, sketched the sign of the cross over her chest. "Yes. You're probably here because of, um, Helene's death as well. Poor dear." Opal cleared her throat. "Helene wasn't an active member of the church, and Hugo, he stopped attending mass years ago, but—"

She held her hands up and waggled them as if to disperse any remnants of her words that might be hanging in the air. "I—I didn't really know Helene and what happened to her was just awful."

"But the Laroche family is still a part of the congregation?" Bentz asked.

"I—I really don't know. I don't see them but, you know, I'm not here twenty-four/seven. I really should get back to work." She stood quickly.

Bentz knew the interview was over, so he handed Opal his card, asking her to call him if she thought of anything else that might be relevant.

"Oh, I will," she promised, then ran a hand lovingly over the bench as she stood and added, "I guess I'd better get going. Those pews won't polish themselves and I promised Father Anthony that I'd be finished today."

Again, Bentz saw the gardener, farther away, casting a wary look over his shoulder. And then it hit him. The man in the flannel shirt was none other than Ned Zavala. Older than Bentz remembered, but definitely the man who had been named the Bayou Butcher by the press. He saw that Mrs. Guidry, too, had noticed the man with the rake.

"Do you know him?" he asked.

"The gardener? Ned?" She shook her head. "Not really. His mother is a member and I think she got him the job." Her lips curled over her teeth. "And you don't need to ask. I know what he was accused of years ago." She gave an exaggerated shiver. "But that's all in the past and he was proved innocent. Right?"

"His mother recanted her testimony."

"Yes, yes, I know." She cleared her throat. "Whatever Mr. Zavala did—what happened—God will cast His own judgment." And at that she crossed herself.

"You know Ned's mother?" Bentz pressed as she took a step toward the church.

"Not really. I mean, I see her around. Or I did; she came to mass every once in a while. But she's sick, in bed for the most part. Cancer, I think." Again she sketched a quick sign of the cross over her chest and cast another furtive look over her shoulder, but Ned had moved through the trees to the small cemetery.

"How long has Ned worked here?"

"Um . . . maybe six months, possibly a little longer. I'm not sure. You'll have to ask Father Anthony."

"So Father Anthony hired Ned Zavala?"

"Yes, yes, I think so. I mean, yes, Ned started working after Father Anthony became the priest here. But that's all I know about it." She twiddled the cross dangling from the chain at her throat.

"How long have you known Father Anthony?" he asked, having already checked. The priest had come to Our Lady of the Grove nearly six years earlier, after nearly five years in Dallas, Texas.

"As long as he's been here. We had an interim priest after Father

Lucas left, but he only lasted a few months. Father Anthony has been here for . . . about five years, I think. Yes, that's right, it's going to be six years in February, I think. Yes, that's right, he came right as my Harold was passing, gave him last rites," she said, and her eyes looked past Bentz to a spot in the middle distance only she could see.

"I thought you lived in Florida."

"Oh." She came back to the present. "We did—you know, vacation home."

"And your car, the Alero, was registered there?" he asked, and checked to see that Ned Zavala was still raking leaves in the cemetery. The man in the flannel shirt was farther into the crypts now, but still visible.

"Yes, yes, bought it from a dealership in Tallahassee. Got a good deal on it, as it was a year old, used as a demo. Harold was proud of that, rest his soul." She crossed herself.

"And now you're a full-time resident?"

"Yes. Oh, yes. I couldn't keep up two places." She nodded. "After Harold passed. It was hard. He loved it there so, the fishing you know. But Father Anthony encouraged me to sell." She brightened at the mention of the priest. "He helped me through a hard, hard time, you know. Father Anthony is as fine a man as I'd ever want to meet." Bentz withheld judgment until he, too, met the parish priest in his office a few minutes later.

Father Anthony Creswell was seated at his desk, computer open, reading glasses perched on the tip of his nose, earbuds visible. His brown hair flopped over a high forehead and he looked up quickly when Bentz appeared in the open doorway. "Oh." Off came the bifocals, out came the earbuds, all dropped onto the desk. "I—uh—wasn't expecting anyone. Can I help you?" Closing his laptop in one swift motion, he stood, a tall, lanky man in jeans and a faded T-shirt, who looked more like an outfielder for the Atlanta Braves than a parish priest in his faded, ripped Levi's and T-shirt.

"I hope so." Bentz introduced himself and took the chair that Father Anthony had cleared for him.

"Sorry. Didn't expect anyone today," the priest said as he put the backpack and several books that had been on the folding chair onto a stool near the closet. His office was cluttered, books and papers scattered over the desk, a huge crucifix mounted on the wall behind the desk, a large window offering a view of the parklike grounds. A bookcase climbed one wall and opposite was a closet, the door hanging open, a long black cassock on a hanger and clerical collar hung on a hook just inside the door. "Now, Detective, what can I do for you?"

Bentz had the priest's full attention. Father Anthony sat, leaning forward, elbows propped on the scattered pages upon his desk, hands clasped together, eyes intent, expression earnest.

Bentz went through the same questions he'd asked Opal Guidry and offered up the same pictures, which the priest studied.

"Wow. Never seen this guy." Father Anthony was much more firm about it than Mrs. Guidry had been. He handed the iPad and pages back to Bentz. "Sorry."

"You're certain?"

"I know every parishioner, every traveling priest, and am usually aware when someone new comes into the church."

"But you don't have cameras on the parking lot or the porch or"—Bentz motioned with a hand to include all the surroundings—"anywhere."

"That's right." Father Anthony flashed a quick, almost humble grin. "We aren't a rich parish here, so we don't spend much money on frills—or extras. Besides, this is a house of worship, a sanctuary where everyone is welcome, no one is judged, and a place of peace. We don't need cameras or alarms."

Bentz wasn't sure of that, but changed the subject to Hugo Laroche. "His family belongs to the congregation."

For the first time since he'd stepped into the office, Bentz saw Father Anthony flinch a bit. "I'm sorry, Detective," he said, "but I really don't discuss my parishioners." He smiled. "We kind of have a private thing going, you know. Confidential."

"I saw a bench donated by the Laroche family."

"That was before my time here."

"Did you know Helene Laroche?"

"Of course." He was nodding, eyes guarded.

"And you know what she did on the side, that she was . . . seeing other men."

The warm smile had faded. "What I discuss with the parishioners is confidential, Detective. I'm sure you know that. What is said in the confessional, stays in the confessional, so to speak. Only God and I can hear."

Bentz noted how the priest fiddled with a letter opener on his desk—a stubby knife, then suddenly aware of it, set the knife down on a stack of unopened mail next to the wide ink blotter. Bentz leaned in closer. "You're a young man, Father. Good-looking."

The start of a smile again, but it froze as Father Anthony became aware of what was coming.

"Did Helene Laroche ever come on to you?"

"What?" He appeared shocked, but a telltale blush stole up the back of his neck, invading his cheeks.

"You know what I mean. It's kind of every Catholic girl's fantasy, right? Young, good-looking priest."

A muscle worked in Anthony's jaw. "I don't like what you're inti-mating. If you're asking if Helene Laroche ever flirted with me. Maybe. Probably. It happens." One shoulder lifted in a shrug as if it didn't matter, but his eyes turned steely. "That said, if you're asking if anything, and I mean *any*thing inappropriate happened, sexually or emotionally or whatever, I assure you that line was never crossed. Never. I take my vows very seriously."

"But she might not have," Bentz said, seeing he'd hit a nerve.

Anthony scraped his chair back. "I have a meeting, with a sick child at St. Ada's Hospital."

"What about Teri Marie Gaines?"

"Who?"

Bentz slipped a picture from his pocket and handed it to the priest.

Anthony studied the photo and shook his head, hair falling over his forehead. "No . . . I don't think so." He handed the snapshot back. "Should I?"

"She was killed recently. Same manner as Helene Laroche."

"Maybe . . . maybe I read about her, but I don't think we ever met. Not that I recall. Now—I really have to run." The priest stood abruptly, extending his hand.

Bentz shook it as he realized he'd run up against a brick wall, but he still had one more question. "You hired Ned Zavala?"

"I did." Father Anthony gave a quick nod, then went about shoving some books into his backpack.

"You're aware that he's an ex-con?"

Anthony zipped his backpack. "Yes, Detective, but again, in the Father's House I don't judge."

"His mother asked you to give him the job?"

Pausing, he let out a breath. "Eileen mentioned it when the previous gardener, Del Olsen, couldn't do the job any longer." He forced another one of his plastic smiles. "It turns out Ned is not only an excellent groundskeeper, he has all kinds of knowledge about local plants, but he's also a handyman. Which really works out. When it comes to fixing things, I'm afraid I have to admit that I'm all thumbs. A major disappointment to my father, who never met a leaking faucet or a broken gate that he couldn't repair." He flashed a grin. Again it didn't touch his eyes. "We're lucky to have Ned here at Our Lady. Now, if you'll excuse me, I really do have to get going." He walked to the closet and opened the door more fully, exposing the hooks where his clerical collar and cassock were hung, then waited as Bentz walked out, and the office door was shut firmly behind him.

But Bentz wasn't finished. He made his way to the cemetery gate and walked through. He didn't see Zavala at first, but as he made his way through the graying tombs and crypts, carved angels and images of the Madonna, and Jesus himself visible in the crumbling marble, he heard the scrape of metal against cement or rock over the soft sigh of the wind.

He rounded the corner of one tall crypt and found Zavala raking around a fountain where an angel stood, wings widespread, head turned heavenward. No water flowed at this moment, but the dark stains running from the angel's eyes made it appear as if she were actually crying.

"Hey." Zavala stopped moving, the tines of his rake no longer scratching the area around the fountain's pool. "What're you doin' here? I ain't done nothin' wrong."

"I saw you working. Thought I'd ask you a few questions."

"I got nothin' to say to you," he said warily. He was a mountain of a man, probably six-three and well over 250 pounds, Bentz guessed. Zavala's face was weathered, his eyes slits in a deeply lined face, his jaw covered in a blond stubble that matched the stringy strands of hair visible beneath his red hat. His plaid shirt was used as an open jacket not quite covering a hole-riddled T-shirt that had once been black but had faded to a dingy gray.

"Did you know Helene Laroche?" Bentz asked.

Zavala started raking again. "No."

"She was married to—"

"I know who she was married to. But I never met her."

"Not even at mass?"

"I said no!"

Bentz took that as a maybe. "What about Teri Marie Gaines?"

"Who?"

Again Bentz retrieved the picture of the dead prostitute from his pocket. "This woman." He extended the snapshot, but Zavala took a step backward and shook his head.

"Nope. Never seen her."

"She—"

"Again, I said no and I git where you're goin' with this, okay? I said, I ain't talkin' to you and I mean it. Not without my lawyer. You son of a bitch! You cost me years of my life! Years! I rotted in prison for somethin' I didn't do! Because you were too lazy to find out what really happened. And now I figure you're doin' it again. That's what you cops do when you don't have a real suspect. You come up with one and ruin his damned life, so just fu—" He glanced at the angel statue in the fountain and shook his head. "—so just leave me the H alone."

Bentz tried another tack. He mentioned the nights the women were killed. "Can you tell me where you were?"

"With my ma."

"Both nights?" Bentz said.

"Every night." His lips tightened, bits of his teeth showing. Small, yellow teeth in a massive face.

"You never left?"

"Ask her."

"I will, and if I find out you're lying—"

"You'll what?" Zavala demanded, his gloved hand tightening around the handle of the rake as he raised it from the ground. The lines on his face became grooves and his eyes seemed to glow with a quiet, hidden fever, a need.

Eyes on the rake, Bentz stepped to one side.

Zavala's jaw was set and he looked as if he might take a swing.

"Try it," Bentz suggested, goading him. Suddenly he was on the balls of his feet, itching for a fight. Let the bastard take his best shot! Large as Zavala was, Bentz was still quick, still worked out with a heavy bag and a speed bag five or six times a week. Urging the bigger man on, Bentz said, "Go ahead. See what happens when you attack an officer of the law!"

Zavala considered, the teeth of the rake pointed skyward, a tic showing near one eye. It was obvious it was all he could do to stop himself. Bentz sensed that if he just gave Zavala a little mental push, the guy would unleash.

"What is it with you and your mother?" he said, goading the gardener. "Maybe you two are in it together."

"What?" Fury leaped in Zavala's eyes.

"A little mother-son team?"

Zavala unleashed, swinging.

Hard and fast, the rake swept down.

Bentz caught the handle in one hand, the rusted tines a mere inch from his face. "Careful, Ned," he cautioned, every muscle tight as he held the gardener's angry gaze.

He'd hit a nerve.

Spittle showed in the corner of Zavala's mouth and he gnashed those tiny, yellowed teeth together as he tried to control himself.

"I get your game, Bentz," he spat. "You railroaded me once. I ain't gonna let it happen again!"

But he wanted to take Bentz down. So bad. Bentz saw the hatred burning in Zavala's eyes.

"Why don't you come into the station and have a chat?"

"And why don't you fuck yourself?" Zavala yanked his rake away, but some of the venom in his words faded. "You talk to my lawyer. You got his name."

"I do. And I will."

"Fuck you!" He spat then, a thin stream of tobacco juice arcing onto the ground.

Glowering at Bentz from beneath the brim of his red cap, he looked about to lunge again, and Bentz braced himself. Then Zavala said, "You know what, I git what you're doin' and it ain't gonna work. So just fuck the hell off." Sneering, he turned, then went back to cleaning the dry leaves and cones off the cement, the tines of his rake scraping like fingers on a blackboard as he worked.

Bentz didn't turn his back on the man as he headed back to the parking lot, didn't trust Zavala as far as he could throw him. The big man was a powder keg, just waiting to be set off.

Bentz wondered about that.

As he reached his Jeep he noticed Opal Guidry getting into her car. She glanced at Bentz, then quickly slid behind the wheel. Without another look in his direction, she hit the gas and drove out of the lot, nearly clipping a Camaro that was speeding down the street.

Bentz watched it all as he climbed into the warm interior of his Jeep, started the engine, and switched on the AC. Before backing up, he gave the church a final glance. Through the dusty windshield he caught a glimpse of Father Anthony standing at the window of his office.

How odd.

The priest had been so insistent he was late to a meeting at the hospital, and yet he'd taken the time to watch Bentz's exchange with Zavala. Now, however, Father Anthony was dressed in his black robe and clerical collar.

Bentz wondered about Anthony Creswell.

No way was the young priest the Rosary Killer. Bentz was sure of that much, because he knew Father John's true identity and that particular psycho wasn't a priest at all. On top of that the true Rosary Killer was older than the man standing in the window.

The thought of a copycat killer tickled his brain. Was it possible?

Father Anthony was young and strong. Surely physically capable of overpowering an unsuspecting victim.

And yet, Anthony Creswell was a true man of the cloth. A believer. Certainly not a murderer.

At least Bentz assumed as much.

There was a line from an old radio show that Bentz had often heard his grandfather quote, something about evil lurking in men's hearts. He couldn't remember the exact quote but it seemed appropriate now as he watched the priest disappear from the window.

"Who indeed," he thought aloud as he backed up, then put his Jeep into drive, pulled out of the gravel lot, and rubbed the back of his neck. He'd originally thought the recent killings of the prostitutes was cut-and-dried, that his old nemesis, Father John, had somehow been resurrected and was haunting the streets of New Orleans once again, but increasingly he was starting to believe it might be something more. Something more complicated. Something more sinister. Something he had yet to figure out.

He thought about Kristi and the attack against her, the murder of her husband and the notes left to terrorize her, notes he was certain Ned Zavala was incapable of creating.

But what about his mother?

And how did this all fit in with Father John?

He couldn't force the pieces of this ill-fitting puzzle together, no matter how he tried.

Frustrated, Bentz left Our Lady of the Grove with more questions than he had answers and only hoped Montoya had fared better. As his partner had suggested, they were following different paths, he on the Father John trail, Montoya trying to root out a separate psychopath who had brutally taken Jay McKnight's life and left Bentz's daughter a wounded widow.

He still believed that Jay's murderer was either Father John or a clever copycat, and somehow connected to his son-in-law's killer. All the evidence at the scenes of the murders of Teri Marie Gaines and Helene Laroche pointed to Father John, but so far Bentz had no real proof that the Rosary Killer had survived. If Father John wasn't responsible for the recent murders, then who? He felt heartburn begin to attack and reached into the console, found an opened roll of antacids, and popped two as he threaded his way through the traffic and drove past the lake, stretching wide, reflecting the sky and meeting the horizon.

He drove past Samantha Wheeler's house, saw that the gates were closed, and felt that he was missing something. Something important.

If Father John were really alive, why hadn't he targeted Dr. Sam? Why would he go after Kristi? Some kind of revenge move against Bentz for nearly killing him? Or Kristi for writing the book?

He rounded a corner, slowed for a jaywalker, and cracked the window, allowing the warm autumn air to flow into the interior.

Nothing was making sense.

Once again, he hoped his partner was having better luck.

CHAPTER 22

Montoya took a final drag of his Marlboro and stuffed the butt in an outdoor ash can near the entrance of the crime lab. One booted foot propped against an exterior wall, he let the smoke drift from his lungs into the clear morning air. Irritation bunched his shoulders and his eyes narrowed on the horizon. If he'd thought he would find any bit of discontent with Jay McKnight's work, or dig up a colleague who hated him enough to kill him, he'd been wrong.

He hadn't.

He'd just been crossing t's and dotting i's, covering every base in the investigation.

The only important bit of information he'd gathered was that there had been some blood collected at the crime scene. Some smeared against the outside of the walls of St. Louis Cathedral that hadn't matched Kristi Bentz's, nor Jay McKnight's. It wasn't even a matter of DNA as those test results hadn't been returned.

So now they knew that the killer had B negative blood, rarer than most and certainly different from the victims'. Montoya had requested medical records on Father John and hoped that there were some and that his blood type would be revealed. Then, at least, they would know whether the murderer who had been lurking at Pirate's Alley had been resurrected from his grave in the bayou all those years ago.

He pushed himself off the side of the building and found his car.

Once in his Mustang, he thought about another smoke. It calmed him and right now he was jazzed.

And so when his phone buzzed and he didn't recognize the number, he answered before he'd even started the Mustang. "Detective Reuben Montoya," and half expected his brother to be on the other end of the connection. He was wrong.

"Yes. This is Vincent Laroche," a deep voice said. "Hugo's son."

"Yeah."

"And I know we're supposed to meet at the department in an hour or so, but . . . Hell. Look, I was wondering if we could speak in private. About my stepmother."

"You have something private to say?"

"Yeah. I think it would be best if we meet somewhere before I connect with my family at the station."

"Where? Your place? Office?"

"No . . . no, oh, God no. Could you meet me at someplace less . . . public?"

Montoya didn't like the sound of that but started his car, glanced in the rearview, and waited for a van to pass before he eased onto the street. "Where?"

"How about on the Riverwalk near the steamboat station? There's a bench there, overlooking the river."

"Sure."

After Vincent Laroche gave more specific directions, Montoya headed to the river and parked not far from the old JAX Brewery in the French Quarter. Once an actual brewery, the huge building had been converted into shops, restaurants, and individual residences. And it was far from private, but Montoya got it. Here, they would blend in with the crowd and obviously Laroche believed that no one would recognize him. Montoya made his way around the building and saw the bench.

No one there. His cell phone rang again. Same number.

"Hey," he answered. "I'm here."

"I know. I can see you."

What? Fuck. Montoya's cop radar went up.

A little late.

"I've got a condo in the brewery." He gave the address. "Come in."

Montoya bristled. "I don't like being jerked around."

"I'm not. Seriously. I'm just being careful."

"Okay."

But he texted Bentz the address and told him if he hadn't heard from him in five minutes, to show up. Then he turned the recorder of the phone on. Just in case. If everything turned out to be cool, he'd turn it off. If not, Bentz would hear everything that went down.

He headed into the building, took the elevator to the third floor, found the unit, and with one hand on his sidearm, rapped on the door with the other.

The door opened quickly, Vincent Laroche on the inside, a tall, lanky man in a baseball cap, three-days' growth of beard shadow where bits of silver were visible, shorts, a T-shirt, and flip-flops. "Detective Montoya. Thanks for coming here. I'm Vincent. Vince." He swung the door wide and Montoya looked inside, saw that they seemed alone, there was nothing out of the ordinary, nothing that appeared dangerous, so he let his hand drop from his service weapon once he'd stepped inside.

"I'm sorry for all of this . . . you know, the secrecy and cloak and dagger stuff," Vincent said, and Montoya noticed that he smelled like a brewery, as if he were actually sweating beer.

"I thought you didn't want to meet at your home."

"I don't. And this isn't."

"Then what?"

"Just another place I keep."

Again, Montoya swept the condo with his gaze. Nothing out of the ordinary in the modern, sleek apartment with an oversized TV, sectional, and small dining table. The door to a bedroom was open and he noticed the corner of what appeared to be a massive bed. Windows stretched along the one wall and offered a view of the river, sunlight glinting on the slow-moving water, and in the kitchen, several empty bottles of Bud stood like soldiers on the counter near the sink.

"Look, I know we don't have much time. I'm scheduled to get to the station with my family and lawyer and . . . Have a seat." He motioned to the couch.

"I'm good." Montoya stood with his back to the wall, able to see all of the doorways. Just in case he missed something. The meeting didn't smell like any kind of ambush, but it didn't smell right.

Vincent Laroche was agitated, had something on his mind. "Okay," he said. "So here's the deal. I'm hoping this conversation is confidential and that it can be avoided later."

"What conversation?"

"About Helene," he said nervously, and scratched his beard. "My—um, my step—my dad's wife." He walked to the window, seemed to study a boat passing on the Mississippi. "She and I . . . well, we knew each other."

"How?"

He sucked in his breath. "I knew her before she got involved with Dad."

"Knew her how?"

"She was tricking. We hooked up and saw each other a few times. I think, well, I know, she heard about Dad from me and she set her sights on him." He lifted his hat from his head, rubbed his hair, and turned to face Montoya. "And then he, you know, got involved with her, divorced Mom, and they were married. Like in less than a year. It was wild. Crazy." Tossing his hat onto the coffee table, he shook his head and appeared beyond distressed.

"And what did you do?"

"Nothing! Watch it go down! Like a goddamned dirigible—a blimp on fire!" He flung up his hands and made an exploding sound deep in his throat. "Ka-Boom! I mean, it was so, so wrong."

"It wasn't working out?"

"What? No! There was no chance of it. Helene married Dad for his money and connections, you know, because he was cool, I guess, a big-time philanthropist, society guy or whatever." He walked to the kitchen, opened the refrigerator door, and pulled out a beer. "You want?"

"No." Montoya held up a hand. "No, thanks."

Vince cracked the bottle and took a long swallow.

"So about Helene," Montoya suggested.

Vince took another swig. "So, she and I, we like, never really broke it off, y'know?" He slid a glance in Montoya's direction. "It just kind of—you know, kept going. We stopped for a while, right before the wedding, but then, after a month or two, once she and Dad got back from their 'honeymoon'"—he made exaggerated air quotes—"well, she kind of came on to me and one thing led to another and then it went on. Hotter than ever and I figured you might find out, but I don't really want to rub it in Dad's face, y'know. He might have suspected, but it was never said, and so why bring it up?"

"It'll probably come out." Helene Laroche as Helen of Joy's death was already high profile and gaining ground in the scandal sheets and gossip platforms. All the old dirt about Hugo dumping his wife for a stripper was resurfacing.

"I know, but I'd rather break it to the family myself. Marianne—she's gonna blow a gasket."

"Did Helene have any regulars?"

"Besides me?" he asked, eyebrows arching. "Who knows?"

"Did she know a woman named Teri Marie Gaines?"

He shrugged. "I don't know. If she mentioned her, I don't remember." He let out a sigh. "It's not like we did a lot of talking, you know what I mean?"

Montoya got it. He asked, "So when was the last time you saw Helene?"

"Last week. The night before she died." Vince motioned toward the bedroom. "Here."

"And did she seem different? Was anything bothering her? Anyone give her trouble?"

"Not that she mentioned. As I said, we, um, we didn't talk a lot."

"What time did she leave?"

"Two-thirty, maybe a quarter to three in the morning."

"She had a car?"

"Yeah. Her Mercedes. In the parking lot." He rubbed the back of his neck. "Look, I'll tell Dad about this. I will. Today. But for now, can we please keep my sister out of it?" He threw back his head and squeezed his eyes tightly together as if imagining Marianne Laroche Petrocci coming unglued. "Just please, let me handle it."

"You'll make a separate statement?"

"Yeah. But not with the family. I think that's weird anyway."

"Unconventional," Montoya admitted, "but it's not that you all were called in; this was a meeting your father's attorney wanted."

"Yeah, yeah, but you wanted to talk to me anyway."

"Of course."

"Okay. It'll happen. Just so we're cool."

Not really, but Montoya had a recording, not that he could use it. In fact if anyone knew about Vince's statement without being read his rights, the whole thing would never see the light of day in court, but before Montoya erased it, he wanted to be assured that Vincent would actually make a statement after the meeting with the Laroche family.

For now, he took his leave.

He climbed into his warm Mustang, rolled down the window, and headed back to the station. As he drove away from the waterfront he wondered if he'd just been fed a line of bull. Was Vincent Laroche telling the truth, or trying to make an end run around the investigation? He'd know soon enough as the meeting with the Laroche family was scheduled in less than an hour. At the first light he was still thinking about Vincent Laroche being involved with his stepmother. The case was getting weirder and weirder, the entanglements beginning to knot.

His cell rang, and from habit, he answered. Ever since Cruz had called him a few days ago, he hadn't ignored any calls to his private number, and because of the fact he knew Cruz was or had been in New Orleans due to the belt he'd left with Kristi Bentz's dog, Cruz would probably soon resurface.

Or at least Montoya thought so. "Detective Reuben Montoya," he said into the phone.

"Oh, well, yeah. Good."

"Who's this?"

"Don't matter."

"Then this conversation is over," Montoya said, though it was a lie. Somehow whoever was on the other end of the line had his personal phone number.

"No—no! Wait. Look." The voice was male, not young, not old. "My name is Jazz."

"Jazz?" Montoya repeated. What kind of a name was Jazz? Probably an alias.

"Jazz who?"

"I said, it don't matter. Look, I'm callin' 'bout Cruz. He's your brother, right?"

"What about Cruz?"

"I'm a friend of his. And I just want to say, he didn't do it. I seen who did and it wasn't Cruz."

"Wait a second. What's your name again and where are you calling from?"

"I told you and I'm not sayin'. I just want you to know that Cruz didn't do it."

"Didn't kill Lucia Costa?"

A pause. As if the caller had been stunned at the use of Lucia's name, shocked that Montoya knew about Lucia and her death. And then a sharp beep behind Montoya made him aware that the traffic light had turned. Pissed, he turned on his dash flasher, making it known he was a cop.

Whoever was behind him in the black Buick backed off.

"I'm asking you, Jazz," he said into the phone as he hit the gas again, "are you saying that Cruz didn't kill Lucia Costa?"

"Yeah, yeah," Jazz said, recovering. "That's what I'm tellin' ya. Cruz was set up. To take the fall."

"The fall?" Montoya repeated, his eyes narrowing as sunlight bounced across the hood of his car. "For whom?"

"Hey, man, that's all I'm sayin'."

"Where is Cruz now?"

"Don't know. Don't wanna know."

"Can I get back to you at this number?" Montoya asked.

The fucker hung up. Quickly, Montoya called back, and—big surprise—got no answer. *Damn.* He'd try to locate the guy, but he knew in his gut that "Jazz" or whatever the hell his real name was had called on a burner phone and even now that cell was probably at the bottom of a river, maybe the damned Trask River.

"Shit." He saw the pack of Marlboros on the console, grabbed it, shook out a filter tip, and lit up. After taking a deep drag, he crushed the pack in his fist. This is how it always was with Cruz.

Never easy.

Always trouble.

Though that trouble usually didn't involve homicide.

"Son of a—!" Montoya tromped on the accelerator and, with his light on his dash still flashing, drove straight to the station.

CHAPTER 23

Montoya strode into the office, kicked out his chair and dropped into it, the smell of smoke from a recent cigarette clinging to him.

"Bad news?" Bentz asked.

"Is there any other kind?" Montoya muttered, then recounted his visit to the crime lab. "So once we hear back on the Rosary Killer's blood type, we'll most likely know if he killed Jay McKnight. It's not a hundred percent, of course, we won't have that until the DNA test results come back, but this will be a strong indicator. In my mind, we'll know. B neg was left at the scene. It isn't all that common."

"So if we find out Father John is B negative, it only means he was possibly there," Bentz said, then added, "Probably."

"We'll see."

"Yeah." He brought Montoya up to speed on what he'd learned at the church.

"So back to the Laroches."

"Right." Bentz glanced at the clock. "They should be here any minute. Coming in with their lawyer." And he'd no more said the word, than he got the call that the Laroche family had arrived. He glanced at Montoya. "Showtime."

"Good." Montoya didn't smile, just got to his feet. Yeah, he was bothered. Big-time. And whatever was eating at him wasn't explained by what he'd learned at the crime lab. Bentz got it. He didn't have to be a rocket scientist to put two and two together; whatever was bothering Montoya was personal and most likely his brother. Again. As he climbed to his feet and grabbed his jacket, Bentz said, "By the way, I took a call. Detective from a county in Oregon. He wanted to talk to you, but when you weren't here they asked for your partner."

Montoya tensed, his face turning to granite. "What did they want?"

"For you to call them back."

"You didn't give them my cell?"

Bentz shook his head. "Figured you could do that." He pulled out the notepad, ripped off the top page, and handed it to his partner.

Montoya glanced at the scribbled note, a muscle working in the corner of his jaw. He stuffed the message into his pocket. "Come on," he said, striding to the door. "Let's do this."

Five minutes later they were inside the largest of the interview rooms and it was crowded.

Bentz and Montoya sat on one side of the table.

On the other side: Hugo Laroche, and his attorney, Alan Thayer. Hugo's children were on either end. This was their meeting, one they'd requested, insisting on coming in together, refusing to be split up, and for now, Bentz decided to hear what they had to say. If he wanted to interview anyone separately, he'd schedule another time.

Marianne was as vocal as ever. Her brother, Vincent, who was a younger, more fit version of his father and obviously quieter than his sister, wore a dress shirt and slacks. Clean-shaven and expressionless, he answered every question asked him, succinctly and emotionlessly, his hands in his lap. Vince's eyes were a little red as he met Bentz's gaze evenly and calmly, while Marianne, true to their first meeting, was as loud and accusing as ever. In the background, through the door, noise drifted in, the sound of saws and nail guns, men shouting, now and then a burst of laughter, all muted, but distracting a bit.

After the quick introductions and Bentz explaining that, as yet, they had no suspects in her stepmother's homicide, Marianne leaned back in her chair, her arms crossed over her chest. "So you're telling me that you have no new leads on Helene's murder."

"The investigation is ongoing," Montoya said.

"I thought you knew who it was, this . . . this Rosary Creep. What was his name?"

"Father John," Vince supplied, still calm and unmoved.

"Right. It's been all over the press. You can't turn on a local station without someone bringing up 'Father John,' and his resurrection from the swamp or something like that. I've seen pictures of the victims from way back when and now . . . now you can't find him?"

Montoya said, "We don't know it's the same—"

"Are you kidding me?" she said, and actually stood.

"Marianne," Alan Thayer said reproachfully. "Please sit—"

"What? Sit down and shut up? Well, no thank you, Alan. I want answers." She jabbed a finger at the tabletop, her rings glittering under the harsh light, her bracelets jangling. "These people came into Dad's house and practically accused him or me or Vince, here, of having something to do with Helene's death." She let out a huff, and as the attorney was still holding up his hand to silently ask her to sit, she plopped back into the chair. "We need answers."

"She's right," Hugo said. "The press have been camped outside the house and I've been contacted not just by friends but by other people on the board of two of the charities I'm attached to. They're . . . Well, they're uncomfortable having the Laroche name attached to them."

"Big surprise! You marry a psycho tramp, some kind of nympho, and it all comes out and what do you expect?" she asked, glaring at her father.

Vincent said, "Marianne, just—"

"Just what, Vince? Huh? Just shut up?"

He cleared his throat and a little flush climbed up his neck. "I couldn't hope for that," he said, glancing at Montoya, "but let's just hear what the detectives have to say."

Marianne rolled her eyes. "I've heard it and it hasn't changed."

"Marianne," her father intoned.

"Oh, God, you're all against me and that's just crazy! We're all on the same side." Then she sent a scathing look at the detectives, indicating that they—the cops—were the enemy. Why was that? Bentz wondered as she ranted on. "Look, we want this wrapped up. Dad's right, it's not good for us to be in the middle of this media circus involving hookers and priests and . . . ugh." She gave an exaggerated shiver. "It's . . . it's too bad about Helene, but there it is. We all have to deal with it. We'd just like you to release the body so we can bury her and move forward."

Hugo visibly winced at her statement, but the attorney didn't interrupt her, and for once, it seemed, emotionless Vincent was in agreement with his sister. He finally asked, "What about Helene's roommate? She had one, right, a place she shared with another woman? I—I read about her. Sherry something-or-other."

"Sherilynn Gordon," Marianne supplied, and glanced at her father. "You know her, right, Dad?"

"We've met."

"Ooooh-kay," Alan Thayer said, slapping his hands on his knees and standing. "Do you have any more questions for my clients? Because if not, we all have places to be. And Marianne's right. The family would like Mrs. Laroche's body released so that we can schedule a service. ASAP." He glanced at Hugo, who nodded his agreement.

"It should be soon," Bentz assured them, as the evidence had been collected, the autopsy finished. "Possibly as early as tomorrow."

"Good!" Marianne said the word, but skepticism was written all over her face; she thought they were being played.

"Let us know." Thayer was scooping up his briefcase. The meeting was over. As Marianne and Vincent scooted back their chairs, Hugo remained seated, his face seeming longer than ever, the lines in his cheeks more pronounced. "Just get him," he said quietly. "Whoever did this to Helene, get him."

"Oh, Dad," Marianne said, her shoulders slumping. "Don't make this into some kind of sad, star-crossed lover thing, okay? This isn't Romeo and Juliet for God's sake. Remember, we're talking about Helene here. Helen of Joy." She cast him a sorrowful glance and then, shaking her head, headed out the door, whispering "Jesus" under her breath.

Montoya escorted them out and Bentz headed back to his office. He'd just sat down when Kristi appeared in the doorway. "Hey," she said, "you got a sec?"

"For you?" He rolled back his chair, smiled up at her, and winked. "Never."

She actually grinned as he waved her into one of the side chairs wedged between the two facing desks and the wall. "What brings you down here?"

"I thought I could buy you lunch."

That was odd. He felt his eyebrow shoot upward. The grin had disappeared and she looked suddenly tired.

"Sure," he said. "Let's do it." He was already on his feet and grabbing his jacket. Once in the hallway, he ran into Montoya, filled him in, and then walked out of the building and three blocks to a little bistro where, at two in the afternoon, they were still serving lunch.

They took a table outside, in an enclosed patio where palm trees in huge pots offered shade and lights had been strung overhead, for the evening crowd. Now the sun was out, bright enough that they each wore sunglasses as they ordered. Bentz decided on a hamburger basket, she a plate of deep-fried prawns, fries, and a salad. A waitress brought them each a sweet tea after they were ordered.

As they were waiting to be served, Kristi seemed to gather herself. "I have something to tell you."

His gut tightened as he braced himself. He expected her to explain that she'd gotten herself into some kind of trouble again, or that she was falling apart because she'd been suddenly thrust into being a widow, or that she was deathly sick—cancer or something.

She shoved her sunglasses onto the top of her head and her eyes were shimmering with tears. But she was smiling and took his hand. "I wanted us to be alone when I told you."

"Told me what?" He was still worried.

"That you're going to be a grandpa," she said, and for a second he didn't know what to say.

Then, still stunned, he said, "But—"

"In the spring. A baby is coming." Tears spilled from her eyes to run down her cheeks. "Jay—Jay didn't know."

"Oh, honey." Springing from his chair, he nearly knocked over the table as he reached her and, bending down, gathered her in his arms. "Oh . . . oh, Kristi. A baby?" And he felt his own eyes becoming hot and wet. Was she serious?

She was nodding. "Yeah. I didn't know it, but—" She sniffed loudly and laughed. "I'm gonna be a mom."

He gave her a squeeze and tried to process it all. A child? His daughter was going to be a mother? As well as a widow. He finally released her as she blinked and wiped her eyes with one of the napkins on the table.

"I know . . . weird, huh?" Then she added. "Well, what isn't these days?"

"Are you okay? Happy?"

"Yeah." She nodded rapidly. "Oh, yeah!" Then she said, "Are you?"

"Of course." He grinned widely and settled back in his chair, then dabbed at his own wet eyes. "It's unexpected. A shock, I guess. But yeah. Wow. A baby." The waitress came then, bringing their meals, interrupting further conversation, and Bentz didn't admit what he really felt, that he was worried sick, even more so now that he knew about the baby. The phrase *Now you're vulnerable* entered his thoughts, but he had the good sense not to mention it. She knew. It was written all over her face, and though he wanted to caution her, to come up with all kinds of paternal wisdom, for once he held his tongue. This wasn't the time.

Instead he hoisted his glass of sweet tea up and encouraged her to do the same. They clinked rims. "To the baby, and ever-growing family."

"To the baby," she said, and for the first time since Jay's brutal death, Bentz saw his daughter smile, her eyes shining with hope along with her tears. His heart squeezed with new fears for the as yet unborn child. "But," he added as he picked up his hamburger, "just so you know, I'm much too young to be a grandfather. Much too young."

Walking to his car in the late afternoon sun, Montoya punched in the number of Detective Wyatt Strange of the Tillamook County Sheriff's Department and waited. He'd already checked the guy out, found out he was legit, and decided he had no choice but to return the call.

Strange picked up on the third ring. "Detective Wyatt Strange."

"Detective Reuben Montoya, New Orleans Police Department. I'm returning your call."

"Oh, yeah . . . Montoya." The guy had a west Texas accent that didn't sound anything like Oregon. "Hey, we're lookin' for Cruz Montoya, and found out he was related to you."

"That's right. Why are you looking for Cruz?"

"I'd like to ask him a few questions. We've got a homicide up here, body found near the Trask River way up in the mountains. Rugged country. Lucia Costa. We think Cruz might be able to help us find out what happened to her."

"He's a suspect?" May as well cut to the chase.

"No suspects, at least not yet. Just a person of interest. Could be Cruz was the last one to see her alive. He might know something that would help us in the investigation. You know where he is? How I might reach him?"

Montoya couldn't lie to the guy, but he wasn't about to give his brother up. Luckily, he didn't know where Cruz had landed. He glanced at his great-grandfather's belt, coiled like a snake and mocking him as he walked a thin line between the truth and lies. "I got a call from him a couple of days ago. Said he was in the Mojave outside Las Vegas, that he was in some kind of trouble—didn't say what it was—and that he was heading east, probably here, to New Orleans. Nothing more."

"Has he called since?"

"No."

"Did you call him back?"

"Yeah. No answer. Kept trying. Now the phone number is out of service."

"Can you give me that number?"

"Sure." Montoya didn't hesitate. He was dealing with the law, for one thing. For another? He was certain Cruz had gotten rid of what was no doubt a burner phone. "Let's see. Here ya go." He rattled off the digits and wished to high heaven Cruz would contact him again.

"Got it. If you hear from your brother, have him get in contact with me," Strange said. "ASAP. As I said, this is a homicide case."

"Will do."

"Thanks." Wyatt Strange ended the connection, which Montoya found odd. He thought the Oregon detective would have a lot more questions for him about Lucia Costa. Montoya had known her most of his life. Her family and his—they'd all grown up together. Then again, Strange probably had all that info. What he wanted was Cruz.

"Join the club," Montoya muttered under his breath. "Join the fuckin' club."

CHAPTER 24

"We'll go later," Kristi promised the dog as she started for the garage. She was already late if she wanted to get to the Newcomers' Worship Event at the New Faith and Glory Church of Praise near Kenner. Dave followed her to the door and she gave him a pat. "Sorry, bud. Hang in. I'll be back in a couple of hours."

She double-checked the alarm and closed the door behind her. Once in the car, she didn't give herself a chance to second-guess what she was doing, just backed out of the garage and drove westward. Her cell buzzed and she saw Bella's name appear on its small screen.

"Hey," she said, using the speaker option.

"Hey." Bella sounded down, which was unusual.

"What's up?" Kristi slowed at a crosswalk when the light turned amber. A bicyclist shot through the intersection and a Prius swerved to avoid the collision. "Wow," Kristi said, her heart racing.

"Wow what?"

"Nothing. Just nearly witnessed a bad accident." The light turned green and Kristi, still jangled, hit the gas.

"Oh . . . okay." Bella sounded distracted.

"Is everything all right?"

"No—um, that's why I'm calling."

Immediately Kristi thought of Sean, Bella's husband, who had a roving eye, and when he had too much to drink, got more than a little handsy. Her fingers tightened on the wheel as she accelerated onto the freeway.

"I'm hoping you'll agree to the TV interview. There, I said it."

"What?"

"I hate to pressure you, Kristi, you know I do, but this is really important and the producer of *Bonjour, New Orleans!* keeps pushing me. She knows we're friends and the story about the Rosary Killer is hot and . . . and really, things haven't been going well at my job."

Kristi glanced over her shoulder, eased into the fast lane, and sped around a white Buick moving ten miles below the speed limit. "What do you mean?"

"Just that. I'm up for review and this, landing you, would be a help."

"I don't know what an interview with me would do with ad sales for the station."

"Oh, come on. More interest, more viewers, more sales. Look, I loathe having to call you, but . . . if you could help me out, I'd like love you forever and I know Renee-Claire would love it."

Renee-Claire Morgan being the host of *Bonjour, New Orleans!*

Kristi saw a sign for her exit and again switched lanes. "Okay, fine. I know I'm going to regret this. But I'll do it." She was already mentally kicking herself as she drove off the freeway.

"Thanks!" Bella breathed. "You're a lifesaver."

"I don't know about that. So when is the interview?"

"Tomorrow."

"What? Wait. No. I need some time."

"Oh, Kristi, please. All you have to do is show up. The producer's assistant has already been in touch with your publisher. She's dealt with the publicity department before and they've already sent materials."

That didn't sound right. Usually the department contacted her *before* any appearances were scheduled. "How did that happen?"

"I don't know, something about your agent, I think."

Zera.

Of course.

"She was supposed to contact you. Anyway, Kristi, we're all set to go! So if you could be at the station at eight tomorrow morning . . . ?"

Kristi's anger burned through her. Her fingers clenched over the steering wheel and she wanted to tell her friend what she could do with the proposed interview. But then she thought about all the times Bella had been supportive, how, especially since Jay's death, her friend had tried to help, to be a sounding board, to try and get Kristi out of the house, and Kristi had rebuffed her, been a lousy friend in return.

"If I agree, then never again, okay? You won't pressure me."

"Right. Right. I know. I know. I swear."

"Okay, I'll be there," she said, and didn't add "under duress" or "but you'll owe me" as Bella had already paid it forward. "I'll see you then." And she disconnected, already regretting her decision. She hit speed dial for Zera's number, but it was after hours in New York and her agent didn't pick up. Kristi left a blistering message and then disconnected.

The sun was sinking low, dusk approaching, as she located the church and pulled into a spot near a streetlamp two blocks down.

"You can do this," she said, giving herself a pep talk as she turned on the recording app on her phone, making sure it could take down everything from her light purse. Then she crossed the lot, clicked the remote to lock her car, and walked into a white brick building fronted with a long, covered porch. On one side a square tower rose to a blocky steeple topped with a spire and cross.

Kristi stepped inside to a wood-paneled vestibule and a sign that read: WELCOME TO NEW FAITH AND GLORY CHURCH OF PRAISE. An elderly woman with dark wrinkled skin, thick glasses, and gray curls handed her a pamphlet. Her eyes narrowed. "Are you a newcomer? I don't think I know you."

"Just checking things out."

"Well here," she said, and handed Kristi a thick packet of papers. "This is information on the church and a short form that we ask you to fill out." She smiled, her top teeth edged in gold. "The reverend, he likes to know who comes in."

Does he? I'll just bet, Kristi thought, but said instead, "Thank you."

"Now you go on in," the old lady whispered. "Take a seat anywhere. The service has just begun." Then she turned her attention to another latecomer and Kristi slipped through a second set of double doors. Silently, she slid into a pew near the rear of the nave. The church was nearly full with parishioners packed onto the smooth wooden pews. Up front the preacher was welcoming everyone, "newcomers and members who have been with us since the beginning."

She watched and felt that the service was as much a show as a religious observance.

Mandel Jarvis was in his element. Still tall and striking, his physique not much changed from his days as a college athlete, his smile just as wide, he wore a light gray suit, black shirt, and lavender tie, and as the doors to the nave closed he led the congregation in a prayer asking the Lord to accept "new and old alike, bless us all." Then upon sending up the prayer in Jesus's name, he looked up and asked the choir to sing. The musicians took their cue, started playing, and after a short intro the choir, in golden robes with white glittering stoles, joined in, filling the church with music as they swayed, nearly dancing on their risers.

People around her started singing and Kristi took up a hymnal and found the right page, though she only pretended to sing as she observed the congregation. Old, young, from all walks of life, it seemed, a diverse group who appeared to adore their leader. He spoke and they listened, raptly, even children, and his voice boomed over the choir when he sang, his hands uplifted to the rafters, his smile seemingly genuine and truly touched by God.

He had everyone in the palm of his hand and he knew it.

His devotion seemed real; she remembered that he'd been an actor, if only briefly before the slaying of his wife. She recalled the high-profile case against him, and as she did, she caught his gaze, saw that he was focused on her.

Her throat went dry, but she stared back at him, refused to be intimidated. Mandel gave a little nod, as if to let her know he'd seen her, then without skipping a beat, spoke to the congregation at large and the newcomers in particular, asking them to take Jesus into their hearts, to join the congregation, to take this first step onto the long, beautiful staircase into heaven.

Near the end of the service, he brought up his wife, the woman he married not three months after Filipa's murder and before he'd been arrested and charged, as the investigation had hit a couple of snags and other potential suspects were weeded out. His second wife, Chandice, had, too, been a model. Originally from Jamaica, she was a statuesque woman with perfect skin, a sexy smile, and intelligent eyes. In a shimmering green dress, she along with their three stepping-stone children joined him at the front of the church and, the entire group smiling, sang the Lord's praises together. The two boys in suits that were identical to their father's, the six-year-old missing a front tooth, the eight-year-old hanging his head until his father touched him on the shoulder. Then he straightened, stood military erect. The youngest, a girl who looked barely two, sported curly pigtails with pink bows that matched her dress. Mandel picked her up and held her as the music started again, and over the introduction, he said, "Friends, come and join me in praising the Lord." And then the choir began singing and he, his wife, and children joined in.

Was it real?

Or all for show?

If Mandel Jarvis had all this—an ever-growing congregation where he was idolized, enough money to live an extravagant life, a loving, healthy family, then why would he, all of a sudden, risk it all to attack her and kill Jay?

Psychotic is psychotic. There is no reasoning process. Don't be fooled!

Kristi had seen enough, and as the hymn came to a close, she looked for the nearest exit.

"Friends!" Mandel said again, louder this time, and when Kristi glanced at the altar again, she found the preacher staring directly at her. Hard. His smile was still in place, his daughter held tight, as he said, "And may we all ask the Lord for his blessing, may all our sins, old and new, be forgiven. May we step away from the past and all the darkness and temptation." His eyes held Kristi's. Dark and intense, his gaze seemed to drill into her soul. A plea? Or a warning? His voice boomed. "May we step forward into the future and the Light. May we *all* follow in Christ's blessed footsteps!"

A chorus of "amens" rang through the nave, and after another prayer and the collection plate being passed, he slipped through a door and returned in a black choir robe to lead the last song while his family returned to their seats. After a final prayer the service was over.

Kristi waited no longer. She hurried out of the double doors and felt Mandel's eyes still on her as she fled—as they had been for the last several minutes of the service. Even through all the good words and shouts of "hallelujah" and "amen, brother," she'd felt a deep-seated animosity and hatred emanating from the pulpit and aimed directly at her.

Outside, night had fallen. Streetlamps glowed and above them she spotted a plane as it rose to the heavens from the nearby airport. Its lights were blinking, the roar of its engines audible over the hum of traffic on the interstate.

Get a hold of yourself!

She took deep breaths and told herself she was imagining it all.

Yet, the questions still dogged her. Was he angry that she'd dared step into his sphere? Or was it deeper? Had he, a family man, ostensibly a man of God, really taken the time to craft notes with Bible verses and leave them to terrorize her? Had he lain in wait for her in that dark alley next to St. Louis Cathedral and attacked her and then turned and used his knife to kill Jay? Physically, he would be capable of murder. But emotionally?

Remember Filipa!

"Hey!" a male voice yelled, and she turned to spy Jarvis jogging rapidly toward her. He ran easily, an athletic gait that belied the fury that knotted his facial features. "Hey. Wait!" In that moment, seeing the black choir robe billowing around him in the night, she froze. Memories of the night in the darkened alley by St. Louis Cathedral flashed through her mind, blazing in bright, angry frames:

She was running through the sheeting rain.

Seeing someone approaching.

Hearing Jay's warning shout.

Catching sight of the glint of a blade.

The agony of pain.

Jay's startled cry.

The roses . . . the roses . . . all around them.

"Kristi Bentz?" Jarvis said, jolting her back to the present. He wasn't even breathing hard, no sweat dotted his brow. "What are you doing here?" His dark gaze bored ruthlessly into hers.

"I came for the Newcomers' Night."

"Sure." He didn't believe it. Glanced back at the church. "Look, I don't know what you're up to, but whatever it is, just stop."

"I thought everyone was welcome."

His lips flattened. Rage sparked in his eyes.

"Look, whatever your game is, it's over. Got it?" His teeth gnashed and then, as if realizing he was showing a face he didn't want seen, he took a deep breath. In that moment a calmness came over him. "I know what happened to you. Read all about it. Saw the reports on TV. And . . . and I'm sorry about your loss."

Now it was her turn for disbelief.

"I wonder where you were that night."

"What?"

"The night I was attacked."

"Oh, this is unreal," he said, throwing up a hand, his temper flaring. "You never give up. Wasn't it enough that you lied about me before? That you threw my life in turmoil and then, just when things had died down, published your damned book and profited from it, once more putting me through hell. And now . . . and now it's all in my face again. That pathetic, fake, twisted TV movie is being aired again." He threw up a hand, looked up at the sky, and let out a deep breath. As if to calm himself, he closed his eyes as his big hands clenched and opened, clenched and opened. Finally he turned back to her. But he hadn't been able to calm himself. His eyes were slits—malevolent, angry slits. "When will it end, huh? When?" he demanded, his lips barely moving. "How dare you come here, to my place of worship?" The reverend was so angry that he was jabbing at the sidewalk with a finger. "So you just leave me alone. You hear me? Leave me the hell alone and stay away from my family!"

"Your family?" she repeated.

"You heard me! Stay away."

"Or?"

"You don't want to know."

"Are you threatening me?" she asked, her own anger rising.

"You're on my turf now," he warned, his eyes glittering in the dark.

"God's turf, I think," she reminded him.

"Watch yourself, girl," he warned. He was starting to walk away in an easy, straight-back stride, but turned to face her, and though his eyes sparked hatred, he flung out, "Have a blessed night."

"Yeah, you too!" Sarcasm dripped from her words.

As she unlocked her car, she reminded herself to be careful, not taunt him or bait him into an attack.

In her mind's eye she saw the scene in the alley at St. Louis Cathedral again. The rain. The dripping poncho. The glinting steel of a knife. Her stomach curdled at the thought. "Dear God," she whispered as she slid into the driver's seat, started the car, and pulled away from the curb. In her rearview she caught a glimpse of the church, the doors flying open, light spreading onto the steps, people flooding through the doors. Good, solid believers flowing into the parking lot, laughing and talking, and all filled with the love of Jesus.

Because of Mandel Jarvis and his family.

For a second she felt not only foolish, but shamed that she would even consider him a suspect.

Then she remembered his first wife.

Filipa had been shot.

Mandel Jarvis could appear to be a man of faith, a family man, a pillar of the community, but he still was, in Kristi's mind, a cold-blooded killer.

"A baby?" Olivia said, a small smile curving her lips as she sat down on the couch, on the opposite end, her legs over Bentz's. He'd come home for dinner and to see Ginny, who was now off to bed, the smell of grilled chicken from dinner still lingering. "Kristi's going to have a baby. Wow. And that makes you—?"

"A grandfather, I know."

"And Ginny?"

"Don't even go there." He couldn't think that his daughter, about to turn one, would be an aunt in the spring. It was mind boggling.

"I was going to say they could be great friends, more like cousins."

There was a twinkle in her eyes that he usually found irresistible, but not tonight. No, this night he was bothered and he didn't want to think how unconventional his family was, all the bloodlines tangled, nothing quite as it seemed. Kristi wasn't even his biological daughter, not that it mattered. He'd raised her as if she was. And now she was pregnant with her dead husband's child.

"Wait. You're not happy about this?"

"Of course I am."

"But—?" She started to sit upright, but he grabbed her calf, massaging the muscle.

"What do you mean, 'but'? She's a widow and will become a single mother, she was almost killed and her husband was, not that long ago. She's getting disturbing notes and some douche bag has been in her house, terrorizing her. Of course I'm happy that she's going to be a mother, I just wish . . . I just wish that for once she would catch a break and she'd have a normal life."

"A normal life?" Olivia said with a chuckle. "Is there such a thing? What do you call normal, the old fantasy about a house with a picket fence, fully employed father, mother at home with two point five kids and a family dog, maybe a cat for good measure?"

"You know what I mean," he grumbled. That was the thing with Olivia. She could see things others couldn't. When he'd first met her, he'd thought she was a kook with a capital K. Turns out the insight he'd scoffed at had really existed and he'd fallen in love with her, head-over-damned-heels. As he rubbed her leg, he remembered that as twisted and messed up as their family was, it was theirs. Uniquely theirs. He only wished it didn't have to be so rough.

"Is there anything wrong with wanting the picket-fence thing for your daughter?" he asked, and she laughed again, a sound that still warmed his heart.

"'Course not. But reality is—"

"What it is, I know. I just wish I could make it better."

"Oh, you do." Her eyebrows knitted in consternation. "You know that, right?"

"I try."

"All you can do, Grandpa," she said, teasing, her lips curving into a taunting smile.

"Grandpa? I'll show you Grandpa." He captured her leg then and as she giggled, rolled over on her and caught her lips with his.

"Promises, promises," she breathed into his mouth, and then kissed him back. Hard. Wanting. Willing.

And for the next few hours, he forgot about the evils of the world and lost himself in her.

Over the sound of crickets chirping and mosquitoes humming, he listened to his radio, hearing the familiar strains of an old song. "Midnight Confessions." The original song was old—over half a century—and yet she played it, some homage to the past, he figured, and the name of her show that started during the witching hour, just as the clock struck twelve.

Fitting, he thought, as water lapped softly beneath this tree house.

Lying on his hammock, suspended over the bayou, he listened to the smooth, calm intonation of Dr. Sam's voice. She was signing off forever in about a week. Tonight, she mentioned it again as she asked those of her listeners who were in need to call her, those asking for her advice. After that, she would be hosting a podcast.

He felt the bitterness rise, bile roiling in his stomach, the bitter taste of her malignant prevarication in the back of his throat.

She needed to be stopped.

He flicked a look over to the peg where his cassock and cincture band draped down the pinewood wall.

Not tonight, he told himself, though he itched to don the robe and feel the clerical collar around his neck. It would be too risky. However, wasn't risk a part of the game? And besides, he couldn't stop himself, felt compelled.

So he picked up the phone he'd stolen, one for which he knew the password, and climbed off the hammock, hearing the nails on which it hung creak a bit as he stood. He'd boat through the swamp, to the spot where he'd hidden his car, and then he'd drive to another place, twenty miles away, make the call, then drop the cell into the water and make his way into the city.

He couldn't pass up the opportunity.

Don't do it.

It would be foolish.

They will be waiting for you.

Bentz will be waiting for you.

Stick to the plan.

Stay the course.

Wait, damn it!

But, despite all the warnings clamoring through his brain, he stepped down the rungs of an old ladder built onto a sturdy tree with thick branches that hung over the water, and dropped lithely into his waiting craft. It rocked slightly as he landed and he quickly untied its mooring rope, grabbed an oar, and began navigating the still, black waters of the swamp. He felt unseen eyes upon him, the creatures of the night watching from the shore, or those more deadly, peering just over the surface of the water, the gators' eyes catching in the glare from his single light, mounted over the prow. Some were huge, massive creatures with sharp-toothed jaws longer than a man's arm, others smaller, still deadly, and staring at him with hungry fascination as he glided past.

So intent was he on his quest, he was heedless of their interest or intent, barely noticed the mosquitoes who wanted to feast on him, was unwary of the snakes coiled in the limbs of cypress trees as he passed below. He refused to listen to the alarm bells clanging through his head.

He paddled on, his oars dipping into the water, the canoe skimming through the bayou, the clink of rosary beads in counterpoint to the deep tonal notes of a lonely frog. A dark, slithering shadow slid past, just beneath the surface of the water. He watched it move, so silky, so strong, so deadly.

He kept stroking.

Sculling.

Moving silently.

No creature of the night would deter him.

No human would stop him.

Not even Detective Rick Bentz.

Especially not that fucker.

CHAPTER 25

D r. Sam felt more than a twinge of nostalgia as she took the last calls of the night. For the most part those who had phoned her at the station were wishing her good luck, telling her how much they enjoyed the show, a couple having regaled her with how her advice had helped them over the years, still others saying they would miss her as they'd listened for years, that hers was the last voice they'd heard before closing their eyes for the night.

So tonight the show had been upbeat, only two serious calls. She'd talked one teenager into seeking professional help as she was dealing with an ex who hadn't been able to accept the breakup and was to the point of stalking her. "Tell your parents, make them talk to the police, even if he's underage, and never be alone until he gets the message and gets help," she'd said, before offering a little more advice and wishing the girl good luck. The other was a man who had lost his partner and was grieving, embarrassed that he'd never come out to his family and acknowledged that he was in love with Gary before he'd passed on. Again, she'd suggested groups the caller could meet with and asked him to have faith in his family's love.

The final call before her sign-off came in. Every call was screened, and through the glass of the soundproof booth, she caught the tech's eye. Jeff, a red-haired twenty-eight-year-old forever wearing a slouchy beanie, caught her eye and gave her a thumbs-up as he put the call through. Information flickered on her computer monitor: the caller's first name—Stacy—then the caller's phone number, and in the final field, a short message indicating what the caller wanted to discuss. In this case it was much like most of the others: Thanks and good luck, Dr. Sam.

There was just enough time for this last quick conversation and then she would sign off. The closing music was already playing lightly in the background.

"Hello, Stacy," she said calmly. "What do you want to talk about tonight?" But instead of a woman's voice filtering through her headphones, she heard a deep male voice, one she instantly recognized, and one that caused the hairs on her nape to stand on end.

"Hello, Samantha," Father John said in a chilling tone that seemed to reverberate through her brain. Her breath caught in her throat and she nearly gagged. "Remember me?"

"What the—?" Bentz stared at his radio as if it had grown ears. He heard Father John's voice clear as a bell. The same bass tone he would recognize for the rest of his life as he'd listened to the recorded calls that had come into Dr. Sam's show all those years ago, when the fake priest had rained terror and caused chaos in the city. He yanked off his headphones and rolled out of bed, waking Olivia.

"What's going on?" she asked groggily, blinking awake.

"Work."

"I know—I figured that, but . . . ?"

"Father John's called in to the station. Dr. Sam's show."

"What? You mean—?" She was starting to wake up.

He was already stepping into jeans and a pullover. "Just what I've been telling you for the past months. He's back. That mother—he's back." Bentz found his keys and walked to the closet, punched in the private code of the wall safe before retrieving his sidearm.

"Where are you going?"

"To the radio station."

"Didn't it sell?" She scooted up in the bed, the old T-shirt she'd taken to wearing to bed outlining her breasts.

Tonight he didn't care.

"This was one of her last programs."

"Oh, yeah." She was nodding, the back of her head rubbing against the headboard as the cobwebs cleared in her mind. "You told me about that."

"So I gotta go." He was stepping into his running shoes.

"When will you be back? Oh, never mind. Sorry, I remember." She slid down the headboard and plumped a pillow. "You don't know."

"That's right."

"Keep me informed. Text me."

"Will do." He didn't even bother kissing her, was out the door, calling over his shoulder to have her reset the alarm, as he stepped into the garage and climbed into his Jeep. That son of a bitch was alive. All these years. But Bentz had known it. Deep down he'd never been satisfied that Father John's body had never been recovered. That whole eaten-by-alligators theory had never really stuck with him. And the second he'd stepped into Teri Marie Gaines's apartment, seeing her dead body with the telltale pattern of tiny cuts around her neck where a rosary had been used as a garrote, he'd been convinced.

Montoya and all the other doubters could just eat crow.

As the garage door rolled up, he told his Bluetooth to call Montoya, but before the call connected, his partner was calling him. As Bentz connected, still backing out of the drive, Montoya said, "I heard."

"You were listening?"

"Of course. I'm on my way to the radio station."

"Meet you there."

Speeding through the near-empty streets, Bentz wondered where the psycho was hiding. Somewhere near Our Lady of the Grove, he thought. Despite what Father Anthony had told him, Bentz had done a quick Internet search of the parish, seen pictures of the priests who had been associated with the parish over the years, none of whom was close to looking like the Rosary Killer. He'd even gone so far as to use the computer to age old pictures of the psycho, but still none of the priests came close to height, weight, or age of the murderer who had supposedly died in the bayou.

Though New Orleans was rumored to be always awake and had more than its share of night people who thrived on the music and bars of the French Quarter, tonight was quieter than usual. The denizens who normally spent the early morning hours drinking and laughing, dancing and exploring the darker corners of Bourbon Street seemed to have decided to stay home or had gone somewhere else. Tonight things seemed quieter. Calmer.

Traffic was light and he pulled into an empty spot near the ware-house where the radio station was located. A patrol car, lights flash-ing, was parked near the entrance, the cop within Kate Donahue, barely more than a rookie, who had already secured the building, though if past experience proved true, Father John was not inside. "We're clear," Donahue said as Bentz made his way to the booth where Samantha Leeds Wheeler, aka Dr. Sam, was still seated at her desk.

"You were right," she said, ashen faced, eyes round with fear, fin-gers rubbing together anxiously. "He's back." She was nodding to herself, staring at a computer screen where a display of all the callers into the program—their names and numbers and reason for their call—was visible. "I'd know that voice anywhere," she said in a whis-per. "He's definitely back, and he hasn't forgotten." Then she looked directly into Bentz's eyes. "And neither have I."

"Okay, I did it," the whore said, and he could tell that she was ner-vous. Twitchy. In her sky-high stilettos, short skirt, tight low-cut T shirt, and jewelry—too much costume jewelry from her bangly bracelets, huge hoop earrings dangling from her earlobes, and ultra-wide beaded choker. Faux pearls, he guessed.

Cheap.

Like her.

"Is there anything else you want, Father?" She asked the question tentatively, obviously worried after she'd called the radio station to get through. She'd connected to WKAM and then he'd taken the phone and left his message with Dr. Sam from the car parked here, in the dark alley, the engine of the old Impala running.

He couldn't tell if she was just the nervous type. She had eyed his cassock and dark glasses warily when she'd gotten into his car at that fleabag of a motel, seemed uneasy about having sex with a man of the cloth. Or maybe it was worse. There was more than a small chance that she'd heard on the news or through the whore grape-vine that the Rosary Killer had returned. She was too young to have heard of Father John, been a grade school kid when he'd become fa-mous and supposedly died in the swamp. Yet she was nervous to be with him, definitely nervous. She might be new to the business,

surely didn't have any of the hard edges he'd associated with prostitutes.

Good.

All the better.

"Yes," he said in a well-modulated voice. "There is definitely more
I want, but not here." He put the old car into drive, eased out of the
back alley behind the boarded over shrimp-processing factory that
had been out of business for years. They were close to the river, here
in an industrial district that would probably soon be gentrified like so
much of the city. But for now, the streets were empty, a few old ware-
houses shoulder to shoulder, the girders of a new building knifing
upward, like some giant erector set, all illuminated by old streetlamps that hummed and spread pools of dim light on the scattering
of vehicles parked on the uneven pavement of the street.

"Where?" she asked tremulously. "Where do you want to go?"

"Don't you have a place?"

"N-no." She was shaking her head, her small face shadowy in the
faltering light from the dash. "My roommate . . . no."

She was lying, of course, and her fingers moved toward the door
handle.

"Why don't we call it a night," she said uneasily. "The call was a
freebie. Just let me off at the corner." She pointed toward the intersection.

"Not yet," he said, and saw the terror mounting in her eyes as he
tromped down on the accelerator, the old Impala taking off like a
shot.

"Hey! What're you—?"

He took the corner a little too fast, and the balding tires of the
Chevy slid.

"You're freaking me out!" she said, her voice tremulous.

Of course he knew that. It was the point. Scaring her a little,
watching the play of fear in her eyes, now round, was part of the
thrill.

No, she wasn't Samantha, but that would come. For weeks he'd
followed Samantha, kept track of her schedule and knew her routine. Had watched, disguised in a restaurant, when she'd used her
cell phone. Memorized the code to get in when her face ID hadn't

worked. She sat talking to different friends and he'd been at a nearby table—an older, bearded man who walked with the aid of a cane, or an elderly woman wearing thick glasses and a shawl, her breasts and teeth and cheek implants all fake. He'd always sat at a dark table, of course, and Samantha Leeds Wheeler aka Dr. Sam had never taken notice. Oh, he couldn't wait to control her, to wrap his bejeweled noose around her long neck, to make her plead for mercy. What advice would she have then?

None.

He would silence her forever.

No one else would suffer the inadequacies and false diagnoses and ineptitude of Dr. Sam.

He tingled at the thought of her begging.

But for now this waifish, naive whore would have to satisfy. If only partially.

The bridge was up ahead and he was pushing the speed limit as well as his luck. He couldn't afford a screw-up now. Couldn't cause any undue attention to himself. Not when he was so close to his ultimate target. He wondered if she—what had she said her name was? Luna? Oh, yeah, right. What a stupid whore-alias. Anyway, he wondered if she would actually jump out of a speeding car as it flew up the ramp and over the thick, black waters of the Mississippi in the wee morning hours. He noticed her contemplating the move, enjoyed her mounting terror, but he'd already jerry-rigged the electronic locks on the doors, securing her in the car. There was a chance she could lunge for the steering wheel, he supposed, but she seemed too freaked out, too frozen for that to happen. And if it did, he'd overpower her. That wouldn't be a problem. She was a weakling.

Easy prey.

And a temporary release.

But there was still more to come, the ultimate triumph. His heart began pounding at the thought of it, of ending Samantha's life. His blood tingled with anticipation at the image of watching her fight tooth and nail, then, of course, lose the battle, and as she realized her death was not just imminent but fated, the fear overcoming her. Then, oh, then she would begin to plead, to beg, to bargain with him. Her fingers would twist in the fold of his cassock as she cried and swore that she would do anything—*absolutely anything*—he wanted if he just spared her and—

"Where are you taking me?" the whore's voice—*Luna's* tinny little whine—interrupted his fantasy. He snapped back to the present and caught a glimpse of the speedometer.

What!?!

The needle was hovering near ninety! If he wasn't careful he'd blow through a speed trap and catch the notice of a roadside cop lying in wait.

No, no, no!

Everything would be ruined!

Starting to sweat, he eased off the gas as they reached the far end of the bridge.

Calm down. Take it slow. Enjoy the moment.

"I asked you where the fuck are you taking me?" the whore demanded in a show of defiance he hadn't expected. She was facing him, her terror still evident, but some other emotion—anger?—burning in those round eyes.

So she was tougher than he'd thought.

Good.

He liked a little fight in them and up to this point she'd been a nearly petrified, weak little sniveling creature.

But maybe not.

Maybe there was a little grit deep inside that tiny body.

He felt the thrumming deep inside, the anticipation racing through his blood, the thought of what was coming, the beads of the home-made rosary, cut glass strung on piano wire, pressing into the soft flesh of her throat. His cock hardened a bit at the thought of what was to come and the glorifying, spiritual act that was still just a precursor to his final, ultimate sanctification.

That could only come with Samantha.

And it would.

Soon.

"Very soon," he whispered under his breath, though he hated this departure from his regular routine. Though necessary as they had to get out of the city quickly, it didn't feel right, like a scratchy sweater that rubbed and chafed.

"What?" his terrified captive asked, quaking in her fear again as the lights of the city disappeared behind them. She was twisting in her seat, looking back through the rear window as New Orleans faded into darkness. "What will come very soon?"

"You will see, my child," he said, telling himself that a change of plan, an altering of routine was good, would keep those who would thwart him guessing. He just had to get his mind around it and he would. They were close now and he could feel that special little thrum in his veins, the twitching of his cock as he contemplated what was to come.

The darkened countryside loomed around them. A car passed, speeding rapidly in the opposite direction, headlight beams washing through the bug-spattered windshield to cast her face in a weird un-worldly light, and in that nanosecond he saw her fear and a flash of something else . . . determination? In the set of her jaw.

But that was wrong.

She was so meek.

Again he felt her tremble, caught just a glimpse of a quivering lower lip. Whatever he'd thought he'd caught sight of was his imagination. This one would be easy, despite the change in venue. He would take her into the swamp, kill her, and dispose of her in the dark water . . . no, wait. The cabin. Where two other bodies were rotting. He'd leave her there along with his trademark hundred-dollar bill because he'd want the cops to know if and when they found her remains, that it was his doing.

Yes . . . it would be difficult. He'd have to kill her, then haul her in the canoe through the winding, treacherous waters of the bayou, deep into the thickets of cypress and muddy, mounded alligator nests, but it would be worth it.

Turning off the main road, he rained on her what he hoped was a beatific smile, and adjusted his reflective sunglasses even though it was the dead of night.

CHAPTER 26

Bentz followed Samantha Wheeler to her house. She'd refused to call her husband, insisting that she would be all right, that she didn't want to wake him or bother her sons, and Bentz had relented. In his Jeep, he'd kept a close tail on her Prius as they eased through the night-dark streets of the city that still pulsed with life in the French Quarter.

She drove through the gates of her home near the lake without incident, but Bentz followed her through.

Ty Wheeler greeted his wife at the back door, a black dog at his side. Wheeler's dark hair was rumpled, his jaw covered in a day's worth of stubble. He was wearing a faded T-shirt from a Nirvana concert and equally washed-out navy pajama bottoms, but his eyes were sharp and intense as Samantha explained about her last caller and Bentz confirmed that he believed Samantha's stalker was alive and back in New Orleans.

"I thought he was dead." Dark eyebrows slammed together. Still standing in the kitchen illuminated at this hour by under-cabinet lights, Ty glared at Bentz. "You shot him. He died in the swamp."

"That's what we all thought," Bentz said, not admitting he'd always had a niggle of doubt because no part of Father John's body had ever been located. "We were wrong."

"Seriously?" Wheeler's gaze moved from the detective to his wife.

Samantha nodded. "Looks like." Her fear had abated somewhat now that she was home, her husband's arm around her, and she appeared to have come to terms with her new reality. "Anyone want something to drink? I could use a glass of wine."

Bentz imagined the taste of a smooth burgundy, or better yet, a smooth double malt scotch, but shook his head. "No, thanks."

Wheeler held up a hand. No. But she found a bottle of white in the fridge, uncorked it, and poured herself a glass. Chardonnay, it appeared. She corked the bottle again, returned it to its spot to chill, and leaned a hip against the center island.

To Bentz, Ty demanded, "So what're you going to do about it—about him, this Father John or whoever he really is?"

They all knew the fake priest's identity, but no one uttered his name. Bentz assured him, "We're gonna bring him to justice."

"Justice." Wheeler snorted. "I liked it better when I thought he was dead and gone."

"I know." *We all did,* Bentz thought, but didn't say it, and took a seat at the built-in banquette when Samantha motioned him to sit down. She then snapped her fingers and pointed the dog in the direction of a large dog bed tucked into a corner near the back door. Rambo sauntered to his spot and lay down, though his dark eyes remained alert.

"So what happened? Where has he been? How has he survived?" Wheeler asked, sliding onto the bench opposite Bentz.

Bentz lifted a shoulder. "Unknown. That's what I intend to find out."

"It's been . . . God, years and years and years!" Wheeler pointed out. "Why the hell would he lie low for so long? And why show up now? Because Samantha's radio program is going off the air? Or because he—what? Just happened to be back in New Orleans? Awoke from a decade-long coma, suddenly remembered he wanted to kill her? What?" And then, hearing himself, held up a hand. "Okay. I'm going off the deep end here."

"Understandable," Bentz said.

"No, it's not. I'm just—shocked, I guess is the right word. Shocked and really sick that he's back." He blew out a long stream of air. "God damn it."

Samantha intervened. "So now what?"

"It might be good if you went away for a while," Bentz suggested. "Take your family and—"

"No!" she cut in. "This is my home. I won't let some freakoid terrorize me into uprooting Ty and the boys. They're in school and we don't really know that the caller was the same psycho. I mean, it sounded like him, but it could have been some kind of digitalized recording or an imposter—a copycat, or—"

"Or he just could be back," Wheeler reminded her, cutting it short. It was as if he'd processed what had happened, got his bearings, and his reporter's instincts had returned. He leaned back in the banquette. "Could this have anything to do with the attack on your daughter? Your son-in-law's homicide? Geez—look, I'm sorry about all that."

"Me too," Bentz said. "Yeah. Me too." Then, "Are all the events connected? Possibly," Bentz hedged, then added, "We're looking into that angle of course, along with several other theories."

"Such as?"

"Nothing real concrete at this moment."

"Damn it," Wheeler said, suddenly darkly serious. "My wife was threatened tonight. She and I—we need to know what we're dealing with."

"As soon as we know anything certain, we'll let you know," Bentz said. It wouldn't help to have Wheeler going off half cocked on information that hadn't been verified. "All I can tell you is that we are looking into all kinds of possibilities, but I'm working under the assumption that the Rosary Killer is back. He's contacted you, Dr. Sam, the way he did in the past, and so the threat is very, very real. I would suggest, just to be on the side of caution, that you and your family take a few days away from the city, just until we sort this all out."

"Agreed," Wheeler said, then looked at his wife. "I think this is nonnegotiable. We'll take the kids over to Disney World. We've been promising them for ages."

"Wait . . . what? No," she said, shaking her head. "I'm not upsetting the whole family, and my job with my new podcast, and yours, Ty. You were supposed to go to Washington tomorrow—wait, I mean today, it's after midnight. So you've got a plane reservation for this afternoon."

"It'll keep."

"But the boys have school and sports and what're we going to do about Rambo? I might not be able to find a kennel for him at the drop of a hat."

"We'll figure it out," Ty said. "Plans can be shuffled. Nothing's set in stone."

"Some things are."

"Nothing that important." His jaw was rock hard, his lips compressed. He pushed himself out of the banquette and walked up to his wife. "I'm not taking a chance on losing you to that psycho, okay? And I don't want the boys here, anywhere close to danger."

She nodded, acquiescing slightly at the mention of her sons and their safety.

"Nothing is worth that."

"You're right. Okay . . . okay." She finished her wine in one long gulp. "We'll go."

Wheeler gave his wife a squeeze. "Good." To Bentz he said, "Just keep us informed. About every damned thing."

"I will," Bentz promised, standing. "And we'll get him. I promise."

"Don't just get him," Wheeler said, his eyes hard. "This time when you find him and take aim and shoot? Don't miss. I want that prick dead."

God help me.

Luna's silent prayer reverberated through her head.

Petrified, she moved, the "priest" prodding her forward, through the thickets and bracken, the tall grass, and marshy ground. Tall cypress rose like pale ghosts and the air was heavy with the scent of earth and rotting vegetation. She shivered. Darkness surrounded them, the only glint of light from the small beam of his flashlight that he swung in front of them where reeds and brambles grew, rough scrub brushing against her bare legs, causing her to shiver. "I want to go back," she said for what had to have been the fiftieth time. "I didn't agree to this—"

"Shut up!" he snarled, and her skin crawled as if a thousand snakes were sliding over her. "I paid for you and you do what I say."

"No—no—I—"

"Don't argue, Luna!" he warned, reaching forward, grabbing her shoulder, and squeezing so hard she let out a yelp of pain. "Just keep going."

This was wrong.

So, so wrong.

She bit her lip and told herself to think. She'd been in tight jams before. You didn't grow up on a working cattle ranch in Wyoming and not get tough. But this—this was different, way different from rounding up strays in the middle of winter, or mending fence, or chopping wood for the fire, or dodging passes from drunken ranch hands.

This was pure evil.

All dressed up in a priest's robe.

But he wasn't a man of the cloth, that much was evident, and she should never have gotten in the car with him. Big mistake. She was far from defenseless, but she put on the sniveling, frail act so his defenses might come down, but now as they were walking through the swamp, she in high heels that sank deep into the soggy, wet ground, she felt real fear. This sick dick was a psycho and he was going to hurt her.

And then he would kill her.

She was sure of it.

Swallowing back her fear, she stumbled forward, bracelets jangling, felt his fingers on her relax a little as the brackish waters lapped at her ankles. Cool water. Filled with creatures. Deadly creatures. But not as dangerous as the man prodding her from behind.

As he swung the flashlight's beam over what appeared to be a rotting dock, he edged her forward up two sagging steps, the wood so soft it gave under her weight, her heels sinking.

"Move it." He gave her a rough push. She stumbled, falling so that her knee scraped over the rotten boards with their rusted, protruding nails, her fingernails splitting and breaking as she caught herself, her palms skating over the wet, weak wood, one shoe sliding from her foot.

"Get up!" he ordered.

He was looming over her, his face pale in the weakest of the shifting moonlight. And in his hand, she saw something winking. Glass? Jewels?

God, no.

Her heart nearly stopped as she recognized the rosary draping through his fingers, bloodred stones barely visible.

"I told you he was back," Bentz said to Montoya. They were at the station and it was after two in the morning, a lot of the surrounding offices' lights dimmed for the night.

"Seems as if."

"Seems? Seems?" Bentz repeated, jazzed. He was at his desk, the quiet of the station at night a balm. No footsteps clattering in the hall, no loud voices, no barks of laughter or constant ring of cell phones, no screaming saws from the construction crew, just a peaceful silence interrupted occasionally with conversation drifting in from the late-night shift. Outside lights glowed through the windows; this city rarely slept, and there was plenty of activity for cops outside or elsewhere in the building, but tonight in their department, it was blissfully quiet.

"It still doesn't fit." Montoya was on his feet, pacing from the window to the door, obviously trying to force the pieces of the puzzle together. "Why would he reappear now? Where's he been? Why is he after Kristi?" He stared out the window and rubbed the back of his neck.

"I don't know what triggered him—maybe the fact that Dr. Sam's show is going off the air. Maybe not. And I sure as hell can't figure out where he's been. If he had been locked up, I think we would have heard." Bentz leaned back in his chair, felt his back pop as he stretched. "And he's after Kristi to get back at her for writing the book, or me for nearly killing him. Or whatever." He stood. "It doesn't have to make sense. He's a whack job."

Bentz walked to the bulletin board where they'd put up pictures of the two known victims: Teri Marie Gaines and Helene Laroche. A map of the area was also pinned on the board and the spots where the bodies had been located marked in red. Places of interest—the bayou by the cabins owned by Cyrus Unger, "CU," the radio station, even Our Lady of the Grove Church were marked, along with the home of Hugo and Helene Laroche and even Vince Laroche's apartment in JAX Brewery noted. Montoya was right, nothing was gelling.

But they were getting closer; Bentz could feel it, that little tingle of anticipation that fired his blood whenever they were close.

He only hoped they could nail the psychotic son of a bitch before anyone else got hurt.

Especially his daughter.

Make that his pregnant, recently widowed daughter.

Yeah, he agreed with Ty Wheeler, and wished that his shot that night in the bayou long ago had found its mark. Next time, Bentz silently vowed, he wouldn't miss.

"I said, 'Get up!'" the man ordered.

Through the hair that had fallen over her face, Stacy stared up at him, dark above the bright beam of light from his flashlight. He was going to kill her. If she let him, he'd strangle her with that damned fake rosary while the bullfrogs croaked and mosquitoes hummed in this godforsaken swamp.

"Now!" he yelled, and something in the bracken behind him rustled, an animal of some kind scurrying or slithering through the woods. For a second he was distracted, glanced over his shoulder, and she caught sight of her dropped shoe. Her fingers wrapped around the narrow arch of the stiletto as she stood, keeping her right hand out of sight.

He swung his gaze back to her and, satisfied that she was obeying, looped the rosary of death over her head.

As he did, she swung upward.

Throwing all of her weight into her shoulder, she thrust the sharp heel of her shoe at his face, aiming for his eye.

"Aaaarrrggh!"

He yowled in pain.

Blood spurted over the shoe and her fingers.

She chopped upward again.

Fast. Over and over.

Bam! Bam! Bam!

"Noooo!" Squealing, he tightened the grip on the rosary, twisting it and cinching it over her throat. But the choker prevented the stones from cutting into her flesh. "You little bitch!" he said through gritted teeth, blood running down his face.

She raised the high heel again and he grabbed the shoe with his free hand.

He ripped it from her sticky fingers, then flung the stiletto into the swamp. "You'll pay for that!"

He dragged her from her feet. Twisting. Grunting. All his muscles coiled.

Her second shoe dangled, then fell off to clatter against the rotting dock.

"Die," he ordered, his breath hot. Heavy.

Despite the choker, Stacy couldn't breathe. She grasped the glittering noose with her fingers, but she couldn't wedge them beneath the heavy wire. Her legs were moving frantically, trying to find ground, but they found only air.

"That's better," he growled.

Satisfied.

Smug.

Another twist.

Oh, merciful God!

Her lungs were tight. On fire.

She tried to drag in a breath.

Could only gurgle.

The holy noose tightened.

Her lungs would surely burst.

She heard popping noises.

From her ears and eyes.

No, no, no!

He shifted, twirling her out over the dark water, dangling her body over the surface where creatures swam and waited.

Just let go.

The voice in her head was so seductive.

Her legs swung beneath her, again over the water.

"*No, no, no! Fight Stacy-girl,*" another gravelly voice ordered her, and in her mind's eye she saw her grandmother, a bit of a woman with long gray braids, weathered skin, and a voice rough from cigarettes. "*Kick him where it counts. Hard. In his balls!*"

She tried to aim her legs, but they were weak.

"For God's sake, scratch the hell out of him!"

As if the old long-dead woman were pushing her, she suddenly flailed forward, lunging for his eyes with her broken nails. She scraped his face, opening an older wound, causing him to scream in pain. "You fucking—"

"Hey!" a male voice yelled from somewhere in the darkness. "What the fuck's going on?"

Stacy saw a bright glow through the trees—a flashlight or lantern's beam.

Her attacker went still, his hands still squeezing her neck. Choking. "Shhhh!" he hissed, as if she could say a word. She couldn't.

"Fight, goddammit!" Granny's voice commanded, echoing in her brain.

With all of her strength, she wriggled.

"Hey, is someone there?" the loud male voice said, and then more quietly, "C'mon, Bobby-Dean, let's check it out. Nah, nah, forget the lines. . . ."

"Shh!" he said again.

An outboard motor roared to life, deafening in the swamp.

Stacy swung her entire body, all of her weight against the man who was intent on choking the life out of her.

Thud!

His grip loosened. "Whaaa—fuck!" He slipped, shoes sliding on the mossy, rotten boards. "You little—" He staggered, trying to catch himself. Twisting, she kicked him hard. Her heel landing against his shin.

"Ow! Shit! You cu—!"

Down they tumbled!

His hands fell away from her neck as they landed.

Thud!

Her head slammed against the rotten boards.

Pain exploded behind her eyes.

The night closed in.

"Fuck!" he spat.

Move! Move! Get away!

"Hey, everything okay?" That deep male voice, sounding far away over the roar of an engine.

No! Everything's not *okay! Help! Please, please help!!!*

But the words wouldn't form. Only gurgled sounds escaped from her throat and he was there! Next to her. Grunting and swearing and . . .

She rolled!

Frantically to the side of the dock. Scrambling. Forcing her unwilling body to move.

"NO!" he yelled.

Feet first, she slid over the edge.

Shrieking in pain, he lunged, his hands finding her hair.

She slid lower.

He grabbed again.

This time his fingers tangled in the rosary still looped over her neck. With a jerk, he pulled her upward while her legs and arms flailed and splashed. "No!" he growled, the noose tightening.

She flung her body backward.

The rosary moved upward, landing under her chin, digging into the soft flesh not protected by her choker.

He twisted it tight and she tried to strike him, to hit and scratch his face as he leaned close.

Still it coiled, like a boa constrictor, squeezing her throat.

He yanked.

Her body rose from the water.

"Fuck, oh . . . shit!" He was doing something with the rosary, cinching it.

The world spun.

She couldn't breathe!

The loud noise thundered in her ears.

Still he was twisting the loop around. "Damn it, I can't—"

He was working the chain, the sharp stones cutting deep.

"Hey! You!" a voice—deep, but far, far away.

The blackness threatened to swallow her.

She couldn't breathe!

Her lungs . . . oh, God, her lungs were going to explode!

She blinked.

The world faded.

A final hard jerk on the noose.

Her head snapped back.

Something gave.

Her choker burst. Pearlescent beads flew into the darkness, plopping like thick raindrops onto the water.

And then the world stopped.

CHAPTER 27

"You've been smoking," Abby charged as Montoya walked into the bedroom. She rolled over and pushed herself up in the bed, her shoulders resting against the padded headboard, her eyes partially open, but catching light from the streetlamp visible through the shades in the shadowy room.

"I quit. You know it."

"I can smell it."

Aw, hell. "Just one," he said, and assumed she could tell that he was lying as he walked to the bed and sat down on the edge.

"You know how I feel about it." A gentle reprimand.

"Yeah, yeah, I know. I know. Shit—it's just this damned case!"

She touched his shoulder. "There's always an excuse if you look hard enough."

"Okay. Right." He turned to her. "No more, I promise."

"Hmmm." Her hand fell away.

"I swear."

"You do that a lot."

"Yeah, I know." He climbed to his feet. "I'll check on Ben and shower."

"Good." Her teeth flashed into a sexy grin. "Do that."

"You are so sassy."

"Only for you, Montoya," she said as he walked out of the room. "Only for you."

His son was sleeping in his crib while nearby the dog was curled on a pet bed positioned under the window. Montoya's head bumped a toy airplane swinging from the mobile hung over Benjamin's crib. A few weak notes of "Fly Me to the Moon" escaped before he caught the plane and the room went silent again. His son was fast asleep, thumb inserted in his mouth, gently sucking. Montoya's heart melted. He wanted to pick the boy up, but resisted. Time enough for that in the morning when Benjamin was awake. For now, Montoya was content to stare down at his innocent, sleeping child, a little soul unaware of the pain, hatred, and ugliness in the world, a world Montoya faced every day.

Maybe he should chuck it all. Grab his tiny family and move to Montana or Alaska or New Mexico, somewhere far away.

"There is good everywhere. There is bad everywhere. You can't have one without the other. Choose your path and stay true. There is more that is sacred on God's earth than is evil." His mother's words came as a reminder, and looking down on his sleeping child, knowing his wife was safe in the next room, Montoya felt the good in the world.

Montoya stripped down in the bathroom and stepped into the shower, letting hot water run over his knotted muscles. He scrubbed his face and brushed his teeth under the needle-sharp spray, a habit his wife detested. Though he tried to concentrate on the good, the sacred that his mother told him about, the evil crept in on Satan's quiet footsteps.

Bentz was wrong.

Montoya felt it in his gut.

Yeah, it looked like Father John, the infamous Rosary Killer, was back and stalking the streets of the city, creating his particular ugly kind of terror, but there was more to it than that. Something else was going on, he could feel it.

Though it seemed that Father John or a copycat was killing prostitutes, the attack on Kristi Bentz and her husband, the cryptic religious notes left in her house, the invasion of her home seemed detached from the ritualistic murders perpetuated by the fake priest. *No,* he thought, lathering his back and shoulders, *there's more to the puzzle than first meets the eye.*

Serial killers had been known to learn from their mistakes, hone their skills, tweak their MOs, but Montoya doubted they would continue on their old path while starting a new one. It was possible, he supposed, pouring shampoo onto his head and washing his hair, but unlikely.

As he rinsed off, he considered the other suspects he'd studied, those who had issues with Kristi Bentz. Though he found no one person who had an ax to grind with her, he'd come up with enemies in the form of the people she'd written about and exposed to the world, especially those who had threatened her. Zavala, Jarvis, and Cooke to name the most obvious. And then there was Drake Dennison, her reclusive rival who hadn't published a book in years. Montoya hadn't forgotten about him as well.

The bathroom had filled with steam as he finally turned off the water and the old pipes groaned in protest. He reached for a towel to dry himself off and felt a hand clasp over his wrist.

"Hey!"

Abby's face appeared in the vapor. Her eyes were wide, no longer puffy with sleep.

"What's going on?" he asked.

"Someone woke me up," she said, "and for once it wasn't the baby." Her lips twitched as she dropped her short robe and stood naked in front of him.

"Oh, yeah? So what're you going to do about it?"

"Hmmm. Punish him, I think." She was nodding, her eyes twinkling. "Yeah, that's what I'm gonna do. Punish him. Hard."

"Oh, right." He scooped her off her feet and she let out a little squeal of delight as he carried her back to the bedroom, her warm body tight against his, her head in the well between his neck and shoulder. "I'll show you who's going to punish whom."

Angling her head upward, she managed to nip at his ear and whisper, "Oh, Detective. Promises, promises . . ."

Stacey opened a bleary eye and saw a white smile gleaming above her. Panic screamed through her body, but she couldn't move, just lay in the cool, shifting water . . . wait, what?

An engine growled loudly, roaring, water undulating in waves, and then went suddenly silent.

Startled, she shifted, felt something hard against the back of her neck. Blinking, trying to focus, she realized it wasn't a faraway smile she was seeing, but a crescent moon riding high overhead, a blanket of stars, and yes, she was in water, cool, lazy water that reeked and smelled of—

Oh, Lord, she was in the *swamp*?

How the hell had she ended up here? And why couldn't she move? And, God, why couldn't she remember anything? She tried to sit up, but whatever was behind her neck, tangled in her hair. . . . She reached up, her mind clearing, the sounds of a bullfrog croaking cutting through the hum of insects.

And the roar had been . . . a boat?

She blinked, tried to piece it all together, but her mind was a jumble.

"Look! Over there! Holy shit, Bobby-Dean! Do you see that?" a deep male voice intoned.

"I see it for sure!" A higher nasal voice, more excited. "Oh, sweet Jesus, it's a girl! Man, oh, man, is she dead?"

"Hope not!"

"What happened to the guy? There was a guy with her. Right?" the higher voice asked. He sounded nervous.

"Yeeeahh." It was a question. And as she blinked, she saw the beam of a flashlight cutting across the still water thick with duckweed and spider lilies.

Panic shot through her.

She tried to move, to get away, but she was tangled against the rotting wood of some pier, her hair and some fishing wire holding her fast, choking her.

"Hey, there, now . . . don't you move . . . we gotcha," the deep voice said, as if she could trust him. Her memory was hazy, clouded, but she had to get away, couldn't trust these faceless men. Couldn't trust anyone. She jerked upward and whatever was caught in her hair held her fast.

No, no, no!

Her heart was a drum, beating a wild tattoo.

Again, she tried to remember how she'd gotten here. Why she was in the swamp as the boat came closer, the sound of oars dipping in water drawing near. She reached up to wrench her hair and throat free of the noose and saw the prow of a boat reach the rotting dock and two men climb onto the slippery boards.

"You'll be okay, now," the huge man said. "We gotcha. We'll take you to a doctor."

His companion, older and hunched over, a wiry man, was a step behind. "Careful, Clive, this here dock's 'bout rotted clean through."

Could she trust them?

No!

Even in her foggy state, she knew she couldn't trust anyone. She tried to get away but whatever was holding her fast wouldn't budge. She kicked and yanked at the thing around her neck.

"Hey, hey there. Don't struggle. Oh, Jesus-God, what the hell's she got around her neck?"

"What're ya talkin' . . . oh, man, oh, man, oh, man."

She felt big hands at her throat and she struggled, trying to get away.

"Hell-fire, girl, you're just makin' it worse."

She swung up at him and he pulled back, staring her straight in the eyes. His hands went up to his sides. "Hey—look it. We're just here to help you. Get you to a doc. Now, come on. Bobby, you got your cell phone? Call nine-one-one."

"No signal," Bobby said, his voice a crackle.

"Oh, shit man, there's a gator!" the big man said. "You got your gun?"

What? An alligator?

In the water?

Next to her?

Oh. God.

She froze.

A scream died in her throat.

Frantically she searched the dark water and she saw it, small eyes catching the flashlight's beam.

The little man scrambled back to the boat.

She felt something move against her leg and screamed, just as Bobby-Dean pulled a long gun from the boat and took aim.

The light played over the water, swinging in an arc.

The swamp went silent.

Something moved.

Inches from her.

The water swirled. A snout appeared.

"Got him!" Bobby-Dean said.

"No!" she yelled, seeing the double-barrel. "Noooo!"

Blam!

The blast echoed through the swamp and Luna sank gratefully back into oblivion.

Stupid, stupid, stupid!

By the dimmed light of the lantern, he nursed his wounds, and even the bayou beneath his cabin didn't soothe him. Tonight there would be no calm. No serenity. No satisfaction that he'd eluded the authorities for all this time. No pleasure in the anticipation of what he'd do to that sick, fake radio psychologist when he was ready.

He'd been an idiot.

Not waiting.

Not keeping to his plan.

Not insisting on going to the damned whore's place. Or some-where else—a safe building. But no, he'd dragged her to the swamp instead, had thought he could dispose of her body with the other two, leave his signature marred hundred-dollar bill there, in that old rotting cabin, so that if and when the three dead were found, the cops would know that he was behind it.

Bad idea.

Nearly fatal flaw.

He sucked in his breath as he applied rubbing alcohol to his wounds and felt the sting. The damned burn of the medication. Served him right. He figured it was his kind of penance, as he then applied an antiseptic cream that didn't burn, actually felt like a balm.

He closed his eyes.

Everything that could go wrong had.

It had been a miracle that he'd escaped, running and thrashing through the swamp to the car and roaring away, nearly hitting a deer that had jumped out of the underbrush.

After all this time.

The years he'd waited.

And in one fell swoop, he'd nearly ruined everything.

He only hoped that she was dead.

And he also hoped those morons in the boat—probably out poaching—found her lifeless and floating.

He wondered if they'd seen him. Could ID him.

Too late to be concerned about it now. He just had to be patient. Wait this out.

It will be all right, he told himself.

It had to be.

CHAPTER 28

"It looks like we caught a break." Bentz's voice was clear, as if he'd been up for hours, but Montoya groaned when he saw that the digital display read 5:13. He listened as his partner explained that a woman had been brought into St. Ada's Hospital with wounds to her neck and body, two men claiming they'd found her being attacked in the swamp, both of them saying the assailant had been a priest. She'd been sedated, but Bentz was already at the hospital waiting to interview her.

"I'll be there in fifteen," Montoya said, then clicked off.

"Don't tell me," Abby murmured into her pillow.

"Gotta go."

"Oh, no . . ."

"Yep." He kissed the back of her head where her curls were all mussed. "That's what you get for marrying an ace detective."

"Ace detective? Oh, save me."

He swatted her rump playfully and rolled off the bed, forcing himself into a fresh pair of jeans and T-shirt, donning boots and a leather jacket before heading outside. The Jane Doe had been admitted to St. Ada's and he made the drive easily, the city in predawn still just starting to stir.

Bentz met him in the parking lot.

"You see her?"

His partner shook his head. "Ambulance took her directly into the ER. The doc says we can see her once she's been examined and put into a room. The good news is that her injuries on the surface aren't life threatening, but either she can't or won't remember what happened."

"How do you know that?"

"Caught up with an EMT who came with her in the ambulance. He spilled."

"And from that you figured she was attacked by Father John."

"Two guys found her in the swamp. Saw what looked like a priest who got away."

"A priest?"

"They said a guy in black robes, but they didn't go after him. They were more concerned with the victim. One stayed with her, the other boated up to a spot in the bayou where he could get cell phone service and called nine-one-one."

"You talked to them?"

"Not yet. I got all this from the deputy who secured the location."

"But you're sure this was Father John?" Montoya asked, wishing he had a cigarette. "MO doesn't jibe."

"She's got a ring of cuts around her neck and sharp red beads caught in her hair." Bentz held Montoya's gaze. "It's him."

"What's she say?"

"Nothing. Remember, she was pretty out of it. Not talking." Bentz glanced up at the stucco building. "This could take a while. Why don't we go talk to the fishermen who brought her in? They're waiting at the station."

"Good. I'll drive."

Bentz climbed into the Mustang and Montoya made short work of the drive. The station was still quiet as there were nearly two hours before the shift changed. Even the construction workers hadn't shown up yet.

The two men, Robert "Bobby-Dean" Clements and Clive Jones, were waiting in an interrogation room with a deputy who had taken their statements. Bentz and Montoya sat down. "We've got it from here," Bentz told the deputy, who left the written statements. He turned his attention to the two fishermen. "I'm Detective Bentz, this is Detective Montoya. We'd like you to go over the story once again, if you don't mind, and we'll have a few more questions."

Both men nodded. They obviously weren't happy about it. Bobby-Dean, the scrawny one with a bad case of acne beneath a scraggly

beard, was antsy, barely able to sit still. He was wearing cut-off over-
alls and a Saints' cap rammed over dirty blond hair and kept glancing
nervously at his fishing partner.

Jones was a bear of a man, as black as his friend was white. He
sported a cleaved eyebrow, a nose that had been broken once or
twice, and a deep, baritone voice. His eyes were gold and intelligent,
his gaze direct as he explained that they'd been out checking their
crawfish traps and heard "a scuffling," then witnessed what they
thought was a man in a black robe.

"Looked like a priest, y'know," Bobby-Dean interjected. He kept
taking off his hat and wadding it between his gnarled fingers before
setting it back on his head and starting the process all over again.

They both agreed upon what they'd seen, could not ID the attacker, swore they thought he'd killed the woman, and hadn't given
chase. "I wish to high heaven I had," Bobby-Dean insisted. "Shit, I
had my daddy's Winchester. Coulda wounded him good."

"Or blown him to bits," Jones disagreed, scowling at his friend and
giving a quick shake of his head as if to shut Bobby-Dean up, then
adding, "We just wanted to get the woman to a hospital."

Montoya asked, "Did she say anything to you?"

"Nothing' much." Again Jones shook his head. "Nothing that made
any sense."

"She was scared. Freaked the fuck out," Bobby-Dean added.

"Anyone live around there? In that part of the swamp?"

Jones shrugged. "Not many. There's a cabin here or there, but
they're pretty much all abandoned."

"Rotted away," Bobby-Dean said, removing his cap again and wring-
ing it in his hands.

They asked a few more questions, got no more answers that
helped out, then, while Jones and Bobby-Dean waited, checked with
the hospital. The victim, Jane Doe as she was still not identified, hadn't
been given a room yet and the doctor wasn't allowing anyone to see
her nor the cops to question her.

"I'm treating her as a patient, not as a suspect, not as a victim,"
Dr. Williams said, and she was as intractable as she'd been when
Bentz had met her in the ER over an hour earlier. A tall, all-business
black woman in scrubs, her irritation visible in the tight line of her
lips, she'd stared straight into Bentz's eyes and told him in no uncer-

tain terms that he was to leave her patient alone until she determined it was safe for the Jane Doe to be interviewed, "and not a second before," she'd warned him in the waiting room of the ER while a nurse was with the victim. "Now, if you'll excuse me, I have a patient who needs my attention," and she swept through a wide set of double doors, her lab coat billowing behind her as she'd left Bentz to call Montoya and meet him in the adjoining parking lot.

So here they were.

The station was slowly coming to life, cops and members of the construction crew arriving, footsteps and voices audible, the smell of coffee wafting in.

Once the interview with the fishermen was over, they asked Clements and Jones to show them the place where they'd witnessed the crime. The fishermen, though not eager, agreed and led Montoya's Mustang in their beat-up Ford Ranger, a pickup with more than its share of dents.

On the road Montoya told Bentz about his doubts.

"It just doesn't all fit," Montoya insisted. "The Rosary Killer always left his calling card."

"The hundred-dollar bill with Ben Franklin's eyes blackened," Bentz said, eyes narrowing thoughtfully. "Yeah, I know. But the rosary beads."

"Glass beads. Not sure if they were from a rosary."

"And the priest's garb."

"Again, just a black robe or coat. And most of Father John's crimes happened inside—at the vic's place."

"Maybe that didn't work this time. For whatever reason." Bentz raked a hand through his hair, more than a few strands of silver visible. "Let's just follow this and see where it takes us."

Montoya shot him a look as he drove across the bridge, the Mississippi flowing steadily and slowly beneath the wide span, boats of all sizes on the river, the city fading behind them. "Okay, but just for the record, I think you're forcing this."

"And I think you're ignoring the obvious."

"Maybe." Still watching the taillights of the Ford pickup, Montoya reached for the pack of cigarettes he'd kept in the console, but found it crumpled and empty.

"You back on those?" Bentz asked.

"No. I slipped up." He dropped the pack.

"Easy to do," Bentz said, and turned away, staring through the side window, avoiding the questions in his partner's eyes while tapping his fingers on the armrest. No doubt about it, Bentz was fighting his own demons.

Hell, weren't they all?

He turned off the main road where the houses faded and the swamp encroached, then took several turns. Finally, the pickup parked on a wide spot in the gravel shoulder. He tucked in behind the truck. "Show us the way," Bentz said to the fishermen, who led them along a thin trail, through thickets and tall grass, deeper into the bayou.

Here in the swamp where the air was thick and earthy, the water was still. Mist was rising, the cypress trees jutting out of the dark water, Spanish moss moving in a bit of wind that breathed across the bayou. As they stepped through the wetlands, Montoya batted at mosquitoes, cattails brushing against his legs, a dragonfly sweeping the surface of the water. Birds chirped from the brush and a great blue heron snapped up a small fish from the water, swallowing it and flying off, feathers glinting through the fog.

A rotting dock jutted into the water, the step to it broken, some of the boards waterlogged and splintered. It was roped off with yellow tape.

"Is this where you found her?" Bentz asked the two men following.

"Oh, yeah." Bobby-Dean was nodding and scratching at his thin beard. "This is the spot. We caught sight of her, right there." He pointed a big-knuckled finger at the edge of the dock. "He was trying to haul her up or somethin'. It was dark, y'know, and we couldn't really tell what was goin' on, but we knew it wasn't right."

They explained again exactly what they'd witnessed and Montoya saw it in his mind's eye, the woman being dragged from the water, the man above all in black, she fighting for her life, he intent on ending it.

But why here?

"You said no one lives around here," Montoya said to the men.

"No one we know."

"Was there a boat here?" he asked. How was the assailant planning to leave?

"Nope."

That didn't make any sense.

"Welllll . . ." Bobby-Dean said, drawing out the word. "There's that old rowboat—we seen it last night, a quarter of a mile up the swamp. It's never been there before."

Jones's eyes narrowed. "You think it has somethin' to do with this?"

"Let's check it out," Bentz said. "How do we get there?"

"I can go get my boat. Easiest way to reach it."

"But, if it was used by our guy, then he had to walk here, along the shore," Bentz said. To Jones: "Go get your boat, but we'll walk. You"—he motioned to Bobby-Dean—"show us the way."

"Uh—" The shorter man looked about to argue, but changed his mind. "Fine," he said, but wasn't happy about it.

Neither was Montoya, especially when he had to swat at a hornet that followed him through the soggy ground. They searched for signs that the would-be killer had stalked through the ground and Bentz pointed out cattails that had been bent. "Coulda been a wild boar," Bobby-Dean said, "or a bear. Probably not a gator."

"Good news," Montoya muttered sarcastically as they rounded a bend, and just past several cypress trees saw the canoe, a small craft tied to a low-hanging branch. "You've never seen this before?"

Bobby-Dean was nodding, adjusting his cap as rays of morning sunlight sliced through the mist to dapple the water. "That's right."

Bentz asked, "And you fish these waters regularly?"

"Me and Clive, yes, sir. This here is our fishin' grounds."

And hunting, Montoya thought, because Bobby-Dean had admitted to having a rifle with him in the night, that he'd shot at a gator who'd been a little too close to the woman they'd been trying to save.

"You got gloves?" Bentz asked Montoya.

"Always." He reached into his back pocket and Bentz did the same. "Let's check this out." A single oar was tucked into the hull.

"Let's test this for prints," Bentz said, a satisfied smile creeping onto his lips.

What were the chances that this craft actually belonged to Father John? "Slim and none" leapt into Montoya's mind, but not so Bentz, who was searching the hull.

And then Montoya found it. The proverbial nail in the coffin in the form of a single bill, folded neatly and tucked into a crack in the wooden stern seat. He plucked the bill from its hiding place, unfolded it, and found himself looking into the blackened eyes of Benjamin Franklin.

CHAPTER 29

This is a mistake.

Kristi pulled into the small parking lot for the television station at seven forty-five and wished she'd never agreed to the interview. She wasn't ready. Wasn't up for it. Not even after getting up at five in the morning, taking Dave out for a run, showering, and downing a yogurt, berry, and banana smoothie. Even the coffee she'd picked up on the drive over hadn't helped. Then again it was decaf. "You did this," she said to her abdomen, as Dr. Vale had suggested she cut out caffeine.

Glancing in the rearview, she saw the indecision in her eyes and hated it. She'd always been a person who knew what she wanted and, if anything, had been impetuous, even daring, but not indecisive. "Get it together," she said, grabbed her purse and stepped into the clear morning.

As it turned out she was the second guest to arrive. She buzzed in at the door, was allowed to enter, and registered before being given a name tag allowing her to be in the station. A harried production assistant with short, tousled hair dyed a faint pink, the barest of lip gloss, and a no-nonsense demeanor named Jen walked her through a rabbit warren of hallways. "The studio is just there," Jen said, pointing to a closed door with a light that glowed with the words "On Air." Then a few more steps down the hallway. "You'll just wait in the green room with the other guests and I'll come and get you before your segment. Right now, you're on second—segment two—but that all depends on if our first guests get through the traffic that's supposedly slowing them down." Her lips were pursed, her expression exasperated, as if she'd heard the same excuse a thousand times and really didn't believe it. "Also, it all depends on if our musical guest shows. Right now that's a pretty big 'if.'" Her lips pulled down at the corners at the prospect as she opened a door at the end of the hall.

Inside the windowless green room, a large TV was mounted on one wall, the current news program being broadcast. Several chairs, a few tables, and a long, faux leather couch were scattered around the room, and a long counter with a coffeemaker, water bottles, and a few snacks dominated one wall. "Help yourself," Jen said, and gestured with one hand to the coffeepot and accoutrements while texting with amazing dexterity. "I'll be back." And, then lifting the phone to her ear, she stepped through the open doorway. "They are? Good. I'll be right down. And what about Bigelow? Have you heard from him . . . ? Okay, then we'll go to plan B unless he surprises us all." Her voice faded and the door finally clicked shut.

Kristi sat in one of the chairs not far from a worn couch where a prim woman holding a long-haired cat upon a tufted pillow was sitting. "Trouble," the woman said, her eyebrows arching over wire-rimmed glasses. Her ash-brown hair was feathered and surrounding a doe-eyed face with a very serious expression that complemented her business suit, glasses, and ankle-high boots. "I'm Dana, by the way," and it was said as if Kristi should recognize her.

Kristi didn't.

When that was obvious, the woman added, "Dana Metcalf?"

Again Kristi drew a blank.

"As in president of PCNOLA."

"Oh." Like that meant anything.

Dana sighed, as if Kristi were an absolute dimwit. "Purrbred Cats of New Orleans, Louisiana," she clarified. "Purrbred rather than purebred." Her eyes twinkled. "It's a play on words. Even though we would never allow an owner to join unless his or her cat had legitimate papers, of course."

"Uh-huh."

"And sometimes people think we're the Personal Computers of New Orleans or the Politically Correct of New Orleans." She tittered and rolled her eyes at the inanity of it all. "If you can believe that!"

Kristi didn't respond.

"I'd give you my card, but I don't want to disturb Mr. Precious, here." She stroked her pet lovingly. "He'd be so upset. Wouldn't you, MP?" she whispered to the cat.

The big gray cat just stared at Kristi, its green eyes unblinking. Definitely *not* upset.

The door swung open again and this time Jen was with two people.

Kristi inwardly stiffened.

Reggie Cooke's imperious gaze landed on her full force. "What the hell is this?" she demanded, her husband a step behind.

"Oh. Dear God." Hamilton Cooke was an inch or so taller than his wife in her heels. Impeccably put together in a jacket, open-throated dress shirt, and slacks, the smile fell from his face as he caught sight of Kristi.

Jen squeezed past them. "If you'll have a seat and wait here until—"

"No!" Reggie turned on the smaller woman. "No way! We won't. I know the drill, but this is an outrage." In full makeup and a black dress with an emerald jacket, she shook her head, her red hair sweeping her shoulders. "An outrage!"

"Please," Jen implored. "If you two will just have a seat, I'll—"

Reggie was unmoved. "I asked you before," she said. "What the hell is this?" Her eyes narrowed on the production assistant before she threw Kristi a suspicious glance. "I suppose this is your doing. First the book and then the movie and now this!"

"What? No! Absolutely not." Kristi refused to be intimidated. She got to her feet and angled her chin upward to meet the lawyer's icy glare. Though Kristi was three or four inches shorter than the current Mrs. Cooke, she wasn't about to be cowed. "Seriously, I had no idea." But Bella had. Kristi didn't doubt it for a second. She wanted to wring her friend's neck for the obvious setup. "This was a last-minute thing and I didn't know who was going to be on."

"Sure." Sarcasm dripped from Reggie's words.

Kristi said, "I was called by a friend who works here to fill in at the last minute." Why was she even bothering trying to explain herself to this stone-cold bitch?

"Oh, right." More disbelief in Reggie's tone. "This station has promoted Hamilton and me repeatedly this week." Before Kristi could say that she'd been a little too busy to keep up with *Bonjour, New Orleans!* Reggie turned to the production assistant. "I'm out. We're both out."

"No, please, Mrs. Cooke—Mr., er, Doctor Cooke, let's all calm down," Jen argued, trying to placate and set things right.

But it was too little too late. Reggie stormed through the door, her high heels clicking loudly down the hall, but Hamilton hesitated and his lips flattened to a razor thin line. He pointed an accusing finger at Kristi. "This is disgraceful," he said, eyes flashing. "But what else could we expect from a money-grubbing hack like you? Feeding off other people's misfortunes. I don't know how you sleep at night."

"And I don't know how you do," Kristi said, half expecting him to lunge at her. The hatred in his eyes burned bright.

"Hamilton!" Reggie's voice called from somewhere in the outer hallway.

"You'd better be careful," he warned Kristi, then turned smartly on his heel to follow his wife.

"Just what I need," Jen said, her voice barely audible. She hurried after them talking loudly, trying to convince them to do the interview. "Mrs. Cooke, please. We're all set for you and Dr. Cooke, the audience would love to—"

The door banged shut behind Jen, cutting off the sound of the rest of her pleas.

"Oooh." From her spot on the couch, Dana sucked in her breath loudly. "Big trouble. They don't like you much," she said to Kristi.

"Ya think?"

"Why?"

"It's a long story." She wasn't about to go into it.

"So then how did this happen?" She motioned in a circle to include all that had just recently transpired. "How did you end up here together?"

"I don't know," Kristi said, but that was a lie. Because she had a pretty good idea of what had precipitated her being here with Dr. Cooke and his wife. It started with the sagging ratings of the morning show, and the host Renee-Claire's fear of either being fired or the show being canceled and then, of course, Bella caving to pressure with the need to save her job, and the sudden reappearance of the Rosary Killer. That coupled with the cable network's airing of the TV movies made from her books made Kristi newsworthy, which she hated.

Though Kristi's appearance was last-minute and not promoted, there was the Internet, where all the segments could be viewed and the murder of Hamilton Cooke's first wife, Bethany, brought up again. Kristi didn't doubt that the Cookes had been asked to be guests on some other pretense, unless Dr. Cooke and his lawyer wife had agreed to be on air to garner public sympathy and pressure as he was petitioning to get his medical license reinstated.

Whatever the reason, it had all blown up.

Dana Metcalf interrupted her thoughts. "Maybe that's why I'm here."

"What?"

"Because they expected a cat fight." Her lips twitched at her own little pun.

"A cat fight? No." Kristi cast her a disparaging glance. Was the woman an idiot? Well . . . the jury was still out on that one.

"That tall woman—I've seen her before." Dana was still staring at the open door while petting her cat. "And the man? A doctor . . . Oh, wait!" The light dawned. "I remember. He killed his wife years ago. Went to jail, and that woman"—she pointed to the door—"she was his attorney. Threw over her husband for him, right? And the husband, he . . . oh, Lord, what was . . . that's right." She looked up, her face alight with discovery. "He's the one they call the Oyster King. Allen Something-Or-Other."

"Aldo Lucerno," Kristi said automatically.

"Yes! Yes! Right! Oh, my God, now I remember. He was angry. Didn't want the divorce. Oh, my! Didn't he swear to kill the doctor or something?" Her doe eyes rounded even further.

Aldo had made many threats, all loud and public. "Or something," Kristi agreed, remembering. While researching the book she'd spoken to Aldo at his business office and he'd been more contained, his anger still seething, but controlled, evidenced only in the flush on his swarthy complexion or a tiny spark in his dark eyes, or the slightest tightening in the corner of his mouth. By that time, Reggie had threatened to sue him for a raft of crimes ranging from tax fraud to domestic battery, and Aldo had clamped down on his verbal attacks.

Dana made tsking sounds. "I always wondered about her. Leaving a prominent businessman for a man accused and convicted, mind you, of killing his wife. What could she have been thinking?"

"Maybe that he was innocent."

"No, no, there's more to it than that," Dana said, still thoughtfully petting the gray cat. "I think she liked the spectacle of it all. Even the fact that he murdered his wife." Dana was shaking her head. She gave a little shiver. "Can you imagine?"

Unfortunately, Kristi could. She'd witnessed Reggie's temper and flair for the dramatic in the courtroom when she was defending her current husband and she'd seen Reggie play to the cameras when giving a press statement about the case, so yes, there was that. Also, Kristi had observed how hard and determined Hamilton could be as he'd sat stoically in the courtroom, not flinching at the sight of his first wife's bloody body when pictures of her lifeless form had been shown to the jury. While their daughter Lindsay had been shuffled from the courtroom before the pictures had been displayed, Hamilton had barely glanced at them, as if in being a doctor, dealing with life and death on a daily basis, he'd become inured to a lifeless body—even his own wife's.

No, it wasn't difficult for her to imagine him killing his wife, Bethany, with the same steely sense of purpose with which he wielded a surgeon's scalpel.

"I wonder who will get their segment," Dana said pensively.

"What?" Kristi was jarred from her musings about Hamilton Cooke to the green room and the cat woman.

"Well, if Dr. and Mrs. Cooke aren't going to agree to be interviewed, then who will fill in for them?"

When Kristi didn't respond, Dana continued. "Well, *Bonjour, New Orleans!* will need someone to interview. They're not going to have Renee-Claire up there alone, now will they? That would be a disaster." Her face was a mask of innocence when she said, "I can do it. I mean, if you don't want to. I can always find something to discuss. Mr. Precious here, is not the only cat I can talk about." She stroked the gray cat tenderly. "Princess Penelope and Ebony and Champagnie are in the car with my husband. I could bring them out. People love to see the difference in the different breeds, you know, and they all have such different personalities. I have a cute story about Ebony. . . ."

She rambled on about cats and Kristi tuned out, not believing for a second that the station would expand the feline segment that was airing due to the cat show that was convening this weekend. Instead Kristi was wondering about Reggie Lucerno Cooke and why she'd been set to appear on the very same day. That had to have been planned. ". . . black cats because of the season as it's almost Halloween, you know. And Ebony is *so* good on television, a natural, if you know what I mean." She was nodding, a smile playing upon her lips. "I have a cute story about her. . . ." Kristi managed a nod and a smile though she couldn't give two cents about any of the felines this woman found so fascinating.

Fortunately, before Dana could launch into more oh-so-fascinating anecdotes about her cats, the producer's assistant returned. Flushed faced, she apologized. "I know this is highly irregular," she said, then cast a disparaging glance through the door to the maze of hallways beyond. "But Mrs. Cooke, though she agreed to do the segment, is refusing to wait here in the green room, so we've shuffled things around and Dr. and Mrs. Cooke will be interviewed in the first segment." She glanced from a clipboard to Kristi. "You're next—as planned—and then, if Mr. Bigelow doesn't arrive, there will be a segment that's been prerecorded about the renovations to the riverboats and the final segment will be you." She nodded at Dana Metcalf. "For the cat expo this weekend. We'll wrap up with that." She glanced up. "Renee-Claire and my producer have already approved the changes and we're set to roll. Okay with you all?"

"Yes, of course," Cat Woman said. "But if you need anyone to fill in more time, I've got three lovely cats—one of them a prizewinner in the SFC—Southland Feline Competition—available. They're all in the car with my husband. He could bring them in. I thought the viewers would like—"

"This one's fine," the assistant said, pointing with her pen at Mr. Precious. "One cat."

"I know, but—"

"Just one. Her."

Dana said quickly, "*Mr.* Precious is a he."

"Fine. Him then. I'll be back to take you to the set at the breaks." Jen glanced at the clock on the wall. "God, where is Tom Bigelow?"

She was texting furiously on her phone again as she exited, the door shutting behind her.

"Well." Dana let out a little huff and pursed her lips. "Okay, I guess," then to Kristi, "Mr. Precious can't handle all this stress. He's a real professional, though I have to be careful with him, you know."

Kristi didn't.

Nor did she care.

The cat hadn't moved an inch on his pillow and seemed content to stare at Kristi with wide green eyes.

"He's a champion breeder—oh, my God—so good. The queens? The female cats? They adore him. He's *very* popular." She was nodding and ran a finger along the fringe of the satin pillow. "And this? We call it his throne." She actually tittered. "It's chilled." Nodding, she added, "Uh-huh. To protect his, you know, privates, to keep him in good shape. For the ladies."

Okay. TMI. Why were they even having this conversation? Kristi wondered if the woman was putting her on or just a bona fide kook. Either way, she wasn't interested in Mr. Precious's love life and quickly turned her attention to her phone to end the conversation. Like right now!

Get me out of here, she thought just as the assistant brought in Tom Bigelow, the missing jazz musician who looked like he'd just rolled out of bed or was still up from a gig the night before. As the assistant tried and failed not to look perturbed, he landed on the far end of the couch while clutching a black instrument case. His eyes were bleary, his hair sticking up at all angles, and he was dressed head to foot in black—jeans, ratty T-shirt, boots, and jacket, all at odds with his wan sleep-deprived complexion. He snapped the case open and withdrew a gleaming saxophone, as pristine as he was grungy.

Eyeing him, Dana scooted a little further away and put a protective arm between her adored cat with his cooled "privates" and the dull-eyed musician.

It all seemed bizarre and all Kristi wanted to do was get it over with.

As soon as possible.

* * *

It just wasn't right, Montoya thought as he drove through the city. No matter how strong Bentz's belief that Father John had returned and was creating his own brand of sick mayhem in the city, Montoya wasn't completely convinced. It all didn't fit. Yeah, the killing of the prostitutes with a rosary—that was all Father John or a damned good copycat, but Jay McKnight's homicide and the attack and subsequent terrorizing of Kristi Bentz McKnight just didn't fit.

He cut through the French Quarter and double-parked near Jackson Square, then jogged through the gates and past the statue of Andrew Jackson atop his rearing horse. The air was fresh, only a few people passing by, the sun rising over the city as he paused to stare up at St. Louis Cathedral, its white sides gleaming, the three black-roofed spires rising upward into the morning sky. Once out of the park, he slowed and walked crisply into the side alley where Kristi and Jay had been attacked. This was what was bothering him. Why would Father John attack here, risk being seen, take a knife to his intended victims?

Victim, he reminded himself. Jay wasn't supposed to be here that night. Kristi was the target and still was, if the notes left in her home were to be believed. He studied the wall where there had been bloodstains, but they'd been washed away, leaving no stain, no physical evidence of the violent attack.

He'd talked to shopkeepers in the surrounding buildings, checked with the church, and the public information officer had put out requests for anyone who had been out in the storm that night, who might have witnessed the attack, or seen the assailant lying in wait or fleeing the scene to call.

So far: nothing.

Father John, the Rosary Killer from another lifetime?

Montoya didn't think so.

He walked back to his Mustang and drove to the station where he found Bentz in their shared office. As puzzled and contemplative as Montoya was, Bentz was the opposite, obviously pumped.

He was drinking coffee from a paper cup and wiping his fingers of powdered sugar, the remains of a beignet visible in the trash can. "We're gonna get him," Bentz told his partner, and there was a spark in his eyes, the same glint of a hunter noticing prey. "We're gonna get him, and this time, this time, that son of a bitch isn't going to get away. Take a look."

He pointed to the maps of the area that he'd taped onto a white board. The one map was of New Orleans. Marked in red were the areas where Helene Laroche and Teri Marie Gaines had been found. Both in the city. Further out was the spot where Jane Doe had been located.

"Okay. Got it. What are the yellow marks?" he asked, but in a second he knew. "Where the bodies were found the first time he was here."

"Right," Bentz said. "The only one out of the city is Jane Doe, but I figure he might have been spooked—had her make the call and then get out of the city. But look over here." He pointed at the second map of the larger area. Montoya understood. He saw places he'd never forget, including Father John's original lair, now long gone. Bentz pointed it out. "Here's where he was, years ago, and then over here"—he drew a line to another spot—"this is Cyrus Unger's cabin, where we caught the image of the Impala when he tried to rent a spot." Montoya was nodding. Again, Bentz drew an imaginary line with his finger to another area, deep in the bayou. "This is where Bobby-Dean Clements and Clive Jones found Jane Doe on that dock, and this"—again his fingers slid across the map—"is the direction the attacker ran, presumably toward this road." He tapped the small lane that cut from the larger road running through the parish.

"So you're thinking Father John lives somewhere in the triangulated area."

"He's familiar with it."

Montoya eyed the map. "Big area."

Bentz was nodding, his eyebrows drawing together as he sipped from his cup. "Yep. But we'll concentrate on here." He touched the spot indicating the dock where Clive and Bobby-Dean had seen the attack on Jane Doe. "Start searching there and fan out. I've got a team on it."

"In the swamp. Already?"

Bentz nodded. "Yeah." He met Montoya's eyes. "It's time to nail the sick son of a bitch." Bentz chewed on the edge of his cup.

"You heading out there?"

"We both are. But first, we need to head to the hospital and talk to his latest victim. She's awake, and surprisingly," he said, scooping up his phone and keys, "other than the knock on her head and her throat bruised and cut, she's okay. Might be released today."

"Really?"

"Yeah, really. So let's go." Bentz was already heading for the door. "Let's see what Jane has to say."

CHAPTER 30

With a knot twisting in her gut, Kristi watched the first segment of *Bonjour, New Orleans!* from her spot in the green room while Dana Metcalf prattled on about cats. Tom Bigelow had poured himself a cup of coffee from the pot on the counter, downed it, then poured a second. He was cradling the cup in his lap, and the shot of caffeine from his first swallows didn't seem to be working. He sat on his corner of the couch, long legs propped on a coffee table. He kept nodding off, then jerking awake, and trying vainly to stay awake only to doze again.

Dana caught Kristi's attention, pointed to the listing cup, and mouthed, "He's going to spill that," as if she, unable to move because of Mr. Precious, wanted Kristi to pluck the cup from Bigelow's slack hands.

Kristi ignored the cat woman and read the closed captions of the program in progress. As expected Reggie fielded most of the questions, which centered around the reason for the couple being guests. Reggie Cooke and her ex-husband, Aldo Lucerno, were on the board of St. Ada's Hospital, neither having resigned despite their divorce, and there was a fund-raising effort coming up, a benefit with a Halloween theme for the season. Reggie enthusiastically invited the public to buy tickets, attend, and most of all, she added with a wink, bring their checkbooks and credit cards!

Of course during that time, Hamilton Cooke was brought into the conversation that included a discussion of his attempt to have his medical license restored. Though Hamilton retained his ever-stoic expression and sat stiffly, almost awkwardly, Reggie's face lit up at the prospect of the restoration. Hands folded in her lap, she leaned forward, as if warming up to Renee-Claire, and smiled.

". . . just a matter of time. Hamilton is an excellent surgeon and he's been fully exonerated in the unfortunate death of Bethany." She grew sober. "The tragedy has taken a huge toll on the family, not only for Hamilton but for his, our, daughter now, Lindsay, who by the way, is in college and planning a career in medicine herself." Reggie visibly brightened again.

Hamilton did not. He even sent what appeared to be a warning glance at the mention of his daughter's name, but Reggie ignored it.

Renee-Claire said, "So Beth's death was an accident."

"Of course. Slipped on the marble tiles of the shower." Reggie's smile turned a little harder.

"And your daughter, Lindsay, found her mother." Renee-Claire had turned her attention fully to Hamilton. "Isn't that right?"

"Yes," Reggie said, trying to take control.

But the host of the program zeroed in on Hamilton. So did the camera. "And what did you do? You were outside, yes?"

Hamilton nodded. "I heard Lindsay screaming, I ran into the house, assessed the situation, and tried to help Beth. Lindsay called nine-one-one." He said it without any emotion, and as the camera panned away Kristi caught a glimpse of Reggie's hand on her husband's knee, her fingers tightening over the crease in his pant leg, adding pressure as if in silent warning.

What was going on here?

"And you lost your license when you were charged and convicted of homicide," Renee-Claire said.

"That conviction was overturned," Reggie snapped, her grin tight. "And, we came here to talk about the benefit at St. Ada's," she reminded the host.

"That you still support with your ex-husband. We asked him to appear today, but he declined."

"You did what?" Reggie's smile slid from her face. This wasn't what she'd expected.

"You were still married to Aldo Lucerno when you represented Dr. Cooke in his appeal, isn't that correct?"

"This has nothing to do with—" She caught herself, straightened her shoulders. "What is this? We came here to promote the benefit at the hospital, charity work for the good of St. Ada's and the city, not to rehash our private lives nor discuss Hamilton's career."

"Yes, yes, of course," the hostess said, backing off a bit. "It's just that New Orleans has always been fascinated by your story. You and Aldo were—high school sweethearts?"

"College and that's ancient history," Reggie said crisply. "We were young. Foolish. And then, of course, I met Dr. Cooke." She turned her eyes to her husband.

"Didn't the true-crime book about Dr. Cooke, *The God Complex and Murder,* written by our next guest, New Orleans's own Mistress of True Crime, Kristi Bentz, detail it all?"

"Excuse me?"

"Everything from the death of Bethany Cooke, to Dr. Cooke's murder trial, and your taking on his appeal and falling in love."

A light of understanding flared in Reggie's eyes. "There was no murder," she said crisply.

"No God complex, either," Hamilton interjected.

"Good. Let's discuss it in our next segment."

Reggie's face fell, but the camera cut to Renee-Claire, who handled the segue easily. "As I said, our next guest is the author of that book and several others, including *The Rosary Killer*, a book about a murderer who was presumed long dead and could, just could be stalking the streets of our fair city again. That's right, author Kristi Bentz is here with us in the studio. She's the daughter of Detective Rick Bentz of the New Orleans Police Department and she recently was a victim herself and is still recovering from an attack that tragically took the life of her husband, Jay McKnight. She's here to talk about the attack, the airing of several movies made for television that were drawn from her books and, of course, about *The Rosary Killer,* her best seller, which will be rereleased soon.

"That's all coming up next after a short break, so stay right here." The screen filled with the covers of both the books that the host had mentioned.

Oh. Dear. Lord.

The knot that had formed in Kristi's gut grew just as the door opened and Jen, the production assistant, motioned to Kristi. "Let's go." To Tom, "You too. We've got chairs in the wings."

"Oh—okay." He nearly toppled his coffee as he roused, spilling a little on his crotch and not seeming to notice as he grabbed his sax.

"What about us?" Dana asked, stroking the cat.

"Next segment. Sit tight. I'll come get you." She cut Kristi a look that said all too clearly that Reggie had insisted Kristi be nowhere near her.

Jen led them through the doors to the studio with its soaring open ceilings, now unoccupied news desk, and two cameras positioned around a set decorated like a typical New Orleans living room. "You," she said to the musician, "take one of those chairs." She motioned to a row of folding chairs in the darkened area of the studio, then guided Kristi to one of the modern armchairs on the set.

Reggie and Hamilton Cooke were nowhere to be seen, but the host, Renee-Claire, was looking at an exit door and frowning. She spied Kristi, pinned a smile on her face, and said, "Hi, I'm Renee-Claire," and shook Kristi's hand. "Apparently Dr. and Mrs. Cooke had somewhere else to be."

"Anywhere else," Kristi said, and for the first time the hostess smiled. "No love lost?"

"None," Kristi said, and told herself to get through this.

"And you use your maiden name. Is that right?"

"Yes, I kept it for the purpose of writing."

"Okay, got that."

"Twenty seconds," a voice from behind the cameras shouted.

"Okay. I'll introduce you and then we'll get into it," Renee-Claire said as she sat arrow straight in the chair.

The segment was counted down and then Renee-Claire was smiling into the camera. "Our next guest is New Orleans's premier crime writer who has encountered more than one serial killer herself. She's the author of *The Rosary Killer* and *The God Complex and Murder*. Please welcome author Kristi Bentz."

The camera zeroed in on Kristi.

"You can do this," Jay's voice was so loud she nearly looked to see if he was behind her, then she settled in to the interview.

"So, you've always been around crime," the hostess said, "as your father is a detective. Is that why you were interested in writing these kinds of books?"

"Yes," she replied, and answered a few more simple questions about living in New Orleans and writing true crime, feeling more comfortable on the set. Then the interview took a darker turn.

"Recently you survived a horrendous attack that put you in the hospital and took your husband's life. Can you tell our viewers about that? Some people are saying that the attacker could be like the reincarnation of a serial killer who dressed up as a priest and murdered his victims. Can you confirm that?"

She dodged the question. "The police are investigating. That's all I can say right now."

"But you were there! The killer tried to take your life!"

"Yes."

"And, as I understand it, your husband saved you."

"That's right," Kristi said, reliving those last horrid moments of Jay's life and the reason he'd come looking for her, that they'd had one of the worst fights of their marriage. She remembered running out to the car, her final words to him ringing through her ears: *"I don't know why I ever married you!"*

"Ms. Bentz?" a voice asked, and Kristi blinked back to the present.

"I asked you if you're planning to write a follow-up book to *The Rosary Killer*."

"I'm not sure yet," Kristi said, recovering. "I'm discussing it now with my agent."

"I'm sure it would be another best seller! Just like both the original book and *The God Complex and Murder*, the story about Dr. Hamilton Cooke, our last guest. These best sellers can be viewed through our sister station or by streaming. You won't want to miss either one!" Again both book covers showed on the screen. "Thank you, Kristi Bentz," the hostess said as the camera focused on her again. "You all will want to stick around because coming up we have one of New Orleans's premier saxophone players, Tom Bigelow, here to play his most recent jazz composition, and later on I'll interview Dana Metcalf, president of a local cat breeders club, and her prizewinning Persian cat, Mr. Precious. They are here to tell us all about the upcoming cat show this weekend, which would be the perfect outing for the whole family!"

The program cut to commercial and Kristi's microphone was un-hooked by Jen, who then motioned Bigelow onto the set.

Less than five minutes later, Kristi stepped into the parking lot and spied a black BMW idling at the exit to the lot. Hamilton Cooke was behind the wheel. He cast Kristi a look replete with hatred. As she stared at him, he raised his hand, pointed his finger like a gun and pretended to fire directly at Kristi. Then he trod hard on the accelerator and his Beemer roared into traffic.

Kristi noticed that his wife wasn't in the passenger seat. Instead Reggie Cooke was stepping out of the interior of a sleek, red Mercedes parked just two slots from Kristi's Subaru.

Reggie's expression said it all: she was pissed. "We need to talk," she said as Kristi approached.

"Okay."

"I don't like what happened in there." She gestured to the building housing the television station.

"Neither do I."

"You set it up."

"No." She thought about trying to explain, but decided it would do no good.

Reggie obviously thought she was lying, but Kristi didn't care. She'd already said as much as she was going to. "I can't believe that little bitch brought up Bethany and Aldo. Ancient history. Nothing to do with now." She was nearly gnashing her teeth. "Anything for a buck, you know. To keep ratings in the stratosphere no matter what. No matter whom you hurt. And you—that's your bread and butter, isn't it? Exposing everyone's little secrets, creating lies, all to sell a few more copies."

"I told you—"

"I know what you said. So, what? Now you're trying to tell me that this was what—random?"

Kristi reached her car and opened the door. "No. I doubt that. I'm saying I had nothing to do with it." She slid inside. "But it's over now."

"Is it?" Reggie glanced back at the huge brick building housing the television station. "I hope so."

At this point, there was no reason to continue the conversation. Kristi closed the door and started the engine. She was still infuriated with Zera for setting this up behind her back and yeah, the producer had to answer for manipulating the guests, but it was over. For now. And if Hamilton Cooke still felt the sting of his original sentence, too damned bad. The reversal of his conviction upon appeal because of some technicality his new wife had discovered didn't alter the facts of the case or change Kristi's opinion.

In her heart of hearts she believed Hamilton Cooke was a stone-cold killer.

From the passenger seat, Bentz swore under his breath. "The press. Already." He eyed the news van as Montoya found a parking spot in the lot adjacent to St. Ada's Hospital.

"It's only gonna get worse." Montoya cut the engine. "You've got to get over your attitude, man. The press can help us getting the word out. If we get a composite of the guy who attacked our victim, they can get it out on TV and the Internet, social media. Don't fight it."

"I just don't like to be pressured," Bentz grumbled as he climbed out of the car and headed inside St. Ada's. He was walking briskly and Montoya, pocketing his keys, jogged to keep up. As he did, his cell phone buzzed and he saw it was the station. "Montoya," he said as they walked through the doors.

"Brinkman," the detective said, and Montoya felt an instant dislike coursing through his veins. He and Brinkman had never gotten along.

"What's up?"

"Just got a call from a hooker," Brinkman said, and Montoya braced himself for some kind of off-color joke.

"Yeah?"

"Her roommate never showed up last night. I figure that's not a big deal, but she said the missing woman is young, about twenty, blond, and new to the profession."

"This woman have a name?"

"Goes by Luna for her clients, if you know what I mean." He sniggered on the other end of the connection and Montoya didn't respond. Brinkman was a good cop, but a slimeball. "Her real name is Stacy Parker. Grew up in Wyoming on a ranch outside Casper. Been in New Orleans less than a year, but the roommate says she never stays out overnight. The latest she's come in before was around three, maybe three-thirty."

"Where does she live?"

"A motel, the All-Day-All-Night Inn. It's a dive a few blocks off the Quarter. The place rents rooms by the day, week, month, and probably hour. She shares the place with the hooker who called it in, Louisa Abernathy, who, by the way, goes by Red. I've already sent a couple of uniforms over there." He rattled off the address as well as Louisa Abernathy's number, which Montoya typed into his phone as he ended the call.

He was standing in the vestibule of the hospital, one side of the wide hallway the admissions desks, the other a waiting area where people were seated in low-slung couches and chairs, potted palms in the corners, long tables scattered with magazines. He saw the sign for the elevators and noticed a sculpture, a bronze bust inset in a wall niche. The sign beneath the sculpted head read: CARLO LUCERNO, FOUNDER.

Lucerno.

As in Aldo Lucerno, the Oyster King?

As in Reggie Lucerno Cooke's former husband?

He caught up with Bentz at the elevator bank. Montoya relayed Brinkman's information on the ride up to the third floor where a tall, bald man in scrubs and a lab coat was just coming out of the victim's room. His name tag read: "Douglas Baines, MD."

He paused at the sight of them and the detectives quickly introduced themselves, showing ID and stating that they needed to talk to the patient in 326. "Five minutes," the doctor said, holding out a big palm, his fingers outstretched to indicate the length of time. "Five. She's still under sedation. Been through trauma and needs her rest."

"We just need to ask her a few questions."

"Good luck," the doctor said. "She's not giving us much information. Not even her name. Driving admissions crazy. Maybe you two can get somewhere with her. But still, five minutes."

"Got it," Bentz said.

They walked into the room where the woman, a petite blonde with bandages at her throat and bruises on her face, lay in the hospital bed. She stared at them with wide, frightened eyes.

When they introduced themselves, she looked away. "I don't have anything to say," she said, her voice a rasp.

"What's your name?" Bentz asked.

Nothing. But she knotted the edge of her bedsheet in one hand.

Montoya asked, "Are you Stacy Parker?"

She closed her eyes for a second. "Oh, God."

Bentz said, "We're trying to help find the man who did this to you."

"I don't want to talk to you." Her eyes had opened again, but she avoided Bentz's gaze to stare through a single window that looked over the parking lot.

"We need to find him," Bentz persisted, his tone even. "We think he's killed two other women, maybe more, and we need your help. Before he hurts anyone else."

She acted as if she hadn't heard, but Montoya noticed her worrying her lower lip. Indecisive. "Was your attacker a priest?"

She swallowed, then made a face as if the action pained her. With difficulty, she cleared her throat. "I don't want my family to find out," she said. "My mom and dad in Wyoming. They don't need to know."

"We won't inform them," Bentz said. "But I can't vouch for the media."

"Oh, Lord." Again she bit her lip and her fingers were working the edge of the sheet like crazy. "The man, he was dressed like a priest," she finally admitted. "I'm not Catholic, but he wasn't a man of God. No way." Her eyes slid away. "It was a disguise or a fetish or whatever."

Bentz asked, "Did he ask you to call in to *Midnight Confessions* and talk to Dr. Sam?"

"I only spoke with the person who answered," she said. "Then I handed the phone to him and he did the rest." She swallowed and looked about to cry. "I'm sorry," she said in a barely audible whisper.

"Tell us what happened," Montoya suggested, and after a moment's hesitation, the dam broke. She explained about him calling and setting up a meeting, then how she got into his car. When asked how he got her phone number, she didn't know, but figured he found it on the Internet.

"Common knowledge." With a shrug, she continued how she'd met him in the French Quarter just off Bourbon Street, how he'd taken her to a parking lot behind a warehouse to make the call, then driven her across the river to a parking spot near the bayou and forced her to walk to the dock where he put a noose in the form of a rosary over her head and the struggle ensued. ". . . I wounded him, I know I did," she said a little more emphatically. "I kicked and scratched, broke a nail even, but if those fishermen hadn't come along . . . I don't think I'd be here. They, um, they saved my life."

"Is this the man?" Bentz asked, and handed her a composite picture of the man who claimed to be Father John way back when.

She studied the photo carefully. "I don't know. It was dark. He wore sunglasses and when I knocked them off, there was all the blood and I was just trying to get away. I never got a real good look at him, but yeah, it could be."

They asked a few more questions and found out she didn't know any of the other victims, had never met Helene Laroche or Teri Marie Gaines. For the first time since they'd stepped into the room, Stacy looked Bentz straight in the eye. "Get him," she said. "Please get him."

"We will," Bentz assured her.

"Good. Because the man is evil. I'm telling you: evil."

CHAPTER 31

"Think of it as an opportunity," Zera said when Kristi finally reached her late in the afternoon. "I know, I know, I should have contacted you first."

"Damn right you should have." Kristi reached into the refrigerator and pulled out a bottle of vitamin water.

"I tried."

"You did?"

"Once," Zera said, sounding hassled. "Check your voice mail. It's not like you've been all that easy to reach lately. And when I couldn't get through, I just went for it. I've worked with that producer before and there's nothing wrong with getting your name out there again, you know, in anticipation of the new book and to promote the old ones *and* the TV shows."

"The new book—?" She cracked open the bottle. "Oh, on the Rosary Killer," she said, remembering.

"Right. You were going to send me something. An idea?"

"I haven't gotten around to it yet." Kristi eyed the clutter in her office, the open notebooks, glowing computer, and tossed into the mix, copies of the books she'd written and given to Montoya.

"Well, for crying out loud, don't take forever. We have to strike while the iron's hot."

"And you're turning this conversation around, getting away from the point."

"Okay, I hear you. No more interviews without your permission first."

"Absolutely. I thought that was understood. The way we do things."

"Got it."

"And don't ever get my friend to coerce me."

"Hey, wait! That's not the way it went down. She contacted me."

Kristi believed it. "Okay. Just check with me in the future."

"Promise," her agent said. "And you get me that outline."

"Fine," Kristi agreed. "Later." She cut the connection and decided that Zera was right, she did need a new project. And wasn't Jay's murder the most important story to follow, the mystery to solve? Wasn't making Jay's killer face justice of prime importance? Instead of being mad at Bella and Zera for forcing the issue, she should thank them because now she had a path forward.

You bet she'd write the story of the Rosary Killer, right after she made him pay for murdering her husband.

She picked up the book about Father John and skimmed some of the pages. It was true that everything was pointing to him as the killer, that he'd survived being shot in the bayou and had waited until just the right time to strike again.

Leaning back in her chair, she saw Lenore leap just before the kitten landed on her lap. "Hey there, little one," she said, as Lenore climbed to her shoulder to settle and purr into Kristi's ear. "I love you, too," Kristi said, petting her tiny head before flipping open the book to its middle and finding a black and white shot of the man who had pretended to be a priest. He was about the right height and build of the man who had attacked her and killed Jay, but something was off about that. Why would he wait so long to return? Was he injured? Out of the country? Surely if he'd been incarcerated, her father would have known of it, so why now? And why come after her?

Because of the book? She ruffled through the pages. That didn't seem right; the book and the tie-in TV movie had been years before.

But the movie's being replayed. Over and over again. On cable. On the Internet. Streaming.

Was the attack generated because she'd immortalized his sins in her book or possibly because her father had thwarted him from his original purpose, hunted him down, exposed him and, everyone had thought, killed him in the bayou? Then why attack Kristi? Why not go after Bentz himself?

Did he think killing Kristi would emotionally wound her father and that would be his supreme triumph?

Implausible. She stroked the kitten as she thought.

Then there was the MO. All wrong. The attacker in the wet poncho might not have been dressed as a priest at all.

But neither was Father John.

It didn't seem right.

Didn't fit.

Three other books were on the desk. Her gaze landed on *American Icon/American Killer.*

Mandel Jarvis.

As Lenore stretched, then moved from her shoulder to the desk, Kristi thought of the football player turned preacher and remembered how he'd threatened her, then she remembered seeing him in the church with his family surrounding him. Had he really found God? Would he risk the good life he'd created to stalk Kristi and kill her? Why?

She drummed her fingers on the edge of the desk and the kitten batted at them. Kristi, lost in thought, barely noticed. Mandel Jarvis throwing everything away to hunt Kristi down didn't seem right either. Not at this moment in time. She remembered thinking someone had been waiting by her house the other night, how Dave had bristled at a figure in the alley.

Mandel?

Was that his style to go lurking in the shadows?

He'd killed one person—well, that anyone knew about—he wasn't a serial killer, so why go after Kristi now?

Again, it didn't make sense.

As for Ned Zavala, the "Bayou Butcher," he was more likely. Anyone who could cut people into pieces . . . and he was mean. Major chip on his shoulder. She didn't buy his mother recanting her testimony and placing the blame on her recently deceased husband, no matter how unhinged and brutal Corrin Hebert had been. She picked up her notes on the *Bayou Butcher* and found her notes that Zavala had indeed threatened not only her, but her father as well. "You'll regret this," he'd yelled to Bentz, and he'd been led in chains out of the courtroom once the verdict had come down. "I'll see to it! You'll regret the day you were born."

And when Kristi's book had come out, she'd received letters from him while he'd been incarcerated. All on lined paper, all in pencil. She found those letters in a file now and looked through them. Five in all, the first being furious and threatening and then less so. She'd received the last one two years before he'd been released and nothing since. And his letters had been written in a stiff printing. As if he were still in grade school. There were some references to God and Jesus, but no specific Bible verses were included.

If Zavala were the killer, again the question was, what would have set him off? Why would he sneak around in the pouring rain to attack her and murder Jay? Again she thought of the prerelease of the TV movie. Was that enough to ignite him? She leaned back in her desk chair.

Did it make sense?

Did anything?

Her head was beginning to pound with the thoughts swirling through it. She felt like she was treading water, moving ever faster and getting nowhere. She scraped her hair away from her face and searched in a drawer until she found a rubber band. As she formed a loose bun with her fingers and snapped the band into place, she saw a copy of *The God Complex and Murder* lying under an open spiral notebook.

"Hamilton Cooke," she said aloud, and picked up the book. He was a cold one. She remembered meeting his eyes this morning when he'd walked into the green room at the station.

If looks could kill . . .

Yeah, she'd be dead already.

He hated her, and Reggie, she, too, despised Kristi and let her know it, but would either of them put everything they had at risk out of what—vengeance? Some kind of warped view of the world? Hamilton was a killer, Kristi felt it in her bones every time she saw him, but Reggie?

It took a deep, simmering rage to wait in a downpour and attack a target, then turn the attack on a second person—but that might have been just self-preservation. She stretched her arms over her head. The notes to her—meant to terrorize.

Not really Reggie's style.

But Hamilton Cooke? What about him?

Something bothered her when she thought about him. What was it she was missing? She went through her notes again, searching for . . . what? She wasn't sure.

Was it something to do with his wife? His first wife? The one who he swore had injured herself in the shower, hitting her head and bleeding out? The autopsy showed that she'd had a blood thinner in her system, but she'd been prescribed it by her doctor who was not her husband. Kristi had always wondered if he'd given her extra medication, then wounded her, made it look like an accident and then watch her bleed out, only to go back to his "yard work" when he knew his daughter was going to find her mother.

What kind of cold bastard did that?

Would he come after Kristi now, years later? Risk his new life with his new wife? Could his rage have smoldered so long or was it Reggie, her white-hot temper, finally exploding? But why? And why now?

Was it because Hamilton Cooke wanted his medical license back and he believed that her book had thwarted him? Had his seething, simmering rage with her finally caught fire? Had he snapped?

She picked up the book, studied the cover where Hamilton Cooke's visage in cruel black and white seemed to stare back at her.

What about the religious overtones of the messages she'd received? She knew that the whole family attended church and gave time and money to St. Ada's, but so what? But wasn't there something in Hamilton's background? She thumbed through the pages to the section on his childhood.

On the surface he'd had it all: good looks, brains, and an athletic body. He'd been a star basketball guard, gotten a scholarship to a private Catholic college, gone on to medical school after a fleeting thought of going to the seminary.

"How about that," she said, biting her lip and thinking hard, trying to imagine Hamilton Cooke as a priest. "Dear God," she whispered. It had been there, at the college, where he'd first met Aldo Lucerno, whose family donated heavily to the college.

Old rivals?

Who ended up marrying the same woman?

Dave padded up the stairs and stared at her.

She patted his head.

He whined and made a move toward the door.

She checked her watch. "I did promise we'd go for a walk, right?" At that the dog did a couple of quick twirls, then shot down the stairs, and ten minutes later Kristi was outside, jogging with the dog at her side, breathing in the cool evening air and feeling her head clear. She had her flashlight with its jagged rim in one pocket, a small aerosol can of mace in the other.

Just in case.

She ran to the river, passing pedestrians, avoiding puddles, feeling herself begin to sweat, her muscles lengthening, and she decided tonight she would run farther than usual, to the French Quarter, then walk back.

What was she missing?

Her heart was pumping, the sun low in the sky when she reached Jackson Square. She paused, breathing hard, and stared across the square to the cathedral, its three spires knifing upward. The tallest tower was in the middle of the church, a huge clock face mounted over arched windows and wide doors, its elegant spire topped with a cross that seemed to pierce the thin clouds.

Why here? she wondered, thinking of the attack as she walked through the park and observed the white cathedral. Was it just because whoever had stalked her knew her routine or did this cathedral have a deeper meaning? Something she couldn't quite grasp. Bits of the messages slipped through her mind:

The wages of sin is death

The day of vengeance is . . . mine

Take vengeance upon her

Though she hadn't planned it, she crossed to the cathedral, tied Dave to a bike rack, and said, "I'll be right back." Then she slipped through the massive doors and stared into the apse, a huge, beautiful expanse with arched, painted ceilings, stained glass windows, row upon row of pews, and the gilded altar. As ever, she was awed by the beauty of the cathedral and truly did feel as if God had blessed this house of worship. Her throat closed as she walked to the votive candle display and lit a candle for Jay. "Rest in peace, my love," she whispered. "Go with God. We love you." She touched her abdomen, thinking of her unborn child, made the sign of the cross, then bent a knee at the altar, which seemed acres away, and dashed a tear from her eye.

She exited and found Dave, patiently waiting, his tail brushing the sidewalk as she approached. "Let's go home," she said, and cleared her throat. Night was slowly but steadily closing in and it would be dark before she reached her house.

Whoever had attacked her hadn't ruined her reverence for the cathedral, and though she wasn't particularly religious, she did find comfort in prayer. She crossed the street, walking briskly. The attacker may have taken Jay's life. But she wouldn't let him ruin hers. No way. No how.

She was more certain than ever that whoever was behind the assault had intended to kill her and wouldn't give up. Right now, he was toying with her, hoping to scare the life out of her. Enjoying her pain.

What had Mandel Jarvis said?

"Watch yourself, girl."

She would, all right, she thought, and tugged on Dave's leash for the long walk home. She'd watch herself, but she wasn't backing off.

"That's my girl," she heard her husband say, though his voice was as faint as the slight breeze rolling off the Mississippi.

CHAPTER 32

"I don't like workin' with the cops," Bobby-Dean said as they cruised through a narrow stretch of the bayou, a spot that was unfamiliar to him. Clive was at the tiller, eyeing the thick vegetation.

"Better to keep them on our side."

"Are they? Are they really?" A mosquito was buzzing around his head and, quick as a rattler striking, he nailed that tiny son of a bitch, caught it in his hand and squeezed, then discarded the insect's tiny body with a flick of his finger. A smeared drop of blood showed on his palm. Probably his own from that little sucker.

The sun was getting lower, afternoon slipping away, clouds gathering. The air was sticky, warmer than it should be at this time of year. Bobby-Dean peered into the brambles and brush. They'd already passed several abandoned cabins—shacks, more like—that had deteriorated to the point that they were little more than rotten heaps of boards and a few bricks, places where only raccoons and skunks, wasps and snakes would call home. He didn't like poking into them, was always certain some damned creature, mad at the prodding, would leap out at him, or maybe a swarm of angry yellow jackets would erupt.

No, sir. He didn't like this.

He didn't like it one bit.

And he sure as hell wasn't comfortable working with the damned police. Bobby-Dean knew from experience you just couldn't trust those cocksuckers as far as you could throw 'em.

He squinted past the prow of the boat, eyes narrowing as sunlight dappled the water, casting shadows. Dragonflies buzzed above the dark bayou, wings snapping as other insects buzzed and fish rose from beneath the surface. Bobby felt a little chill whisper up his spine, a bit of a warning that he always felt when he was nearing danger. He'd felt it seconds before he'd caught sight of that sick son of a bitch trying to kill the blond woman on the dock last night, a frisson of apprehension, and he felt it now, as if a ghost were passing across the back of his neck.

Raising a hand, he said, "Hold up."

"Wha—?"

"I said hold up." There was something here, something not quite right, something he could feel.

Clive cut the engine and the boat drifted, spider lilies and duckweed parting as the prow cut deeper into the shadows.

Was it his imagination, or had everything gone quiet? No fish jumping, no frogs croaking, even the damned insects were no longer humming. All Bobby-Dean heard was the sound of the boat cutting through water and the escalated beat of his heart. The back of his throat went dry.

"What is it?" Clive asked.

"Shh!" Bobby-Dean strained to listen. He'd grown up in these parts and the sounds, smells, and sights of the bayou, the feel of it all, was an integral part of him. But today . . .

Maybe they should just get the hell out.

Leave this work, whatever the fuck it was, to the cops. What were they looking for anyway?

"Anything suspicious, y'know, anything that looks outta place." That's what the deputy in charge, a big, rawboned woman in aviator sunglasses, had told the boaters and people on foot, some with dogs as they went searching for what? Other victims? A hideout? Bobby-Dean didn't know and he wasn't all that keen on finding out.

"You see somethin'?"

Damn that Clive, he never talked when ya wanted him to, but if ya told him to be quiet, hell, he kept runnin' his mouth.

"Don't know."

Maybe it was nothing.

But then why weren't the birds chirping?

Not even a crow cawing.

He studied the cattails and the undergrowth as the boat moved slowly through the umbra, passing by some rotted boards just under the water, the remains of a dock or pier, just as the boat jolted, the prow hitting a submerged piling.

Clive said, "What the—?" as Bobby-Dean caught the first glimpse of a flash of white beneath the water. Something—oh, Jesus. He let out a sharp little scream as the water moved, the spider lilies parting to expose a skull lying faceup just under the surface.

"Shit!" He actually jumped back, the boat tipping slightly before righting.

But his gaze was fastened on the bones—definitely a skull devoid of flesh, definitely human. Blackened eye sockets and nasal cavity, grotesque smile missing more than a few teeth.

"Jesus, Mary, and Joseph!" Clive whispered, making a quick sign of the cross over his barrel chest. "Let's get the fuck outta here."

"No—no. Make the call! To that deputy! Make the fuckin' call!" Bobby-Dean felt his insides turn to water, but he knew they had to stay here, by the eerie bones. The cops and everyone around would think of them as local heroes for the discovery.

And that had to be worth something.

Cruz started to turn in to the motel, but spying the cop cars at the end unit, decided to keep his Harley on the street and roared past. He didn't know what was going down, but didn't like it. Though he had paid for his room for a week, he never left any of his belongings in the room. He traveled light by necessity, so it was easy enough to stuff two pairs of jeans and a couple of shirts and shaving kit into his saddlebags.

Adjusting his sunglasses against the bright October sun, he wondered what his next move should be.

Sooner or later he'd have to give himself up, and he figured he'd be best off with his brother, an officer of the law, at his side. Well, except for the fact that he'd fled the scene of a homicide, driven across too many state lines to count, and was now considered a fugitive.

That had been his choice rather than face the consequences of his actions in Oregon. But he had a friend working out the details of what really went down, so maybe he'd get lucky.

He couldn't run forever.

But maybe, just maybe, for a little while longer.

* * *

Bentz's stomach roiled.

It was all he could do not to throw up right there on the bayou as he stared at the body submerged in the water. From what he could see, he guessed the skeleton was a woman, small frame and long gray hair, but the sex wouldn't be determined until the lab analyzed what was left of the bones. From the way they'd been picked clean, he thought they'd been there a while.

"This place gives me a case of the willies," Montoya said, staring at the remains of the woman.

They were seated in one of three boats that had been sent to the area where the skull had been first seen by Bobby-Dean Clements and his friend Clive Jones, the very two fishermen who had seen Father John attacking Stacy Parker just the night before.

Those two men were still here, in their own boat drifting nearby, watching as divers went into the bayou to retrieve what they could. It wasn't that the water was all that deep here, but all of the area had to be explored and examined and the sun was setting, the bayou still aside from the sound of a few birds in the trees and voices from the search team.

Bentz popped three antacids from a roll he kept in his pocket and scanned the thickets and underbrush surrounding the water. Brambles and vines grew thick and he spied a huge clump of vegetation that seemed out of place. "Take us down there," he said to the officer at the rudder.

"You got it." The deputy manning the boat eased them closer. "What is that?" Bentz said, motioning to the mass of weeds where several cypress rose, Spanish moss draping downward.

Montoya lifted the sunglasses from his eyes and squinted, focusing on the weedy thicket. "Vegeta—Maybe more. Christ, is that a chimney stack?" he asked.

"Or was," Bentz said. "Let's get more people down here." As they drifted closer, he studied the swell of brush and dense foliage rising out of the swamp waters, a spongy island of wet earth.

"Let's check it out."

"Careful of gator nests," the deputy warned as she guided the boat closer.

Montoya stepped out, his boots sinking deep, water lapping over the tops. Bentz joined him and together they pushed their way through the cattails, reeds, and water to dryer land.

"Dark as hell here," Montoya said, and pulled a flashlight from his pocket. He trained the beam past the brambles, toward the smokestack. "Oh—here we go." The beam cut between the vines and onto the remains of rotted wood siding, a splintered window frame, and what appeared to be the remains of a small shanty or cabin, all broken down, flattened by the weight of the foliage that had engulfed it. "You think she"—he hooked his thumb backward to the area where the body had been found—"belonged here? Lived here?"

"Don't know." But Bentz didn't like it. He caught a glimpse of a yellow jacket nest partially visible in the wood, the wasps flying in and out and holes for other critters of the swamp, and . . . oh, shit . . . was that a hand? "I think we got another one," he said as Montoya swept the beam of his flashlight onto a stack of broken-down boards. The remains of a human hand were visible, bones gray and partially covered in dirt, parts of some fingers missing, but definitely a human hand.

The flesh on the back of his spine crawled. "What the hell happened out here?" he said as a hawk flapped into the swamp and settled onto the branch of an overhanging cypress.

"Nothing good," Montoya said as the beam of his light caught in the glitter of stones. Bloodred, they sparkled on a chain wound through what was left of the fingers, a muddy cross dangling from the thin links twined in the bones.

Bentz's blood ran like ice water through his veins as he stared at the remains of the rosary.

"He was here," he said to Montoya. "Father John. He was here."

"Maybe. But these two. They've been dead a long time."

"Doesn't matter. We need to rope this off, it's a crime scene."

"It's the damned bayou."

"I don't care, he was here," Bentz said, and looked across the bayou, fifty feet or so, where Bobby-Dean and Clive's boat idled. "Hey!" Bentz shouted. "You! Come over here!"

Bobby-Dean had the gall to point a thumb at his chest in a *who-me?* gesture and Bentz waved him over. "Yeah, you! Both of you! Come on over here!" He ordered the deputy to find a way to rope off the area and to have the CSI team come and check out the swampy island and destroyed cabin. "No telling what else we'll find in there," he said, and the eerie feeling that had been with him earlier dissipated, was chased away by the stronger sensation that they were getting somewhere, that the hunt was on and this time, the fake priest was the prey.

Once Clive Jones's boat had reached the island, he cut the engine. "What is it?" Bobby-Dean asked warily.

Bentz cut to the chase. "There's another body here."

"Oh, fuck, man." Bobby-Dean ran a hand through his thin beard. "I knowed it."

Montoya asked, "How did you know it?"

"When we found that body. I . . . I was afraid it was Maizie."

"Who's Maizie?" Montoya wanted to know, and Bentz waited.

Bobby-Dean glanced at Clive. The big man nodded, then looked away, swatted at some insect that was bothering him and, Bentz noted, had begun to sweat. He mopped his head and stared into the brambles covering the remains of the shack.

"Maizie Ledoux," Bobby-Dean said. "Married to Willard." He glanced at the island and Bentz got the feeling that the bony hand he'd seen belonged to Willard.

"They lived around here. Never stayed in one place long, near as I can tell, sold alligators and game and she . . . she dabbled."

"Dabbled in what?" Bentz asked, and noticed that Clive's face clouded over.

Bobby-Dean cleared his throat as a crow, high up in a cypress tree, let out a plaintive caw. "Well, I guess what you'd call it is the, um, dark arts."

"Dark arts?"

"Voodoo," Clive said. "That's what they said, but no one knows for sure."

"When was the last time you saw them?"

"That's just it," Bobby-Dean said. "It's not like anyone saw them. Not regular, for sure, and they kind of squatted, you know, moved around, you never really knew where they were."

"Was there ever anyone else with them?" Bentz asked.

"Like a kid?" Bobby-Dean said, and both he and Clive were shaking their heads.

Montoya said, "Like anyone."

Bobby-Dean rubbed the back of his neck. "Nah. They were loners, you know."

"Not right." Clive was serious. "No one wanted to hang out with them. Just did their business—whatever it was—and left."

"They have relatives or friends?"

"Look man, I didn't know them. Nuh-uh. I just heard about 'em. Saw 'em maybe—what?" He looked to Clive, who was shaking his head. "Maybe four—five times?"

"In how long?" Bentz asked.

"Oh—Geez, I don't know." He lifted his hat and squared it on his head. "Years. Long as I can remember, I guess. As I said, they came and went. Months would go by and you wouldn't see 'em."

"Years," Clive corrected.

"So when was the last time you saw them. Either one of them," Bentz said, and the two men looked at each other.

"Maybe, what?" He looked at Clive. "Three years."

"Uh—yeah." The big man was nodding his agreement. "Little less. Christmas time. We seen 'em, no—just Maizie I think." He was frowning, thinking, eyebrows drawn together. "Down tryin' to sell bait to CU. He rents cabins around here. Cyrus Unger."

"We know him."

"That's right," Bobby-Dean agreed. "I remember cuz CU had that old light-up Santa outside his office he always puts up at that time of year."

The deputy drove them back to the spot where they'd hiked in and they made their way back to Bentz's Jeep. Once they changed into regular shoes, dumped their boots and placed them in the back, they took off, heading back to New Orleans.

"We're gonna get him," Bentz said, flipping down his visor as they rounded a curve and the setting sun was in his eyes. "I can feel it."

"If we can find him."

"We will." Bentz was sure of it.

It was only a matter of time.

He had to move.

Now!

The damned cops were closing in. But that was fine. He was ready.

He'd been planning this for so long. They were in for a big, big surprise.

And so was she.

In his rowboat, he slid through the water, the moon his only guide.

Stroke.

He was anxious, but knew everything was in place. He'd been preparing for this moment for years. Years! And now it was about to come to fruition.

Finally.

The cool of the evening chased through the swamp, a soft breeze ruffling the leaves and causing the Spanish moss to sway ghostlike overhead. Insects buzzed and, somewhere hidden in the cypress trees, an owl gave off soft hoots.

He kept rowing.

Through the labyrinth of bayous, around trees and islands, slipping unseen by the few cabins where lights still glowed in the windows, he rowed steadily.

Quickly.

With purpose.

Stroke.

His craft cut through the water easily, but he was beginning to sweat and the injuries that whore Luna had inflicted ached, the scratches to his face, the bruise on his shin. They were healing, but the scrapes on his face were still visible. He'd have to cover them before he initiated the next step of his plan.

If only she'd died as she was supposed to. But instead she'd survived, been taken to the hospital, probably told all she knew to the cops.

Well, fine.

She didn't know all that much.

And he was ready.

Still, it was irritating. A glitch in his perfect plan.

Because of those damned fishermen her death had been interrupted, he'd been injured and barely gotten away. But he had escaped. He took heart in the fact that he'd survived, that God was with him on his mission.

Stroke.

Under some low-hanging limbs, the moss trailing its light fingers over his scalp, he rowed and insects swarmed and a bullfrog croaked mournfully. He had packed his most precious belongings with him, the beads and piano wire, his hunting knife and his disguises—clothes and makeup—all neatly tucked into his duffel bag.

His destination was all part of his plan. He just hadn't intended to move to his new hiding spot quite so soon. But it was ready, and maybe, just maybe, these sequences of events were preordained, maybe God, a test. And he'd passed with flying colors. Maybe he should be grateful rather than annoyed.

He'd been following Dr. Sam at a distance, seeing that cops patrolled her house more often, even spying more cop cars than usual as she left the studio. That was his fault for showing his hand.

But the cops, especially Rick Bentz, were thick as thieves, so he'd had to tread carefully, wear the disguises. He'd managed to change plates on the Impala again. It was simple enough to slip through the parking lots of big box stores and remove a plate, then reattach it to his Impala, but he'd taken care there, too, as these days there were cameras everywhere.

Another reason he had to up his timeline.

As he thought of his plan and Rick Bentz, always dogging him, he decided it was time to turn the tables on the detective. Bentz, like the fake radio shrink, needed to pay for his sins. Too bad his kid wasn't killed in that attack that took her husband's life.

Maybe he could do something about that.

Stroke, stroke.

Yes, he thought, the night feeling like a cloak around him.

Bentz's Achilles' heel had always been his family. Even more important to him than his reputation as a cop.

So why not kill two birds with one stone?

Yes, yes! His spirits soared.

He would set his plan in motion tonight. There was no time for rest and recovery. Because he had so much to do. So very much. He couldn't be distracted. Nor waylaid.

Time was of the essence.

Stroke. Stroke.

Around a final bend, he caught a glimpse of his destination and his heart soared at the sight of a small, forgotten monastery. In truth it was never completed, and what had been built had fallen into ruin, crumbling into the surrounding water, the only access by water. But time hadn't completely destroyed the building, the rock walls and rotting timbers. He'd managed to save what he could, salvaging the heart of the ruins, and here, he thought, he would be safe to finish what he'd started so many years ago.

He smiled. Sent up a quick, precise prayer for guidance.

Stroke. Stroke. Stroke.

Soon, so very soon, he would have his long-awaited vengeance.

CHAPTER 33

"Okay, okay, I forgive you," Kristi said into the phone as she crossed the trolley tracks on the way back to her house. Dusk was settling over the city, Kristi's heart rate was back to normal, and Dave was trotting beside her.

Bella let out an unconvinced sigh. "I feel like a loser."

"Get over it."

"So you're not mad?"

"No. I'm not. Not anymore. I told you, I was pretty pissed to be set up for the interview that way, but I'm over it."

"Seriously?" How many times did Kristi have to tell Bella that she wasn't angry?

"It was an awful thing to do. Blindsiding you like that. And with Dr. Cooke."

"Again, just so it doesn't happen again."

"It won't. Oh, no. It won't." Kristi rounded the corner to her house and eyed the coming darkness. Pumpkins and lanterns were glowing, patches of light from the windows on the street, a few cars passing under the streetlamps.

It appeared quiet.

It appeared safe.

And yet she felt her nerves tighten.

Glancing down at the dog, she noted that he wasn't on guard tonight, his hackles weren't up and he wasn't staring down into the neighbor's alley.

Good.

"Okay, but drinks are on me," Bella said a little more brightly. "This weekend—oh! How about Halloween?"

"Can't. It's Ginny's birthday."

"Oh. Right. I forget you have a sister. She's just a baby."

For a second Kristi thought about blurting out that she was going to have a child herself, but held it back. Better to tell Bella in person. "Right. She's turning one, so I really need to be there, but maybe the next week?"

"I would love it. I need some girl time. To be honest, things aren't great with Sean right now. I don't want to bug you about it, you know, since you lost Jay so recently, but sometimes . . ." Her voice faded for a second, then she cleared her throat. "Just so you know why I can't lose my job. Anyway, the first weekend in November, right? I'm holding you to it. I'll call Sarah and Jess, too."

"Good." May as well tell the whole group her secret before she began to show.

"I'll see you then." Bella cut the connection just as Kristi reached her house. She let herself in, disengaged the alarm, and poured herself a tall glass of water while Dave lapped noisily from his dish near the back door. After running through the shower, slipping on pj's, and paying attention to Lenore, she made a microwave dinner that tasted like cardboard, drank a bottle of juice, and wished for a glass of wine. Those days, at least for the next year, were long gone.

As she pulled the kitchen trash can from under the sink, she recoiled from the odor. "Wow." How long had it been since she'd emptied it? Didn't want to think, just pulled the plastic sack from the bin, tied it, and carried it through the garage. Dave, of course, padded after her as she slipped outside to the area where she kept the big bins. As she did, Dave barked loudly.

"What?"

He was staring at the plastic garbage can. Still barking.

"Shh! Stop!" She looked around.

No one.

And she'd flipped on the light in the garage, illuminating the area. No one was hiding anywhere nearby.

"You're being silly," she said, and hoisting the bag with her right arm, unhooked the bungee cord and flipped open the lid with her other.

A sharp hiss came from within, and as she was about to drop the bag into the can, she saw, coiled on the bottom, a huge snake with a triangular head, reptilian eyes staring up, jaws open to expose the white inside its mouth.

No!

Quick as lightning, the cottonmouth struck!

Shooting upward!

Mouth open!

Fangs exposed!

Kristi leaped back. "What the—!?"

The lid fell back onto the tub as the snake's head hit it.

She dropped the garbage sack.

Shit, shit, shit!

Thump! The can hopped as the snake struck the side.

Then again.

Thump! Thump!

Each time Kristi jumped backward, certain the snake would pop out. Heart thudding, she slid on spilled yogurt, caught herself, and kept her eyes fastened to the tub. *Trap it! Trap it inside!*

With Dave barking his fool head off, her fingers shaking, she reattached the bungee cord that held the lid in place, then backed away. The tub teetered wildly with the writhing and striking of the snake within while her own heart was knocking fast and hard.

"What's going on?" A male voice came out of nowhere.

She whipped around and faced the same man who'd found Dave in the park and brought him home: Cruz Montoya. Dressed in leather jacket and jeans, his black hair mussed, he stood only inches from her.

"What're you doing here? How'd you get in here?"

He glanced at the still-moving can. "Maybe I'm here to save the day."

"Oh, for the love of God, no! No. This is no time for jokes!"

He was staring at the tub. "What's in there?"

"You don't know?"

"How would I?"

"I don't know, maybe you put it in there." The can rattled ominously.

"Put *what* in there? Whatever it is, it's mad as hell."

"It's a damned water moccasin!" she said.

"A water—? Where the hell would I get a snake?"

"Where would anyone? In the bayou. Or wherever! But right now," she said, tamping down her panic and pointing at the bin, "it's in there! It didn't just crawl in there itself and you're here and—"

"Why would I put the snake in there?"

"I don't know. Why would anyone?" Her throat was tight, her words strangled as they crossed her tongue. She thought of the warnings, the recent attack. "Someone's trying to make me go insane," she said, backing away from Cruz as the idiot unlatched the cord and opened the can for a peek.

"Shit!" He slammed the lid down again.

"Holy crap! I told you!" She stopped backing up as she felt something squishy beneath her feet. A rotting banana on the sole of her running shoes.

Great. Just. Great.

"Why are you here?" Her heart was still pounding wildly, adrenaline firing her blood, but she wasn't freaking out any longer.

"I came to see you."

"Me? You don't even know me—are you sure you had nothing to do with . . . with that?" She pointed at the garbage bin, now quiet.

"Of course not."

"Well, who? Who would do that?"

"Someone who wanted to scare the hell out of you."

"Mission accomplished!" She wasn't shaking, but her pulse was in the stratosphere.

"I'll get rid of it."

"The snake?" she said, tempted to let him deal with the problem. "Seriously?"

A cynical smile lifted one side of his mouth. "I've dealt with worse."

"Oh, right." For the first time she really looked at him, really saw the grim set of his jaw, his eyes drawn to the garbage can. She wondered aloud, "What're you doing here? And don't give me any BS about wanting to see me."

Dave had quit barking and, head down, tail wagging, slowly approached Cruz. Traitor, she thought.

"Just came by for my belt." Quick answer. A lie.

She didn't believe him for a second. "Your brother has it."

Bending down to scratch Dave behind his ears, Cruz said, "So you know who I am."

She sent him a how-stupid-do-you-think-I-am look. "Well, yeah. I managed to put two and two together."

A bit of a smile touched his lips as he straightened. "I can get that snake back to the wild."

"You'd do that?"

He lifted a shoulder. "Why not?"

"Why? Why would you do that for me?"

He didn't answer.

"Wait a second. You want something. I knew it!" She felt her eyes narrow suspiciously. "What is it?"

"Okay. The truth is, I could use your help."

"*My* help? How?" She eyed him. What was his game? "I already told you I don't have your belt."

"Yeah, yeah, I know. I got that," he said, pushing his hair from his forehead. "But I'm hoping that before I get in contact with my brother—which I will, and soon—I might need a place to lie low for an hour or two."

"A place—? Like here?" She was dumbstruck. "You want to crash here?"

"Not crash, but just hang out until I figure out my next move."

"Why? I know you're in some kind of trouble. I got that feeling, but I understand that's always kind of your thing, right?" When he didn't respond, she added, "So now you want me to aid and abet?" She couldn't believe it. "My dad's—"

"I know who your dad is. Rick Bentz. Partner to Reuben Montoya. Who you already reminded me just happens to be my brother."

"And you want me to lie to them and let you stay here—"

"Not lie." He shook his head. "Not stay."

"Just equivocate."

"Or say nothing."

Was he nuts? "I can't—"

"Fine. I get it. Dumb idea." He was backing away, palms out. "I just knew that you don't exactly shy away from trouble."

"So you, what? Thought you could take advantage of that?"

He was dead serious. "Well, there could be a story in it."

"I write true crime."

"I know. Think about it. A whole new homicide for you to put into book form."

"An exclusive?"

"Sure." He shrugged.

"You're involved. In a homicide."

"No," he said, and was dead serious, "but I'm gonna find out who is. Think about it." And then he asked, "So you're okay now?" He motioned to the now-silent and unmoving garbage tub.

No. I'll never be okay. Not again. Maybe not ever. "Sure."

"Good. Then you should call the police."

"I will."

He nodded.

He was opening the gate that led to the front of the house. "You sure you got this handled?" He pointed at the unmoving tub. "You got this handled?"

"Now." She nodded. "Yeah. Thanks."

"Okay, then I'll see ya around." And he was gone, through the gate, his footsteps quick and fading as she reached for her phone and put a call in to her father.

"Odd," she said aloud. Cruz was lying. She sensed it. So why had he really dropped by? She whistled to Dave and headed inside, wondering why Cruz had suddenly appeared, wondering who had dropped a cottonmouth into her trash, and more importantly, why. She didn't think Cruz had left the snake in her trash only to appear . . . no, that didn't make any sense.

"Par for the course," she said as she punched in her father's cell number.

Nothing was making sense these days.

Nothing at all.

Bentz was jazzed.

He felt his blood flowing through his veins, the way he always did when he knew he was about to bring a scumbag to justice. On the drive back from the bayou he was putting the pieces of the case together in his mind. Some clicked neatly into place, others he had to force, but he knew he was on the right track. Soon they'd nail Father John, the fake priest.

Once he'd parked his Jeep in the station's lot, he and Montoya headed inside. It might be a long night ahead of them, but Bentz didn't care. The long hunt was coming to an end. Finally.

The station was still buzzing with cops coming and going, talking and laughing, passing through the metal detectors, swapping stories, most in full uniform, boots loud on the floor.

Stripping off his jacket as he walked past the draped plastic curtains of the area of the station that was being renovated, he saw workmen putting lids on paint cans and folding ladders to be stacked in the corners, Bentz said, "I'm telling you we're dealing with that same fuckin' maniac."

Once inside their shared office, Bentz eyed the map of the bayou he'd mounted on the wall. Taking a pen from his desk and uncapping it in his teeth, he surveyed the area and marked the spot where they'd found the remains of Maizie and Willard Ledoux. Though the bodies still needed to be formally identified, Bentz believed the two fishermen.

"Maybe." Montoya wasn't completely on board.

"No 'maybes' about it," Bentz said, tapping the map of the bayou with his finger. "Father John is back." The location of Maizie and Willard Ledoux's bodies and home only added to his conviction that somehow Father John had survived all these years. "And dollars to donuts he killed the Ledoux couple. Don't know how or why or if he knew them, but he did it. We need to find out how long they've been dead—Jesus, has Father John been here all these years?" He traced his finger around the bayou. "My guess is that he's here—somewhere in the swamp. It's where he feels most comfortable, but now that we've got a victim who survived and the spot where she was attacked, he might move." He sat in his chair and leaned back, tenting his hands and thinking. "But my guess is he won't go far."

"What about Dr. Sam?" Montoya asked as he fired up his laptop.

"I still think she's in jeopardy. Otherwise he wouldn't have had

Stacy Parker call in to her show before he took her out to the swamp."

"Uh-oh." Montoya was reading the screen on his computer.

"What?"

"Records was able to locate all the info on the Rosary Killer in the archives." He was frowning, the screen reflecting in his eyes.

"And—?"

"And his medical records indicate his blood type was O positive." He met Bentz's concerned gaze. "The blood that was found at the scene where Kristi was attacked and McKnight was killed—found on the cathedral walls—was B neg."

Bentz thought about it. "Father John is our guy. We know that."

"You know that. He could be a damned good copycat."

"Don't think so."

Montoya met his gaze. "Then we've got ourselves two killers now, don't we? The one killing prostitutes and the person who killed Jay McKnight."

"Jesus, Joseph, and Mary," Bentz said as his cell phone rang. He recognized Kristi's number and clicked on. Before he could say a word, she said, "I think you'd better get over here, Dad. And bring someone with fish and wildlife or whatever. Somebody left me a cottonmouth as a little gift."

"What?" he said, reaching for his jacket. "We're on our way! And, Kristi, don't mess with it."

"No worries there, Dad."

He cut the connection. "Come on," he said to Montoya.

"What's up?"

"I don't know. But get animal control on the phone and have someone sent over there who can deal with snakes. Send them to Kristi's house. Let's go!"

"Snakes—?"

Bentz was already out of the room. "I'll explain on the way."

And he did. While breaking the speed limit, his light on his dash blinking, he drove straight to the Garden District and pulled into Kristi's drive. She was waiting near the garage and walked them along the side path to the gate and area where she kept her trash bin. "You don't have to look," she warned. "It's a cottonmouth."

"How the hell did it get there?" Montoya asked, ready to open the lid.

"Don't!" Bentz warned. "Fingerprints."

"Yeah, and a poisonous snake!" Kristi reminded them. "And I don't know how it got here, but I don't think it slithered in on its own." She cast the tub a disparaging glance. "I only lifted the lid once to drop in this"—she motioned to a half-full garbage bag, its seam split—"and found my little friend. He made a valiant attempt to strike me, but missed."

"Jesus," Montoya whispered.

"Are you okay?" her father asked.

"No." She shook her head. "But I will be."

"Someone from animal control is on his way," Montoya said, looking at his phone. "Be here in ten."

"Good." Bentz didn't think the snake could escape with the bungee cord holding the lid in place. "Let's go inside." As they walked through the garage to the kitchen, Bentz felt a slow-burning rage coursing through him.

Probably the same psycho who killed Jay.

And now, it seemed, not the Rosary Killer.

They'd barely gotten inside, a shaken Kristi offering water or coffee or soda, when the animal control truck rolled up to a stop outside. "Here we go," Bentz said, and they all returned to the garbage tub. The officer, Alex Johnson, was a burly black man with an easy smile and dark eyes.

"Someone called in about a snake?" he asked.

"In there." Kristi pointed. "Water moccasin."

"How big?"

"Don't know. Big enough."

"Any chance I can take the tub? Since it's already contained?"

"Fine with me." Kristi didn't care if she ever saw the garbage bin again. "All it has in it is the snake. I cleaned the can out last week and the garbage hasn't been picked up yet this week."

"Then I'll bring the container back when we've gotten the snake back to where he belongs," Johnson said. "Just let me take a peek at him. Y'all step back." They did, and when the big man raised the lid, he let out a low whistle. "Yeah, that's a cottonmouth all right. A big fella. But there's somethin' else in here. On the lid."

"What?" Bentz asked.

"An envelope? Like an invitation of some kind? Taped to the inside here."

Bentz's heart nose-dived. "Ah, hell."

Beside him Kristi sucked in her breath and shook her head. "Again?" she whispered.

"Son of a bitch." Montoya's voice was barely audible.

Johnson said, "Let me see if I can get it without getting him all agitated again." To the snake: "You behave."

"Wait," Bentz said, "I think you'd better remove the snake from the bin. We're going to need to dust it for prints and examine it. Evidence."

"Got ya," Johnson agreed.

In the distance Kristi heard the sound of a motorcycle roaring to life and run through its gears as it sped into the night.

Johnson went back to his truck, returned with a long-handled hook, a bag, and a cage. Then while they watched from a safe distance, he flipped open the lid and, using the long hook, snared the angry snake, then deftly slid the twisting serpent into a huge bag that he quickly secured. "Anything else?" he asked with a grin. In his hands the bag wiggled and shook as the snake tried to get free.

"That's it. Just the one," Kristi assured him.

"Okay. Anytime," Johnson said, hoisting the writhing bag and heading back to his truck, parked at the curb in front of the house.

As he drove away, Kristi said to her father, "I never noticed the envelope. All I saw was the snake."

Montoya was nodding. "He would've caught my attention, too."

Bentz was already putting on gloves and removing the envelope, tape and all from the lid.

The card was the same as the others, the deckled paper, the single black rose drawn in ink, but the Bible verse was different:

> *~The righteous will rejoice when he sees the vengeance; He will wash his feet in the blood of the wicked.*
> *Psalm 58:10-11~*

CHAPTER 34

"You're telling me this is not Father John's work?" Bentz demanded, once they'd gathered in Kristi's kitchen. He was upset and Montoya didn't blame him. Bentz's kid had barely survived a brutal attack in which her husband had been killed and now she was being targeted.

"Did he ever leave notes before?" Montoya countered as Kristi offered soft drinks or coffee or water. "You got a Diet Coke?"

"Sure." She found a bottle in the refrigerator and handed it to Montoya.

Bentz held up a hand. "I'm good," he said, but it was a lie. Bentz was anything but "good."

"I just think we have to separate what's happening to Kristi from the homicides of Teri Marie Gaines and Helene Laroche and the attack on Stacy Parker. Those, I agree, look like the work of Father John, and the fact that he had Stacy call in to the station so he could connect with Dr. Sam on her radio show—yeah, it's either Father John or a damned good copycat." Montoya cracked open his cola and took a swallow. "But what's happening with Kristi. Nuh-uh. That's a different dude."

Bentz rubbed the back of his neck, obviously struggling with the idea. To his daughter, he said, "Tell me that with your new security system, you have a camera that covers that area?"

"I do." She seemed a little nervous about it.

"Let's take a look."

"Okay. I've got it hooked up to my phone. An app. Wait a second." She pulled the phone from her pocket, then opened the app and found the area in question. She hesitated, scrolled a bit, and fiddled with the footage. "Let's see, nothing . . . nothing . . . I'm backing up. It doesn't show anyone—oh, wait. Oh . . . Oh . . . God." She handed the phone to Bentz. "This is a couple of nights ago, when I was out for a run. I, um, I came back and I thought I saw someone in the alley across the street. The dog was with me and he barked like crazy, but when I looked again, no one was there. But look at the date and time. This is literally less than ten minutes before I got home. I haven't been to that side of the fence until tonight when I was taking out the garbage."

Bentz and Montoya studied the screen. Sure enough a man— well, it looked like a man, but that wasn't for certain; a tall woman could have been caught in the camera's eye. It was just a few seconds. He slipped through and unlatched the gate by reaching over, opened a large case of some kind, dropped the snake into the can, then hurried away, his face never full on to the camera's eye, a black overcoat and pants, a hat low over his eyes. Bentz kept the footage rolling, seeing nothing but a neighboring cat in one frame and a lumbering opossum in another.

"It ends here," Bentz said.

"What—no . . ." She came around the counter and took the phone again. "See, this is where I open the can and see the snake." Again, she handed the phone to her father. "Then I jumped back and must've hit the camera because everything seems to go screwy after that."

Montoya watched and saw, just as she said, her image opening the can, then screaming and dropping the garbage sack, the dog barking wildly as she snapped the lid down and rehooked the cord holding the lid in place.

"We'll need a copy of this," Bentz said. "Maybe the lab can enhance the images and we can get a better picture of the guy."

"Maybe, but he kept his face turned, because he probably spotted the camera," Montoya said.

"We'll check the neighbors, street cams. He must've driven here. I mean, he was carrying a snake for crying out loud—a big snake." Bentz backed the footage up again and looked at the carrying case from which the snake was deposited. "Maybe we can get something on the bag. Or shoe prints. Or fingerprints on the lid of the can or envelope."

"He was wearing gloves," Montoya said. "Avoided the camera. The envelope was pretaped, you saw how he slapped it under the lid. The whole thing took less than five minutes and then . . ." He looked at Kristi. "And then he waited for you to return?"

"I don't know. It might not have been the same guy, but someone was out there. In the alley across the street. Between the big square blue house—the two story—and the cottage."

"I'll go check it out."

Montoya left through the front door, checked the area around the house and across the street to the alley, walking the length of the short gravel strip and coming out on the far end, another quiet street. Reaching into his pocket for his pack of cigarettes, he came up empty and headed back to the spot across the street from Kristi's house where, tucked behind a single pine, he could view her front porch, one of the few on the street without any Halloween decorations. From his vantage spot, he could see from one end of the block to the other and he imagined whoever had dropped the snake into her garbage can waiting for her.

But who?

He'd dismissed Father John—not his style.

There had to be a reason whoever was attacking her was doing it now, and he knew that all of Jay's and Kristi's family members were out—none had a reason and all had alibis. As for friends or enemies, he found none except the disgruntled author Dennison Drake, whose career had been upended and surpassed by Kristi Bentz, but Dennison had a solid alibi for that night—the reclusive author had been in New York with his agent.

He considered Vince Laroche and his secret affair with his step-mother, who tricked by the name of Helen of Joy. He was a slimy character, no doubt about it, but Montoya didn't see Vince tangled up in the other murders. Would he kill her just to shut her up, use the other prostitutes' murders as cover? No. Montoya doubted that Laroche would understand Father John's MO, nor would he know how to perfectly stage the Rosary Killer's victims.

Montoya, like Bentz, believed the Rosary Killer was back. He was even discounting a copycat. The homicides they could attribute to the fake priest were too much like the originals. Montoya's gut twisted at the thought. He'd believed for so many years that Father John was dead.

But he didn't believe the fake priest was behind the attack on Kristi and her husband. Jay, he was certain, just happened to be in the wrong place at the wrong time. Someone had intended to kill Kristi Bentz that night.

That left, as far as Montoya could see, the subjects of Kristi's true-crime books as primo suspects. There were three, besides the Rosary Killer, whose crimes were being aired on the poorly shot TV movies with B or C list actors. The trouble was, they all had alibis.

Mandel Jarvis, the ex-pro ball player turned preacher featured in *American Icon/American Killer,* had been with his aunt who was in a care facility in Baton Rouge.

Ned Zavala of *The Bayou Butcher* fame had been in the area but, according to his mother, had been with her, in the house, all night long. She didn't sleep well and his snoring kept her up. According to her, Ned had fallen asleep early, on the Barcalounger in front of the flat screen TV. It was a thin alibi as Ned's mother wasn't exactly known for telling the truth, but for now it would suffice. Montoya had already been poking around with the neighbors, all of whom said they "thought" Ned's pickup had been parked outside the single-wide where his mother resided.

Then there was Dr. Hamilton Cooke, the "brilliant" surgeon who was the star of *The God Complex and Murder* and had taken his own wife's life. The doctor had been tried, convicted, then his conviction overturned with the help of the woman who would become the second Mrs. Hamilton Cooke. His alibi was his wife, who swore he'd been with her all night long. It was an alibi that couldn't be broken but, in Montoya's opinion, was weak. And Reggie had given up her first marriage, put her career at risk, suffered through the scandal because of her love for the doctor. What more would a little lie harm, especially if it meant preventing her husband from ending up behind bars again, and her personal life from being thrown in front of the public, her career tarnished yet again?

He thought again of the cards left for Kristi. The snake coiled and waiting in her trash.

Did Hamilton Cooke have a penchant for black roses, fancy paper, and quoting the Bible as well as handling a poisonous snake?

Somehow, it didn't seem the good doctor's style.

But it was someone's style. Montoya was hell-bent to find out which of these losers knew about snakes.

"I know, I know," Kristi said, raising her palms as if in surrender. "I get it, but I'm *not* leaving my house, okay? That's what he wants. To scare the crap out of me, but I'm not going to give in to him." She stared at her father, silently daring him to argue as he sat at her kitchen counter.

Bentz stared right back. Not backing down. Frustrated.

She knew what he was thinking because he'd told her often enough: she could be as stubborn as her mother. He glanced at her abdomen and again she realized what was going through his mind: that now it wasn't just her life that was on the line, it was the child she was carrying. She knew that, too, and without thinking, placed a hand over her abdomen. He was right, but that psycho had killed Jay, who had made the ultra sacrifice to save her. It was payback time.

"I'm saying," Bentz went on with measured calm, "that you bunk in with Liv and Ginny and me, just until we crack the case."

"Then he wins, Dad. Don't you see? That murderous son of a bitch wins!"

"Think of the baby."

"I am! What kind of a mother cowers because she's getting nasty notes, or gets snakes left in her garbage bin? And what kind of a chicken-shit person does those things?"

"A sick one. A dangerous one. And you were attacked. Your house was broken into. Your husband was killed."

"I know that! You don't have to remind me, okay? I've got the dog. I've got the security system." She thought about the claw hammer tucked under her pillow. "And Jay . . . Jay has—had a gun."

"I thought you were anti firearms," her father said.

"I am. Jay wasn't. And I know how to use it." She let out her breath. "You made sure of that."

"This isn't about courage and proving yourself or anything else. It's about your life."

"I get that, Dad. Don't you think I get that?"

"Kristi, just listen to reason—" At that moment his phone rang and he glanced at the screen. "Sorry—I need to take this."

Thank God. Their argument was on its way to escalating to the stratosphere as they were both so muleheaded. She knew that; he did, too. It was just the way it was. She found a sparkling water in the refrigerator, opened it, and took a long swallow as she listened in to her father's one-sided conversation. Noticing Lenore peeking out of the bookcase in the living room, she went to the kitten and picked her up. "What're you doing hiding? Come on and join the party." But the cat was having none of it and wriggled, hopping to the floor and sliding under Jay's favorite chair. "Okay," she said, "have it your way."

Taking another drink, she turned back to her kitchen and her father, who paced from the living room to the garage door and back again. His face had darkened, eyebrows slammed together, jaw tight. "You're sure? Everyone? . . . Well, find the ones who checked out, maybe they saw something. . . . Yeah, I know the kind of place the All-Day-All-Night Inn is. They rent rooms by the second and don't get into checking ID. Wouldn't matter. Most of the clientele don't use their real names anyway." He was talking, listening, and ever moving. "And the roommate who called in the Missing Person Report? What's she have to say? . . . Nothing? She saw nothing? Great." He rolled his eyes to the ceiling. "What about the other 'residents' and I use the term loosely . . . Unobservant lot, eh? . . . Yeah, I know they all get jittery around the cops, but someone saw something . . . Oh, yeah? Just left even though he'd paid in advance?" Her father stopped walking. "You got a name? . . . Crap, sounds like a phoney, but check it out and what? . . . A Harley? That he parked *inside*? What kind of a nutcase is he? Must have somethin' to hide. Like a lot . . . Yeah, let's find him. Who knows? He might be our guy."

Kristi listened to the conversation and her heart nearly stopped. Her mind was spinning as she remembered Cruz Montoya had looked like he'd just gotten off a motorcycle and she'd heard an engine fire up, though it was after her father and Montoya had arrived. And what about the time when he'd found Dave and brought the dog back to her—hadn't she heard a big bike's engine start?

Was it a coincidence?

Hell no.

Because Cruz had come here looking for a place to stay. Because he couldn't hide out at the motel any longer.

So why didn't she just blurt it out? Tell her father her suspicions?

Because, damn it, he'd brought Dave to her. Because he'd been willing to tackle getting an angry water moccasin out of her trash bin.

She was sure he hadn't been playing her.

Okay, pretty sure.

But she wasn't ready to give him up.

Yet.

Montoya tapped at the slider and she jumped. Again she thought of Cruz and how he resembled his brother. Same dark hair, same strong jaw, same attitude.

She unlocked the door, letting him inside.

"You okay?" Montoya asked. "You look like you've seen a ghost."

"Just still trying to settle my nerves," she lied, and Montoya's eyebrows drew downward.

"I thought you'd, you know, gotten a hold of yourself."

"I did, but then . . . well, I'm fine now." She drew in a long breath and told herself to be cool.

"Find anything?" Bentz asked as he disconnected and pocketed his phone.

"Nah."

"Just got a call from the motel where Stacy Parker was staying. No one saw anything, of course, but there are a few MIAs—one guy in particular. Left the day it all came down, didn't return, and had prepaid in cash, of course. And get this, he drove a Harley and kept it in the room with him."

"Huh." Montoya said, and Kristi saw that he, too, was digesting the info and probably wondering about his missing brother.

Bentz went on, taking a seat at the island. "I called the lab. They're picking up the garbage container and this." Bentz pointed to the envelope and card with its damning rose drawing and Bible verse, tape still intact, now wrapped in a plastic bag. "Maybe we'll get lucky. Maybe he left a fingerprint on the tape or the card."

"He hasn't before," Montoya pointed out.

"Yeah, well, maybe this time he was careless." Bentz scowled and Kristi saw that he didn't believe it for an instant.

Neither did she.

CHAPTER 35

Montoya was too wound up to end the day and for once he didn't have to rush home. Abby and Ben had spent the day with another new mom and infant and both were exhausted. She'd called to say Ben was asleep, she was turning in early, watching a movie in the bedroom. "You're on your own for dinner," she'd told him. "And if I'm asleep when you get in, don't wake me, okay? Ben, either. He was getting fussy tonight. Needs his sleep."

Which worked for Montoya because he wasn't ready to shut down for the night. Not after coming so close to a writhing, scary cottonmouth. So who would have access to a large snake? Who would handle a water moccasin? He'd checked the Internet and had come up with an answer:

Ned Zavala.

As much as Montoya had dismissed the big man earlier, he kept coming back to all the reasons Zavala could be behind the attacks. Zavala lived near the bayou, was used to dealing with reptiles, so he was Montoya's first guess. The trouble was the person in the footage he'd seen from the camera pointed at the container at Kristi's house was much slimmer than Zavala, who was a bear of a man.

Still, the man hunted alligators and creatures of the swamp. If anyone could capture a water moccasin, it would be good old Ned.

Montoya decided to pay the Bayou Butcher a visit.

At the table in one of her favorite cafés just outside the French Quarter, Samantha Wheeler checked her watch. She was running late because her dinner with Caroline had gone longer than she'd planned, but then that was more usual than not. She and Caroline never seemed to run out of conversation. They were old friends from college, one of the few she'd kept after her first marriage had dissolved, so they kept in touch, usually meeting on the last Thursday of the month for dinner and drinks and just to catch up.

Tonight had been no different.

"I really need to run," Sam said, finishing the last of her wine, taking out her phone and texting her husband to tell him she was on her way. "I hate to cut this short, but Ty's with the boys and he's got an early flight in the morning, so I'd better get home and take over so he can get a few hours' sleep. He's going to meet us at Disney in a couple of days."

"Vacation?" Caroline asked.

"Yeah." It was just a little lie. They'd tried to leave earlier, but their work schedules and flights had held them up longer than planned. "A bit of R and R. We'd hoped to go earlier but work and life got in the way."

Caroline was nodding, streaked hair shimmering under the low lights. "Oh, don't I know. I've got to go, too. I've got an early meeting in the morning and Lars gets a little antsy if I'm like two minutes late." She rolled her expressive eyes—big and blue, the lids shaded a smoky gray. Lars was the most recent of a string of boyfriends, all of whom had been on the possessive side, at least as far as Samantha was concerned. Caroline had been married for ten years, divorced her husband for cheating, and then had taken up with a series of boyfriends looking for "Mr. Right" or "Mr. Okay," who, in Sam's estimation, were no better than her husband had been. In fact, some had been worse.

Caroline's phone buzzed and she checked it. "Oh, Geez. Guess who's asking where I am?" She smiled coyly, as if his overt possessiveness was cute. Sam had already told her what she'd thought about a man checking up on *his* woman, and it hadn't gone over too well, so she held her tongue.

"I'd better hustle." Caroline opened her wallet and reached for her credit card when her phone buzzed again. "Oops." She shoved her card back into its slot, pulled out a couple of bills, and put them on the table. "You mind settling up?" she asked, slipping her arms through her jacket, standing, and bending to give Sam a quick hug and kiss on the cheek.

"No problem."

"You're the best! Okay, good, *ciao!*"

Samantha was already fishing in her purse while Caroline, in heels and a short skirt, wended her way agilely through the tables, side-stepping patrons and waiters and hurrying through the door.

At that moment, someone fell against the back of her chair, then clipped the edge of the table, jostling it. Plates with crusts of uneaten bread slid and smashed onto the floor. Glasses toppled. Ice cubes skittered across a widening pool of water. Flatware followed, clattering loudly.

The surrounding conversations ended abruptly.

"So sorry," a gruff voice apologized. A bearded old man with a walker. Wearing a cap and horn-rimmed glasses, he looked confused. "Didn't mean to . . ."

"Oh, dear!" a woman in her seventies at a nearby table muttered.

"It's okay," Samantha said to the bearded man, who had somehow managed to stay on his feet.

He doffed his cap and shuffled off, pushing the walker toward the front of the café. A waiter held the door open for him while a busboy hurried to her table and started sopping up the spillage with a heavy towel. A waitress with her hair pulled back in a long braid was right behind him. "Get the mop. We don't want anyone slipping." She was already swiping at the tabletop. "I've got the table, you get the floor."

"Here," said the seventy-ish woman at the neighboring table, and handed the waitress a spoon that had slid under her chair as the busboy returned with a rolling bucket and mop.

All in all it was chaos for the next five minutes.

"I'm late," Sam said to the waitress once the table was cleared and dry and the busboy had swabbed the area after picking up glass. "Would you mind?" She handed her credit card to the girl with the braid.

"Oh, sure. No problem." She took the card and made her way to the bar area where she totaled the bill and ran the credit card as the busboy pushed the mop and bucket out of the dining area. People at nearby tables began talking again and the waitress returned with

Sam's credit card and receipt. "Is this"—she motioned to the soggy bills on the table—"a tip?"

"Uh-huh." It was more than she would normally leave, but she just wanted to get out and she figured the wait staff deserved the extra cash for all the commotion.

"You sure?"

"Yes. Thanks."

"Thank you!"

"You're welcome." Sam grabbed her jacket and purse and headed for the door.

Outside it was cool and dark, streetlights glowing, signs in other restaurants and shops adding illumination. She'd parked two streets over in a lot and was halfway there when she reached for her phone.

It wasn't in the exterior pocket where she always kept it, so she figured she'd tossed it into the larger space in her bag. Riffling around inside, her fingers touched lipstick tubes, her wallet, and keys. No phone. "What the devil?" She slowed. Had she left it on the table? Was it knocked off and had it possibly skittered across the floor in all of the confusion? She remembered texting Ty and then what? Had she just left it on the table?

Well, crap!

Just to make sure she hadn't missed it in the bag, she pressed the button on her watch that was linked to the phone and heard a soft beep.

Not from inside her bag, but from somewhere nearby. Really? She'd dropped it and hadn't heard it land? Maybe while getting her keys out of her bag. Disgusted with herself, she kept pressing the button on her watch, the reactive beep getting stronger as she searched the concrete.

And there it was.

On the ground right next to a narrow spot between two buildings. How had that happened?

She bent down to pick it up, and just as she did, she sensed something—a movement in the corner of her eye and the rustle of leaves. "Wha—?"

He lunged.

From the narrow space between the two buildings a dark figure leapt. She started to scream, but the air was cut from her lungs.

One strong arm held her tight, his gloved hand reaching up to cover her mouth. With his free hand he jabbed something cold and hard against her neck. Panicked, she tried to scream, to react, to kick and flail. Instead she felt fifty thousand volts scream through her body! Shock waves jolted across her skin and down her limbs. Shuddering and convulsing, she had no control, but somehow he—her attacker—slapped duct tape over her mouth and zip-tied her wrists and ankles despite her flailing and body parts that were out of her control.

No, no, no!

Inside she was screaming, but heard only gurgled, muffled noises coming from her throat as he dragged her along the dirt path between the two buildings to a small, pockmarked parking area. She lost a shoe, felt broken asphalt scrape against her heel.

Fight, Sam, fight! Don't let him do this to you . . . don't! Fight back. He's going to kill *you! Fight, damn it!*

But she couldn't. Despite the warnings in her head, her body refused to comply. He lifted her from the ground and stuffed her into the backseat in a matter of seconds.

"Hey!" she heard someone yell as if from under water. *A man,* she thought. Then quick hard footsteps. Someone running!

Oh, please! Help!

Too late!

He slammed the back door shut, climbed behind the wheel, and gunned it as he pulled the driver's door shut.

No! God, no! Help me. Someone help me!

Her mind was jangled, her heart racing, her thoughts a jumble, but she knew she was in trouble. Big trouble.

"Hey! Hey!" A sharp male voice frantic but farther away.

She tried to kick at the door, but her feet wouldn't work.

"What do you think—"

He hit the gas.

Thud!

The car bounced as if he'd driven over a berm or rock or something hard.

She was thrown against the back cushions.

She tried to yell, but her words were garbled and muted behind the tape.

Get up! Kick! Scream! Fight back!

But her body was useless, her brains half scrambled. She couldn't think straight, couldn't make her body move, but one thing was certain, she thought as she saw the streetlights through the car's windows as he drove through the city: Father John, that madman who had nearly killed her years before, was finally going to finish the job.

She blinked.

Tried to think.

Tried to work her hands out of the zip-ties, but they were tight around her wrists and her hands weren't doing what she wanted anyway. The same with her feet. They were nearly immobile.

However her hands were tied in front of her and that was a mistake, probably because he hadn't had much time. Still she was pretty sure that if she could get control of her quivering, unreliable body, she would be able to at the very least take the tape from her mouth with her fingers, then either scream or try to unlatch the ties with her teeth.

He took a corner a little too fast, and the car rocked and slid, fishtailing, and then she noticed the beard and hat, tucked into one of the backseat pockets—the psycho's disguise. He'd knocked into her table on purpose and in the melee, he'd grabbed her phone before shuffling out of the café. Her heart sank even further as she recognized how she'd been duped. Her gaze moved to the far pocket, on the back of the passenger's seat. It held a rosary, glittering beads dangling from it. They sent a drip of terror through her bloodstream as she saw the winking cross swaying from the deadly noose.

Oh. God.

Still quivering, her body seizing, she realized then that she was on her own.

No one was going to rescue her.

If she couldn't find a way to save herself, she was most certainly doomed.

CHAPTER 36

Kristi reviewed the security tape for the fifth time. Try as she might, she couldn't determine who the prick was who had dumped a damned snake into her garbage bin.

"Jerk-wad," she muttered, then absently patted Dave's head as he'd come up to her office and placed his nose on her knee.

She was over this!

Whoever was terrorizing her needed to back the hell off.

But they wouldn't.

Not until she did something about it.

Not until she faced the freak.

Don't be crazy.

You're not just putting yourself in danger.

Think about the baby.

She'd be careful. Of course she would. And it wasn't as if she wasn't able to defend herself. She'd practiced tae kwon do for years, though admittedly, she was a bit rusty. She pulled out her phone, looked again at pictures of the cards she'd received. Studied them.

So neat.

So precise.

So threatening.

Not exactly Ned Zavala's style; the Bayou Butcher was a brute of a man, not known for his light touch.

As for Father John, she had no idea where that psycho was, and though he had always been more refined than Zavala, she didn't fit the profile of his victims, all prostitutes except for Dr. Sam, his ultimate target. Was it possible that he might be behind the cryptic notes with their religious references? Yes, but unlikely.

Nor did she see Mandel Jarvis, busy and outgoing as he was, scripting the notes with the roses. And he had a good thing going with his family and church. He'd threatened her after her trip to the New Faith and Glory Church of Praise, but it was reactionary, she thought, because she'd crossed the line, stepping on his turf. She remembered how he was with his wife and children. She couldn't rule him out with any certainty, but Pastor Mandel was definitely on the back burner.

That left Hamilton Cooke.

She thought about it as she pushed back her chair and walked down the stairs and into Jay's office, which remained nearly the same as it had been when he'd last sat in the chair with the creaking roller. The police had taken his laptop and a few other items for their investigation, but the pictures and awards remained, the books in the case, the tie he'd left slung over the back of his chair. She'd never put it away and now she stopped, running her fingers over the silk fabric. Her throat grew thick and she blinked rapidly. The horrible words she'd flung at him, "I don't know why I ever married you," echoed through her brain.

She imagined him huddled over the desk, books scattered around him, reading glasses on the end of his nose reflecting tiny images of his computer screen. "But I do know," she whispered now, fighting tears. "Because I loved you, Jay. I still do."

"I know."

Jay's voice sounded so much clearer in here—in his room—and if she closed her eyes she could imagine the scent of his aftershave and the faint sound of his laughter.

"Oh, baby," she whispered, and sniffed, her emotions so suddenly raw again. She had to pull herself together. Maybe Bella had been right when she'd suggested a grief counselor. Maybe . . .

But now she knew that she had to move forward.

And that meant ending this reign of terror that had her in its grip. Whoever was behind Jay's death had to pay.

Newly resolved, she dropped his tie over the back of his chair again and walked to the closet, where she pulled the gun case down from the top shelf, set it on the corner of the desk, and snapped it open.

The SIG Sauer was waiting.

She pulled the pistol from the case and felt its weight, remembering balking when Jay had brought it home. "No firearms," she'd said. "We're going to have kids someday and—"

"—and we'll keep it locked and safe. Promise." He'd flashed a little smile. "Look, Kris, we probably won't ever use it, never take it out of the case. But just in case we have to, it'll be here. I don't like some of the letters you've been getting and there are just so many nuts around."

"Nuts who can break in and steal it or use it on us."

"That's not going to happen."

In that respect, he'd been right. So now she was here, in his office, gun in hand, ready for battle.

The irony of the situation didn't elude her.

As she felt the heft of the gun and practiced aiming it, she planned her next move. First off, she planned to have a conversation with Hamilton Cooke. Of all the people who could be behind the attack, she couldn't dismiss the skilled surgeon.

Cooke was precise.

He liked to play head games.

And he hated Kristi.

She located the extra clips for Jay's pistol on the upper closet shelf.

But would Hamilton Cooke handle a snake? Where the hell would he get one? From an accomplice? But who? Was that even likely?

Her thoughts turned to Cooke's wife. What about her? Was she involved? Reggie was a tall woman. Could she possibly have been the attacker that night? Her heart turned to stone as she remembered the fire in Reggie's eyes as she'd confronted Kristi in the parking lot of the television station. And more precisely she recalled how only seconds before, Hamilton Cooke had pointed his finger at her like he was aiming a gun, before speeding out of the very same lot.

Could they be in it together?

Their hatred of her could be so intense that it was possible.

But anything was.

And she needed answers.

It was time to have a chat.

She snapped a clip into the handgun, then took two more clips from the shelf.

Pocketed both.

What are you doing? Expecting a shoot-out? her saner, more rational mind nagged.

She didn't know, but she wanted some form of protection.

"Now or never," she told herself, checking to make sure both dog and cat were safely inside and the security system was engaged. She went into the garage, hit the switch to open the door, and slid into her Subaru.

"Just be careful, Kris. Be damned careful." Jay's voice was faint, but she could hear it.

"I will," she whispered to her dead husband, and touched her abdomen. "Promise."

Ty Wheeler's voice was frantic. "It's Sam," he said from the other end of the wireless connection. "She didn't come home."

Bentz, already worried sick about Kristi, was driving home after dropping Montoya at the station and had gotten a call. He had answered hands free when he'd recognized Ty's name as it appeared on his phone. "How long has she been gone?" He was driving through the heart of the city, traffic thick, pedestrians on every corner, streetlights turning night to day.

"I don't know. Three hours, maybe. She went out. To have dinner with her friend, it's a usual thing, but she texted she was on her way home, and she hasn't shown up. I've called. I've texted. Nothing." His voice was edged in fear. "Caroline—that's the friend she had dinner with—I phoned her and Caroline said she left the restaurant first because she was running late. Sam was settling up—paying the bill, I guess. Anyway, I know it hasn't been that long, but it's just not like her. And she has work tonight. She wouldn't be this late. She was gonna come home and help with the boys, then head to the studio." He sounded beyond distraught and Bentz didn't blame him. "So, of course, I called the restaurant. The waitress remembered her because there was some kind of commotion at her table as she was leaving. It was bumped and dishes went everywhere, so anyway, the waitress said she left about an hour and a half ago. There's a time stamp on her credit card receipt.

"And here's the real worry," he said. "She has a locator on her phone. She and I each do, and hers is nowhere near the restaurant or home. It's in the bayou."

"Jesus," Bentz whispered. "But we can track her, from the device."

"I'm already on my way."

"Whoa. Hold on. This is a police matter," Bentz said, thinking of the brutality of the killer.

"Yeah, I know that. But it's also my wife. Do any of you have an Apple watch or iPhone?"

"Yeah. This number."

"I'll link you up. All you have to do is accept."

"Got it."

A second later he got an alert.

"We're on our way."

Bentz flipped on his emergency vehicle lights and hit the gas. Ty Wheeler's concern was infectious. "Keep trying to reach her!"

He disconnected, pulled over to the curb, and eyed the screen with its map of the area. "I'll be damned," he said under his breath. The pulsating red dot indicating the location of Samantha Wheeler's phone was in the swamp and not far from Cyrus Unger's place. Probably half a mile from where they'd come across the bodies, what were presumed to be the rotting remains of Maizie and Willard Ledoux, though there had yet to be an official ID.

Father John's work.

Bentz was sure of it.

And now the maniac had Samantha Wheeler.

Bentz called for backup, and as he did, he added, "And a boat. We're gonna need a boat."

Through the old car's windows, Sam saw the lights of New Orleans fade to darkness. The Chevy picked up speed; she heard the whine of the tires on pavement and the smooth rumble of the engine.

She didn't want to think where they were going or what he was going to do to her when they got there.

Somehow, someway, she had to save herself. Her convulsions had stopped and the quivering in her limbs had lessened, but there was still a problem getting her muscles to do what her mind wanted. She was frantic, her breathing wild, her heart trip-hammering crazily.

Try, Sam! You've got to try!

Clamping her jaw tight, she concentrated. Attempted to move her fingers and kept one eye on the back of his head.

Come on, come on.

She gritted her teeth. Told herself she could do this.

Felt one finger move.

That's it! Keep going!

Another finger wiggled.

Good! She was beginning to sweat, felt perspiration break out across her forehead. All of the fingers of her right hand were moving slightly. Responding. *Think, Sam. Make them work. And don't let him know. He can't know that you are gaining control of your body again!*

To that end, she forced herself to shake a bit, to mimic how her arms and legs had reacted, to tremble every so often. Just in case he was listening.

The car drove onward and every so often he'd look over his shoulder. Once she gave a little shudder as if she were still having convulsions and he seemed satisfied, turned to face the windshield again, his eyes on the road.

Slowly and silently she worked. Moving both hands and eyeing the rosary dangling so close to her. If she could somehow reach it, sit up and loop it over his head, she could throw her weight back and choke him with his own damned weapon.

He might lose control of the wheel.

They could crash.

Or he could get the upper hand.

But so what?

He was going to kill her anyway. She had no doubt of the heart-stopping fact. So she kept trying, reaching forward. Missing. Her fingers just brushing the dangling cross and causing it to swing faster.

Miles rolled by.

Frustration mounted. Why couldn't she reach it?

She felt the car decelerating. Oh. God. She swallowed back her fear. Had he reached his destination? Was it too late? Again panic

surged through her. She had to work fast or she'd have no chance.
No chance at all.

She reached again.

Missed. A fingertip swiping the cross.

It swung, still out of reach.

Come on. Come ON!

He turned a corner, the tires crunching on gravel.

Damn!

She felt the car slow, turn, then move faster again. The sounds of
the bayou reached her ears, the smell of wet earth and brackish
water seeped into the car.

Sam's heart sank.

It was over.

She took another pass at the rosary just as the car suddenly shud-
dered to a stop and he flung open the door and the interior light
flipped on.

She kept her hands in front of her. She forced her body to twitch
more convincingly and rolled unfocused eyes toward him. Silently
she prayed he didn't realize she had some, if only a little, control of
her body.

He hesitated and then, to her horror, took out his damned stun
gun, pressed it to her neck, and as she let out a weak "No!" jolted her
again.

No, oh, no! Her body spasmed wildly and he slammed the door,
locked the car, and took off on foot.

Shaking, her brain unable to focus clearly, she was aware enough
to know that couldn't be right. What was his plan? To leave her in the
car? Alone? Surely not. She'd recover and break out.

He would be back.

And soon.

The only reason he hadn't killed her was that he wanted to take
his time, to torture her, she was sure of it. In the darkness, she heard
crickets and frogs, smelled the deep, dank odor of the swamp. He'd
brought her to the bayou, but where? And why?

*To kill you slowly. To extract his own, sadistic punishment. Don't
let him, Sam.*

With all her concentration, she tried to set her jaw to steady herself, to get her hands to work, to take control. But her teeth rattled. Her muscles convulsed. Her eyes seemed to wiggle in their sockets.

You can do it.

You can.

You have to. For yourself. For Ty. For the boys.

Her heart wrenched at the thought of her sons. She couldn't imagine not ruffling their hair, or teasing them, or holding them close when they were hurting. And Ty . . . oh, God, she wouldn't think of not seeing him again, not kissing him or touching him. Tears filled her eyes, but she wouldn't break down. She couldn't. She had to find a way to get free, to save herself, to see her family again. She forced back her fear.

Seconds ticked by, then minutes.

How long had he been gone?

Five minutes? Ten? Twenty?

She had no way to tell time, but slowly her control was returning. She stretched her fingers and most of them complied.

Come on. Come on!

Her legs, still twitching, were heavy. Awkward, but she could move them slightly.

And her arms . . . yes, they were responding!

Sweating from the effort, she fought to steady herself and reach for the rosary.

The car beeped.

Interior lights flashed on, nearly blinding her.

She started, pretended that there were still some tremors in her body. He cast a glance her way, but slammed the door shut, started the car, and hit the gas, rapidly backing up, hitting the brakes, then switching gears, punching the accelerator.

Sam was thrown backward and forward and in that moment, her fingers scraped the back of the driver's seat. The cross caught between her fingers.

As the car bumped and shimmied onto the smooth pavement of the parish road, she tugged. Like a snake sliding out of its den, the rosary finally slithered from the pocket to twine through her waiting fingers.

CHAPTER 37

I pace.

Back and forth, back and forth, over and over again as the television glows, mocking me. I feel the old anxiety building with every passing moment. I've been patient, but my patience has worn razor thin. I know it's risky, but I can't wait any longer.

I click off the television after watching the segment of *Bonjour, New Orleans!* with Kristi Bentz over and over again. I can nearly recite the personal, provocative questions from that twit Renee-Claire. The whole segment was intended to embarrass me all over again. And it did. Even now I can feel my blood boiling, a tic starting near my eye. I touch my face to stop it and feel the scab, now nearly healed, from Kristi Bentz's umbrella, but still visible. She nearly took out my eye with that pointed tip.

Bitch!

I rewind the show again, this time to Kristi Bentz's segment, and there she is talking about *her* book, *her* story, as if it wasn't my life she'd exposed, baring all the flaws for the whole damned world to see.

The tic becomes stronger.

Humiliating, that's what it is!

Embarrassing.

But the program holds a sick fascination for me and I can't seem to stop myself from sitting here, in my private quarters, replaying the whole mortifying, disgraceful show. I've even suffered through the segments with the near-dead-looking saxophonist and the inane cat lady with her nearly comatose feline on his tufted pillow.

But those parts of the show were only filler; the real show was the drama of Hamilton Cooke, Reggie, and that bitch Kristi Bentz.

That's why viewers have tuned in.

Revulsion curdles my blood.

I rewind once more, seeing the disjointed images reverse in quick jerky movements, the sound a garbled babble until I reach the interview again. Then I study the screen as a smiling Renee-Claire asks her guests questions, each more personal than the last. The host is loving it, too, nearly creaming herself. I can see it in Renee-Claire's eyes, so bright with interest at exposing all the dark, scandalous secrets of her guests' lives.

No more.

I clench my teeth.

Tonight it ends.

No more pain.

No more suffering.

Time for retribution.

I lick my lips in anticipation.

I've waited so, so long.

With new fortitude, I walk to the small closet, find my poncho, ski mask, and dark glasses inside. After I'm dressed, I see that the television is still on, the vile program running, and I hit the pause button on the remote.

The screen freezes on a frame filled with a head shot of Kristi Bentz. She looks intent, her eyes wide, her auburn hair gleaming under the studio lights.

Beautiful.

Smart.

And, I think, pulling on my gloves, soon to die.

Cruz knew he shouldn't return to Kristi Bentz's place. Going back was sure to be trouble. Big trouble.

Astride his Harley, he sped along the streets of New Orleans, kicking the bike into a higher and higher gear, listening to the engine whine as he considered the open road. Soon he would reach the interstate and he could leave the Big Easy in his dust.

There was no reason to return. No *sane* reason.

If he did, he would be playing with fire.

Yet he was compelled.

For a reason he didn't understand.

"Hell."

He pulled a 180 and turned his bike around, heading back to the heart of the city, and ignored the blare of the horn from the driver of a cherry-picker truck that he zoomed past, the lights of New Orleans calling, a siren song he couldn't ignore.

He thought about Kristi Bentz and told himself that what he felt, a connection, was all in his head, a damned figment of his imagination. His jaw tightened. But who else did he have to turn to?

His family?

All of his siblings had their own lives.

What about his cop brother?

Cruz scoffed at the idea. Reuben had an obligation to his family and his duty as an officer of the law. He shouldn't have ever reached out to him. That had been a mistake. A major mistake. One, he was certain, that would haunt him.

As for his friends, he wouldn't drag any that remained into this mess. It was too dangerous and he'd already left a few in Oregon who knew too much for their own good. That bothered him. More than he wanted to consider right now.

So it came down to Kristi Bentz. Maybe he could strike a deal with her.

The agreement would be simple: if she helped him, he'd grant her an exclusive on her next book, one he was certain would become a best seller.

If he survived.

He gunned his Harley, leaving behind the laughter, bawdy jokes, and forever-celebration of the French Quarter where earlier he'd hidden in a dark bar, a hole in the wall. For a few hours he'd nursed a single beer, melding into the crowd, sitting near a raucous group of partygoers while he tried to figure out his next move. He'd turned a dozen options over in his mind: Should he stay in New Orleans or leave? Talk to his brother and take a chance that Reuben wouldn't send him to Oregon, or try and disappear? Turn himself in, or keep running, forever looking over his shoulder?

None of the options were viable.

So he kept coming back to Kristi.

Not a great option, but the best he could come up with on the run.

No one would suspect that she would be his contact; her father was a cop, partner to Cruz's brother.

At least Cruz hoped that was the case.

He drove a winding path and tried to figure out where he could ditch the bike where it wouldn't be readily noticed, yet handy should he need it. He considered a few options, then landed on the parking lot of a motorcycle store about a quarter of a mile from her house. It neighbored a dive-bar and would blend right in.

He thought about the jump drive hidden deep in his saddlebag. His ticket out, should circumstances play the way he hoped. He would offer it to her and when she opened it on her computer, she'd see a grainy image of what had gone down that night near the Trask River in Oregon.

His insides still turned cold at the thought of it.

At the image of Lucia in the water.

Jesus, he missed her.

Slowing as he came to an intersection, he spied the bike store, situated, as he remembered, next to the bar. He stopped, boots on the ground, motorcycle idling, and surveyed the adjoining parking lots. Both places of business had cameras mounted under the eaves of the buildings, but those on the bar seemed all for show, not even pointed over the lot. Still, the cameras gave him pause and he zeroed in on an area that was slightly protected by a hedge and offered some cover from the street.

It would have to do.

He eased through the intersection and into the lot. Checking to see that no one was watching, he cut the engine, unlocked one of the bags, and searched in a side pocket. His fingers found what he was looking for. He pulled out the jump drive, stuffed it into the front pocket of his jeans, then, remembering the deadly snake left in Kristi's garbage can, he quickly withdrew his Colt Mustang Pocketlite and slipped it into the pocket of his jacket.

Just in case.

"I told ya. My boy wasn't involved in any of that shit!" Eileen Hebert pointed a long, gnarled finger at Montoya as he stood on the listing porch of her single-wide mobile home, he on one side of a rusted screen door, she on the other.

On permanent blocks on a piece of land that bordered the bayou, the Hebert home was surrounded by small sheds and coops, and a longer, dilapidated, but more permanent structure that had once housed the freezer and body parts of the victims of the Bayou Butcher. Two hounds of indeterminate breed had howled when he'd knocked on the door and now stood on each side of Eileen. Her face was gaunt and chalky, her body slight, a few sparse wisps of gray hair visible at the edge of a knit beanie. She wore a housedress over jeans and a dark, disapproving expression.

Montoya wasn't put off. "I'd like to talk to Ned. Is he here?"

"Jesus Christ, don't you need a warrant or somethin'? I ain't lettin' you in here."

"Mrs. Hebert—"

"For Christ's sake, let him in, Ma," a deep male voice yelled from within the trailer.

"No, I—"

"Just do it and get it over with," the voice, presumably Ned's, argued.

"Hell." Eileen snorted. "I don't like this," she muttered. "Don't like it one bit." But she moved out of the way, unlatched the door, and the suspicious dogs let down their guard, their tails beginning to wag.

"Fred. Go lie down. You too, Wilma," Eileen ordered. "Go on . . . git! Find yer beds!"

Begrudgingly the dogs obeyed, both curling up in a ratty dog bed tucked near the slider door on the far side of the room where the gold shag carpet was worn thin and didn't look as if it had recently, if ever, seen a rug shampooer. The house smelled of stale cigarettes and bacon grease.

Ned was seated in a dirty recliner positioned in front of a massive flat screen that nearly blocked the living area from the kitchen. A second recliner sat next to the first, a narrow TV tray separating them. On the tray was a pack of cigarettes, several crumpled paper napkins, and two paper plates, orange grease spots visible, crusts of bread going stale. But the most important thing was the fact that Ned's right leg had been fitted with an orthopedic walking boot that rested on the footrest of his worn La-Z-Boy.

Montoya asked, "What happened?"

"Broke my damned foot, that's what happened," Ned growled.

"And he's been pissy ever since." Eileen closed the screen door with a clang of metal.

"Probably needs surgery." Ned reached onto the TV tray for a pack of Camels, scraped the pack off the tray, and sent it wobbling.

"When did that happen?"

"Yesterday." He scowled, rubbed the side of his face where three days' worth of stubble was growing, then he shook out a cigarette and jammed it into his lips.

"Don't you be smokin' in here," his mother warned, and he sent her a look as he grabbed his lighter from the tray and flipped the footrest down, struggling to his feet and almost hopping to the dirty slider.

If Ned was faking his pain and inability to walk, he was doing a damned good job of it, and seemed to wince as he pushed the door open.

As he did, the hounds shot to their feet, barking noisily as they streaked outside, across a sagging deck, and shot past the tumble-down sheds before disappearing into the surrounding thickets. From inside one of the coops, startled chickens clucked and squawked.

"Idiot dogs," Zavala said, the cigarette jumping in his lips as he talked. "It's Ma's fault, if you ask me. She babies 'em. Won't make 'em behave. They ain't trained like the huntin' dogs we had when I was growing up." He lit up then, and in the flicker of his lighter his face grew haunted, as if walking down that particular memory lane was a dark and twisted road. The lighter clicked closed and he drew in a deep lungful of smoke. He balanced his good hip against a railing that didn't look as if it would hold his weight.

"So what the hell do you want from me?" Ned asked. "I already talked to that dick-wad Bentz at the church. So what're you doin' here harassin' me? I got nothin' to hide. Nothin'."

"Not harassing. Just double-checking," Montoya said. Then he got into it, asking Zavala about his whereabouts.

According to Zavala he'd either been at work at the church, or here, tending to the place, or, just last night, he'd stopped in at

Corky's, a local bar, for two beers. "You can ask the bartender, that would be Corky hisself. He was tendin' last night.

"After that, I drove home, here, and that's when I stepped into a hole out here, dug by either the dog or some critter. Anyway, I knew it was there, but it was dark and I stepped in it, twisted my leg, and busted up my foot in a couple of places. Sheeeit." He took another drag from his smoke and gazed up at the dark sky where a few stars were just visible.

"Look, man, you gotta believe me. I don't know nothin' about what's goin' on—them murders. It ain't me. Just like it wasn't me before. So, come on, get off my case."

"Just a few more questions."

"Yeah, yeah, there's always a few more, ain't there?"

Montoya ignored his complaints and brought up Kristi Bentz.

"That one," Zavala said as smoke streamed out of his nostrils. "She's a piece of work now, ain't she? The apple don't fall far from the tree with her. Nosey little bitch and she got it all wrong, y'know. I never killed no one. You got that." He glowered as he took a final pull on his cigarette, then dropped it onto the deck and squished the butt with the heel of the boot on his good foot.

"Fuck!" He sucked in his breath at the pain of shifting his weight. "Just what I need is to be laid up. Fuck!" The dogs, still making noise in the darkness, came bounding back, causing the chickens to squawk again.

"Fred! Wilma! Hush!" Zavala yelled as the hounds, toenails scraping against the weathered decking, rushed madly through the still open door where, Montoya noted, Eileen Hebert was loitering as she eavesdropped.

"Anything else you need to know?" Zavala asked, hobbling toward the door as his mother slipped noiselessly toward the far end of the house. "Cuz if there is, you can do what I told yer damned partner to do and talk to my lawyer."

"Just one thing," Montoya said. "You advertise on the Internet—Craigslist and through Facebook—that you sell baby alligators."

He stopped as he reached the slider, steadying himself on the door frame. "That's right."

"Anything else? Like other animals—I heard you have chickens."

"Those are for the eggs. Yeah, I sell what I can, what I catch. Frogs.

Turtles, sometimes." One of the dogs—Fred—came up and looked up expectantly. Zavala leaned over and petted his head, causing Fred's tail to swipe back and forth. "But I don't sell puppies," Zavala said, straightening and stepping gingerly inside. "Hell, I wouldn't breed those two hounds fer nothin'. Puppies would turn out dumb as shit."

"What about snakes?" Montoya asked.

"Sure." Zavala lifted a big shoulder. "If I got one."

From the corner of his eye Montoya saw a movement as Eileen came around the corner from what Montoya guessed was the bedroom area. One side of her housedress sagged, the pocket bulging.

A gun?

Montoya's heart stilled. His muscles tensed.

Had she gone to the back and picked up a small pistol?

"I think we're about done here," Eileen said, her lips thin. She nodded toward Zavala. "Ned, here, needs to rest. Same with me. I ain't been well."

Montoya's eyes never left her.

"Cancer, ya know. Ned, he takes good care of me. We take care of each other. And we don't need no one comin' out here, rilin' up our dogs, makin' me jumpy, and askin' all kinda questions that we don't need to answer."

The bulge in the pocket moved.

What?

Moved?

As whatever it was inside was alive?

In a chilling flash he remembered the stark white of the water moccasin's open mouth, its needle-like fangs.

"What have you got there, Eileen?" His own sidearm was holstered at his shoulder. He could retrieve it in a split second.

Would that be too late?

The bulge moved again.

"I heard you asking about the little gators." She smiled coldly and reached into her pocket.

"Stop!" Montoya ordered. "Hands up. Where I can see them!"

"I was just gonna show you an itty-bitty baby."

As she began to withdraw her hand, Montoya drew his weapon, aiming it straight at her heart.

"Whoa!" Ned yelled, nearly falling down as he held out his palms. "Put down the fuckin' gun! Great God almighty! Put it the fuck down!"

Eileen's graying eyebrows twitched up. "No need for that," she said, staring blithely down the barrel of Montoya's service weapon. She pulled a baby alligator from her pocket and the tiny creature stared at him with unblinking reptilian eyes.

"Jesus, Mom. Why?" Ned said, and looked as if he might have a heart attack, his face drained of all color.

Eileen stroked the back of the alligator's head with one finger, but she stared straight at Montoya and said reproachfully, "Don't tell me, Detective, that yer scared of this tiny thing."

The woman was nuts! And enjoying this.

Montoya lowered his weapon.

"Jesus, Ma, what're ya thinkin'?" Ned demanded, and reached for his pack of Camels.

"Maybe you want this little guy for the missus," Eileen suggested to Montoya, her smile twisting with cold humor. To her son, she added, "Serves him right for bustin' in here and askin' all sorts of questions."

"He didn't bust in, Ma. We let him in."

"You did."

"Holy shit!" Ned dropped into his chair and rubbed both hands through his hair. "Are you crazy?" Then to Montoya, "Just leave."

"In a minute." Montoya had come this far, out to this bayou away from town, and just suffered Eileen's cruel and dangerous sense of humor, so he wasn't quite ready to take off just yet. "All I really need to know is if you sell snakes." Montoya's heart was still thudding in his chest, his blood pumping, his muscles tight, and he kept his eyes trained on Eileen. She was small, but he didn't trust her, didn't know what else she might find amusing. Or worse.

"I sell 'em when I can." Ned lit up. "If I got any."

"You don't smoke in here!" Eileen said, her voice in the stratosphere. "You take that vile habit outside!"

Ned ignored his mother's screech and took a long drag, before shooting smoke from the corner of his mouth.

"You go outside," she ordered, and the dogs were already at the door again, whining and dancing, ready to shoot out across the deck once more.

"What about recently?" Montoya pressed, his eyes still on Eileen as he asked Ned, "Anyone come wanting a snake?"

"Careful," Eileen warned, her voice low.

"Matter of fact I did sell one," Ned said, bragging as he defied his mother and blew another cloud of smoke toward the dingy ceiling. "A nice sized cottonmouth. Just last week."

CHAPTER 38

*S*critch.
S Scritch.
Scritttcchh.

"What the hell?" Reggie said, slamming her book shut. She'd been sitting by the window reading *The Stand,* by Stephen King, one of her favorite novels of all time. The window was cracked and she had been vaguely aware of the rush of the wind through the magnolia tree in the yard and the soft sound of crickets, but now . . . a grating, scratching noise that was so damned irritating and distracting. She'd heard it somewhere before. She was certain of it. And it had always, always bothered her.

Thankfully, it had stopped, and she wondered if it was her husband. Hamilton had been so twitchy lately, anxious to the point of paranoia. And that interview on television, what a cluster-fuck that had been. Reggie had thought, or hoped really, that the interview would showcase Dr. Hamilton Cooke, the wrongly accused surgeon who was desperate to return to medical practice to help the ailing, to once again become a stalwart pillar of the community.

It could happen.

He was after all handsome and charming, or could be when he wanted to be. None of his attributes had been shown in the television gig however.

That calculating bitch of an interviewer—Renee-Claire—had set them up to allow Kristi Bentz in the same studio. Of all the nerve! As if Reggie would ever agree to be on television with that twisted little bitch! Even now, just thinking of the interview and how it had been derailed, a near disaster, made her blood boil. She reached for her glass of wine, took a final swallow, then called to the kitchen. "Hamilton, be a dear and pour me another?"

When there was no response, she turned her head toward the kitchen and said a little louder, "Hamilton?"

An hour before, she'd left him at the stove where he'd been creating some kind of late dinner that neither one of them needed. She always fought her weight, ran six miles every morning, then worked out with weights three times a week to keep her figure as lean as it had been at twenty. Lately she'd noticed, though she hadn't mentioned it too many times of course, that Hamilton, always athletic and trim, had started developing a bit of a paunch. It wasn't too bad, yet, but this new hobby of his—trying to master the art of French cuisine—wasn't helping. He needed to step away from the gas range and hone a strong workout routine that included either swimming or biking daily as well as basketball and golf. He needed to get back into sports and paying attention to his physique rather than worrying about creating the perfect boeuf bourguignon or worse yet, crème brûlée. Good Lord, how many calories were in that tempting but evil dessert? Like seven million—give or take?

"Ham?" she called again, but obviously he couldn't hear her over the megawatt, industrial-sized fan that he'd insisted they install. It rose above the eight-burner gas range and the pot filler he'd had plumbed into the wall. That of course, required a new backsplash for the entire kitchen, all with imported tiles.

No doubt about it, Hamilton and his new interests were starting to bug her.

She reminded herself not to fall into that trap. He was just going through a rough patch and once he was focused again—and it better be soon—all would be well.

Although, he did have a wandering eye. She knew that all too well. It worried her, sometimes consumed her. Tonight though, right now, she pushed those wayward thoughts aside. At least for the moment.

She and Hamilton, they were on the right track. She knew it. Once he had his medical license reinstated, he'd return to the fit, suave, ultra-handsome, athletic man she'd married so eagerly. His practice would take off and he might become a celebrity doctor, have his own podcast, even a cable TV show. Why not?

Shoot for the stars! That had always been her motto and she saw no reason to abandon it now.

She kicked away the ottoman as she stood and stretched. Leaving her novel dog-eared and open on the side table, she picked up her empty glass and walked through the dining room. In the kitchen the fan was roaring and the smell of tangy bouillabaisse tickled her nostrils. Her traitorous stomach even rumbled. She ignored it. This decadence had to end!

"Hamilton?" she called.

Only the light over the stove was illuminating the kitchen.

How odd.

Also, the pantry door hung open.

Why? So unlike her husband.

The bottle of Merlot was still open on the island, a red ring visible and staining the marble countertop.

She frowned.

Hamilton knew better. In fact he was as nit-picky and meticulous—even anal—about his kitchen as he had been in the OR at the hospital.

What the hell?

And what was this note card with a black rose etched on its front, like a damned wedding invitation for vampires? Good God. Was he now into calligraphy as well as attempting to become the next Julia Child?

She opened the note and read the scripted words:

> *~Thou shalt not commit adultery . . .*
> *Exodus 20:14~*

What?

Now Hamilton was writing down Bible verses? About adultery no less.

She knew he liked being on the board at St. Ada's, but this—? Quoting the Old Testament? Writing it down in some creepy, cryptic funereal missive?

Had he gone completely around the bend?

His own glass of wine, left near the stove, was untouched. The stew on the burner was roiling wildly, blue gas flames curling over the bottom of the pan. To top it all off, she noticed fine marks on the counter suggesting that he'd marred it. Recently. She knew the scratches hadn't been there yesterday. Now, she ran her finger over the smooth surface, feeling a series of the barest of grooves. Was this the cause of that damned scratching sound? As if he'd sharpened a knife on the counter? For the love of God, what had Hamilton been thinking? What was wrong with him?

"Ham?" she said again, and felt a breath of distress blow across her nape.

Where was he?

What had been that horrid scratching sound?

As she turned toward the door of the darkened pantry, hanging ajar, she felt all of her nerves tighten.

"Hamilton?" she said again, slightly irritated as she turned off the stove and that Mad Max of a fan. The noise receded and now she could hear the erratic beating of her heart. "This isn't funny."

She passed by the knife block near the stove and pulled out the long fillet knife, though that was ridiculous. She was in her own home with her husband and . . . Oh, God. Was the back door open? Just slightly? Unlocked? She strode to it and found the dead bolt un-engaged and thought maybe Hamilton was outside.

Had he ducked out for a cigar? Another bad habit that had to be broken.

Or had he dashed outside to the garage to get something out of his car?

She stared across the lighted brick path to the old carriage house that served as their garage. Was the side door of the garage open as well?

Why?

The hairs on her nape rose and her throat was suddenly dry as sand. She grasped the hilt of her knife in a death grip.

"Darling?" she called anxiously again, and heard the scrape of a shoe on the floor behind her. He'd been inside all the time! "What do you think—?" She turned then and saw the glint of a knife's short blade.

"What?" she whispered, recognizing the oyster-shucking tool for what it was.

She gasped, her eyes meeting his. "NO!"

The razor-sharp edge slashed across her throat. "Oh, yessss. 'Darling,'" he mocked.

She swung her own knife, its long blade plunging through his clothing to the flesh below. She tried to slice, but her legs wobbled.

She was blinking, light-headed, blood pouring from her throat.

Her knees buckled.

As she dropped, she saw blood bloom on his shirt, then she fell backward.

Bam! Her head banged hard against the cold Italian marble of the floor. She heard the crack of her skull.

With difficulty she looked up at familiar, intimate eyes. He smiled and said, "Yes, dear? I think you wanted something? What was it? Another glass of wine? I'm afraid it's too late for that."

And then the blackness consumed her.

The swamp closed in on them.

Bentz and Ty Wheeler were with several deputies in one boat, a reluctant Bobby-Dean and Clive in the other as they knew the bayou like the back of their collective hands and could navigate the dark waters. Bentz had argued against Sam's husband being a part of the team, but Ty had been insistent and there had been no time to argue, so Bentz had broken protocol again.

The boats moved slowly through swamp that was thick with duckweed and salvinia in the water, cypress trees rising like pale totems to the starlit sky. Spanish moss dripped and danced overhead and Bentz couldn't help wondering what it hid in its folds. Rat snakes were known to hang from branches, and though not deadly, not something Bentz wanted dropping on his head.

He was already tense at what was going down.

He only hoped they weren't too late and that Samantha Wheeler was still alive. Oh, God, please.

He felt the weight of his sidearm in the shoulder holster beneath his thin jacket and strained to see in the surrounding darkness, just a few flashlights illuminating their way. They'd cut the engines of the boats and now were drifting, oars aiding as they moved in closer to the target, the area where Samantha Wheeler's watch indicated she was being held.

Now that they were this close, Bentz wondered how the killer had slipped up. Such a simple mistake. But maybe Father John had been out of the mainstream so long, off the grid if he'd been living with Maizie and Willard Ledoux as it now seemed, that he wasn't aware of all the technological advances that had exploded exponentially over the past decade or so.

Whatever the reason, they were closing in and Ty, who had been watching the face of his iPhone, held up a hand and pointed ahead of the boat, fifty yards or so, where a huge tree leaned out over the water, thick branches creating a canopy over a portion of the bayou.

Bentz glanced at the phone's screen, then nodded, and Ty dimmed its light. The hastily created plan was simple:

Divers would slip into the water, reach the hideout, and attempt to break in, just as Bentz identified himself and they flooded the lair with blinding light. It was risky. Bentz had no idea if Samantha Wheeler was dead or alive, or hanging by a thread.

He wanted to be the one to nail Father John, would have loved to go into the bastard's hiding spot, weapons drawn, guns blazing, but he'd agreed to this plan because it was the safest for the captive. He motioned to the next boat and the divers silently entered the water.

Now, the true waiting began.

It would all be over in ten minutes.

The longest ten minutes of Bentz's life.

"Hello?" Kristi knocked on the front door of the huge home owned by Reggie and Hamilton Cooke. She'd jogged the few blocks to their house and seen the lights aglow, the gate unlocked. Cautiously she'd walked up a sweeping drive and walkway to the wide front porch where large pots of colorful flowers were still in bloom and palm trees swayed far above the two-storied home. However, unlike all of the other houses on the street, the Cooke estate showed no signs of the season, no pumpkins or jack-o'-lanterns on the front porch, no fake headstones or zombies digging up from underground decorating the neatly trimmed shrubbery and understated lighting.

She pounded louder, and pressed the bell, hearing the dulcet sound of chimes from within. Yet no answer.

Maybe they realized who was knocking on their door and chose to ignore her, though that wasn't exactly Reggie's aggressive style. She peered in one of the sidelights surrounding the door frame and saw no movement inside, just a two-storied foyer where a huge, crystal chandelier winked high overhead, and to one side, through a wide arch, the living area where Kristi saw neatly spaced and expensive furniture, a white couch flanked by floral chairs surrounding a marble-faced fireplace.

She waited, tried the bell again, and after a few minutes with no response, not any sound from within, took a lit pathway around the side of the house, past locked French doors to the rear, where a long lap pool stretched across the back patio and a breezeway connected an older, detached garage to the main house.

The door to the garage was partially open and she peered inside.

Two cars: Hamilton Cooke's black BMW and his wife's sleek Mercedes were parked side by side.

So it appeared the happy couple was at home.

Kristi didn't hesitate.

She made her way to the back door, knocked loudly again, and as she did the door swung inward.

Really?

The front door locked tight, the back door completely unlatched.

She felt more than a second's misgiving, her heart knocking slightly, but she ignored it.

"Careful, Kris," Jay's voice, which had been silent for a while, now warned her.

She slipped his gun from her pocket.

"Hello?" she called again. "Anybody home?" Nerves tight as piano wires, she stepped into the kitchen. Lit only by the over-stove light and filled with the aroma of tangy herbs and fish, the dim room was quiet. A pot of some kind of stew sat under the lights and a bottle of wine stood open on the island, a full glass near the stove.

This was wrong.

So wrong.

She reached for her phone just as she saw the blood. Thick and red and smeared on the marble of the floor.

She froze.

"Get out! Get out now!" Jay's voice was clanging in her ears. *"Call the cops!"*

But what if someone was hurt? From the amount of blood, it seemed that someone had been horribly wounded.

"Hamilton Cooke's a doctor! He can handle it. And if not, his wife will. She's pretty damned efficient." Jay's voice seemed to reverberate through the house. *"Call the damned cops, Kristi, and get the hell out. Now!"*

She took one step toward the door when she heard the moan. Low. Almost unworldly. Emanating from the pantry.

Oh. Jesus.

Hardly daring to breathe, her weapon now fully drawn, she eased over the bloody marks to the pantry and tipped the door open with the nose of her gun.

"Oh, God," she whispered as the door opened and light spilled into the dark interior. On the floor beneath the shelves of neatly stacked boxes of cereal, rice, oatmeal, and cans of tomato paste and diet cola, were two bodies. Lying almost entwined, blood thick and smeared on the floor and some of the cabinets.

Kristi's stomach clenched as she recognized Reggie Cooke, lying in a thick, red pool of blood. She was staring fixedly, but a gurgling sound passed through her bloody lips and her left hand twitched.

Still alive!

But not for long.

Kristi saw the color fading from Reggie's face, a curse Kristi had lived with. She could see the life bleed out of a person as they lay dying.

"No," she said. "Hang in there!" But already she was looking at the second body. This time she did wretch, felt bile burn up her throat. She swallowed against the sour taste and stared at Hamilton Cooke, who lay near his wife. He was already dead, his white polo shirt soaked and stained, his tan slacks dark with the blood that had drained from the gaping wounds to his torso and crotch. His eyes were open, his mouth rounded, his face set in an expression of shock.

"Oh, God, oh, God, oh, God," Kristi said.

Kristi yanked her phone from her pocket and, still holding the

gun with one hand, started to plug in 9-1-1 as she knelt beside Reggie. "I'll get help," she whispered, knowing in her heart of hearts it
was too late for the lawyer. "Stay with me. You just stay with me."

At that moment the door to the pantry swung wide.

The operator answered. "9-1-1. What is your emergency?"

A shadow stretched suddenly across the interior of the pantry,
blocking the light from the kitchen.

"Too late!" a deep voice said.

Before Kristi could raise her weapon, Aldo Lucerno kicked it hard.
Crack!

Pain scorched through Kristi's hand.

The gun went flying. It clattered against the glass bins of flour and
sugar and fell to the floor.

"I wondered if you'd show up here," Aldo said, and she noticed
the knife in his hand. A short-bladed weapon used for shucking oysters. Sharp. Deadly. Smeared in blood. "Good. Saves me the trouble
of hunting you down!"

She was crouching, ready to spring. Her eyes on the knife, her
hand throbbing.

"Nine-one-one," the voice squawked from her phone, and quick
as a cat striking, he swiped the phone from her and smashed it on
the floor.

"Now that I have your full attention," he said.

"We need to get help," she argued.

"Too late."

"But—" She wanted to tell him that Reggie was still alive, that
there was a slim chance that she could be saved, but she knew it
would fall on deaf ears. In fact, he might finish the job. Instead he
was focused on her.

"You sent me the notes," she charged, stunned, not realizing the
depths of his depravity, his humiliation. "And the snake."

"Gifts."

"Not gifts. Warnings. And no thanks." She had to figure out how to
get past him. He filled the doorway to the pantry and there was no
other way out that she could see. But if she could get to her gun. It
was somewhere in the back of this closet, but she'd have to trip over
Hamilton Cooke's body to retrieve it—that was if she could find it.

She didn't dare take her eyes off Aldo, couldn't see the pistol in her peripheral vision.

Think, Kristi, think.

You've been in tight spots before! You have to save yourself. More than that, you have to save the baby! Think of the innocent child you're carrying!

"I don't understand," she said, hoping to keep him talking, trying and failing to keep her panic level.

The gun! Where was it? *Where!?*

"Oh, sure you do. Don't play dumb with me. You know why. You profited from my pain," he said. "You and your damned book were everywhere besmirching my family's name, making money for the shame that I suffered! It wasn't bad enough that she," he spat out, glancing at his dying ex-wife, "she flaunted her affair, having it play out on national TV, that she left me for a convicted murderer, but then you had to keep it going. Publishing a book. Agreeing to a made-for-TV deal, getting rich off my family's disgrace!"

Kristi couldn't believe it.

He was this disturbed? He'd harbored a grudge, letting it fester and grow until it became an obsession, a need for revenge. Recalling the horrid notes he'd left, the deadly snake, she felt a new rage. He had no right to terrorize her, no right to take her husband's life. For the first time she noticed the wound on his face, remembered attacking him with the umbrella, felt the rage that he with his damned knife had destroyed her future.

"But why now?"

"Because it was all happening again!" he exploded as if she were an imbecile. "You were just on television! And that cheap piece of . . . that made-for-television movie where I'm played as if I'm a damned idiot? On over and over again. Do you know what that does to my reputation! I'm a proud, upstanding citizen. I own a company. I'm on the board of charities and all of you"—he waved his knife to include his dying wife, her dead husband, and Kristi—"you need to pay."

She couldn't let him get away with it.

She shifted slightly, onto the balls of her feet, still crouched, protecting her belly, and swallowed back her fear. All the while, she fastened her gaze to his knife. "So you killed—?"

"My cheating wife? And her lover?" he said, as if she should understand. "Of course I did! We were married in the church and she defiled her vows, took up with a known killer," he spat out the words. "And as I said, you opened my life, my pain, my suffering to the world. You destroyed my privacy and my life!" His face was twisted brutally. "So, you too, Kristi Bentz, must pay for your sins. Tonight."

CHAPTER 39

Bentz's skin crawled. He stared at what had obviously been Father John's lair, but the little cabin in the tree had been stripped bare, only a sleeping bag lying on a bed built into the wall and a small table and stool in the middle of the small, rough-hewn space.

And on the table was a phone.

Dr. Samantha Wheeler's cell phone.

Left here purposely to taunt and tease, to let Detective Rick Bentz know he'd failed.

Bentz felt sick inside.

He'd been duped by Father John.

Again.

And Samantha Wheeler's life was still very much in danger.

If she wasn't already dead.

"Rope it off," he told deputies, both of whom were still in wet suits, the first to have crept up the rickety ladder, a few well-spaced boards nailed into the trunk, and observed the now-empty space.

"How?" one asked, looking around the darkened bayou.

"I don't know. Figure it out. Get the crime scene team here!" He was angry and frustrated. Played for a fool. Enraged, trying to think straight, he climbed down the rickety ladder and heard a night bird cawing loudly, cackling, as if the swamp itself were laughing at him.

His jaw was so tight it ached. He stepped into the waiting boat.

"Not here," he confirmed to Ty Wheeler, who had already heard the news a few minutes earlier and had demanded to look for himself when the deputies had told them the makeshift cabin had been empty. Bentz had convinced him to wait in the boat as they couldn't take a chance on disturbing whatever evidence might have been left behind.

"If not here, then where?"

"Not far." Bentz was thinking aloud.

"So bring in more cops!" Wheeler yelled. "Light this place up! Find her!" His face was white in the night, his expression haunted, as if he knew the worst was yet to come. "Find her," he repeated.

"We will," Bentz promised. Deep in his heart, he wondered if it was too little, too late.

Emergency lights flashing, Montoya stepped on the gas and his Mustang blew through two amber lights on his way to Kristi Bentz's house. All the while he was on the phone, nearly yelling into the dash through his Bluetooth connection to the station. "That's right! I want BOLO on Aldo Lucerno's car. A 2014 Bentley." He rattled off the license plate he'd memorized.

"Got it," the dispatcher acknowledged.

Montoya took a corner a little too fast, skidding a bit, the rear end of his car fishtailing. "And keep trying Bentz. He's gonna want to know about this."

"Roger that."

Montoya cut the connection and swore under his breath. He knew his partner was out in the bayou somewhere chasing his own white whale in the form of Father John, but damn it, Bentz would want to know that Aldo Lucerno was the killer who took Jay McKnight's life while attempting to murder Bentz's daughter.

Montoya had seen the evidence for himself. Not only had Ned Zavala admitted that he'd sold a water moccasin to Aldo just the week before, but he'd described the spot where he'd delivered the snake. Montoya had located the place, and without worrying about protocol had broken into Aldo's sanctuary, his lair.

The small apartment was hidden on the property, not far from Aldo's grand, Italianate, much larger house with its elaborate, square tower and bracketed cornice, and manicured grounds where palms and magnolias shaded gardens with fountains. Painted pink, and on the verge of ostentatious, the home was at odds with the tiny apartment Montoya had discovered. The apartment had been devoid of life, but candles burned and on an ancient writing desk, he'd discovered writing tools, black ink, and a stack of deckle-edged paper identical to the kind used in the notes to Kristi Bentz.

Montoya didn't understand the sick-o's motive or how he thought he could pass biblical judgment on Kristi; he only knew that he had to warn her.

Before it was too late.

With a crank to the Mustang's wheel, he turned onto her street in the quiet residential neighborhood graced with well-kept lawns and porches sporting Halloween decorations. He shot into Kristi Bentz's driveway and stood on the brakes, out of the car just as it screeched to a stop. He tried her phone again and was sent directly to voice mail.

"Oh, come on," he growled, then walked to the front door and pounded, announcing himself. "Kristi. It's Reuben Montoya."

Inside, the dog started barking and raising a ruckus.

"Come on, come on!" He waited. Paced. Glanced at his watch, then stared straight up at the camera mounted on the porch's overhang. "It's me!"

He texted her.

Again, nothing.

Once more, he called his partner. "Come on, Bentz, this is important."

Once more, he didn't get through.

"Son of a—!"

Frustrated, he rammed a hand through his hair, spun on the porch and noticed movement—a flickering in the shadows. Not here at Kristi's house, but in the alley across the street. In the very spot Kristi had thought she'd once spied someone spying on her place.

"Hey!" Montoya yelled, but as quickly as the figure had appeared, it vanished, racing through the Garden District, almost disappearing between the houses before his eyes.

Montoya didn't think twice.

He took off at a dead run.

The car was slowing.

From the backseat of the Impala Sam heard the shift in the rumble of the engine's motor, sensed the change in movement.

She swallowed back her fear. She had to do this. Silently she tested her fingers and her hands, then shifted her body. Little by little as the time passed, she was gaining control.

Oh, please.

But if he stopped again, he'd zap her, send however many thousand volts through her body.

Or worse.

She didn't know where he was taking her, but it wouldn't be any place good and she'd never get another chance to stop him.

She stretched the heavy rosary between her fingers. It wasn't standard by any means. The stones were sharp, honed by this maniac, and they were strung over something stiff and heavy, like piano wire or heavy-duty fishing line, something guaranteed not to break no matter how taut it was strung, no matter how much pressure was applied, no matter how much his victim fought.

She silently vowed not to be the next victim.

As the Chevy slowed, she gathered her strength.

The car turned suddenly, banking, and once more tires crunched on gravel, the whole car bouncing on what she assumed was a little-used lane. She heard weeds scraping the undercarriage beneath her, felt the entire body of the Impala lurch when a tire struck a pothole or large rock.

Dear God, where was he taking her?

She knew she'd have one shot and one shot only. If he caught a glimpse of her in the rearview mirror, he'd be able to react, so she kept a low profile.

She smelled the swamp. Stronger here, the brackish water, wet earth, and realized that wherever he was taking her, it would be the last place she would ever see.

Unless she killed him.

And she could. She was certain of that harsh fact.

But she'd have to act soon.

Before it was too late.

She took in a quick breath, praying her body would comply with the commands of her brain.

The car slowed even more, creeping now, brambles with limbs scraping its sides.

Now, Sam! You have to do it now!

It was now or never.

And she was ready.

Three, two, one!

She sprang.

Leaping forward, forcing her arms over the headrest and his head, her fingers scraping the ceiling of the car, she looped the chain around his neck and pulled with all of her strength.

"Hey—what?" he yelled, the car sliding as his foot slipped on the gas pedal.

She threw her weight backward.

"No . . . oh, shit." His voice was strangled.

She tugged harder.

He let go of the wheel.

Stepped on the accelerator.

The car careened forward, crashing over brush and rocks, tearing through branches and vines.

She caught a glimpse of his face in the rearview. Panicked eyes, whites showing, glared back at her in horror and surprise.

"Die, bastard!" she hissed through clenched teeth. "Die!"

His eyes bulged with panic.

He flailed wildly, scraping and tearing at the thin, cutting noose at his throat.

Sam's arms began to ache with the effort, but she didn't give up.

"You—you . . . stop," he ordered, his voice strangled. He clawed at his self-made noose, scratching frantically.

The car jerked and tires spun as he struggled, his feet kicking, alternately pressing against the gas and the brake, throwing them both back and forth as he struggled.

Don't let go. Do not let go!

Her arms were screaming with pain, the rosary digging into her fingers.

He fought and gasped.

She jerked harder.

Ignoring the ache running across her shoulders and down her forearms.

Gritting her teeth.

Never letting up.

Die, you bastard, die!

Pressing her back hard against the backrest, she yanked, sweating.

Straining. Trying to get her legs to press against the back of the driver's seat for leverage, so she could lie down and create more pressure.

She heard him squeal and felt a moment's satisfaction.

Finally, he was getting something back for all the pain he'd inflicted, all the people he'd killed!

She knew that she was his ultimate target. He'd said so years before, blaming her for giving his sister advice when she'd called into *Midnight Confessions.*

His sister had been tormented, mentally tortured, and this man, this fake, ungodly impersonator of a priest had blamed Dr. Sam for her death.

But that was wrong. His sister's death had just been an excuse for him to exercise his own sick passion, his compulsion for murder.

And now she would end it.

Except that it wasn't working.

To her horror she realized he'd reached behind his head and wedged a finger into the small space between the rosary and headrest. Just as the car picked up speed. Had he hit the accelerator on purpose? The Impala rushed forward, careening crazily, tearing through brush.

"No!" she said aloud. "Oh, God, no!"

Bam!!!

The car slammed against a tree, glanced off, tires spinning.

Momentarily she lost her grip, the chain sliding through her fingers, razor-sharp beads slicing her fingers.

Forcing herself, she caught the rosary again, grasping hard. But it was too late. He'd taken advantage of the momentary slack.

A second finger joined the first.

Tugging against her.

No, no, no!

She pulled again, throwing herself against the backrest, pulling tight.

Yowling in pain, he flung his whole body forward and screamed, blood visible on his fingers as he ripped the rosary from her hands.

The car plunged into the swamp and the rosary slipped through her fingers.

He was out the door in a second, standing knee deep in the water and weeds. Samantha cowered away, but there was no hope as he opened the back door, leaned inside, and pressed the cold, horrid stun gun against the side of her neck.

Her body jolted and she was quivering again, but she heard his words clearly. "Now, *Doctor*, it's your turn to die."

Aldo lunged.

His sharp oyster-shucking knife raised, he swung at Kristi.

She rolled at the last second, her body a ball.

She knocked his feet out from under him, felt his blade glance off her shoulder.

Aldo slipped on the bloody floor to land atop his dead rival.

Adrenaline burning through her blood, Kristi scrambled to her feet, sliding in Cooke's blood and stumbling. She broke her fall by grabbing a shelf, felt a glass jar, and hurled it at Aldo as he tried to stand.

He ducked. The jar flew past him to crash against a wall in the kitchen, shattering on the floor.

She found another jar. Threw it fast.

Again the jar went sailing to smash with a thunderous crash against the floor.

The gun—where the hell was the gun?

Aldo struggled to his feet and feinted as her fingers scrabbled for another weapon, anything. A can. She flung it at the man who had killed her husband, the deranged psycho who had tried to kill her, the murderer who had butchered Hamilton and Reggie Cooke.

The can hit Aldo in the chest and he swayed for a second. "Shit! You bitch!"

She fumbled for another weapon, a smaller jar. She threw it.

It bounced off him to smash against a row of bottles that clattered and fell onto the bodies on the floor with soft, sickening thuds.

Before she could grab another jar, he closed in, swiping with his knife as if he were brandishing a machete in the jungle. Kristi backed up on the bit of floor by Hamilton's head.

"Nowhere to run," he taunted, swiping again and lunging. The knife glanced off the arm of Kristi's jacket, fabric rending.

She spun on one foot. Aimed high with the other. Tried to kick him in the face.

He was too quick.

He grabbed Kristi's arm as she spun and tried to kick high again.

Quick as a cat he grabbed her ankle and she spun onto the floor again, landing this time on Reggie, the woman's body giving a bit, the tiniest of cries passing through her lips.

She was still alive?

The gun. Jay's pistol. Where had it landed? *Where?*

Frantically she searched the small, crowded space as she lay atop the dying woman's body.

"There's no escape," he warned her, and as she glanced up, she saw the evil gleam in his eye, the bright light of satisfaction as he moved his deadly weapon from one hand to the other. Waiting to strike, his eyes holding hers.

He's enjoying this. The sick prick is actually enjoying this.

She tried to scramble to her feet, but something warm touched her hand. A finger? Reggie's hand? Oh, dear God. Near her ear, she felt warmth. Reggie's shallow, slowing breath. In that second she felt something press into her hand—not Reggie's fingers, but something cold and hard and sharp. Oh, Jesus, was the near-dead woman sliding a knife to her, a long, slim blade that sliced Kristi's skin as she fumbled for the hilt?

"Kkkiiiillll him," Reggie whispered almost silently, just as Aldo, his own bloody weapon hoisted high, leaned down to finish her off.

Kristi twirled the fillet knife so that the blade was upright. He slashed down and she feinted with her body. Slid away from Reggie while she still held the fillet knife with its long cruel blade erect.

"Ah!" He saw his doom in that split second, but landed on the blade, it cutting through flesh—muscle and skin, scraping against a bone in his rib cage.

"Aaaarrrggh," he roared, the knife in his fingers swinging in a wide arc. Kristi, trying to stand upright, dodged to one side. She felt the sting of his short blade scrape through her hair to the back of her neck.

But Aldo wasn't finished; he was trying to find his feet while blood oozed from his gut and his own legs were tangled with those of his ex-wife. "You—you—you die tonight!" he vowed. He raised up, a wounded animal.

"No!" another male voice thundered, and with a resounding crack, a gun fired. Aldo twitched, dropping his weapon, blood spraying from his mouth as he fell with a thud onto Reggie. Her eyes blinked and, beneath him, she stared at Kristi.

Oh. No. No. No!

Kristi's head whipped around as she clambered to her feet.

Cruz Montoya stood in the doorway, a gun in his hand, still pointed at Aldo, who was lying unmoving. There was blood, so much blood. And bodies. Oh, God! Everywhere Kristi, shaking, felt the urge to heave.

"Are you all right?" Cruz asked, lowering his weapon and helping her into the kitchen.

"No," she admitted, and managed not to throw up. "No."

"It'll be okay."

"It'll *never* be okay!" she said, in a voice she didn't recognize.

"Kristi," he whispered, and she thought he might fold her into his arms.

"Freeze!" another sharp, male voice commanded. "Drop your weapon and put your hands over your head."

Cruz didn't hesitate. His gun fell to the floor, landing with a sharp thud. Hands raised, he turned, and Kristi looked past him to find Reuben Montoya, both hands on the gun he had aimed at his brother, standing in the kitchen. Backlit by the light over the range, he was in silhouette.

"Are you all right?" he demanded, his gaze still centered on his brother, though he was speaking to her.

"No—yes. I don't know."

Cruz said, "We need an ambulance!"

"More than one from the looks of it." Montoya's face a mask of determination and regret, his eyes dark and somber. Still he kept the muzzle of his gun trained on his brother's heart, and said clearly, "Cruz Montoya. You're under arrest."

CHAPTER 40

"I want you to look at this footage one more time," Bentz said to Bobby-Dean and Clive as they clustered around his Jeep at the end of the gravel road where he'd parked. Ty Wheeler had reluctantly and angrily been forced to leave with a deputy. Bentz was in the swamp with the two fishermen, his iPad balanced on the hood of his SUV. He hit play on his iPad and the drone footage began to play, footage he'd thankfully downloaded hours before so he didn't need to depend on Wi-Fi for it to be viewed.

So now, here in the damned bayou, mosquitoes swarming, he waited, hoping beyond hope that one of the two fishermen would locate something out of the ordinary, something he'd missed.

In time.

The minutes stretched out. Bentz drummed his fingers on the hood. Finally he asked, "You see anything?"

The images had been taken in daylight, the drone riding high over the swamp to video the thick vegetation and dark water. A few cabins dotted the meandering shoreline and pelicans skimmed the water looking for fish that rose occasionally. Alligators and egrets, a deer leaping through the shadows appeared as the drone flew. Piers jutted into the water, a scattering of boats, but mainly reeds and brush, exposed roots, alligator nests, and duckweed between the tall, ghostly cypress.

Clive complained, "We've been over this. Like, what? Five times."

"Take another look," Bentz encouraged, his frustration mounting. "You know where we are, right, where we're parked?"

"Sure." Bobby-Dean was nodding, adjusting his cap. He pointed one finger at the screen. "That's Old Man Ross's cabin. I recognize his boat."

Clive grunted his agreement. "Yep. And there"—he nodded at the screen—"that's Dot Miller's place. It's just half a mile off Junebug Lane, right by Sugar Corners."

He'd heard that much before. "And what about this?" Bentz asked, feeling a spike in his adrenaline. "Is this—Cyrus Unger's bait shop?"

Scratching his cheek, Clive squinted. "Sure is."

"Uh-huh." Bobby was nodding. "Yep."

"And what's that?" Bentz asked, pointing to a cluster of trees at a bend in the water. Nearly covered by brush, it rose like a hill that shouldn't be in the flat area around the swamp.

"Oh—that?" Clive scowled.

"Don't rightly know," Bobby-Dean said, and slapped at a mosquito that was buzzing near his face. "What you think, Clive?"

"Humph." Clive's lips curved down as he shook his head. "Not sure. Ain't no hills out here. Nuh-uh. But maybe an old barn fallen down. Somethin' like that."

"It's falling down all right," Bobby agreed, studying the screen. "Something pretty big. But doesn't look like a barn. No barn I ever seen. I don't know." But he was thinking, his face pulled together and creased, a hand scratching beard stubble. "Can we get a closer look somehow?"

"Sure." Bentz zoomed in, focusing on the mound of the obviously overgrown rubble and wondering why they hadn't seen the hillock of overgrown, mossy timbers or whatever before. It had been hidden mostly by the canopy of trees.

"Oh, I know," Bobby said, and snapped his fingers as the light dawned in his mind. "Didn't recognize it from here up top." He glanced at Clive. "Ain't that the ruins of the old monastery?"

"The what?" Clive stared at the screen. "What're you talkin' about?"

"A monastery?" Bentz repeated, and felt a little sizzle of adrenaline at the thought of anything Catholic and religious being here. "There's a monastery here?"

"Nothin' ever came of it." Bobby looked at his friend. "Don't you remember? There was talk of it when we was kids. The old folks laughed about it. Some rich guy donated some land to the church, years ago—maybe a hundred, like around the turn of *last* century or so. But the deal was, the guy would only give the church the property if they agreed to build a monastery on it."

Clive thought hard, but was nodding. "You're right." He leaned in closer to the screen. "The way I heard it was the rich old dude, the guy who owned that piece of property, he had a kid who was a priest or somethin'."

"Right. That's the way I heard it," Bobby-Dean said. "The upshot was that the deal was struck, and the church tried like hell to build a big ol' monastery, but couldn't do it cuz the ground wouldn't hold. No matter what they did, they couldn't find bedrock out here in the swamp, so after years of plannin' and tryin' and frettin', the whole kit and kaboodle was scrapped and left to rot." He jabbed a finger at the screen. "Dollars to donuts, that's what's left of it."

"Yep. That's the way I heard it." Clive was nodding.

"Then let's go," Bentz said, feeling a surge of hope, that there was a chance for Samantha Wheeler yet. If only. "You know the way?" he asked.

The two men shared a look.

Bentz repeated, "I asked if you could take me there."

"Yeah. I guess," Clive said, but he sounded reluctant.

"Then what's the hang-up?"

"Oh, shit, Clive," Bobby-Dean said, staring at the bigger man. "Don't tell me you believe all that voodoo BS, do ya?"

"What voodoo BS?" Bentz asked.

Clive frowned. "No—guess not." But he made a quick sign of the cross in the darkness.

"The way it's told," Bobby-Dean said, "is that the place is haunted or cursed or whatever. It's all just a loada' crap o'course, but I guess Clive, here, believes it."

"My mama did." Again he made the sign of the cross.

"Don't care," Bentz said, feeling time running fast. "A minute or so ago you couldn't even remember it existed, so pack away any of your fears, okay? Let's go! What's fastest? Boat or car?"

"Six o' one, half a dozen of t'other," Bobby said.

Clive shook his head. "Nah. Car's faster."

"Good." Bentz grabbed his iPad, jogged around the nose of his Jeep to the driver's side, and threw open the door. The two men stood rooted to the spot. He started the engine, rolled down the window, and ordered, "Get in! And I mean now!"

"You can't arrest him!" Kristi argued, standing next to Cruz at the door of the Cookes' pantry. She couldn't believe what was happening! For the third time, she asserted, "Cruz just saved my life!" She was fired up, her heart still pounding as there were still three dead bodies in the pantry, some kind of stew cooling on the stove, blood still smeared all over the marble floor.

The whole situation was bizarre. Outré. Something out of a horror movie or very bad nightmare.

Montoya was undeterred.

He'd already snapped handcuffs on his brother, checked his pockets, and relieved him of a pocketknife, then checked on the condition of Aldo Lucerno as well as Reggie and Hamilton Cooke. He'd called for backup and an ambulance, then read Cruz his rights as sounds of sirens screamed closer and closer.

The ambulance would be too late, though.

Hamilton had already been dead, lying in a pool of his own blood when Kristi had arrived. As for his wife, Reggie, she, too, had passed. In the second after Reggie had pressed the knife into Kristi's hand and softly demanded Kristi kill Aldo, Kristi had witnessed Reggie's color drain from pink to gray. Aldo, too, had turned an ashen color as Kristi had driven the fillet knife deep, a split second before Cruz had fired his gun and finished the job.

Cruz hadn't killed Aldo. His soul had already been passing to the afterworld compliments of his ex-wife's blade and Kristi's deep thrust. Her slice had been fatal. Aldo would have died within the next few minutes before Cruz had shot him.

Yet, who knew how much damage Reggie's deranged ex could have inflicted in the short space of time between the deadly thrust and his actual collapse and death? Could he have taken Kristi's life and that of her unborn child, if not for Cruz's fateful bullet?

Probably.

No one would ever really know.

But Kristi believed Cruz's dead-on shot had saved her life even if it hadn't been necessary to end Aldo's.

Again, she pleaded. "Please, don't. He saved my life!"

Impassive, Montoya didn't take his eyes off his brother, but said, "Cruz just killed a man."

"No—it was me," Kristi argued. "I stabbed him. It was fatal. He would have—"

"I know what you did." Montoya cut her off as the shriek of sirens reached her ears. "I saw it all. You and Cruz, both of you will have your chance to give a full statement."

Kristi seized up the argument. "If you saw it, then you know he was only saving me. Saving my child's life!"

"Your what?"

"I'm pregnant!" she said, and for the first time since that horrible, excruciating night she felt tears burn in the back of her eyes. How close had she come to losing this baby? Jay's baby?

Montoya tried to clarify, "You're—?"

"Yes!" And she felt the weight of two sets of eyes upon her, both Montoya brothers registered their surprise.

Cruz took a chance, turning to face her. "Jesus. Pregnant? And you came here and—?"

"I had a gun. It's in there." She hitched her chin toward the pantry that was now a morgue. "It's . . . it was Jay's."

"But a baby?" he whispered, stunned.

"I know. I know. Dumb. But here we are."

A muscle worked in Montoya's jaw. "The law is the law," he said, and Kristi didn't interrupt him even though, by her father's account and her own experience, she knew Reuben Montoya didn't always play by the rules and was known to bend the law to the breaking point. "Cruz shot Aldo Lucerno and he's wanted in another state. Oregon."

Cruz nodded and said to Kristi, "It's okay."

"What? Are you kidding? No, no, it's not okay." She shook her head. "It's not okay at all!"

"The way it has to be." Cruz sent her a look, his eyes holding hers. "I'll be fine. Pet your dog for me."

"What? My dog?"

"Dave."

"I know, but—?" What was he talking about? What did Dave have to do with anything? The sirens were close now. Screaming. Blue and red lights flashed from the front of the house.

"I stopped by your house and got him all riled up," Cruz explained. "So please." Again he sent her a steady look. "Let him know it's okay. Pet him for me." His eyes, still intent, tried to convey some silent message, one she was supposed to read. He repeated, "For me."

"Okay, but . . ." Pet the dog? For him? She didn't get it. She was lost.

Footsteps thundered outside, sounding like a herd of wild horses.

"The cavalry," Montoya said, and for the first time since showing up at the Cookes' house, a bit of relief was visible in his sharp features.

In a second, two cops burst through the back door. "Police!"

"It's clear!" Montoya yelled. "Drop your weapons. Where are the EMTs?"

"Right behind us," the first cop, a short woman, replied. She holstered her sidearm.

"Get them in here," Montoya ordered. "Now!"

Sam shivered, her body still jerking from the third time Father John had stunned her. He'd sent over a hundred thousand volts through her before rolling her convulsing body in a tarp and dragging her into this godforsaken place—a cavern converted to some kind of bunker—in the swamp somewhere.

Water dripped from what appeared to be warped, rotten timbers holding up the remains of a ceiling. A small stream trickled across the flat stones of the floor where dozens of votive candles lit the wide chamber. Their tiny flames flickered and cast shifting shadows on the crumbling stone walls. Everywhere, permeating the air, was the smell of dank, moist earth.

He'd tied her to a simple straight-backed chair, the only piece of furniture on the uneven rock floor. But he'd had difficulty controlling her quivering body, her bonds not as tight as he'd intended as she couldn't "sit still!" as he'd commanded when lashing her to the chair.

Her wobbling wrists were bound to the chair's back where it met the seat, her legs, still trembling, strapped as best he could to its spindly legs. She was immobile aside from her head and he, that vulgar excuse of a man who dared wear the robes of a priest, who had the audacity to call himself "Father," slowly circled her. There was nothing holy about him, nothing the least bit venerated or hallowed. He was evil personified and worse yet, that wicked, malignant soul was garbed in the dressings of the blessed along with reflective sunglasses that didn't hide the scab running down one side of his face.

A monster.

A grotesque, evil monster moving around and around.

Methodically.

Sometimes chanting, sometimes not, but ever-wailing in deliberate, ever-narrowing concentric circles as Sam whipped her head around, back and forth, trying to keep him in her vision and knowing what he intended.

A slow and savage death.

She tried and failed not to give in to the fear.

Don't go there, Sam. Don't!

You know all this about him.

You always have.

Now, keep a cool head. You have to find a way to fight him! To thwart him! To save yourself!

How? Oh, God, how?

Her options were limited, but she couldn't give in. She tried the cords tying her feet and hands and they loosened, but not enough! She was still bound to the chair.

Frantic, her pulse pounding, her heartbeat wild, she forced her mind to think, to come up with a plan, *any*thing.

You can do this, Sam. You can. Think! There must be a way to trip him up!

Maybe? Maybe if she somehow tripped him up, played a mental game with him, even angered him to break his concentration, she could find a way to turn the tables or get free.

If she could throw him off track, he might possibly make a mistake.

She hoped.

At the very least she would gain some time and maybe then she could think more clearly, her brain able to control her limbs that still were twitching in their bonds.

Oh, if only!

But the spasms were less frequent and she thought she might be able to move her fingers a bit, though she didn't dare try.

She tried to speak. "W-w-why?"

"Why did I bring you here? Why have I kept tracking you?" he threw back at her. "You know why! Your poisoned advice killed my sister."

"N-N-No—no it didn't."

He sent a look that could cut through stone as he passed in front of her, the hem of his cassock wet, dampness wicking up the fabric with each step, blood still dripping from his neck where the sharp stones had cut into his neck, showing an intricate red pattern on his skin. He'd aged in the years since she'd first met him, and the struggle with her and effort of dragging her in a tarp over the rough, sodden terrain had taken its toll on him. He was breathing hard from the effort, his face pale as a specter.

"And—a-and the others?" she demanded.

"The others?" he snarled, disappearing behind her as she turned her head as far as possible to keep him in her field of vision.

"The women you killed!"

"Practice."

"Bull," she spat out, finally taking control of her tongue. Her legs and arms, too, felt more in control. "You got off on it."

He appeared on the other side of her and shot her a glance. His entire demeanor was angry. Defiant. "They were whores," he spat.

"And you're a killer."

"Sent by God."

"Oh, yeah right," she said, baiting him, but no longer caring, her passion overtaking the fear that still pulsed through her. She pushed hard on her wrists, tried to get the cords to give way. "God's will is just your excuse."

"I was doing His bidding."

"By dressing up and playing a priest?" she said, eyes watching him, the bonds at her hands looser, she thought. "Why now?"

"It was time. You were closing down your program."

"But it's been years."

"I was waiting for a sign," he said.

"And did you see it?"

"Of course. You decided not to stop. You were going to continue. I prayed that it would be over, that once your program ceased, so would you, but you weren't going to."

"The podcast," she whispered. "That's a crap excuse."

"A sign," he corrected, his voice steady.

He disappeared from sight, walking behind her again, and she whipped her head around so that she could see him again. "Pretending to be holy. Do you really believe that?"

"I'm—"

"A liar and a murderer! That's what you are. You killed innocent women and—"

"Not innocent," he spat out, angrier still. "Those little whores were far from innocent! Evil women! Harlots of Satan!"

"According to you."

"And the Father!" He was in front of her now once more and visibly agitated, his lips tight, a tic developing near one eye, visible at the edge of his dark lenses. He stopped to stare at her.

A good sign?

Or a bad omen?

As dire as the situation was, she had to keep him talking, if only for her own satisfaction. As long as he was talking, he wasn't killing her.

"The Father speaks through me."

"You wish! This is all playacting, and you know it! The fake robe, the fake name, the fake reasons for doing what you do! You're a fraud! I know it, you know it, and believe me, God knows it. It's sacrilege that you dare to wear the robes of good men, true believers who have given their lives to Him."

"You know nothing!" he argued, his eyes flaring, his upper lip quaking, his fingers clenching and flexing over the deadly chain in his hand.

She flexed her legs. Stretched the ties. Her wrists were raw from the strain of trying to escape, and as if he noticed her struggle, he smiled slightly. Not a beatific play of the lips, but a wide, leering grin.

He thinks he's won.

He thinks I'm already dead.

Think again, prick!

He started walking again, around and around, closer and closer, into her field of vision, out of it, his countenance appearing all the more evil in the glimmering light of the dying candles.

Her throat was dry with fear, her heart was drumming to the beat of a thousand drums as she tried to keep her gaze on him, to watch his every move, and knowing that each time he circled her, he was bringing her closer to death.

And she'd fight him tooth and nail to the end.

Don't let him out of your sight!

He won't draw this out forever, Sam. You have to do something. Something now!

If only she knew what.

"Shit!" Bentz stood on the brakes.

Shuddering, the Jeep slid wildly as Bentz cranked hard on the wheel to avoid plowing into the car stopped dead in front of them.

"Hey!" Bobby-Dean yelled from the backseat. "Watch the fuck out!"

Clive whispered, "Holy Christ, man!"

Grinding to a stop, spraying gravel, and nearly ramming into the back end of the old Chevy, the Jeep missed the rear bumper of the Impala by less than an inch. In his headlights, he recognized the car, its fender dented in several places, one tire axle-deep in water, as Father John's vehicle.

His blood ran cold. "Stay here," he told the two men, and slid his gun from its holster, then stepped outside where the sound of the bayou—the insects buzzing, frogs croaking, water lapping—greeted his ears. He reached into his vehicle again and grabbed his flashlight to switch it on and sweep its bluish beam over the landscape.

Near the Impala, the vegetation had been flattened, a trail of bent weeds indicating that something or—more likely someone—had been dragged deeper along what had once been a road but was now only ruts with stones and exposed roots, a protrusion of drier land jutting into the swamp.

His heart pounded an uneven cadence.

This was it.

This was the place where Father John lay in wait. He knew it. Could feel the bastard.

With his free hand, he tried using his cell phone, got no reception, and swore under his breath. "Son of a bitch."

He turned back to his Jeep. "Changed my mind," he said, focusing on Clive. "Get out. Walk—no run—until you get a signal and dial nine-one-one. Tell them Bentz needs backup and give them the address."

"This place ain't got no address," Clive complained as he and Bobby-Dean climbed out of the rig, the interior light cutting through the darkness.

"Then explain where it is. But go. Go fast!"

Bobby-Dean was already jogging up the double ruts.

Bentz didn't have time to wait. Samantha Wheeler was either being tortured or dead already. He took off, using the flashlight's beam as a guide as he swept it back and forth over the thick ferns and vines that clogged the road. Half jogging, he kept to the trail, what had once been an access road and now was little more than a break in the thick weeds.

If only he wasn't too late!

Pulse thundering in his ears, he hoped to high heaven that Bobby-Dean and Clive, not the most responsible people he'd ever met, had the good sense to call 9-1-1 for backup. ASAP.

God help me.

God help Sam!

Around a final bend, he saw it.

A dilapidated structure loomed in the darkness, a broken-down behemoth now covered in vines and brambles and ferns growing wild, water tupelo and cypress trees ringing the area, rising tall, like ghostly sentries surrounding a castle.

From somewhere nearby an owl hooted and he heard the whir of a bat's wings overhead as the ever-present Spanish moss danced eerily from the thick branches. He didn't think of water snakes or alligators, or bears or pumas, just forged on, taking a thin land bridge, the swamp encroaching, surrounding the massive pile of rubble, water tupelo trees vying with the cypress in the bayou.

He swept his flashlight carefully over the muck and followed the drag marks to the pile of debris and saw an opening where once there had been a door, and now was just a dark hole. His insides turned to ice as he thought of Samantha inside with the madman who intended to exact his painful vengeance upon her.

Was he too late?

He'd soon find out.

Bending slightly, he slipped through the gaping maw of what had once been the monastery.

Total darkness enveloped him and he heard the steady drip, drip, drip of water on what had once been a stone floor and the scratch of claws, unseen rats, he figured, as they scurried out of his path.

The roof had collapsed partially, and he couldn't stand upright. He used the flashlight sparingly, hoping not to announce his presence with the bright rays. Feeling his way forward, stumbling twice, he saw, through cracks around what had once been a door, an eerie wavering light.

Bentz's heart clutched.

He doused his flashlight for good.

Inching forward quietly, he realized he was seeing another sagging doorway, this one leading further inside what was left of the building.

His weapon drawn, Bentz sent up a quick, silent prayer to a God he'd left years before. *Please, don't let me be too late.*

Father John was directly behind her.

Sam felt his presence and her skin crawled.

He'd stopped.

Completely avoiding her peripheral vision. She swung her head as far as she could, back and forth, trying to spot him, but it was impossible. If he stayed directly behind her, if he was not moving at all and very close, he was invisible to her.

Her heart thudded.

Her nerves were frayed.

And her hands—good Lord—her hands still could break free!

Though the chair wasn't bolted down and rocked a little when she twisted within it, there was no way she could make it turn and keep up with him. It scraped, moved slightly, but she couldn't see directly behind her.

Did she hear something over the sound of running water and the thundering of her heart?

Sense something other than the monster's slight breathing?

Or, more likely, was she feeling unfounded, bitter hope?

She strained to listen and heard the slightest scrape of a shoe again. This time only inches from her, just out of her field of vision.

No, no, no!

She felt his breath upon the top of her head, riffling through her hair.

Panic spiraled through her.

She whipped her head around, the chair rocking more, scraping against the stone floor, but he stayed at her back.

"Where are you—"

In that instant she felt a sudden whoosh of air as he flung the rosary over her head to circle her throat.

No!

Oh, God, no!

Razor-sharp stones bit into her flesh, cutting off her air.

She strained.

Couldn't breathe.

Was freaked beyond freaked!

Her arms strained, stretching the ties at her wrists! Tugging. Hard!

But they couldn't stretch their bonds. Try as she might, she couldn't reach up to pull the unholy noose from her neck!

Panic rose.

Her lungs were on fire!

The chair rocked with her struggles.

"Hold still!" he hissed.

No!

This was not the way she was going to leave this earth.

Never this way!

She was rasping, trying to drag in the slightest bit of air.

She thought of Ty. Of her children. Of the life she'd planned for herself. Images of the boys on Christmas morning, their faces aglow, of the last time they'd been to the beach together as she'd watched her sons skim board in the lapping tide, of the way Ty's arms felt around her, how his strength would seem to flow into her body, how kissing and making love to him transported her . . . Oh, God . . . and the memories yet to be made, the camping trips, or vacations . . .

Disney World and beyond. And now it was all turning to dust, ending with her life. . . .

No, no, no!

Her lungs were ready to burst!

She struggled as he pulled hard on the chain.

The chair wobbled, rocked crazily. The beads sliced deep.

Hot blood trickled down her neck.

His breath ruffled her hair. "Good-bye, Doctor Sam," he snarled against her ear, "It's time for you to die!"

Bentz witnessed it all.

From the partially collapsed hallway where he was hunched over, he stared into the candlelit cavern and saw Father John behind Sam, who was tied to a chair, the deadly rosary wrapped around her neck. He saw the panic in her eyes as the maniac behind her tugged hard on his unholy noose.

Aiming his weapon, hoping to get a clear shot, he yelled, "Police! Stop! Hands in the air." And then he called the bastard by his name.

Father John froze.

He glanced up.

Startled.

"Hands over your head!" Bentz yelled.

Samantha, struggling for breath, rocked her chair back against her assailant.

"Whaaat?" Father John yelled as he fell backward, losing his footing on the wet stones.

He slipped, pulling Samantha by the noose over him as he yanked on the rosary.

Bentz flew out into the cavern.

The killer was struggling to kill her, his head flung back, the cords on his neck visible as he stretched the rosary.

Gasping and flinging her body weight in the chair, Samantha struggled, but her face, which had been so red, was draining of color.

Bentz didn't wait.

Father John's head was exposed.

He aimed.

Fired.

Blam!

The gun blast echoed loudly in the chamber.

Father John's head popped backward, his sunglasses flying off. His body jerked once, and then went slack. Sam was still in the chair, lying over the now-dead form of her captor. Still was fighting to breathe.

Bentz rushed forward, yanked the noose of bloodred beads from her neck, and heard, as if in the far, far distance, the wail of sirens over her own ragged gasps for air.

"You'll be all right," he assured her, though he didn't believe it himself. "You're going to be okay."

He righted the chair, cut her bindings with his jackknife, and she scooted across the wet stones of the floor, scrambling as far away from the inert form of Father John as she could.

"Ty?" she croaked. "Where's—?"

"With the boys. He'll be here." With one last look at the dead man to make sure that he wasn't moving, he knelt beside her, noticed the deep red gashes all around her throat, cuts in the unique pattern of a rosary. "Hang in. You're going to be all right. It's over," he told her, and sent up yet another prayer that he wasn't lying, that now, finally, the Rosary Killer was dead. Now and forever.

CHAPTER 41

The next afternoon, as the sun was sending rays through the dirty office windows, Bentz was seated at his desk at the station. He held his badge in one hand, rubbing it, thinking of the years he'd spent on the force, wearing this piece of metal, being shielded by it, believing it made him the man he was. Now it was time to turn it in. As he sat in his desk chair for the last time, he heard rattling as the painting crew tore down sheets of plastic that had been a barrier from the construction zone.

The renovation to the department was about over. After more than two months of delays, Montoya would have his own office again.

With a new partner.

Hopefully a younger partner.

Unless Bentz chickened out.

So far he hadn't. He'd promised Olivia that he'd hang it all up, kick back and enjoy life, and spend more time with the family. "If you really can't give it up," she'd told him, "you can go into private practice."

"Become a private dick?" Bentz had scoffed at the idea. "No way!" Now, though, he was rolling it around in his mind. It would be safer and something to do. He really didn't see himself spending hours upon hours fishing or trotting Ginny to toddler preschool, or taking up—what? Gardening? Bow hunting?

"Give me a break," he muttered.

Montoya walked into the office just then, grim as he had been since the day before when he'd arrested his brother and sent him off to Oregon.

"You okay?" Bentz asked as Montoya dropped into his chair.

"Do I look okay?" New lines bracketed his mouth and eyes and he appeared not to have slept for a week.

"You look like shit."

"Feel like it, too." Scowling, he glanced out the window.

"You don't believe he did it."

"Who? Cruz?" Montoya wrapped a hand around the back of his neck. "I think Cruz is capable of a lot of things, some of it pretty fu— effin' shady. But murder?" He gave his head a sharp shake. "No way."

"So what're you gonna do about it?"

"What can I do?" Montoya picked up the belt that was coiled on his desk.

"You tell me."

"Haven't decided yet." He stretched out the tooled leather. "See here," he said, pointing to a spot in the belt where the stitching had pulled away, the front separating from the back and creating the slimmest of pockets.

"Yeah? So what? Old leather separates."

"If you say so." But Montoya rubbed his finger over the stitching. "All of the rest of it is tight. Strong. Sturdy." He eyed the opening. "Just one spot that completely split, and the ends of the binding? Not frayed." His eyes narrowed. "It almost looks like the stitching was intentionally cut."

"Why?"

"Dunno."

"But you think that's significant?"

"Might be. And I think it's worth asking my brother about." He snapped the belt once, then coiled it neatly again.

"You gonna talk to him?"

"Yeah. Eventually." Leaning back in his chair and closing his eyes, Montoya added, "But first let him deal with the cops in Oregon." He nodded to himself as if agreeing to a thought that had crossed his mind. "See what they find out." Opening his eyes again, he stared up at the ceiling, and in the ensuing silence, Bentz heard the painters still packing up, talking to each other, footsteps retreating down the hallway.

It had been a long night and a day that seemed to go on forever. He'd found Samantha Wheeler in the old, nearly forgotten monastery, being choked by Father John. Bentz hadn't thought twice about finishing the job he'd started years ago, and killed the murdering son of a bitch.

This time there was no doubt.

The man who'd pretended to be a priest had left this earth to meet his maker.

As for Dr. Sam, she'd been taken to the hospital, treated for her contusions and terror, gave her statement in a voice that barely worked, and insisted she wanted to go home ASAP, so after one night at St. Ada's she'd left and was insistent that she would end her radio show and start her podcast as planned. Despite the fact that her voice held a gravelly edge to it. She was taking control of her life and no "freak of a fake priest or anyone else" was going to stop her. She had even indicated to Bentz that she and Ty were taking that planned Disney trip "come hell or high water or monsters dressed up in holy garb." She'd had fire in her eyes as she'd held her husband's hand in the hospital and Bentz believed her.

There was talk of the Laroche family dedicating a park in Helene's memory. Her husband, Hugo, was still dealing with his grief, and while his daughter, Marianne, had been quoted by the press as saying "good riddance to bad news," Hugo's son, Vincent, had been more somber and remarked that Helene was a "sensitive soul" and he would miss her.

Stacy Parker aka Luna, who had nearly been killed by Father John, had given up her streetwalking life in New Orleans and had packed up and moved back to Wyoming, telling Bentz that she wasn't "a city girl after all." She was going back to college. Or business school. Or even ranching.

Who could blame her?

Bentz cracked his neck. After seeing Dr. Sam to the hospital, he'd spent most of last night and this morning with Kristi. Montoya had filled him in and his heart had nearly stopped when Bentz had realized how close he'd come to losing her, to losing his first grandchild.

But Kristi was, if nothing else, a fighter. His older daughter had seemed remarkably together after all she'd been through. "One day at a time," she'd told him with a sad smile.

Once more he'd offered up his residence as a place to pull herself together and she'd told him flat out she *was* together and she wasn't going anywhere.

Aldo Lucerno, the man who had killed Jay, Hamilton Cooke, and Reggie, was himself dead. Kristi saw no reason to fear living in her home. "I think I'll be okay, Dad," she said, despite a new bandage to her shoulder. "No more notes or snakes, black roses or ugly little knives. Okay? You can relax. I'll be fine."

He wanted to believe that.

He wanted desperately to believe that she would be all right.

But he didn't think he'd relax. Ever.

Still, Kristi had the presence of mind to bring Jay's gun with her on her visit to the Cooke house the night before. The police had found the pocket pistol wedged between the cans of tomato sauce and boxes of beans. He only hoped she'd never have a reason to use it.

Now he looked at Montoya across the expanse of their two desks. "You gonna be all right?" he asked his partner as he reached for his jacket.

"Sure." Montoya rolled his chair away from his desk. "Why not?" His voice dripped with sarcasm.

"We solved a couple of cases," Bentz reminded him.

"And found a new one."

He was talking about his brother and the death of Lucia Costa. Cruz was definitely in trouble on that one.

"Not our jurisdiction."

"I know." Montoya didn't seem convinced.

Thankfully, he'd been integral in helping save Kristi's life. Montoya had learned from Ned Zavala that Aldo had bought a cottonmouth just the week before, but when he'd tried to locate Aldo, the man was nowhere to be found. Not in his home. Not in the apartment at the back of the property where Montoya had discovered the damning note paper, ink, and religious artifacts. From Lucerno's place, Montoya had driven to Kristi's house to warn her and had seen a figure lurking in the nearby alley. That figure hadn't turned out to be Aldo Lucerno. Instead Montoya had followed his own brother to the bizarre and bloody scene at the Cookes' home.

Though Cruz had fired the shot that killed Aldo, Reuben had been there to make certain the bastard was dead and that justice, such as it was, could be served.

And now Cruz was on his way to Oregon to face whatever was waiting for him.

"I gotta run." Bentz stretched out of his chair. "It's Halloween and Ginny's first birthday."

Montoya sucked in his breath. "You can't miss that, man. Not for anything."

"Not if I want to stay married." Grabbing his jacket, he added, "And I do." Eyeing his partner, he added, "Maybe you should call it a day, too."

"I will. Soon."

Bentz hesitated and Montoya sent him a get-outta-here look. "I'm fine."

Not certain he believed his partner, Bentz left anyway.

Montoya was a big boy. He'd figure out whatever he had to with his brother.

Bentz found his Jeep in the lot and drove directly to a toy store. He double-parked on the street and headed inside. He couldn't go home empty-handed—not on his kid's first birthday, so he eyed the racks of stuffed animals quickly. Since it was Halloween, he settled on a huge black cat that he was certain Olivia would deem inappropriate, paid for it, and after melding into the traffic that had piled up, drivers sending him hateful glances, he drove home.

His wife and baby daughter were waiting by the front door.

He raced up the steps. "Happy birthday, Ginny," he said, holding out the huge stuffed animal, its green eyes wide.

Gleefully, his daughter said something unintelligible and opened her arms wide.

Bentz ignored Olivia's what-were-you-thinking expression as Ginny smiled widely, showing off her two bottom teeth and hints of matching uppers.

"That's right, honey, it's a kitty," Bentz said.

"You think that's what she said?" Olivia asked.

"Absolutely." He gave his wife a quick kiss, then carried both the oversized stuffed animal and his daughter to the living room. "And she loves it."

"That she does." Olivia followed him into the living room. "We just have to find a place for it."

The front doorbell rang.

"Trick-or-treaters already?" he asked, noting that the sun had yet to set.

"Nope." Olivia opened the door and Kristi walked inside. She was carrying a pink box with a white bow and offered it up, along with a kiss for her sister.

"Happy birthday, Gin-Gin," she said, and the baby's eyes lit up at the sight of her.

"I didn't know you were coming," Bentz said. "I mean, you had a rough night."

"And miss Ginny's first birthday?" She waved his concerns away. "What kind of a big sister would I be if I didn't show up?"

Bentz felt his heart swell—Jesus, he was beginning to get soft!— but he was pleased, felt a warmth seep through his veins at the thought that they—all the members of his little ragtag family—were all together. All safe.

Ginny tore into her present, a little shorts outfit, a book, and a hand puppet in the shape of a witch complete with wart on her nose. "Not everyone has a birthday on Halloween," Kristi explained, donning the puppet and touching Ginny on her nose. The little girl squealed in delight.

At that moment, the doorbell chimed.

"Here we go," Bentz muttered.

Sure enough. When Olivia answered the door, a chorus of small voices shouting "trick or treat" echoed through the house. It seemed normal. Part of a regular life.

Bentz figured he'd get used to it.

Kristi spent an hour with her dad, Olivia, and Ginny, then drove home.

Telling herself that she should be relieved, even relaxed now that she would no longer be harassed or stalked by Aldo Lucerno, she still had trouble letting go—despite all the assurances she gave her father.

She'd gone over the notes she'd taken for *The God Complex and Murder* and wondered how she'd missed that Aldo had been so humiliated by Reggie's affair and what he considered Kristi's exploitation of it. How had she not seen that he would turn to murder? Yes, he'd been brusque and threatening when she'd originally interviewed him, but she hadn't seen anything that hinted he was a psychopath.

Did it matter now?

He was dead.

As was everyone associated with that horror story. And of course her agent had called, Zera insisting she write two more books. "At the very least. *Rosary Two* is a given, right? We've been talking about it, but now, there's this new twist, a whole new crime book about the Oyster King, right? I mean, who better to write it than you?"

"Who indeed," Kristi said, answering her own question as she pulled into her garage, walked into the house, and was greeted by both Dave and Lenore, the first with ridiculous kisses that washed her cheeks, the second by soft little figure eights between her ankles. "Hey," Kristi said, rubbing the dog behind his ears and promising him a walk in the morning as she let him out the back door. She observed him running the length of the backyard to end up doing crazy zoomies at the door and taking off again. All the while, Kristi petted the kitten, listened to her purr, and felt a warmth of satisfaction.

For once she didn't feel the pull of a glass of wine and settled for three pieces of bite-sized candy as she spent the next two hours answering the door and seeing every Halloween costume imaginable. From a two-year-old who could barely walk in his octopus outfit with eight outstretching tentacles, to a group of teenaged boys in Jason and Michael Myers masks who could barely mumble "trick or treat" before taking their candy and dashing off the front porch and wheeling away on skateboards. Bert and Ernie arrived, followed by Garfield, SpongeBob, a flapper, and a variety of Disney princesses. Her favorite was a toddler bumble bee who was more preoccupied with her wings than the candy.

As she finally turned off the light for the night, she smiled and patted her abdomen. Not this year, and probably not next, but in two years, watch out. There would be a new trick-or-treater in town. Baby McKnight would be ready for a candy grab!

Her phone buzzed with a text from Bella asking about coffee.

Want to meet for coffee? Please? My treat. Then several emojis of cups of java and ending with a happy face blowing hearts as kisses.

Kristi and Bella had already had a short conversation about what Kristi had been through and Bella apologized again for setting her up with Hamilton Cooke and Reggie. "It's just awful about them. Thank God you're okay!"

Was she?

Would she ever be?

Time would tell, she figured, and texted back:

You got it. How about Magnolia's? Saturday at 10:00? Maybe Sarah and Jess can join? It was time to mend some fences over a hot latte and the latest gossip. And Kristi would let her friends in on her little secret, that she would soon be a mother. She felt it was time. She was ready.

Later that night, she curled in her bed and Dave whined to join her.

"Sure, why not?" she said, "but let's take this off." She unhooked his collar so that she wouldn't hear his ID tags rattle as he shifted around during the night. As she did, she felt a bulge in the leather collar. "Don't tell me this is ruined already." She gave the dog a glance of reproval as she turned the collar over and saw that it was marred. It had been sliced to create a small pocket and within the tiny space a minute thumb drive had been wedged.

"What the—?" She had trouble retrieving the drive, it was wedged in so tight. "Who put this here?" And then she remembered Cruz Montoya's final words to her: "Pet him for me." And again, "for me," as he'd stared at her with some unspoken message she hadn't understood.

Now, she thought, she might.

She threw back the covers and quickly padded barefoot up the stairs.

Dave was right on her heels, toenails clicking behind her.

Once in her office, she switched on a light and fired up her laptop. "Now, what is this?" she asked the empty room, and when the computer was up and running, Kristi slipped the thumb drive into a port and hit play.

For a second she didn't understand what she was seeing, then she realized it was a night scape, near a river, a woman running along a river's edge and someone, a big man, chasing after her before tackling her and dragging her deeper into the water. The woman fought, flailing and kicking up water, splashing and hitting, but the man just dragged her deeper into the river and held her head down until she was unmoving. Then he let go and her body floated downstream to disappear in a wild swirl of frothing water as she hit the rapids.

"Dear God," Kristi whispered, horrified.

What the hell was this? Evidence of a woman being murdered from the looks of it. She watched it again and felt cold to the bottom of her soul. Cruz had obviously left her with this for a reason. But why?

She bit her lower lip and glanced out the window to the dark night beyond, her own reflection a ghost reflecting on the glass. She turned back to the computer and watched the footage one more time.

"Help him, Kris," she heard, clear as a bell, as if Jay were standing right next to her. Once again, she peered up at the window, expecting to see his pale image next to hers in the watery reflection.

Of course he wasn't there.

She was alone.

Totally alone.